F
Berry

Berry, Steve,
1955-

The patriot threat.

DATE			

THE
PATRIOT
THREAT

ALSO BY STEVE BERRY

COTTON MALONE NOVELS

The Lincoln Myth
The King's Deception
The Jefferson Key
The Emperor's Tomb
The Paris Vendetta
The Charlemagne Pursuit
The Venetian Betrayal
The Alexandria Link
The Templar Legacy

STAND-ALONE NOVELS

The Columbus Affair
The Third Secret
The Romanov Prophecy
The Amber Room

EBOOK ORIGINALS

"The Tudor Plot"
"The Admiral's Mark"
"The Devil's Gold"
"The Balkan Escape"

THE PATRIOT THREAT

STEVE BERRY

MINOTAUR BOOKS

NEW YORK

www.minotaurbooks.com

Book designed by Steven Seighman

Library of Congress Cataloging-in-Publication Data

Berry, Steve, 1955–
  The patriot threat / Steve Berry.—First edition.
      pages   cm
  ISBN 978-1-250-05623-8 (hardcover)
  ISBN 978-1-4668-6260-9 (e-book)
  ISBN 978-1-250-07136-1 (international edition)
  1. Political fiction.   I. Title.
  PS3602.E764P38 2015
  813'.6—dc23

                          2014040122

Minotaur books may be purchased for educational, business, or promotional use. For information on bulk purchases, please contact Macmillan Corporate and Premium Sales Department at 1-800-221-7945, extension 5442, or write specialmarkets@macmillan.com.

First Edition: March 2015

10 9 8 7 6 5 4 3 2 1

For Sam Berry,
my father

ACKNOWLEDGMENTS

This is my first novel with Minotaur Books, part of Macmillan Publishers. The experience has been wonderful. My sincere thanks go out to John Sargent, head of Macmillan, Sally Richardson, who captains St. Martin's, and my publisher, Andrew Martin. Also, a sincere debt of gratitude is offered to Hector DeJean in Publicity; Jeff Dodes and everyone in Marketing and Sales, especially Paul Hochman; Jen Enderlin, the sage of all things paperback; David Rotstein, who produced the cover, Steven Seighman for the excellent interior design work, and Mary Beth Roche and the folks in Audio.

As always, thank you Simon Lipskar for another great job.

And to my editor, Kelley Ragland, it's been a joy getting to know you.

A few extra mentions: Meryl Moss and her extraordinary publicity team (especially Deb Zipf and JeriAnn Geller); Jessica Johns and Esther Garver, who continue to keep Steve Berry Enterprises running smoothly; M. J. Rose, one of the original members of the Plotters Club; and Richard Stamm, curator of the Smithsonian Castle (for pointing me toward a clever desk).

As always, to my wife, Elizabeth, who remains the most special of all.

This novel is dedicated to Harold Earl "Sam" Berry, who is the namesake of Harold Earl "Cotton" Malone. How each acquired his respective nickname remains a mystery.

What's not in doubt is the effect both men have had on my life.

No feeling in the world is greater, more ennobling
and more sacred than patriotism.

—KIM IL-SUNG, ETERNAL PRESIDENT
DEMOCRATIC PEOPLE'S REPUBLIC OF KOREA

THE
PATRIOT
THREAT

PROLOGUE

Franklin Roosevelt hated being in the same room with his infamous visitor, but he appreciated the need for them to talk. He'd been president four years, but three weeks from now history will mark his second inauguration, the first held on January 20. Before that the oath had always been taken on March 4, commemorative of the exact day, in 1789, when the Constitution first took effect. But the 20th Amendment changed that. A good idea, actually, shortening the time after the November election day. Too much of a lame duck made for a dead duck. He liked being a part of change. Hated the way anything was once done.

And he particularly despised any member of the "old order."

Like his visitor.

Andrew Mellon had served ten years and eleven months as secretary of Treasury. He started with Harding in 1921, then worked for Coolidge before being eased from office by Hoover. He completed his government service with one year as ambassador to the Court of St. James, finally retiring in 1933. Mellon was a staunch Republican, then and now one of the wealthiest men in the country, the living embodiment of "old order" wisdom the New Deal longed to change.

"Here, Mr. President, is my offer. I hope it can be carried out."

Mellon handed over a piece of paper.

He'd invited this pariah to afternoon tea because his advisers had cautioned him that *you can kick a mean dog only so long.*

And he'd been kicking Andrew Mellon for three years.

It started just after his first inauguration. He'd instructed the Bureau of Internal Revenue to audit Mellon's 1931 tax returns. There'd been departmental resistance to his over-exercise of presidential power—words to the effect that Internal Revenue should not be used as a political weapon—but his directive had been carried out. Mellon had claimed a $139,000 refund. The government found that he owed $3,089,000. Charges of tax evasion were brought, but a grand jury declined to indict. Undaunted, Roosevelt ordered the Justice Department to proceed civilly and a trial was held in the Board of Tax Appeals, involving fourteen months of testimony and evidence. It had ended only a few weeks ago.

They occupied the Oval Study on the second floor, his favorite spot in the White House to conduct business. It had an overcrowded, lived-in look from packed bookcases, ship models, and a confusion of paper piled everywhere. A fire raged in the hearth. He'd abandoned his wheelchair and sat on the sofa, Attorney General Homer Cummings beside him. Accompanying Mellon was David Finley, a close associate of the former secretary.

He and Cummings read Mellon's offering.

It laid out a proposal for the establishment of an art museum, to be located on the National Mall, which Mellon would erect at his own expense. The building not only would become a repository for Mellon's own massive collection, it would also accommodate future acquisitions.

To be called the National Gallery of Art.

"Not the Andrew W. Mellon Gallery?" he asked.

"I do not want my name publicly associated with the building."

He appraised his visitor, who sat ramrod-straight, head held high, not a muscle moving, as if presidents still bowed to his every whim. He'd always wondered why three would choose the same man for their cabinet. He could understand the first—Harding, a weak and inept fool—and maybe even the second—Coolidge, who'd finished out the term after Harding had the good sense to die two years into office. But in 1924, when Coolidge earned his own four years, why not select a new Treasury secretary? That made sense. Every president did. Then Hoover repeated the mistake, reappointing Mellon in 1929, only to finally be rid of him three years later.

He said, "It states here that the gallery will be managed by a private board of nine trustees, five appointed by you. It was my understanding that this institution would be administered by the Smithsonian."

"It shall be. But I want the gallery's internal operation to be wholly independent of the government, as the Smithsonian currently enjoys. That point is non-negotiable."

He glanced at his attorney general, who nodded his assent.

Mellon's offer had first been made a year ago. The building would cost between $8 and $9 million. Mellon's own art collection, valued at $20 million, would become its nucleus. Other quality works would also be acquired and displayed, the idea being that Washington, DC, might become one of the principal art capitals of the world. Mellon would endow the institution with $5 million, the income from which would be used to pay the salaries of the top administrators and to acquire more works. The government would perpetually pay for building maintenance and upkeep. There'd been months of behind-the-scenes negotiations to iron out the details, all leading up to this final gathering. Attorney General Cummings had kept him informed, but there'd been little give-and-take. Just as in business, in art Mellon drove a hard bargain.

One point was still troublesome, though.

"You have specified," he said, "that all of the funds for the building, and for the art, will come from your charitable trust. Yet it is this trust that we contend owes the people of this country over $3 million in back taxes."

Mellon's stone features never flinched. "If you want the money, that's where it is located."

He could tell he was being played. But that was all right. He'd asked for this encounter. So—

"I wish to speak to Mr. Mellon alone."

He saw that his attorney general did not like the idea but knew it was not a request. Both Cummings and Finley left the room. He waited until the door was closed and said, "You do know that I despise you."

"As if I care what you think. You're insignificant."

He chuckled. "I've been called arrogant. Lazy. Stupid. A manipulator. But never insignificant. I actually take offense to that one. I fancy myself to be quite relevant to our current economic predicament. One, I might add, you bear some responsibility for creating."

Mellon shrugged. "If Hoover had listened, the Depression would have been a short one."

It was going on seven years since that fateful Friday in 1929 when markets crashed and banks failed. Hoover was gone, but the Republicans lingered, still in control of Congress and the Supreme Court, enough that his New Deal policies were being dealt one legal blow after another. He'd confronted so many obstacles that he'd decided to make peace with his enemies, which included this devil. But not before he had his say.

"Let me see if I recall. As secretary of Treasury you advised Hoover to liquidate labor, stocks, farmers, and real estate. Purge all of the rottenness out of the system. Once done, according to you, people will work harder and live more—how did you put it—moral lives. Then you said that enterprising individuals will pick up from the less competent."

"That was sound advice."

"Coming from a man worth hundreds of millions I could see how you would feel that way. I doubt you'd have the same attitude if you were starving and out of work, with no hope."

He was actually surprised by Mellon's physical appearance. The face had drawn gaunt, the tall frame even thinner than he recalled. The skin was pale as lead, eyes tired and longing. Two heavy furrows ran at angles from the nostrils to the corner of the mouth, obscured partially by the trademark mustache. He knew Mellon to be eighty-one years old, but he looked over a hundred. One fact was clear, though—this man remained formidable.

He plucked a cigarette from the box on the side table and slid it into an ivory holder. The sight of its soft tip between his clenched teeth, held at a jaunty forty-five-degree angle, had become a sign of presidential confidence and optimism. God knows the country needed both. He lit the end and savored a deep drag, the smoke heavy, each inhalation producing a comforting ache in his chest.

"You do understand that there will be no change in our position relative to the matter presently pending in the Board of Tax Appeals. Your gift will have no affect on that litigation."

"Actually, it will."

Now he was curious.

"The National Gallery of Art will be built," Mellon said. "You cannot, and will not, refuse to do this. My gift is too much to ignore. Once opened, the gallery will become the premier place for art in this nation. Your petty tax trial will be long done. No one will ever give it another thought. But the gallery—that will stand forever and never be forgotten."

"You truly are the mastermind among the malefactors of great wealth."

"I recall that quote of yours, describing me as such. I actually took your words as a compliment. But coming from a professional politician, interested only in votes, it matters not to me what you think."

He said, "I am saving this country from the likes of you."

"All you've done is create a blizzard of new boards and agencies, most overlapping already existing departments. They do nothing, other than bloat the budget and increase taxes. The end result will be disastrous. More is never better, especially when it comes to government. God help this country when you're done with it. Thankfully, I won't be here to see those wretched consequences."

Roosevelt savored more tobacco before noting, "You're right, to refuse this gift would be political suicide. Your friends in the Republican Congress would not take kindly to that. And, I'm told, since the gift *is* yours you may set its terms. So your grand national gallery will be built."

"You weren't the first, you know."

He wondered what the old man meant.

"I did it long before you ever thought of it."

Then it hit him.

James Couzens, who'd died two months back, after fourteen years in the U.S. Senate. Thirteen years ago Senator Couzens launched a congressional probe of tax rebates provided to companies owned by then Treasury secretary Mellon. The investigation revealed Mellon had not divested himself of control over those companies, as he'd pledged to do prior to entering government service. There'd been calls for Mellon's resignation, but he'd weathered the storm and Coolidge reappointed him in 1924. That's when Mellon turned the Bureau of Internal Revenue on

Couzens, whose audit revealed $11 million in back taxes. But the Board of Tax Appeals reversed the decision and concluded that, actually, Couzens was entitled to a refund.

"Was that not your greatest humiliation," he told Mellon. "The appeals board sided completely against you. Your vendetta against Couzens was exposed for all that it was."

Mellon stood. "Precisely, Mr. President."

His guest stared down at him with eyes black as coal. He prided himself on dominating a room, able to take command of any situation, but this statue of flesh and blood made him feel nothing but uncomfortable.

"I'm dying," Mellon said.

That he had not known.

"Cancer will kill me before the next year is done. But I have never been a man to whine or cry. When I held power, I used it. So you have, after all, done to me, your apparent enemy, nothing different from what I did to mine. Thankfully, I still possess the money and means to hold my own. I do want to say this, though. I destroyed my enemies because they tried to destroy me. Mine were all defensive strikes. Your attack against me was clearly offensive. You chose to hurt me simply because you could. I have done nothing either to or toward you. That makes our fight . . . different."

He allowed the nicotine flooding his lungs to calm his nerves and told himself to show not a speck of concern or fear.

"I've left my country a donation of art. That will be my public legacy. For you, Mr. President, I have a separate, more private gift."

Mellon removed a tri-folded sheet of paper from his inner coat pocket and handed it over.

He accepted the note and read what was typed on it. "This is gibberish."

A cunning grin snuck onto Mellon's face. Nearly a smile. What a strange sight. He could not recall ever seeing this man project anything other than a scowl.

"Quite the contrary," Mellon said. "It's a quest. One I personally created just for you."

"For what?"

"Something that can end both you and your New Deal."

He gestured with the paper. "Is this some sort of threat? Perhaps you've forgotten who you are addressing."

His error of two years ago had already become abundantly clear. What was the maxim? *If you try to kill the king, make sure you do.* But he'd failed. Attorney General Cummings had already advised him that the Board of Tax Appeals would rule against the government, and for Mellon, on all counts. No back taxes were owed. No wrongdoing had occurred.

A total loss.

He'd ordered his Treasury secretary to make sure that any announcement of that decision be delayed for as long as possible. He didn't care how it was done, just that it was. Yet he wondered. Did his visitor already know?

"A man always has two reasons for the things he does," Mellon said. "A good one and a real one. I came here today, at your invitation, to be frank and honest. Eventually all the people now in power, yourself included, will be dead. I will be dead. But the National Gallery will always be there, and that is something this country needs. That was my *good* reason for doing what I have done. The real reason is that, unlike you, I am a patriot."

He chuckled at the insult. "Yet you readily admit that what I'm holding is a threat to your commander in chief."

"I assure you, there are things you do not know about this government. Things that could prove . . . devastating. In your hand, *Mr. President,* you hold two of those."

"Then why not simply tell me and have your pleasure now?"

"Why would I do that? You've allowed me to twist in the wind these past three years. I've been publicly tried, humiliated, labeled a crook and a cheat. All while you abused your office and misused power. I thought it only right to return the favor. But I made my gift a challenge. I want you to work for it, just like you've made me do."

Roosevelt balled up the paper and tossed it across the room.

Mellon seemed unfazed. "That would not be wise."

He pointed the cigarette holder like a weapon. "On the campaign trail, back in '32, many times I saw a placard in business windows. You know what it said?"

Mellon kept silent.

"*Hoover blew the whistle. Mellon rang the bell. Wall Street gave the signal, and the country went to hell. Hooray for Roosevelt.* That's what the country thinks of me."

"I prefer what Senator Harry Truman noted of you. *'The trouble with the president is he lies.'*"

A moment of strained silence passed between them.

Finally, Roosevelt said, "There's nothing I love as much as a good fight."

"Then this will make you a happy man."

Mellon reached into his pocket and removed a crisp dollar bill. "It's one of the new ones. I'm told you personally approved the design."

"I thought the old money needed retiring. A bit of bad luck associated with it."

So the Treasury Department, in 1935, had redesigned the $1 bill, adding the Great Seal of the United States along with other stylistic changes. The new bills had been in circulation for just over a year. Mellon removed a pen from another pocket and stepped to one of the tables. Roosevelt watched as lines were drawn on the face of the bill.

Mellon handed over the dollar. "This is for you."

He saw that Mellon had drawn two triangles atop the Great Seal's reverse face. "A pentagram?"

"It's six pointed."

He corrected himself. "A Star of David. Is this intended to mean something?"

"It's a clue from our history. There were men in our past who knew that a man like you—a tyrannical aristocrat—would one day come along. So I thought it fitting that history"—Mellon pointed to the bill—"and that anomaly begin your quest. As you can see, the formation of the two triangles joins five letters. O S A M N. It's an anagram."

Roosevelt studied bill. "Mason. They form the word *Mason*."

"That they do."

Against his better judgment he had to ask, "What does it mean?"

"The end of you."

Mellon held a military bearing, standing tall, head still cocked down, as if openly mocking his commander in chief's inability to stand. A hissing log from the fire burst from the flames and spat at them.

"*A strange coincidence, to use a phrase, by which such things are settled nowadays.*" Mellon paused. "Lord Byron. I thought it apt here, also."

His guest moved toward the door.

"I'm not through speaking with you," Roosevelt called out.

Mellon stopped and turned back. "I'll be waiting for you—*Mr.* President."

And he left.

THE
PRESENT

ONE

VENICE, ITALY
MONDAY, NOVEMBER 10
10:40 P.M.

COTTON MALONE DOVE TO THE FLOOR AS BULLETS PEPPERED THE glass wall. Thankfully the transparent panel, which separated one space from another floor-to-ceiling, did not shatter. He risked a look into the expansive secretarial area and spotted flashes of light through the semi-darkness, each burst emitted from the end of a short-barreled weapon. The glass between him and the assailant was obviously extra-resistant, and he silently thanked someone's foresight.

His options were limited.

He knew little about the geography of the building's eighth floor—after all, this was his first visit. He'd come expecting to covertly observe a massive financial transaction—$20 million U.S. being stuffed into two large sacks destined for North Korea. Instead the exchange had turned into a bloodbath, four men dead in an office not far away, their killer—an Asian man with short, dark hair and dressed as a security guard—now homing in on him.

He needed to take cover.

At least he was armed, toting his Magellan Billet–issued Beretta and two spare magazines. The ability to travel with a gun was one advantage that came with again carrying a badge for the United States Justice Department. He'd agreed to the temporary assignment as a way to take his mind off things in Copenhagen, and to earn some money since nowadays spy work paid well.

Think.

He was outgunned, but not outsmarted.

Control what's around you and you control the outcome.

He darted left down the corridor, across gritty terrazzo, just as another volley finally obliterated the glass wall. He passed a nook with a restroom door on either side and kept going. Farther on a maid's cart sat unattended. He caught sight of a propped-open door to a nearby office and spied a uniformed woman cowering in the dark interior.

He whispered in Italian, "Crawl under the desk and stay quiet."

She did as he commanded.

This civilian could be a problem. *Collateral damage* was the term used for them in Magellan Billet reports. He hated the description. More accurately they were somebody's father, mother, brother, sister. Innocents, caught in the crossfire.

It would be only a few moments before the Asian appeared.

He noticed another office door and rushed inside the dark space. The usual furniture lay scattered. A second doorway led to an adjacent room, light spilling in through its half-open door. A quick glance inside that other space confirmed that the second room opened back to the hall.

That would work.

His nostrils detected the odor of cleaning solution, an open metal canister holding several gallons resting a few feet away. He also spotted a pack of cigarettes and a lighter on the maid's cart.

Control what's around you.

He grabbed both, then tipped over the metal container.

Clear fluid gurgled onto the hall floor, spreading across the tile in a river that flowed in the direction from which the Asian would come.

He waited.

Five seconds later his attacker, leading with the automatic rifle, peered around a corner, surely wondering where his prey might be.

Malone lingered another few seconds so as to be seen.

The rifle appeared.

He darted into the office. Bullets peppered the maid's cart in deafening bursts. He flicked the lighter and ignited the cigarette pack. Paper, cellophane, and tobacco began to burn. One. Two. He tossed the burning bundle out the door and into the clear film that sheathed the hall floor.

A swoosh and the cleaning liquid caught fire.

Movement in the second room confirmed what he'd thought would happen. The Asian had taken refuge there from the burning floor. Before his enemy could fully appreciate his dilemma Malone plunged through the doorway, tackling the man to the ground.

The rifle clattered away.

His right hand clamped onto the man's throat.

But his opponent was strong.

And nimble.

They rolled, twice, colliding with a desk.

He told himself to keep his grip. But the Asian pivoted off the floor and catapulted him feetfirst into the air. His body hinged across his opponent's head. He was thrust aside and the Asian sprang to his feet. He readied himself for a fight, but the "guard" fled the room.

He found his gun and approached the door, heart pounding, lungs heaving. Remnants of the liquid still smoldered on the floor. The hall was clear and wet footprints led away. He followed them. At a corner, he stopped and glanced around, seeing no one. He advanced toward the elevators and studied the transom, noticing that the position-indicator displays for both cars were lit 8—this floor. He pressed the UP button and jumped back ready to fire.

The doors opened.

The right car was empty. The left held a bloodied corpse, dressed only in his underwear. The real guard, he assumed. He stared at the contorted face, obscured by two gaping wounds. Surely part of the plan was not only to eliminate all of the participants, but to leave no witnesses behind. He glanced inside the car and spotted a destroyed control panel. He checked the other car and found that it had also been disabled. The only way out now was the stairs.

He entered the stairwell and listened. Someone was climbing the risers toward the roof. He vaulted up as fast as caution advised, keeping an eye ahead for trouble.

A door opened, then closed.

At the top he found an exit and heard the distinct churn of a helicopter turbine starting from the other side.

He cracked open the door.

A chopper faced away, tail boom and fin close, its cabin pointing out to the night. The rotors began to wind fast and the Asian quickly loaded on the two large sacks of cash, then jumped inside.

Blades spun faster and the skids lifted from the roof.

He pushed open the door.

A chilly wind buffeted him.

Should he fire? No. Let it fly away? He'd been sent only to observe, but things had gone wrong, so now he needed to earn his keep. He stuffed the pistol into his back pocket, buttoned it shut, and ran. One leap and he grabbed hold of the rising skid.

The chopper powered out into the dark sky.

What a strange sensation, flying unprotected through the night. He clung tightly to the metal skid with both hands, the chopper's airspeed making it increasingly difficult to hang on.

He stared down.

They were headed east, away from the mainland, toward the water and the islands. The location where the murders had occurred was on the Italian shore, a few hundred yards inland, a nondescript office building near Marco Polo International Airport. The lagoon itself was enclosed by thin strips of lighted coast joined in a wide arc to the mainland, Venice lying at the center.

The chopper banked right and increased speed.

He wrapped his right arm around the skid for a better hold.

Ahead he spied Venice, its towers and spires lit to the night. Beyond on all sides was blackness, signaling open water. Farther east was Lido, which fronted the Adriatic. His mind ticked off what lay below. To the north, ground lights betrayed the presence of Murano, then Burano and, farther on, Torcello. The islands lay embedded in the lagoon like sparkling trinkets. He curled himself around the skid and for the first time stared up into the cabin.

The "guard" eyed him.

The chopper veered left, apparently to see if the unwanted passenger could be dislodged. His body flew out, then whipped back, but he held tight and stared up once more into icy eyes. He saw the Asian slide open the hatch with his left hand, the rifle in his right. In the instant before rounds rained down at the skids, he swung across the undercarriage toward the other skid and jerked himself over.

Bullets smacked the left skid, disappearing down through the dark. He was now safe on the right side, but his hands ached from gravity's pull. The chopper again rocked back and forth, tapping his last bits of strength. He hooked his left leg onto the skid, hugging the metal. The brisk air dried his throat, making breathing difficult. He worked hard to build up saliva and relieve the parching.

He needed to do something and fast.

He studied the whirling rotors, blades beating the air, the staccato of the turbine deafening. On the roof he'd hesitated, but now there appeared to be no choice. He held on tight with his legs and left arm, then reached back and unbuttoned his pant pocket. He stuffed in his right hand and removed the Beretta.

Only one way left to force the chopper down.

He fired three shots into the screaming turbine just below the rotor's hub.

The engine sputtered.

Flames poured out of the air intake and exhaust pipe. Airspeed diminished. The nose went up in an effort to stay airborne.

He glanced down.

They were still a thousand feet up but rapidly losing altitude in something of a controlled descent.

He could see an island ahead of them. Scattered glows defined its rectangular shape just north of Venice. He knew the place. Isola di San Michele. Nothing there but a couple of churches and a huge cemetery where the dead had been buried since the time of Napoleon.

More sputtering.

A sudden backfire.

Thick smoke billowed from the exhaust, the scent of sulfur and burning oil sickening. The pilot was apparently trying to stabilize the descent, the craft jerking up and down, its control planes working hard.

They overtook the island flying close to the dome of its main church.

At twenty feet off the ground success seemed at hand. The chopper leveled, then hovered. Its turbine smoothed. Below was a dark spot, but he wondered how many stone markers might be waiting. Hard to see anything in the darkness. The chopper's occupants surely knew they still had company. So why land? Just head back up and ditch their passenger from the air.

He should have shot the turbine a few times more.

Now he had no choice.

So he let go of the skid.

He seemed to fall for the longest time, though if memory served him right a free-falling object fell at the rate of thirty-two feet per second, per second. Twenty feet equaled less than one second. He hoped that the ground was soft and he avoided stone.

He pounded legs-first, his knees collapsing to absorb the shock, then rebounding, sending him rolling. His left thigh instantly ached. Somehow he managed to hold on to the gun. He came to a stop and looked back up. The pilot had regained full control. The helicopter pitched up and maneuvered closer. A swing to the right and his attacker now had a clear view below. He could probably limp off, but he saw no good ground cover. He was in the open, amid the graves. The Asian saw his predicament, hovering less than a hundred feet away, the downwash from the blades stirring up loose topsoil. The helicopter's hatch slid open and his attacker one-handedly took aim with the automatic rifle.

Malone propped himself up and aimed the pistol using both hands. There couldn't be more than four rounds left in the magazine.

Make 'em count.

So he aimed at the engine.

The Asian gestured to the pilot for a retreat.

But not before Malone fired. One, two, three, four shots.

Hard to tell which bullet actually did the trick, but the turbine exploded, a brilliant fireball lighting the sky, flaming chunks cascading to the ground in a searing shower fifty yards away. In the sudden light he spotted hundreds of grave markers in tightly packed rows. He hugged the earth and shielded his head as the explosions continued, a heaping mass of twisted metal, flesh, and burning fuel erupting before him.

He stared at the carnage.

A crackle of flames consumed the helicopter, its occupants, and $20 million U.S. in cash.

Somebody was going to be pissed.

TWO

Kim Yong Jin stood on one side of the bed, holding the intravenous bag. His daughter Hana watched him from the other side.

"I imagine this is something you have seen before," he quietly asked her in Korean.

By *this* he meant the strong asserting themselves over the utterly weak. And yes, he knew she'd borne witness to that too many times to count.

"No comment?" he said.

She stared at him.

"No, I suppose not. The fish would never get into trouble if he but kept his mouth shut. Right?"

She nodded.

He smiled at her intuition, then returned his attention to the bed and asked, "Are you comfortable?"

But the older man lying before them did not reply. How could he? The drug had paralyzed every muscle, numbing nerves, freeing the mind. A tube from the IV bag Kim held snaked a path down into a vein. A valve allowed him to control the flow. No danger existed of anyone ever knowing that it had been administered since their captive was a diabetic, one more needle mark hardly noticeable.

"I don't suppose it matters if he's comfortable or not," he said. "Silly question, actually. He's not going anywhere."

Indifference in the face of dominance was a trait he'd inherited from his father—along with sparse hair, excess weight, a bulbous head, and a private passion for decadent entertainment. Unlike his father, who managed to succeed his own father and lead North Korea for nearly a quarter century, Kim had been denied that opportunity.

And for what?

Visiting Tokyo Disneyland?

Two of his nine children had wanted to go. So he obtained false Portuguese passports and tried to gain entry. But an observant border officer at Narita International Airport caught the deception and he was detained. To secure his release, his father had been forced to personally intervene with the Japanese government.

And it cost him.

He'd been disinherited, dropped from the line of succession.

Where before he'd been the eldest son, entitled to the reins of power, afterward he was disgraced. And twelve years ago, when his father finally died, Kim's illegitimate half brother had taken his place as head of the military, chairman of the National Defense Commission, and supreme leader of the Workers' Party, wielding absolute control over Democratic People's Republic of Korea.

What was the wisdom?

Only a bad plowman quarrels with his ox.

He glanced around at the suite.

Not as luxurious as his penthouse two decks above, but still way above average. He and Hana had just spent ten days cruising the Adriatic and Mediterranean Seas, stopping in Croatia, Montenegro, Sicily, and Italy, waiting for the old man lying before them to make a move.

But nothing substantial had occurred.

So now, on the last night, as the ship sat docked in Venice and the several thousand on board were ashore enjoying the sights, they'd come to pay Paul Larks a visit. All it had taken was a knock on the door and Larks had been easily subdued.

"Mr. Larks," Kim said in a congenial voice, "why are you on this trip?"

"To right a wrong."

The voice was strained, but the answer definitive. That was the thing about the drug. Truth was all the brain could reveal. The ability to lie ceased to exist.

"Which wrong?"

"One my country has done."

Another annoying aspect was that usually only the question asked was answered, nothing much was ever volunteered.

"How long have you possessed the documents that right this wrong?"

"Since I worked for the government. I found them during that time."

This man had once served as an undersecretary of the American Treasury Department, having been quietly forced out less than three months ago.

Kim asked, "Was that before or after you read the book?"

"Before."

He, too, had read *The Patriot Threat* by Anan Wayne Howell. Self-published two years ago, with no fanfare or notoriety. "Is Howell correct?"

"He is."

"Where is Howell?"

"I'll meet him tomorrow."

"Where?"

"I was told he would find me after I left the ship."

"Did you not come here to meet with Howell during the cruise?"

"That was the original plan."

A curious reply. "Were you to meet anyone else?"

"The Korean. But we thought it best not to do that."

"Who is *we*?"

"Howell and I."

He was puzzled. "Why?"

"It's better if we keep this among Americans."

Now he was agitated. *He* was the Korean. "Where are the documents that right the wrong?"

Larks had carried a black Tumi satchel around since the first day of the cruise. On deck. To meals. Never had it left him. Yet it was nowhere in the suite. Hana had already searched.

"I gave them to Jelena. She said the right password."

The name was unfamiliar. A new participant. But he wanted to know. "Tell me what the password is."

"Mellon."

"Like a fruit?"

"No. Andrew Mellon."

He caught the irony, but still asked why that label had been chosen.

"He was the custodian of truth."

Only someone who'd read Howell's book would understand that observation.

"When did you give Jelena the documents?"

"A few hours ago."

This was a problem, for sure, as retrieving these papers was partly why he was here. Weeks ago he'd tried from long distance to coax them from Larks with no luck. Then he'd conceived the idea of a meeting overseas. A rendezvous that might not only provide the written evidence he sought, but lead him to the instigator of it all. Anan Wayne Howell. Author of *The Patriot Threat*.

"Does Jelena know Howell?" Kim asked.

"She does."

"And how will she deliver the documents?"

"She'll meet Howell tomorrow, after leaving the ship."

Clearly, things had not gone as planned. But he'd expected bumps along this treacherous road. Dealing with odd personalities and desperate people came with risk.

"Who are you?" Larks asked suddenly.

He glanced down to the bed.

The drug had worn off faster than anticipated, but he'd kept the dose light so the old man could communicate readily.

"I'm your benefactor," he said. "The Korean." He did not mask his contempt at the label.

Larks tried to rise, but Hana restrained him. It took little effort to keep the older man down.

"You've disappointed me," Kim said.

"I have nothing to say to you. This is an American problem. We don't need people like you involved."

"Yet you accepted my money. Came on this trip, and I heard no complaints."

He twisted the valve, allowing more of the drug to flow downward. A fog quickly reappeared in Larks' brown eyes.

"Why did you turn on the Korean?" he asked.

"Howell thought it best. He was suspicious."

"Of what? Was not the Korean your friend?"

"These wrongs do not involve foreigners."

"What wrongs?"

"Those done to Salomon, to Mellon, to Howell, to all the people. They're ours to solve. Sadly, it's all true."

Kim increased the flow, which would allow Larks' mind to completely surrender free will.

"What is all true?" he asked.

"The patriot threat."

He knew the term from the book, but the question had always been—was it real, or just the fantasy of some fringe author bent on wild conspiracies? He was literally betting his life that it existed.

His phone vibrated in his pocket.

He handed the IV bag across the bed to Hana and found the unit.

"The helicopter exploded over the lagoon," a man reported. "We were too far away to know anything, but we did see a man jump onto the chopper as it lifted off. We're headed by boat now to where it exploded."

"Twenty million dollars gone?" Kim asked.

"It seems so."

"This is not good."

"Like we have to be told. Our payment just went up in flames."

The men had been hired on a 50 percent commission.

"Find out what happened," he said.

"We're en route."

More problems. Not what he wanted to hear. He ended the call and stared down at the bed, thinking about the courier Larks mentioned.

"There may be a way to find the woman," he said to Hana. "This Jelem."

She handed the IV bag back to him.

"Tomorrow," he muttered. "When Howell appears."

Which meant Paul Larks was of no further use.

So he opened the valve all the way.

THREE

Stephanie Nelle entered the department store and marched straight toward women's apparel. The mall was on the north side of town, not far from Magellan Billet headquarters. She'd never been much of a shopper, but occasionally she enjoyed an evening or a Saturday afternoon browsing, something to take her mind off her job. She'd led the Magellan Billet for sixteen years. The intelligence unit had been her creation, twelve agents, employed by the Justice Department, who handled only the most sensitive investigations.

All good people.

But something was wrong.

And it was time to find out what and why.

She caught sight of Terra Lucent across the store and navigated the aisles toward her. Terra was a petite woman with copper-colored hair, one of four administrative assistants the Billet employed.

"You want to tell me why I'm here," Stephanie said as she drew close to her employee. "And shouldn't you be asleep?"

"I appreciate you meeting me. I really do. I know it's unusual."

"To say the least."

She'd found a note on her desk that asked her to come to Dillard's at 5:30 and tell no one. Terra had worked for her a number of years, assigned the graveyard shift because of her levelheadedness and dependability.

"Ma'am, this is important."

She registered concern on the younger woman's face. Terra had recently divorced, for the fourth time. A bit unlucky in love, but she was good at her job.

"I have to report something. It's not right what's happening. Not right at all."

She caught the dart of the other woman's eyes as her gaze raked the store. Only a few employees and a couple of shoppers milled about.

"Are you expecting someone?"

Terra faced her and licked her lips. "I just want to make sure we're alone. That's why I asked you to come *here*."

"Why the note? Could you not have called? Or just talked to me at the office? Why all this secrecy?"

"I couldn't do any of those."

The words were riddled with apprehension.

"Terra, what's going on?"

"Late one night, about ten days ago, I'd gone to get myself a drink from the cafeteria. We were shorthanded, so I took the cell phone with me in case anyone called. I always smoke downstairs, outside. But when I'm there alone—I know we're not supposed to smoke on the floor—I can't leave for long when no one else is there. I leave the door open so I can hear the incoming bell ding, and go down the hall to smoke."

Billet rules required that someone always monitor the office. Agents were issued specially programmed laptops and iPhones since encrypted emails and text messages were one of the quickest and most secure forms of communication.

"Why don't you just smoke in the office?"

She shook her head. "You'd smell it. No way."

Her affinity toward anything with tobacco was no secret, and federal law forbid smoking in the building anyway. "Forget about the cigarettes and get to the point."

"Ten days ago, like I said, I was in the alcove at the end of the hall. I cracked the window to let the smoke out. I finished and headed back to the office. That's when I saw him. He flashed a badge and made threats. He said he was from Treasury."

"How did this man get in the building?"

"I checked the electronic registries the following day and there was no record of anyone entering at that hour."

Every door was protected with a swipe lock that required a keycard for entrance. Which meant whoever *he* was had friends in the right places.

"What was he doing there?"

"He wanted computer access."

"And you gave it to him?"

Terra nodded.

"How long was he in the office?"

"Half an hour. He used a terminal in the conference room. After he left, I looked, but its directory was wiped clear."

"And you've waited till now to tell me this?"

"I know, ma'am. But I thought it was some emergency he was handling."

"I can't believe you've done this."

Disappointment clouded her employee's face. "I know. But . . . he made me keep quiet."

She didn't like the sound of that.

"I wrote a bad check, ma'am. It was when I was divorced the last time. The store took a warrant. I made good on it, but I was still arrested. This guy knew about all that. He told me he'd keep quiet and everything would be okay. I wanted to keep my job. I knew the arrest would be the end of my security clearance. The check was over $500. A felony. The charges were eventually dismissed, but I wasn't going to take the chance. My children have to eat. So I did what I had to, but then he went too far."

She was listening.

"He came back a few days later and wanted more computer access— this time on *my* ID." Terra paused. "I gave it to him. None of this is right. And he wants access again, tonight."

She considered the information, then asked, "Is that all?"

Terra nodded. "I'm so sorry. I really am. I've tried hard to do right by my job. I know you trust me—"

"You've broken every rule."

Terra's eyes reddened.

At the moment she needed this woman to be her ally, so she made clear, "We'll let it pass—for now—provided you do three things."

"Anything, ma'am."

"Tell no one what you just told me. Give him access tonight. And tell me everything he says and does from this point on."

Terra's face brightened. "Of course. I can do that."

"Now go on. Get out of here and get some sleep. Your shift starts in a few hours."

Terra thanked her again and left.

That was a first. Never had Billet security been breached. Her unit had always been a tight one, without incident, the list of its successes far outdistancing any failures. That winning percentage had also bred jealousy among her colleagues. But Treasury? What did they want among Billet files badly enough to blackmail one of her employees?

Whatever it was, she had to know.

She slowly made her way out of the department store. Terra strolled thirty yards ahead of her. They entered the mall's towering glass-topped atrium, which directed shoppers in four directions toward retail stores on two levels.

Stephanie caught sight of a man on the second floor.

Slim, thin hair, dressed in a dark suit and white shirt, standing propped against the railing. He immediately fled his position and started walking, one floor above, paralleling her direction. Terra hustled down the sparsely populated mall toward another atrium that housed the food court. Doors there led out to the rear parking lots. Stephanie's gaze darted upward and she caught glimpses of the man still following. When they reached the atrium, Terra turned left for the exit doors, and the man bounded downward on a semicircular staircase. As he rounded the risers and approached the ground floor, Stephanie slipped her cell phone from her pocket.

The man came to the last step.

She pointed the phone, centered the image, and snapped a picture, quickly lowering the unit. The man found the terrazzo and turned for the mall's rear exit. No question. He was after Terra. She caught sight of a security guard sitting at a table drinking from a coffee cup.

Something hard nudged her ribs.

"Not a sound, or your employee there might not make it to work tonight."

She froze.

Terra left through the mall exit.

The man ahead of her stopped and turned back. A smile filled his face. The phone was still in her grasp, down at her side. The first man stepped toward her in a slow stride and reached for the unit.

"I don't think you'll be needing that."

FOUR

MALONE SPRANG FROM THE GRASS, HIS LUNGS RAW FROM PANTING the dry night air. Luckily he had avoided the stone markers that stood at attention all around him when he fell. The helicopter debris continued to burn, not much left but charred bits and pieces. A fading glow from the blaze illuminated the way through the graves to the church. There should be a boat dock near there, perhaps even a night watchman some-where on the island. But where was he or she? That crash should have attracted some immediate attention. Surely it had been noticed across the lagoon in Venice. Police would soon be on their way, if they weren't already. Waiting for them didn't seem like a good idea. He needed to leave. His task had been to simply observe and report. But wow—had that gone wrong.

Once a year, on the birthday of their Dear Leader, North Korean insurance managers sent a gift of $20 million in cash, all generated by fraud. Things like transportation accidents, factory fires, floods, and other catastrophes within North Korea, most of which either never happened or were manufactured. Every insurance policy within North Korea was issued by the state-owned KNIC. To spread its liability KNIC sought out reinsurers around the world willing to accept a portion of its risk in exchange for hefty premiums, and those companies were found in Europe, India, and Egypt. Of course, each of those entities assumed that

KNIC would have evaluated its risk and written its policies accordingly, wanting to minimize exposure. After all, that was the whole idea of the insurance business—to pay out as few claims as possible. But that was not the case here. Instead, KNIC made sure there were expensive claims the reinsurers would have to honor. In fact, the more disasters the better. To avoid drawing undue attention, claims were systematically generated against differing reinsurers. One year the focus was on Lloyd's, the next Munich Re, then Swiss Re. Every claim was carefully documented, then sped through puppet courts in Pyongyang where the outcome was never in doubt. It helped that North Korean law made it impossible for reinsurers to send their own investigators to check anything.

All in all, it was the perfect scam, one that generated annual revenues topping $50 million, some of which was used by KNIC to keep the scheme going, the rest paid into Dear Leader's pockets.

Twenty million dollars, annually, for the past four years.

Bags of cash had arrived in Pyongyang from Singapore, Switzerland, France, Austria, and, this year, Italy. Sent to an entity called Bureau 39 of the Korean Workers' Party Central Committee, created to collect hard currency and provide Dear Leader with funds independent of a virtually nonexistent national economy. Intelligence reports indicated that the money financed things like luxury goods for the country's elite, missile components, even the production of nuclear weapons. Everything an enterprising young dictator might need.

Stephanie wanted this year's money transfer witnessed, as that had never been possible before. American intelligence had learned its location—Venice—so she told him to leave the cruise ship and head inland.

He'd wondered about the coincidence.

How did that money transfer just happen to occur while he was already in Venice?

The answer to that question had not become overly important until the shooting started. Now the cash was ashes and all of the participants to the payoff dead. So he'd like to know.

His mind searched for everything he knew about his current location.

Isola di San Michele was once two islands, but a canal between them had been filled long ago. Napoleon created the cemetery in 1807, when he ordered Venetians to stop burying their dead within the town. A Renaissance church and a former monastery remained from that time. A high brick wall guarded its shores, the dark outline of tall cypresses rising above it. He recalled one other anomaly. The burials were squeezed tight, the dead guaranteed only a few years' rest. After a decade the remains were exhumed and stored in ossuaries, making room for more bodies. One of the notice boards that listed the timetable for exhumations stood to his right.

He popped the magazine from his Beretta and replaced it with a spare from his pocket. Then he started walking toward the church, making no pretense of silence. A series of gardens studded with cypress trees and more monuments lined the stone-paved walkways. Some of the graves were gaudy with domes and sculptures and wrought iron. Some were stacked in terraces like filing cabinets. Amazing how audacious people could be with death.

The kink in his leg began to work itself out. He was too damn old to be dropping from helicopters. He was supposed to be retired—after a career in the navy, law school, then a dozen years at the Justice Department working for Stephanie Nelle's Magellan Billet. He quit three years ago and now owned an old-book shop in Copenhagen. But that hadn't stopped trouble from finding him. This time, though, he'd found it, as he'd willingly accepted Stephanie's offer to freelance. The past few weeks had been anything but pleasant. He'd heard not a word from Cassiopeia Vitt. They'd dated for the past year, but parted ways a month ago when trouble had once again found them both in Utah. He'd thought maybe after she cooled down they could work it through. He'd even called her once, but she did not answer. He did receive an email, though. Short and sweet.

Leave me alone.

Obviously, her bitterness still retained fire.

So he did as she asked, and a chance to roam the Adriatic and Mediterranean for ten days on the U.S. government's dime had seemed like a good respite. All he had to do was keep an eye on a former Treasury

official, Paul Larks, who might lead him to a man named Anan Wayne
Howell, an American fugitive. The Justice Department wanted Howell. So he'd stayed close. Larks was pushing seventy, walked with a
slight stoop that reminded him of his old friend Henrik Thorvaldsen, and
had kept to himself during the cruise, which had made him think that
whatever was supposed to happen would happen in Venice. Then the dis-
patch from Stephanie, sending him to the Italian mainland, arrived.

And disaster followed.

He approached the lighted church, its white marble façade overlook-
ing the lagoon. Everything was closed up tight. He rounded one side and
spotted a boathouse. A dim light burned inside, illuminating one of the
sleek, low-riding runabouts that had made Venice famous.

"Stop right there," a male voice said in Italian.

He turned to see a heavyset man in uniform bobble up in the dark.
He still held his Beretta, which he quickly shielded behind his thigh.

"Are you stationed here?" he asked the man in Italian.

Languages were easy for him, the advantage of both living in Europe
and having an eidetic memory. He was fluent in several.

"Were you in that crash?"

"*Si*. And I have to leave the island."

The man came close. "Are you hurt?"

He nodded and lied, "I need a doctor."

"My boat is there. Can you make it to the dock?"

He'd heard enough and revealed the gun, aiming it straight at the
man.

Hands went into the air. "Please, *signor*. That is not necessary. Not at
all."

"The keys to the boat."

"They are on board. In the ignition."

"I need you to go back to wherever you stay and call for help. Tell
them about the crash. Right now, do it."

The unarmed guard did not need to be told twice. As the man hustled
off, Malone made his way down to the dock and onto the boat.

The keys were indeed in the ignition.

He powered up the engines.

KIM REMOVED THE NEEDLE FROM LARKS' ARM. THE OLD FOOL HAD proven to be nothing but trouble. They'd spoken on the phone and communicated by email many times. He'd listened with patience to all the rants. Larks was angry with his government for a multitude of lies. Eventually Kim had revealed to Larks that he was Korean, not realizing that might be a problem. After all, Howell had bought them together, all of them supposedly kindred souls bound by the same interest. Larks himself was a widower who'd alienated his bosses—forced to retire after thirty-plus years of government service. He had no children and little other family. He was, for all intents and purposes, forgotten. Now he was dead. But two vital things had first been learned. Larks had passed his cache of documents on to a woman named Jelena and Howell would be in Venice tomorrow.

His cell phone vibrated again.

"We watched with night-vision glasses," the voice reported in North Korean. "A man definitely jumped onto the chopper and hung from its strut. The pilot tried to lose him, but couldn't. He dropped off, onto a small island, then we heard shots, and an explosion. That same man, still holding a gun, just left the island in a boat."

With the chopper down, its occupants killed, and all of the men at the cash transfer, he assumed, dead too, the loose ends were certainly tied—except for whoever was in that boat.

True, the idea had been to steal the money.

But with it gone—

"I recommend you kill him," he said.

"I agree."

FIVE

STEPHANIE SIZED UP HER ASSAILANT. HE WAS GOVERNMENT, OF that she was sure. Career man. Nearing retirement. And confident. Too much so, actually, since they were now sitting in a mall food court.

"I love Chick-fil-A's," he said, gesturing with the sandwich he held. "When I was a kid my mother would buy them as a treat for me and my brothers."

He seemed pleased by the memory. The other man—the one with the gun—sat at a nearby table. Though it was dinnertime, the tables were nearly empty.

"Is there a reason you've assaulted the head of an American intelligence unit? Your man over there threatened me and one of my people."

He kept eating his sandwich. "The two pickles are the key. Just the right amount of dill flavor to spice up the chicken."

She realized he was trying to get under her skin, so she asked, "What are you? DEA? FBI?"

"That hurts."

But she knew. "Treasury?"

He quit chewing. "I was told you're a smart lady."

Any other time she'd tell this moron to go to hell. But that was the thing about fishing. If you dangled the right bait at the right time, what you were after just might swim by and sneak a nibble. And this fish had done just that. "Why does Treasury think it can threaten a fellow federal agent and hold her against her will?"

He shrugged. "You can leave whenever you want."

"You must have friends in high places."

He grinned. "Best kind of job security."

That meant the secretary of Treasury. "All this sounds like a conspiracy to me."

"Only in the best of terms. Done to get your attention. And see how well it worked? Here we are, sharing dinner."

"You're the only one eating."

"I offered and you said no, so don't blame me that you aren't having any of this good ol' American food."

He sucked a swallow of Coke through a straw, then returned to his sandwich. His cockiness was weighing on her, as if she and the Magellan Billet were insignificant. But she'd encountered the attitude before. Of late that arrogance had all but disappeared since, for the past two years the Billet had been at the forefront of nearly every major intelligence success. It helped that the White House had total confidence in her unit, a fact that had not gone unnoticed by her colleagues.

"Who wants to get my attention?" she asked.

"Now, we just met, and I have a rule about kissing and telling, so why don't we just say that they're all good people and leave it at that." He laid down his sandwich. "We figured you and your employee Ms. Lucent were not here for the sales on women's wear."

"So you listened in on our conversation?"

"Something like that. She seems like a loyal worker, coming to you and confessing like that."

"She'll be an ex-worker soon."

"I figured. That's why I decided it was time for us to chat."

"About what?"

"Why is Cotton Malone in Venice?"

Finally, the heart of the matter. "We just met and I have a rule about kissing and telling, so why don't we just say that Cotton's good people and leave it at that."

He smiled at her mocking. "We have a comedienne here. A real Carol Burnett."

She dug in and readied herself for the fight she'd been hoping for.

"People wonder about you, Stephanie. Where you stand. What's important. My boss—one of those good people I mentioned—defended you. He said Stephanie Nelle serves her country with honor. She's a good American."

He popped the last bite of sandwich into his mouth and she hoped he wouldn't lick his fingers. But he did, then dried the tips with his napkin.

"I know a lot about you," he said. "You've got a law degree and twenty-eight years at Justice. Before that you were with the State Department. You've been around, that's one reason you were tagged to start the Magellan Billet. Experience and know-how, and you've done a heck of a job. Your agents are some of the best America has on the payroll. That kind of thing gets noticed."

"Even by important people like you?"

He caught her sarcasm. "Even by me. You know, I love Chick-fil-A ice cream. Want some?"

She shook her head. "Trying to quit."

He motioned to the other man. "Get me a cone and some more napkins." The man headed off for the serving counter.

"Your minions always do your errands?" she asked.

"They do whatever I say."

He seemed proud.

"You still haven't said what you want with me."

"And you haven't answered my question. What's Malone doing on that cruise?"

"I sent him."

"Stay away from Paul Larks."

Now it was her turn to play dumb. "Who's that?"

He chuckled. "Do I look stupid?"

Actually, he did.

The man returned with the ice cream and Chick-fil-A Man started licking the sides. "Wow, that's good stuff."

As the other man withdrew, she asked, "What's Treasury's interest in Larks? He was forced out three months ago."

The man's tongue continued to attack the cone. "He copied some documents. We want them back. We're also looking for a guy named Anan Wayne Howell. I think you know the name?"

That she did.

"We think Larks will lead us to him, but not with your guard dog on duty."

"Tell the secretary of Treasury he needs to take all this up with the attorney general."

He found the cone and bit into it. "I'm not an errand boy."

No, he wasn't. He was a fool, which made him even lower on the pole. He finished the cone and again licked his fingers.

She averted her eyes until he finished.

He stuffed the balled napkins, the Styrofoam cup, and the foil-lined jacket for the chicken sandwich into a paper bag. Then he stood, bag in hand, and threw her a glare that was devoid of all whimsical humor. "Remember what I said. Stay away from Larks and call Malone off. We won't warn you again."

"We?"

"People who can cause you problems."

She kept her cool. "I need my phone back."

He found the unit in his pocket, dropped it to the floor, and shattered it with the heel of his shoe. With his trash in hand, he and his companion strutted away.

She watched as they left the mall.

Pleased the fish had not only nibbled the bait, but swallowed it hook, line, sinker—even the whole damn boat.

SIX

VENICE

MALONE FIRED UP THE INBOARD MOTORS, WHICH SPUTTERED THEN, as he readjusted the throttle, roared to life. He backed the launch out of the boathouse. The V-hull looked to be a fifteen-footer, all wood, and he could feel the engines' powerful hum. He knew little about the lagoon except that its navigable routes were defined by lighted pilings, *bícoles,* there to help boats avoid the mudflats, tidal islands, and salt marshes. Merchants and men-of-war had plodded these waters for centuries, the currents fed by the ebb and flow of the sea, so treacherous that no enemy had ever taken Venice by force.

He decided to follow the lighted route and head back toward town, then round the main island for the cruise ship dock that sat on its west end. When he'd left the ship earlier, water taxis and private launches were ferrying people to and from that dock. Another one would not be noticed.

He found the lagoon and shifted the throttle from reverse to forward. Boats were no strangers to him. His late father was career navy, achieving the rank of commander. He'd matched that rise, spending nine years on active duty before being reassigned to the Magellan Billet. Back in Copenhagen he occasionally rented a sloop and enjoyed an afternoon on the choppy Øresund.

He swung the bow around.

Another boat appeared from the darkness, its profile rushing straight at him at high speed. In the dim light he saw two men, one aiming a gun his way. He dove down as pops rang out and bullets thudded into the windshield.

Where the hell had they come from?

He yanked the wheel hard right and headed away from Venice, toward the island of Murano and its glass factories, which lay just northeast of Isla de San Michele. A channel about half a mile wide separated the two locales, marked with more *bicoles,* their lights signaling a path north in the darkness toward Burano and Torcello. He pushed the throttle forward, and the diesels' even roar knifed the bow across the calm water.

His assailants were behind him, but gaining, both boats scudding across the surface in clouds of noisy spray. He found the channel and stayed between the lights on either side, the path about fifty yards wide and illuminated like a fairground. He could take the two men behind him, but he needed room to maneuver—and some privacy would be good. That helicopter crash had certainly attracted attention, and the guard on San Michele had surely called the authorities by now. Police boats could come from anywhere at any time.

He turned east, then back north, heading away from Murano. The boat behind was gaining. He still toted his gun with a full magazine, but hitting anything from a pitching deck in the dark, while trying to stay in the channel, seemed unlikely. Apparently his pursuers had come to the same conclusion, as no more shots had been fired.

The second boat swept in close.

One of the men leaped across, slamming his body into Malone. He lost his grip on the wheel. They tumbled to the deck. The boat veered left. He catapulted the man off him and tried to regain control, but his assailant lunged. In the darkness he noticed Asian features, the compact frame hard as steel. He swung around, pivoting off the wheel, and kicked the man in the face, sending him reeling toward the stern. He stuffed a hand into his back pocket, found his Beretta, and shot the problem in the chest. The bullet's recoil propelled the body over the side and into the water.

The second boat remained on him, pounding into the starboard side, trying to maneuver him out of the channel. They were racing along, still within the lights that defined out of bounds. He needed this over. Who these people were was anybody's guess. Were they on the side of the folks who'd come to receive the $20 million? Or part of the team that stole it? Apparently somebody had worked a lot of planning for tonight. The only thing they hadn't anticipated was a retired freelance agent screwing everything up.

He veered right, kissed the second boat, and grabbed his bearings. He was past Burano, near Torcello, in a quiet, darkened part of the lagoon. The lights of Venice burned miles to the south. He held the wheel tight and readied himself.

The hull was slammed again and recoiled.

Then another crash.

He worked the wheel and pressed his boat tight against the other, both craft racing ahead toward the right side of the channel. He kept close and did not allow the other boat any room to maneuver. The other driver's attention seemed focused on him.

Big mistake.

He forced them more right, closer and closer to the edge. The next *bicole* was less than half a mile ahead and he intended to give his assailant a choice. Crash into it or go farther right, out of the channel. Left was not an option. The other man was all shadow, shaped similarly to the first one.

He continued to force the other craft over.

The piling approached.

A hundred yards.

Fifty.

Time for his attacker to choose.

Malone leaped left from his boat into the channel. He hit the water feetfirst and surfaced just as the boats crashed into the concrete tripod piling, both hulls vaulting skyward, engines whining, propellers beating only air. They careened down and splashed the water on the channel side, but did not float long, quickly sinking, their engines' wild chaos drowned to silence.

He breaststroked to the far side of the channel and found a sandbar only a few yards beyond the defined perimeter, the water barely knee-deep.

He suddenly realized how close he'd come to disaster. He searched the darkness for the man from the other boat, but saw and heard nothing. He stood in the lagoon, a good mile from the nearest shore, eyes burning, hair plastered to his skull. Only the silent islets, the faraway buildings of Venice, and the dim line of the mainland could be seen. Overhead, he caught the lights of a passenger jet homing in for a landing. He knew this water was not the cleanest in the world, nor at the moment the warmest, but he had no choice.

Swim.

He heard the growl of an engine, back toward the south, the direction he'd come from. No lights were associated with the sound, but in the darkness he caught the black outline of a boat cruising his way. He still carried his Beretta in his pocket, but doubted the gun would be of much use. Sometimes they worked after a dousing, sometimes not. He shrank down in the water, his feet now encased with a soft layer of muck.

The boat eased closer, cruising at the edge of the channel.

The nearest light was five hundred yards away at the next piling. The one that had been positioned here, nearby, had been obliterated in the crash.

The boat stopped, its engine switched off.

Another sleek V-hull.

A sole figure stood at its helm.

"Malone. You out there?"

He recognized the voice. Male. Younger. Southern accent.

Luke Daniels.

He stood. "About time. I wondered where you were."

"I didn't expect you to go Superman on me, flying through the sky."

He freed his feet from the muck and trudged closer.

Luke stood in the boat and stared down at him. "Seems the first time we met you were pulling me from the water in Denmark."

He stretched an arm up for some help. "Looks like we're now even on that one."

SEVEN

KIM POURED HIMSELF A GENEROUS SPLASH OF WHISKEY. HIS PENT-house suite two decks above Larks' was a four-room monstrosity filled with mahogany and rattan furniture. He'd been impressed by the size and grandeur, along with its amenities like rich food, ample drink, and a massive spray of fresh flowers provided each day. The in-room bar came stocked with some excellent regional wines and American brown whiskey, both of which he'd also enjoyed.

A grandfather clock with Westminster chimes announced the presence of midnight and the beginning of November 11. Pyongyang was seven hours ahead, the sun already shining there on Tuesday morning. His half brother, North Korea's Dear Leader, would be rising for another day.

Kim hated him.

While his own mother—kind and well bred—had been his father's lawful wife, his half brother sprang from a long-standing affair with a national opera star. Both his father and grandfather had kept many mistresses. The practice seemed perfectly acceptable, except that his mother hated infidelity and became clinically depressed at her husband's callousness. She eventually fled the country and settled in Moscow, dying a few years back. He'd been there with her at the end, holding her hand, listening to her laments of how life had treated her so cruelly.

Which it had.

He could say the same.

He'd been educated at private international schools in Switzerland and Moscow, first earning the respected title of Small General, then Great Successor. From living overseas he acquired a taste for Western luxury, particularly designer clothes and expensive cars, again not unlike his father. Eventually he'd returned home and worked in the Department of Agitation and Propaganda, then was assigned to head the nation's Computer Center, where North Korea waged a covert cyber-war on the world. Next he would have garnered high military appointments, moving closer and closer to the center of power. But the incident in Japan cost him everything. Now, at fifty-eight years old, he was all but nonexistent. What had been the harm? He'd just wanted to take two children to Disneyland.

"We cannot rule without the army," his father said. "It is the foundation of the Kim family's hold on national power. My father acquired their loyalty and I have maintained that. But after your antics, they have no confidence in you."

He felt an illogical mixture of shame at his error and pride in his stubbornness, so he truly wanted to know, "For what reason?"

"You are irresponsible. You always have been. Life to you is what you read in those adventure novels. What you write about in those wild stories of yours. The plays and shows you watch, they are all nonsense. None of it is real, except in your mind."

He hadn't realized his father knew of his private passions.

"You do not possess what is required to lead this nation. You are an incessant dreamer, and there is no place for those here."

To him generals were like schools of fish, each floating in tune with the other, none ever wanting to risk swimming alone. What one did, all did. They were useless, except in times of war. But war was the last thing on his mind.

Lost confidence in him?

That was about to change.

His father had been a mercilessly practical man, depressing in appearance. He'd cut his hair in a short military style and, in public, wore drab Mao suits that looked ridiculous. His half brother emulated that style, another inept fool, thirty-nine years old, homeschooled by his whore mother and shielded from the world. But that had proven an unexpected advantage. While Kim had been sent abroad for an education, his father's two other sons, both illegitimate, had been able to grow closer to him. The adoration that had once been his alone became spread among his siblings. And when he'd embarrassed his country on the world stage, those pretenders became players.

He glossed his throat with more of the whiskey.

One bright side, though, had emerged from tonight. No $20 million U.S. would be making its way to Pyongyang for any birthday. His half brother had ruled long enough to have amassed his share of enemies. Thank goodness loyalties ran shallow in North Korea. Some of his half brother's enemies had become his friends and quietly reported the details of this year's tribute. He'd intended on stealing the money and depriving his half brother of the funds, hiring a criminal group from Macao to handle the task. Now that money was gone. But for him, its destruction served the same purpose. Thankfully, personal finances were not an issue. He had more than enough monetary resources. On that score his father had not failed him.

He refilled his glass with more whiskey.

He'd actually never met his half brother. Custom required that a leader's male children be raised independently of one another, the oldest son always favored. He'd heard that his half brother openly thought of his older sibling as an overweight, careless playboy, incapable of any serious responsibility, no danger to him at all. But underestimating him would be his half brother's undoing. He'd gone to great lengths to create that carefree public image. He'd found that being considered an unimportant, embarrassing disgrace—a drunkard—brought with it freedom of movement. It also helped that he lived in Macao, out of the limelight, and never openly interfered in North Korean politics. From time to time the press would seek him out, but his comments were always silly and nonsensical. He was, for all intents and purposes, dead.

He smiled.

What a glorious resurrection he was about to experience.

The look on his half brother's face would be worth the indignities he'd been forced to endure.

And all thanks to Anan Wayne Howell's *The Patriot Threat*.

Law and finance had always interested him. He liked how they were so intricately related, especially within the United States. Americans prided themselves on a strict adherence to law. *Stare decisis,* they called it. *To stand by that which is decided.* Most legal systems around the world rejected the concept, and with good reason since it came with a flaw. What if adherence to "that decided" meant disaster? Did you follow the law then? Not in North Korea. But the Americans? They would be a different story.

He emptied his glass with one long swallow.

His laptop sat on the table before him, its screen filled with a page from *The Patriot Threat.* He'd been rereading a part of it earlier before visiting Paul Larks. He studied the passage once again.

By an executive order signed in 1942, Franklin Roosevelt taxed all personal income over $25,000 ($352,000 in today's value) at 100%. Can you imagine? Work hard an entire year, make good decisions, earn a respectable income, then give everything over $25,000 ($352,000 today) to the government. Congress disagreed with FDR and, in its infinite wisdom, lowered the rate to 90%. Eventually, tax rates were changed by Presidents Kennedy and Reagan. Kennedy lowered the top rate to 70%, Reagan plunged it to 28%. Following each of those tax cuts, government revenues skyrocketed and investments increased. Both the 1960s and 1980s were times of great innovation. The first President Bush raised the top rate to 31%, Clinton climbed even higher to 39.6%, the second Bush cut it to 35%. Currently, the top rate has returned to 39.6%. Taxes on personal income account for 82% of all federal revenues. Corporate income taxes contribute another 9%. So over 90% of federal revenues come from the taxation of income.

What was the proverb?

A crafty rabbit has three caves.

Just another way of saying—scatter your money and your attention.

When he was stripped of all rights to succession, his father's propaganda machine had gone to great lengths to scandalize him publicly. He'd been ordered to accept the insults in silence, then move abroad. His father had wanted him gone.

That was fourteen years ago.

His father died two years after that, his half brother immediately taking the title Dear Leader and assuming absolute control.

And that could have been the end of it all.

But a few months ago, while prowling the Internet, he'd accidentally discovered Anan Wayne Howell, one of those events that could only be described as fortuitous. After scanning through the website, he'd downloaded Howell's book and read every word, wondering if it might be his ticket out of obscurity. *Dreamer?* Why not? He possessed something his half brother would never enjoy.

Vision.

And that had allowed him to realize the potential from Howell's radical thesis. One problem existed, though. Howell had not been seen or heard from in three years. Kim had to find him. Originally, he'd thought this trip was the way to make that happen. Now his only lead seemed the woman with the black leather satchel and a possibility that Howell might appear tomorrow.

He poured more whiskey.

When he'd tried to visit Disneyland in Tokyo it had not been solely for his children. He was a fan, too. So much that a framed print hung on his office wall back in Macao. It depicted Walt Disney himself, above a statement the visionary was noted for saying—*It's kind of fun to do the impossible.*

That it was.

Hana stepped inside from the balcony, where she'd retreated once they'd returned from Larks' room. Solitude had always been her friend. Of all his children she seemed most like him. She was twenty-three years old and, sadly, life had not been kind to her. Many scars remained in a sullenness that refused to leave her.

"You need to see this," she said in Korean.

She spoke so little that he always listened to every word.

He followed her back outside.

Below, he caught sight of a motor launch rounding in from the channel, making its way down a narrow man-made waterway that led to a concrete pier. Water taxis abounded, depositing passengers who were making their way back toward the ship's gangway.

The new boat slowed.

They stood a hundred feet above it, concealed by the night, and he could see two men, one he recognized.

The annoying American.

Hana had spent the past ten days keeping close to Larks, their task complicated by a man who seemed to be doing the same. She'd managed to snap a photo, and sources in Pyongyang had informed them that his name was Harold Earl "Cotton" Malone. Tall, trim, broad-shouldered, with sandy-colored hair. A former navy commander who'd worked twelve years for an intelligence unit called the Magellan Billet, part of the U.S. Justice Department. Malone had retired three years ago and now owned an old-book shop in Denmark.

So what was he doing here?

Malone had followed each time Larks had left the ship, wandering through Dubrovnik in Croatia, Valletta on Malta, and Kotor in Montenegro.

"Seems Mr. Malone has returned," he said.

They knew he'd left the ship a few hours ago, Malone's absence making their visit to Larks possible. The missing leather satchel still weighed on his mind. There may indeed be a way to find it, but the nosy American below could be a problem.

"He'll check Larks' room before heading to his own," he said. "He's done that every night." He handed her a keycard. "I took it earlier when we left. I thought it might come in handy."

She accepted the offering with the same pointed silence he'd come to expect.

"It's time to deal with this problem."

And he told her what he wanted done.

She nodded and left the balcony.

EIGHT

Atlanta
6:20 P.M.

Stephanie turned onto the graveled driveway of her house. She lived forty miles north of Atlanta on the shores of Lake Lanier, in a stone cottage surrounded by tall pines that overlooked the placid water.

She stepped from the car and retrieved a newspaper at the end of the drive. She'd left so early this morning that it had not yet arrived. The cool evening air was typical November, and as she walked around to the backyard she listened to birds serenading one another while they searched for dinner. The attorney general of the United States sat on a terrace lined with autumn flowers.

Her boss was sipping on a mug of something steamy and smiled when she spotted Stephanie. "I see you made it out in one piece."

Stephanie slid back one of the metal chairs and settled into its thick cushion. "It was interesting, to say the least."

Harriett Engle was a recent appointee, previously Kentucky's senior senator. When she'd announced that her fourth term would be her last, President Danny Daniels had asked her to resign early and serve as his third attorney general. He hadn't fared well with two previous AG choices. One had proven a turncoat, the other inept. Harriett seemed the exception. Smart, savvy, competent. Initially, Stephanie and Engle had not hit it off—too much testosterone between them—but they'd eventually come to an understanding.

"You have a lovely home," Harriett said. "You were smart when you bought this place."

That she was. She'd left the key where Harriett could find it.

"After I was sworn in, I read your file," her boss said. "You've been a single woman a long time. Do you think you'll ever stop missing him?"

Her husband, Lars, had taken his own life years ago. Thankfully, with Cotton Malone's help, she'd settled all her disputes with the past. "We lived apart for a long time before he died. Still, his death hit me hard."

Harriett smiled. "My husband passed a few years ago."

She already knew that. Engle was approaching seventy, her age belied by the presence of high cheekbones, a ruddy tone, and bright-green eyes. Her blondish-gray hair, raked flat against her scalp and twisted in a knot, lay as smooth as marble. Some might say a surgeon had restored some of her youth, but the allegation would be a lie. That was simply not this woman's style. Stephanie had come to know that Harriett's sly smile offered no clue to her mood, and usually contradicted her true emotions. Also, a disarming, grandmother-like voice masked an intellect first nurtured in law school, then refined at the Harvard Kennedy School of Government.

"Tell me what happened," Harriett said.

And she reported the events from the mall ending with, "Chick-fil-A Man seemed to like his job. But I'd never have such half-assed, pathetic fools working for me."

Contrary to what was said during the show staged in the department store, Terra Lucent had promptly reported the first contact made by Treasury and the blackmail attempt. That information had been passed up the line to Harriett, and they'd allowed the incursion into the Magellan Billet to find out what was going on. The encounter at the mall had been arranged by Stephanie to flush out the problem, knowing that Terra was most likely being watched. Audio surveillance of their meeting seemed a given, which was why the mall had been chosen for the locale. Once Chick-fil-A Man knew Terra had confessed, it seemed reasonable that Treasury would make a move.

And it had.

"They're definitely focused on Paul Larks," she said. "And they don't want Cotton around."

All of which seemed puzzling. Cotton's task had been simple. The U.S. attorney for the Middle District of Alabama had requested the Billet's assistance. Standard procedure called for the names of all federal fugitives to be provided to the National Security Agency. The label Anan Wayne Howell was an unusual combination, easily flagged, and had been detected during NSA's routine international telephone surveillance. From that the FBI had learned that Larks would be traveling to Venice to board a cruise boat and meet with Howell. Three years Howell had been on the run, and the U.S. attorney thought this might be a good opportunity to snag him. So Stephanie had hired Cotton to shadow Larks and see what developed. A typical in-and-out scenario that should have been without drama.

"I'm told Mr. Malone can be a handful," Harriett said.

"That's true. But he gets the job done." She paused. "The secretary of Treasury has apparently decided that these missing copies are so important, he's willing to threaten and coerce members of another intelligence unit. Interestingly, the secretary doesn't feel he can simply ask us for the information. On both incursions into my files, they've only gone after the reports Cotton has made from that cruise."

"They want to know how close he's getting."

"To what?"

"I don't know, but it's time to find out."

Harriett located her phone and punched in a number. The unit was on speaker, and her boss laid it on the table as the line rang and a female voice answered, "Office of the Secretary of Treasury."

"It's the attorney general of the United States. I need to speak to the secretary."

"I'm sorry but he—"

"Please tell the secretary that either we speak now, or he can speak to the president later, after I report everything I know on Paul Larks."

A full two minutes passed before a male voice said through the speaker, "All right, you have my attention."

Everything that had happened was reported, then Harriett said, "Joe, we set your man up to see how far you were willing to take this."

"I guess I shouldn't be surprised. This is not my forte."

"What's going on?"

"Just like my agent said, we believe Larks copied some sensitive documents from Treasury archives. The breach was only recently discovered, and we want them back."

"What kind of documents?"

"The classified kind."

"I need more than that, Joe."

"Not on this phone."

Stephanie realized that *classified* did not necessarily mean "top secret." Still, you didn't discuss either on an open line.

"We're after a fugitive," Harriett said. "That's all. He was indicted in federal court for tax evasion, tried and convicted in absentia. He fled the country just after his trial started, and really pissed off the local U.S. attorney. His name is Anan Wayne Howell. For us, this isn't a big deal."

A few moments of silence passed.

"Unfortunately for me, Harriett, it is a big deal. There's more here than you realize."

Stephanie heard the strain in the secretary's voice.

"I gather that," her boss said. "But you've gone about this all wrong."

"Perhaps. But it had to be done."

"How does Kim Yong Jin figure into the equation?"

That was a new name. Twelve hours ago Harriett had specifically directed her to send Malone inland to observe a North Korean cash transfer. Some background intel on an insurance fraud scheme had been provided, which she'd passed on to Cotton. But there'd been no mention of Kim.

Harriett said, "You told me about that money transfer and that Kim Yong Jin was in the neighborhood. You asked if I had an asset near Venice, knowing, of course, that I did. Then you asked me to send that asset over to witness the transfer."

More news to Stephanie.

"What I wanted was to get Malone off that ship."

It seemed the man on the other end of the line definitely knew more than they did.

"Can you be at the DC federal courthouse at 11:00 P.M.?" the secretary asked. "Sixth floor. I'll leave word with security to admit you."

"I'm bringing Stephanie with me."

"I'd prefer you not."

"That's non-negotiable. She's my eyes and ears."

Another pause.

"All right, Harriett, we'll do this your way."

The call ended.

"You never told me about Kim or that Treasury *wanted* Cotton at that money transfer."

"I was told not to. Stupid me respected that request."

"How did Treasury know Cotton was even on that ship in the first place?" she asked. "Their first contact with Terra came *after* the cruise left port."

"I'm assuming they have someone there, watching Larks, too. Once they tagged Malone, they zeroed in on the Billet."

Thankfully, she'd taken precautions and ordered Luke Daniels to provide backup in case Cotton ran into trouble. Still, she was baffled. "What's going on? This is a lot of trouble for some copied documents. What's so important?"

"I don't know. So let's get our butts to Washington and find out exactly what we've managed to get ourselves into."

NINE

Hana Sung stared at the closed door for Paul Larks' suite. Her father had once again thought ahead and prepared them for any contingency. He was smart, of that she was sure.

But why would he not be?

He was a Kim.

She had faithfully learned the family history. The first Kim, her great-grandfather, had been born near Pyongyang. Legend said he was the son of a poor farmer, but actually his father was a teacher with an above-average income. He fought the Japanese in the 1930s when they occupied Korea, and was there in 1945 when the Soviets liberated the country. His greatest mistake was not insisting that his allies claim the entire peninsula. Instead Stalin respected an agreement made with Roosevelt, dividing the country in half, creating the more populated, agricultural south and the industrialized north.

That first Kim became the north's Great Leader and ultimately convinced Stalin that he could retake the south. In 1950 he led the Fatherland Liberation War, but American intervention had prevented reunification. Eventually, as she now knew, a cease-fire had been arranged, the country remaining divided, the war never over. Interestingly, if anyone in North Korea were asked about the outcome of that great conflict, they would unhesitatingly declare that the south invaded first and Kim had won. Ignorance seemed to be a national trait. But who could blame the people? Everything they saw and heard was controlled.

The second Kim easily assumed power and bestowed the name *Eternal President* on his father, taking *Great Leader* for himself. The cult of personality that had started with the first Kim only intensified with the second. A philosophy of self-reliance labeled *juche* became a national obsession. The country gradually withdrew into itself, looking increasingly only to Kims for salvation. A mistake, but one few within North Korea would ever realize.

She'd been taught that the first Kim was a mighty general who rode a white horse and carried an enormous sword that could fell a tree as if slicing bean curd. He turned pinecones into bullets and grains of sand into rice, crossing rivers upon paths of fallen leaves. Both Kims showered the people with fatherly love. They portrayed themselves as noble and caring, even immortal. And in a sense, they were. Both rested in the magnificent Palace of the Sun, inside glass sarcophagi, their heads upon pillows, a workers' flag draping their bodies. She'd visited there twice. A surprisingly emotional experience, made even more so by the fact that their blood flowed through her veins. *The spiritual pillar and lighthouse of hope. Prominent thinker-theoreticians. Peerlessly illustrious commanders. A solid foundation for the prosperity of the country.* That was how the Eternal President, Great Leader, and Dear Leader all described themselves.

And she wondered.

Would that praise include her, too?

She doubted it.

Her father had sired nine children, with only three being legitimate. She fell into the illegitimate category. At twenty-three, she was the youngest. The others were all married, with children of their own, still living within North Korea. They'd abandoned their father once he fell from grace. She alone had stayed with him. Her mother had been his mistress, one of many he'd maintained back when he was still in line to rule.

So no offspring of their's would become a Kim.

Instead, she was Hana Sung.

Hana referencing the number one, singular, important. Sung meaning "victory." Her father had eventually wanted her to change it, but she'd politely refused. And he hadn't insisted. A flaw in him, for sure, since he never could insist on much of anything. Yet he could kill a helpless old man without a thought, and order another, who'd interfered with the money theft, eliminated. Was that a contradiction? The world thought him stupid and lazy, a drunk and a gambler. She'd come to know those were but carefully crafted illusions.

Her father was a Kim.

And this third generation, which included his half brother, was just like the first two.

But what about the fourth?

Her own life had taken a difficult path. She had no real identity except what others had imposed. She'd been alive, but not really a person. More a piece of property, used by others for *their* needs, never her own.

And of late, that fact had begun to bother her.

She studied the corridor.

Given the hour few people were around, only a handful coming and going from the staterooms that lined the outer side.

She'd noticed the American, Malone, early during the cruise. He'd stuck close to Larks, but had made no attempt to locate her father. Which made her wonder. Did Malone know about him? Or about her? She'd concluded that he did not. Which made his presence even more puzzling. A few minutes ago her father had told her exactly what he wanted done, and she would do it. Following his orders, at least for a little while longer, seemed the prudent course.

She approached Larks' suite and used the keycard for entrance.

The door opened and she quickly stepped into the darkened space.

Hopefully, Harold Earl "Cotton" Malone would be along shortly.

TEN

Malone hopped from the boat. Luke Daniels worked the throttle and kept the hull close to the concrete dock.

"I'll need you back here by 7:00 a.m.," he said.

Luke threw him a salute. "I've missed taking orders from you, Pappy."

He smiled. "Like you ever did."

He'd never cared for the nickname, one Luke had used from the first day they met. Of course, he called the younger agent Frat Boy, a label Luke had not particularly liked either. And while Malone was on contract, here for a limited engagement, Luke worked for Stephanie Nelle and the Magellan Billet full-time. He was a Southerner, ex-military, the nephew of President Danny Daniels, which seemed not to mean much of anything to either Daniels. He and Luke had first met in Denmark a month ago and finished up their mission in Utah. When they parted ways in Salt Lake he'd told Luke that he looked forward to their next encounter. He just hadn't known then that it would be so soon.

On the boat ride to the cruise terminal Luke had explained more of what was happening. The $20 million had been slated for a charter jet out of Venice's airport straight to North Korea. The United States and Europol had finally decided to build a case on insurance fraud, and some eyewitness testimony could be vital. Of course, no one had anticipated a theft.

"How was it that cash transfer just happened to be here in Venice?" he'd asked Luke.

"That I really don't know. I was in Rome and Stephanie told me to get my butt over here. That's when I called you. My orders were to help the old guy out, if he got into trouble."

"Is that how Stephanie put it?"

"Close enough."

He bid Luke goodbye, found the gangway, and passed through a security point that included a metal detector. His gun had been left with Luke for tomorrow, no way to keep it without drawing unwanted attention. The staff tossed him a few odd looks, considering that his hair was damp and askew, his clothes mud-splattered and smelly from the splash in the lagoon.

"Crazy water taxi," he said, adding a smile.

It was just after midnight, but plenty of folks were still coming and going, enjoying their last few hours aboard. He hadn't experienced much of the ship's nightlife, as both he and Larks had been early to bed. His room was on the same deck as Larks', albeit at the other end.

Once on board he grabbed an elevator to the ninth floor and exited to an empty hallway. He'd kept a careful watch the entire cruise, but doubted Larks had noticed. The older man had seemed oblivious to anything and everything, staying to himself, most times toting a black leather Tumi bag. He'd also memorized the facial image of Anan Wayne Howell that Stephanie had provided, but had caught no sight of the fugitive. There'd been a lot of distractions, though. The cruise ship held three thousand passengers, and every port had been a madhouse. He'd thought that day in Split he was about to strike pay dirt, but Larks had left the Croatian café alone, after waiting two hours, connecting with no one. What was so important about Howell? He'd been told only that the man was a federal fugitive who'd ticked off a local U.S. attorney, fleeing after the start of his trial. But Malone knew the deal. Contract help was told only what they needed to know. And frankly, he was not interested in delving real deep here. For him, this was a mental diversion. The chance to make some quick, easy money. Nothing more.

But things had definitely escalated.

Nine men had already died.

He decided to make a final check on Larks' room. He'd left the ship right before the early-sitting dinner, heading for the mainland hours before the scheduled deal, reconnoitering the building and gaining access while its doors were still open for the day. Then he'd waited patiently until it was time to head for the eighth floor. He should call Stephanie and report what had happened, but Luke had assured him that he'd handle that. Next, he ought to head back to Copenhagen and his bookshop.

But that came with a problem.

He could not deny that he missed Cassiopeia Vitt. Loneliness, for him, was like a periodic disease. He'd just grown accustomed to having someone special back in his life, but now she was gone. He'd been divorced awhile. His ex-wife still lived in Georgia with their teenage son, Gary. Their marriage had not ended easy, and it had taken some effort for them both to find peace. Life was good between them now. Unfortunately, he could not say the same for himself and Cassiopeia. And being back at the bookshop would only provide him more time to think about that failure.

He felt grimy from his dip in the lagoon. He'd rinsed off the mud from his trousers and shoes while on the boat ride, but he definitely could use a shower and some sleep. Tomorrow he'd be ready to follow when Paul Larks debarked. He'd see where the older man would lead him, and if that was to the airport and a flight home, then his temporary job would be over.

He approached the door to Larks' suite. Pricey accommodations for sure, and he'd wondered how a former civil servant could afford them. Everything was quiet and he was about to leave when he noticed the door was ajar. Each cabin came with an electronic lock and spring-loaded hinges that ensured the latch engaged. There was also a dead bolt for added security. Larks' had been engaged, its steel extended, cocking the door open.

Odd.

He checked his watch. 12:48 A.M.

Larks had been an early-to-bed guy for the past ten days.

Nothing about this registered right.

He stepped close and listened, hearing nothing. He gently knocked and waited for a response. None came. He rapped his knuckles again, this time loud and insistent. Still no reply. He pushed the door inward and stepped inside. The suite was dark, some ambient light spilling past the glass doors to the balcony and more from the hall outside.

"Mr. Larks," he said, his voice low.

A short entranceway led into the main salon, an open doorway to his left into what was most likely the bedroom. He saw the outline of someone lying down. One arm was draped over the mattress edge, the hand angled askew.

He checked for a pulse.

None.

Paul Larks was dead.

He wondered about the Tumi satchel and stepped out into the salon, making a quick search and finding nothing. Back in the bedroom he scanned the bathroom and closet, switching the lights on, then off.

No satchel.

He left the bathroom light on and came back close to the bed. No evidence of violence was anywhere to be seen. He wondered if Larks had simply died of natural causes. But if so, how coincidental would that be? On the bedside table he spotted an insulin kit with syringes. He was about to reach for the phone and call for assistance when something pricked his right leg.

Sharp.

Stabbing.

Like a needle.

He recoiled.

The room spun. His mind fogged. Muscles throughout his body began to surrender their strength. His legs buckled. Stunned and dizzy he fought for balance. His knees found the carpet. The world blinked in and out and he saw a figure emerge from the other side of the bed. Someone had been beneath the mattress. That sight made him think of another night, from a few years ago, in southern France. Dark and windy, when someone had been shooting at him.

Cassiopeia Vitt.

Their first encounter.

And then before he blacked out, like in France, this time he also thought he saw the outline of a woman.

ELEVEN

Kim switched on his laptop and settled down in the chair. His suite came with several rooms, including a dining area with a polished mahogany table. He'd ordered dinner—some gazpacho, braised pheasant, and an array of cheeses, complemented by a Loire wine and aged claret. Most of his meals had been enjoyed right here, which had allowed him to keep a low profile. His only ventures out had been to the spa for several delightful treatments. He'd hoped that a jovial European atmosphere aboard ship might open the lines of congeniality among himself, Howell, and Larks. But none of that had occurred, and the presence of a former American agent had changed things even further. Now Hana would deal with Malone. He was fortunate to have her. North Korea was indeed a man's world, but that did not mean a woman could not be useful.

The laptop announced that it was ready to work.

He'd first written while in college, and quickly discovered that he liked the experience. An English professor told him that all writers had a little voice in their head, one that didn't say *write a bestseller* or *sell lots of books,* it simply whispered for them to write every day. If listened to, the voice went silent. If ignored, the urge never relented. He'd long ago learned to listen to the voice. Writing freed his soul and allowed his imagination to wander. When his father had stripped him of his birthright, writing had been what saved him. And where reality had seemed always defined by others, his creative life could be shaped exactly as he wanted.

His rereading of *The Patriot Threat* and his visit with Paul Larks had sent his thoughts reeling.

He needed to soar.

The envisioned scene became clear.

The day his father disowned him.

"You will not succeed me."

He'd expected a rebuke, maybe even some discipline, but never those words.

"Your actions have caused me disgrace and embarrassment. My advisers have concluded that you must be replaced."

"I was unaware that you listened to advisers. You are our Great Leader. Only your word matters. Why do we care what others think?"

"And that is why you cannot succeed me. You have no understanding of what it takes to rule this nation. My father led this country and tried hard to reunify it. He invaded the south and fought the great war and would have prevailed, if not for American intervention. His leadership is still remembered. Five hundred statues are erected in his honor. After every wedding newlyweds find the nearest likeness of him and lay flowers at his feet. His body rests in a glass coffin where hundreds of thousands come each year to pay their respects. You could never garner such feelings from the people."

He did not agree, but he stayed silent.

"What were you thinking?" his father asked. "Going to Japan and an amusement park? What possessed you?"

"The love of my children."

"You show love for your children by not dishonoring your parents. That way they see in you what you expect from them. You have shown your children nothing but disgrace."

He'd had enough of the insults. "I am a patriot."

His father laughed. "You are a fool."

"Who will take my place as Great Successor?"

"One of your brothers will assume the role."

"You're making a mistake. I'm not incompetent. Quite the contrary, I am my father's son."

"If you were my son, your judgment would be far better."

"And what is yours, Father? You continue to prod the south, threatening war, causing nothing but discontent. You spend all of our money on weapons and bombs, while the

people starve. You constantly threaten the Americans with disaster, yet never do a thing to assert yourself. And why? Because you can never allow our soldiers to invade the south. Once there, they would see how well fed the people are. How good they live. They'll realize immediately the lies you have told them. You forget, Father. I have seen the world. I know the truth. So what are you, but a paper tiger."

"I am the leader of this nation."

"Which means nothing outside this nation. I was educated far from here, at your insistence. I know what the world thinks of us. We are laughed at—thought of as idiots. We are regarded like naughty children who require discipline. You say I have brought disgrace to you. What disgrace have you brought to us all?"

"I see that my decision is the right one. Your brothers would never speak to me like this. One of them will be worthy."

He felt empowered, not afraid to say, "They will be you. Another paper tiger, threatening everyone, doing nothing, being laughed at. That is your legacy, Father. It will not be mine."

"You are a dreamer. You have been all your life. You stay lost in your self-centered world. Your mother was the same. Neither of you will ever accomplish a thing."

"My mother taught me to actually do something. That is why she lives in Russia. She could no longer take your insults and indiscretions. Her marriage meant something to her. So she acted. Now one of your bastards will rule? Fitting. Some say you were a bastard child, too."

Anger flooded his father's face. "You and I will never speak again. Do not come in my sight."

"That will be my pleasure. But I want you to remember something."

He stared hard into his father's eyes.

"I am no paper tiger."

He reread the scene and liked the approach, though it was not entirely accurate as to the real confrontation with his father after the Tokyo Disney incident. He'd actually been beaten, his father watching as underlings pummeled him. And as he lay on the floor with broken ribs and blood gushing from his nose, his father had coldly told him that he would be disinherited.

He'd said nothing then.

No challenge at all.

This version of history was much better, and since his father was long dead no one of importance existed to contradict him. One day, when the people read of his exploits—and they would—history would note that greatness had been his destiny from the start.

The door opened and Hana entered.

He'd instructed her on how to lure Malone into Larks' room, then hide beneath the bed and wait for him to draw close. The American would do as he predicted, of that he was certain. Understanding human nature was another of his passions.

"He's down," she said. "But first he searched for the satchel."

Searching told him something. He had no idea who the American was working for or why he was interested in Larks. But on the off chance that he might be here for the U.S. government, he'd opted not to kill him. That would only bring more attention, which was the last thing he wanted. The better way was to slow Malone down, complicate his life, and being found with a dead man would accomplish both.

"His clothes were damp and smelled," she said.

"Any idea why?"

She shook her head.

"Mr. Malone will be unconscious a few hours," he said. "Time for us to get some rest and prepare ourselves." He motioned to the laptop. "First, though, I have something for you to read. Some details between myself and your grandfather. It's important you know exactly what happened between us. I think you will find it enlightening."

TWELVE

UNITED STATES OF AMERICA,
   Plaintiff-Appellee

   v.

ANAN WAYNE HOWELL,
   Defendant-Appellant.

No. 12-2367
United States Court of Appeals
   Eleventh Circuit.

Anan Wayne Howell has not filed a tax return in nearly two decades. An indictment charged him with four counts of willfully failing to file tax returns in violation of 26 U.S.C. §7203. Howell was present at the start of the trial, but voluntarily absented himself from the rest of the proceedings, eventually fleeing the trial court's jurisdiction. A jury in the United States District Court, Middle District of Alabama, convicted him, *in absentia,* and he was sentenced to three years in prison and a fine of $12,000.

Howell is a tax protester. His main argument (presented through his court-appointed counsel) is that he did not need to file tax returns because the 16th Amendment is not part of the Constitution.

Howell insists that the amendment was not properly ratified and that his prosecution under the Internal Revenue Code of 1954, 26 U.S.C. Sec. 1 *et seq.*, was void *ab initio*. Howell only provided the trial court the briefest of explanations, which did not explain why the 16th Amendment is void beyond stating a wild conclusion that the required number of state legislatures never ratified the amendment and that the Secretary of State in 1913, Philander C. Knox, falsified the certification record.

Howell sets forth the following contentions: (1) The text Congress transmitted to the states for ratification provided that, "The Congress shall have power to lay and collect taxes on incomes, from whatever source derived, without apportionment among the several States, and without regard to any census or enumeration"; (2) On February 25, 1913, Secretary Knox certified the 16th Amendment was duly ratified, at least 36 states having tendered ratifying resolutions to the State Department; (3) Knox knew that a number of states had not properly adopted the amendment as submitted; (4) Knox knew he was under a duty to instruct those states that they must ratify a conforming version of the amendment; and (5) no conforming ratification ever occurred. Howell asserts that the ratification of the 16th Amendment did not comply with Article V of the Constitution and that therefore the 16th Amendment is non-existent.

At the outset, we note that the 16th Amendment has been in existence for 100 years and has been applied by the Supreme Court in countless cases. While this alone is not sufficient to bar judicial inquiry, it is persuasive on the question of validity. Thus, for Howell to prevail, we would require, at this late hour, an exceptionally strong showing of unconstitutional ratification. Howell (through his appointed counsel) has made no such showing, only boldly concluding that the amendment was improperly ratified. No evidence has been presented to prove this assertion, nor has Howell cited any factual or legal authority binding on this court (or for that matter on Secretary of State Knox in 1913) for his contention that the 16th Amendment was improperly ratified. In short, Howell has not carried the burden of showing that this 100-year-old amendment was unconstitutionally ratified.

For all of the foregoing reasons, the conviction of Anan Wayne Howell on all counts is AFFIRMED.

KIM STOPPED READING FROM THE LAPTOP'S SCREEN.

After Hana had gone off to bed, he'd again found the opinion dealing with Howell online and studied its wording. While on the run as a fugitive, Howell had published *The Patriot Threat* as an electronic book. No way had ever existed to physically locate Howell. Larks had been his best bet, and the old man had promised that an introduction would happen.

But that had not occurred.

We don't need foreigners involved.

He hadn't expected a rebuke. But Americans could be like that. They exuded an arrogance, a superiority that proclaimed they, above all others, knew what was best. Yet Korean society had existed for many millennia before anyone had ever heard of the United States. Koreans were descended from Siberians who migrated south tens of thousands of years ago. Their culture was ancient and sophisticated, though the political and physical division of the country since 1945 had definitely created differences between north and south. He recognized those, even appreciated them. His father, grandfather, and half brother ignored them. Typical North Koreans knew little to nothing about the outside world. How could they? All communications were controlled both in and out. He'd been fortunate, never having lived long inside that bubble. Unfortunately, twenty million North Koreans could not say the same. His father was so proud of his ability to lead. But who couldn't when you exercised total control over what people saw, read, thought, and believed.

And the penalty for nonconformity?

Death. Or even worse. The labor camps.

Once there, prisoners stayed for life, as did their children and their children. They were taught that they were enemies of the state who had to be eradicated, like weeds, down to the roots. They were worked to death and killed at will, regarded as not even human. That was the legacy of how his family had ruled, and his half brother carried on the same oppressive polices. Two hundred thousand people remained prisoners inside the camps.

He would rule with the people's *true* consent, after *earning* their respect.

Dreamer? Hardly.

But he had to show everyone that he was capable of great things. Where his relatives only boasted of glory, he must achieve it.

He stared again at the screen and *United States* v. *Howell*.

An exceptionally strong showing of unconstitutional ratification. That's what the American judicial system wanted? A new resolve infused him.

Okay.

He'd provide it.

THIRTEEN

HANA TRIED TO SLEEP, BUT BEING ALONE IN A SOFT BED, UNDER-neath clean sheets, remained a strange feeling.

For the first nine years of her life she'd slept on nasty concrete beneath a stinking blanket. When she was a small child her mother had left her alone every day, just after the sun rose. Electricity only ran for two hours, once from 4:00 to 5:00 A.M., then again at 10:00 to 11:00 P.M. The first hour was to allow the preparation of breakfast, which had not been much. Mainly bits of corn, some cabbage, and soup. The second hour was to allow an end to the day with a few chores, a few bites to eat, then sleep. Food evolved into a constant want. There was never enough. Anything could be a meal. Rats, frogs, snakes, insects. Starvation was a means the guards used to maintain control. Nearly every prisoner was stunted by malnutrition—a loss of teeth, black gums, weak bones, and hunched spines inevitable.

She was born an irredeemable slave inside Labor Camp 14, her blood tainted by the crimes of her mother. Its fenced boundaries stretched fifty kilometers north to south, half that east to west, the electrified barbed wire dotted with guard towers and patrolled around the clock. No one went anywhere near the fences. The punishment was instant death, either from the electricity or from bullets. She learned later that there were many camps scattered in the North Korean mountains. Hers, in South Pyongan province, confined over 15,000 people. More than ten times that many filled the rest.

Camp rules were taught from birth. Never escape. No more than two prisoners may meet together. Do not steal. Guards should be obeyed. Anything suspicious must be reported. Prisoners shall work every day. The sexes remain apart. All errors are to be repented. And violators of any rule will be instantly shot.

For nearly half of her life she wore stinking rags, stiff as a board from dirt and grime. No soap, socks, gloves, or undergarments were ever available. She and her mother worked fifteen hours a day at forced labor, and would until the day they died. Malnutrition was the main cause of death, but execution ran a close second. The law had been proclaimed in the 1950s by the first Kim. *Enemies of class, whoever they are, their seed must be eliminated through three generations.* The world outside the fences knew nothing of what went on inside. No one cared. Prisoners were forgotten.

But what had her mother done?

Finally, at age eight, she'd asked.

"My sin was falling in love."

A strange reply, one her mother never elaborated upon.

Together they occupied one room with only a table and two chairs, sharing a kitchen with dozens of others. There was no running water, no bath, and only a communal privy. The windows were gray vinyl that allowed in little light and plenty of weather. Insects swarmed in the summer and the air continually stank of excrement and rot. An allocation of coal, mined by prisoners, provided some winter heat since it was deemed counterproductive to kill too many prisoners at once.

"I'm here," she said to her mother, *"because you fell in love?"*

There had to be more.

But her mother still offered nothing.

The guards taught them that the sins of their parents could only be erased with hard work, obedience, and informing on others. Redemption came from snitching. Tell on rule breakers and you received a few grains of rice. Report a violation and you'd be allowed time to soak in the river.

She came to resent her mother.

Then to hate her. With an all-consuming rage.

She flushed those troubling thoughts from her brain.

Sleep seemed to be finally arriving. The hour was late and she needed rest. Tomorrow could prove decisive. She'd long hoped that her father was different from the other Kims. He liked to say that was the case. The first two had ruled with great cruelty. He should have been next, but he squandered his opportunity. He'd been right in what he said beside Larks' bed. She had witnessed the strong dominate the weak. Every day, until age nine, she worked clearing snow, chopping trees, or shoveling coal. She'd particularly hated cleaning privies—chipping out frozen feces and carrying the clumps with her bare hands to the fields. Early in life she learned to stand straight and bow to the guards, never looking them in the eye. She spent her days finding fault in herself. How many times had she watched newborns clubbed to death with iron rods? The spectacle had been periodically arranged to discourage prisoners from multiplying. After all, the whole idea was to cleanse three generations of incorrect thinkers, not allow another to be born.

In the camp there'd been two classes. Those born there, Insiders, and those sentenced there, Outsiders. The main difference was that Outsiders knew what lay beyond the fences and Insiders had no idea. That knowledge made Outsiders weak. Their will to live disappeared quickly. To Insiders, not knowing about the world actually became an advantage. For them, licking spilled soup from the floor seemed okay. Begging was simply a way of life, betraying a friend just part of surviving. Their own guilt, shame, and failure was what dominated their thinking. Unfortunately for Outsiders, they remained paralyzed with shock, revulsion, and despair.

And while her life had unfolded behind those fences, hidden from the world, she now knew that Kims had lived as princes, wanting for nothing. Her father proclaimed himself on a mission of redemption. But she wondered what would happen when he achieved that goal. What would he do when power was finally in his hands?

She'd read what her father had written about the day his father disowned him. Whether any of it was true, she did not know. Deceit seemed a Kim family trait. In the camp she'd been taught little about the country's leaders. Only after her release had she learned more, most of it troubling. In the camp the guards had been her sole authority. They taught her what and how to think, when and what to say. So silence became her friend.

Along with truth.

And where before, as a prisoner, she was nothing, now the choices in life were hers.

Which brought her comfort.

And sleep.

FOURTEEN

Stephanie was familiar with this United States court-house. It sat in Judiciary Square, facing south toward Constitution Avenue and the Mall. Nothing about its exterior was noteworthy, the style bland and institutionalized, common to the 1950s when it was built.

She and Harriett Engle had flown from Georgia on the same Department of Justice jet that had brought the attorney general south. It had been waiting for them at an airfield north of Atlanta, not far from Stephanie's house. Originally, the plan had been to flush out Treasury, then deal with things tomorrow after Cotton reported back about both the money transfer and Larks. But all of that changed with the call to the secretary of Treasury. Things became further complicated after Luke Daniels' report, which came during the flight. The twenty million dollars was destroyed and all participants to the transaction were dead.

The mention of Kim Yong Jin's name had also added a new dimension.

Kim had been groomed from birth to assume hereditary control of North Korea. He married young and fathered several children. Gambling was most likely an addiction, as was alcohol. After an incident in Japan with forged passports, his father had publicly proclaimed that his eldest son possessed *less-than-reliable judgment*. That insult had not only branded Kim a failure, but by implication meant that his two half brothers were the *dependable ones*. Eventually the military had thrown its support to one of Kim's siblings and the succession was assured. Kim left North Korea and now lived in Macao, a regular at the casinos, the rest of his time spent in and around China. Reports noted him as gifted in the arts and uninterested in politics. He had a passion for film and wrote scripts and short stories, a familiar figure at Japanese movie houses. He was regarded as knowledgeable of the world, appreciative of technology, maybe even open-minded, but no danger. Little to nothing had been heard from him in a long time.

But something had changed.

Enough that Kim Yong Jin had appeared on Treasury's radar screen.

They entered the courthouse and passed through security, the guard directing them to one of the upper floors. She knew what awaited there. The Foreign Intelligence Surveillance Court, tasked with overseeing all surveillance warrant requests against suspected spies working inside the United States. Most of those applications came from the NSA or the FBI, but Stephanie had appeared before the court on several occasions for the Magellan Billet.

"Treasury seems to have been busy," Harriett said as they stepped into the elevator.

"Did you know they were appearing before the court?"

The Justice Department normally prepared all warrant applications and its lawyers argued them. But sometimes the agencies employed their own counsel.

"This is all news to me," Harriett said.

The court had been created thirty-five years ago, its eleven judges appointed by the chief justice of the United States. One judge was always on call, the proceedings conducted in secret, at all hours of the day and night, behind closed doors. Records were kept, but stayed classified. A few years ago an order from this court was leaked to the press by a man named Edward Snowden. In it a subsidiary of Verizon had been compelled to provide a daily feed to the NSA of all telephone records, including domestic calls. The backlash from that revelation had been loud, so much that cries for reform had gained momentum. Eventually, though, the rancor died and the court returned to business. She knew this to be a place friendly to intelligence agencies and the statistics were overwhelming. Since 1978, 34,000 requests for surveillance had been submitted. Only eleven had ever been denied, less than 500 of those modified. No surprise, really, considering the bias of the judges, the level of secrecy, and the lack of any adversarial relationships. This was a place where government got what it wanted, when it wanted it.

The secretary of Treasury was waiting for them when they stepped from the elevator. The white marble corridor was dimly lit, no one else in sight.

Joseph Levy had the good fortune both to have been born in Tennessee and to have become friends with then-governor Danny Daniels. He earned a PhD in economics from the University of Tennessee and a juris doctorate from Georgetown. He taught for a decade at the graduate level and was in line to become head of the World Bank, but he chose instead to serve in Daniels' cabinet. He was the only one of the original group from the first term still around. Most of the others had moved on to the private sector, cashing in on their good fortune.

"Are you making your own warrant applications now?" Harriett asked.

"I know you're pissed. But I had to do it on this one."

"So help me, Joe. You're going to explain yourself or I'm going straight to the White House."

Now Stephanie realized why her boss had included her. It was no secret that the president showed the Magellan Billet favor. Her agents had been involved with all of the hot issues from the past few years, including a foiled assassination attempt on Danny Daniels himself. So her just being here was enough for the secretary of Treasury to know that whatever he expected to remain secret was about to change.

"We both seem to have stumbled onto the same players, only in a different game," he said. "We've been watching Larks and Kim Yong Jin for a couple of months now."

"You monitored their calls?" Harriett asked.

The secretary nodded. "We started with domestic warrants on Larks' phone. But once Kim made contact from overseas, we obtained more warrants. They've been communicating regularly, and all of this involves that fugitive your U.S. attorney in Alabama is searching for."

"How do you know about Howell?"

"I read the Magellan Billet reports."

"Which you could have simply asked for," Stephanie said.

The secretary tossed her a glare. "Unfortunately, I couldn't."

She wasn't going to relent. "Yet here we are, talking about all of it now."

Annoyance flooded the man's face, but he kept his cool. "That's right. I admit, I have a problem. Some of our long-lost secrets have found the light of day."

"I hope you're going to explain more than that," Harriett said.

"Follow me."

He led them down the hall to a wood-paneled door. Inside was a brightly lit conference room adorned with a long dark table lined on all sides with black leather chairs.

"The judge is waiting on me. We have a surveillance-warrant application that we need processed tonight. I told him the attorney general herself would be coming by and I had to speak to her first. He agreed to give us a little time. You should read something."

The secretary motioned to the table where two piles of paper lay. A title sheet atop both read in bold letters, THE PATRIOT THREAT BY ANAN WAYNE HOWELL.

"It's a printed copy of an ebook Howell published a couple of years ago. Just after his conviction."

"About what?" Harriett asked.

"Taxes. What else? Howell fashions himself an expert on our system."

"You don't agree?" Stephanie asked.

"He's a conspiratorialist and paranoid. Most of what's in that book is garbage. But there are some tidbits that bear noting. I made two copies and marked the important passages."

Stephanie glanced at Harriett. What choice did they have? They'd demanded an explanation and now they were being provided one. But Stephanie had a few more questions. "How did you know Malone was on that ship?"

"Like I said, I read his reports."

"That's not good enough. You came just after that cruise left port. You knew to come looking for those reports. How did you know Cotton was there in the first place?"

"You do realize that you're interrogating a cabinet-level official."

"Who broke myriad laws, all of which carry a prison sentence."

"Answer the question," Harriett said.

"Eyes on the ground, there to watch Larks, but we spotted Malone. So I sent some people over to learn what they could from your files. Hopefully, without drawing attention. But that part didn't work out. As to those laws I broke, I considered the risk worth taking."

She knew that Joe Levy had certainly never been in a fight like this before. His background was law and money. To Stephanie's knowledge he'd never served in the military and had no training in intelligence operations. He was definitely in way over his head. So what had prompted him to take such chances?

"Are you're managing this all on your own?" she asked. "An international intelligence operation run by Treasury agents?"

"I thought it best to keep it internally contained. Paul Larks gave me little choice. Neither did Kim Yong Jin."

"Kim's a nothing," Stephanie said. "How's he a problem?"

"He can read."

An odd response.

Then she got it.

The paper stacks on the table.

"There's also one other reason why I've chosen to involve you," the secretary said. "This whole matter is . . . complicated. It has to be kept here, among us. After you read some of Howell's book, I'll explain further and hope that you agree."

FIFTEEN

Venice

KIM LAY IN THE BED, THE HEAVY GOLD CURTAINS DRAWN, BUT HIS mind would not surrender to sleep. He sensed that he was closing in on his goal, the truth perhaps no longer out of reach. When he'd first stumbled upon Howell's website he'd thought the whole idea fantastical. And his first email to Howell had gone unanswered.

His second, though, brought a reply.

> So good to hear from a fellow sufferer. Sorry to learn, though, of your arrest. It's a great injustice our country heaps on us. I was tried and convicted without me being there. I chose to leave the country before they could get to me. It's a shame we have to pick between our freedom and our country. But the fight must continue and it can't be waged from jail. That's why I wrote my book, which outlines everything I believe. This quandary began long ago, in a different time, when some amazing things happened. Read the book and let me know if it proves helpful.

To garner a reply, he'd changed tack and posed as someone charged with tax evasion, thinking that the ruse might open the door to Howell. And it had.

So he'd sent more questions, as Peter From Europe, all of which Howell answered. In his undergraduate studies, Kim had majored in world history and economics. Both subjects interested him. American history, though, was definitely something new, and he'd spent the past few months reading, readying himself for this moment. Unlike what his father may have thought, he was neither stupid nor lazy. Howell was right. Monumental things might indeed have happened long ago, the seeds of that conflict sown by a man named Andrew Mellon.

Whom he'd learned all about.

Thomas Mellon, a Scots Irish, immigrated to the United States from Ireland in 1818. There he set his sights high and attended college, then read law and became a successful Pittsburgh lawyer. In 1859 he was elected a local judge, a position in which he both excelled and profited. Ultimately he founded T. Mellon & Sons, a private banking concern in Pittsburgh. He fathered eight children, the sixth a boy named Andrew, a contemplative lad possessed of an undeniable confidence.

At age twenty-seven Andrew assumed leadership of his father's bank. Over the next two decades he acquired control of more banks and insurance companies. He then branched into natural gas and aluminum, where he financed the creation of Alcoa. Energy was big business in Mellon's day, and his venture into that realm became known as Gulf Oil. By 1910 the family fortune was over $2 trillion in today's money.

Mellon was a shy, silent, astute man. Those closest to him said he had a dry sense of humor and an infectious laugh, both sparingly shown. He cultivated few friends, but those that he did remained so for life. He smartly recognized early on the value of political influence and became a huge donor to the Republican party. In 1920 one of his closest friends, Philander Knox, a U.S. senator from Pennsylvania, convinced newly elected president Warren Harding to appoint Mellon secretary of Treasury. He served from 1921 to 1932, through three presidents. Calvin Coolidge proclaimed that *the business of America is business*, and the country certainly prospered. Spending and taxes were cut, while budget surpluses abounded. America in the 1920s became the world's banker, with Mellon at the national helm. He could virtually do no wrong. But the 1929 stock market crash changed that perception, and the Great Depression ended Mellon's reign. Franklin Roosevelt and his New Deal hated anything and everything about Mellon and his policies. Roosevelt was so repulsed that he brought charges of tax evasion, but Mellon was exonerated in 1937, three months after his death.

His lifetime achievements were amazing.

Second only to J. P. Morgan as a financier. On par with Carnegie, Ford, and Rockefeller as an industrialist. He created five Fortune 500 companies and endowed a foundation that continues to this day to dole out millions in contributions annually.

But his greatest achievement may have yet to be revealed.

Howell had enticed Kim with that last part. So he'd taken the bait and asked for more, learning from another email that Mellon's secret legacy might not be so easily found.

Suffice it to say Mellon was both ruthless and brilliant. He understood how to both acquire and keep power. But he was fortunate. He ran our economy at a time when things were good. His policies of low taxes and less regulation worked. I feel for your situation, Peter From Europe. I haven't filed a tax return in a long time. I sincerely believe that the law does not require me to. Nor do I believe your American companies have to pay corporate income taxes, either. It's a shame they are being bilked by the government. My lawyer tried to make the argument at my trial that the income tax is illegal but, unfortunately, proof of that may not exist anymore. That's why I fled, and I would encourage you to stay hidden, too. It's the safest course. That way we can keep looking. I've researched this for a long time and I'm convinced I'm right. The proof does exist. Stay vigilant and keep in touch. One day we may find what we're looking for. Thank God for the Internet.

He thought Andrew Mellon sounded a lot like his own father. A cold, practical, indifferent man focused on one thing. For Mellon it was making money. For his father? Unfettered, unrestricted, unlimited power—the ability to control, without question, the fates of tens of millions.

He had to admit, it was a potent aphrodisiac.

As was proving his father wrong.

He would enjoy the day when his half brother fell from grace, when the lackeys in military uniforms pleaded for him to lead. No confidence in him? He'd have them all shot. Because on that day he would have accomplished what no one inside North Korea had ever thought possible, including his father.

He was no paper tiger.

The mountains of North Korea were home to many tigers, their bodies brown with long black lines. Myth said that long ago a tiger and a bear wanted to become human. God told them to stay in a cave for a hundred days eating only garlic and mugwort. The bear stayed the required time and became a woman, but the tiger could not endure the wait and left, remaining a wild animal. Later the bear who became a woman married God's son and gave birth to a son of her own, who became the founder of Korea.

Tigers were courageous, fearless, and majestic. Many North Koreans decorated their front gates with pictures of them. The top of a bride's carriage was draped with a tiger blanket to protect the newlyweds from evil spirits. Women wore a decorative brooch with tiger claws to fend off bad spirits. Rich patriarchs once sat on pillows embroidered with tiger images.

Tigers meant power and courage.

If you talk about the tiger, the tiger will appear. And if you want to catch a tiger, you have to go to the tiger's cave.

His mother taught him those wisdoms.

And he knew what she meant.

The word *tiger* stood for "adversary." Or "challenge." Or anything that seemed out of reach. What a wonderful woman. She'd loved him for who he truly was, unlike his father who wanted him to be something else. He'd spent a lifetime cultivating a worldly personality that seemed unfazed by politics. Few to none knew what he thought or who he was. For him causes would not be taken up with the apparent randomness his family liked to show. His words would not be laughed at or ignored. On its current path North Korea seemed doomed to end by either coup, revolution, or mere ineffectiveness.

He would break the cycle of ridicule and failure.

And be something the world would rightly fear.

SIXTEEN

STEPHANIE SAT AT THE CONFERENCE TABLE, HARRIETT ACROSS from her, the hard copies of *The Patriot Threat* left them by the secretary of Treasury spread out before them.

"I'm going to have a long talk with our U.S. attorney in Alabama," Harriett said. "He never mentioned that this fugitive was a writer."

"And you never mentioned anything about Kim or that Treasury specifically wanted Cotton at that money transfer."

"Which, as I've already said, was a big mistake on my part."

"You have to realize your silence placed Cotton Malone in unnecessary danger."

"Are you always so impertinent to your bosses?"

"Only when my people are on the line."

Harriett smiled. "I assure you. I learned my lesson."

It was approaching midnight in DC, which meant dawn would be coming to Italy soon. Luke had reported that Cotton wanted him back at 7:00 A.M. The cruise ship debarkation could be their break.

She shuffled through the pages, the book's introduction promising "amazing and startling revelations." A quick glance at the table of contents revealed a few chapter titles. "Historical Non-Perspectives." "Can the Courts Be That Stupid?" "A Warning to the IRS." "Political Questions No One Wants to Answer."

"This is some kind of tax evader's manifesto," she said. "Which makes sense, considering Howell's criminal problems. But the copyright date is after his conviction. So he wrote this while a fugitive."

Several spots were marked with paper clips. She found the first tagged section and read.

One of the mysteries of the 1920s was how Andrew Mellon managed to remain Secretary of the Treasury for nearly eleven years, through three different presidencies. One line of thought deals with the fact that Mellon was the first public official to actively engage the Internal Revenue Service as a weapon against political enemies. Audits were routinely conducted to harass opponents. Criminal charges were sometimes brought, as were civil trials in administrative tax courts, all designed to pressure Mellon's enemies. Perhaps he was deft enough at retaliation that even presidents feared him. A modern-day analogy would be J. Edgar Hoover, who managed to retain control of the FBI through six administrations. Some say Hoover's infamous secret files played a major role. Just as with Hoover, several investigations into Mellon's activities ensued and there were even calls for his impeachment, but none ever materialized to anything substantive.

One story persists, though. Which may, more than anything else, explain Mellon's longevity. In February 1913 Philander Knox was the outgoing Secretary of State. A month later a new president (Woodrow Wilson) would appoint his successor. In 1916, Knox was elected to the Senate from Pennsylvania. He was also a candidate for president in the 1920 election, but was defeated for the nomination at the Republican Party convention, eventually working hard to elect Warren Harding. Knox and Mellon were close friends, both from Pittsburgh, and it was Knox who urged Harding to appoint Mellon Secretary of Treasury. The incoming president, like most people in the country, had never heard of Mellon. To that point, he'd kept a low profile. Knox first described him to Harding as a "Pittsburgh banker, highly regarded in Pennsylvania" and active in providing large amounts of money for

Harding's election. Which may have been the only criterion that really mattered. Mellon was selected and took office in March 1921. Knox died in October 1921. Some say that, before his death, Knox passed a great secret on to Mellon and it was this secret that provided the real reason for his longevity.

"I've never heard this before," Harriett said.

"Which means it could all be a figment of Howell's imagination. I read the appellate court's opinion on his conviction. His appointed trial lawyer tried to present some crazy arguments that the 16th Amendment was not legal. The secretary was right. Howell's a wild conspiratorialist. He sees things that simply don't exist."

"I'm beginning to wonder just exactly what does exist."

Stephanie agreed.

So they kept reading.

A fair question would be: Why would Philander Knox give Andrew Mellon anything that might be harmful to the United States? Something that Mellon could use to his political advantage. By all accounts, Knox was a lifelong patriot. He served in three presidents' cabinets, twice as Attorney General (for McKinley and Theodore Roosevelt) and once as Secretary of State (for Taft). Three times he was chosen to serve in the United States Senate from Pennsylvania. By anyone's measure that kind of career would be termed a great success. But to Knox it proved not enough. He was a wildly ambitious man who coveted being president.

Unfortunately, as one contemporary described, "He wants to soar like an eagle, but has the wings of a sparrow." He was generally regarded as intellectually brilliant, but his incisive tongue and pompous attitude made him few friends. Another contemporary said, "He served with distinction, but achieved none." His reputation was mainly confined to Pittsburgh, where he was a favorite among that city's rich elite. Men like Andrew Carnegie, Henry Frick, and Mellon himself regarded him as a friend. President Harding shunned him for selection to his new Republican cabinet in March 1921, which Knox openly resented. He continued, though, to serve in the Senate, representing Pennsylvania for another seven months before dying.

"It seems politics then was not so different than now," Harriett said. "The Senate is still filled with people who want to be president."

"You included?"

"I was the exception. I just wanted to be attorney general."

"Why this job?"

Her boss shrugged. "My time in the Senate was over, and I wanted to have some say in who succeeded me, so moving over here for the last year of my career seemed like a good idea. It gave the governor an appointment to fill my unexpired term. Luckily he listened to me and chose the right person."

"But you'll serve here only a short time."

Harriett smiled. "Not necessarily. Maybe I'll be like Knox and Mellon and another president will keep me on."

Stephanie smiled, and they returned their attention to the manuscript.

Mellon himself never spoke or wrote about how he retained his cabinet position for so long, but after his death a few of his associates speculated. They told the story of how the National Gallery was created, with Mellon donating both the millions for the building and his massive art collection (worth many more millions). Roosevelt hated Mellon and was not happy about having to accept the charitable gift, but the president had no choice. To refuse would have seemed petty and foolish, two things Roosevelt could never afford to be publicly. Decades after Mellon's death, some of his associates finally began to whisper things Mellon had used to maximum political advantage.

By November 1936 Mellon knew he was dying. On New Year's Eve 1936 he met with Roosevelt at the White House. His closest friend, David Finley, accompanied him. Finley would later become the first curator of the National Gallery of Art and the founding chairman for the National Trust for Historic Preservation. We know from Finley that the president and Mellon spoke privately for about fifteen minutes. Finley wrote in his diary that Mellon left that meeting in "an exuberance that I had never before seen upon the man." When queried, his mentor said, "I gave the president a note that I drafted. He crumpled it up and threw it across the room. But it will be interesting to see what he ultimately does with it." Finley tried to learn more, but Mellon remained cryptic. "It's something to occupy him. In the end he'll find what I left. He'll not be able to keep himself from looking, and all will be right. The secrets will be safe and my point will have been made. For no matter how much he hates and disagrees with me, he still will have done precisely what I asked."

"Finley became a Washington icon," Harriett said, "the father of the historic preservation movement. He was the one who fought to save Europe's treasures after World War II. The Monument Men were his creation."

She knew of Finley's reputation. Credible and trustworthy. Not a fanatic in any way. Which gave Howell's account even more importance.

They kept reading the marked passages.

Finley and Mellon were especially close. They worked together at the Treasury Department. In 1924 Finley ghost-wrote *Taxation: The People's Business* for Mellon, which spelled out the then Secretary of Treasury's position on taxes. The book was immensely popular. By 1927 Finley had become Mellon's closest associate, penning his speeches, helping write official Treasury policy, and assisting with Mellon's private art collection. Mellon died in 1937, just as construction on the National Gallery began. The museum opened in 1941, with Finley in charge. Books written by people close to the National Gallery have acknowledged that, even from the grave, Mellon directed a great many details. Finley, remaining loyal, did exactly as Mellon had requested.

"What in the world," Harriett said. "It's like an Oliver Stone movie." She smiled. "And just as short on proof. Lots of vague references to unnamed sources. But I'm not surprised. I've come across things far stranger than this that proved to be true. So I've learned to keep an open mind."

"Is that another lesson I should learn, too?"

"It's just that you've been in this job only a short while. I've dealt with some unique stuff over the years. So the fact that a former secretary of Treasury may have corralled FDR into doing his personal bidding is not all that strange."

They found the final flagged portion.

Little is known as to what happened after that meeting on New Year's Eve 1936. If FDR paid attention to anything Mellon said, there is no record of it that can be found. There is evidence, though, of an internal Treasury Department investigation that occurred in early 1937. Documents I obtained through several Freedom of Information requests contain references to that inquiry, ordered by FDR himself. Unfortunately, documents were withheld from my request (noted as classified) and some that were provided came heavily redacted. What could be so sensitive that so many decades later it must still be kept secret? From the few references that have survived, we know that Roosevelt became concerned about the 1935 redesign of the dollar bill and wanted to know if Mellon had played any part in that process. Unfortunately, no documents that I have been able to obtain can answer that question. Mellon died in August 1937, and Roosevelt's attention focused on ending the Depression and the growing turmoil in Europe. There is no evidence of Roosevelt concerning himself again with Andrew Mellon.

One comment, though, did survive. Not by Roosevelt, but by David Finley. In his private diary, published in the 1970s, Finley recounted his last conversation with Mellon, just days before his mentor's death. Finley accompanied Mellon on a drive from Mellon's Washington apartment to Union Station. From there, a train would take Mellon north to Long Island and his daughter's residence. He planned on spending a few weeks there refreshing himself. Unfortunately, that's where he died. As they passed the

Federal Triangle and the site where construction on the National Gallery had begun:

> *We talked of the 1920s and our days at Treasury. He was so proud of his public service. He'd shepherded America into great prosperity. The Depression was still not his fault. "It should never have happened," he said again. "If Hoover had only listened." We gazed out at the foundation work for the National Gallery. Though I did not know it at the time, that would be his last look at his creation. He spoke of New Year's Eve a few months earlier and our visit with the president. I asked if anything had ever come of that balled-up piece of paper. He shook his head and told me that the secrets remained out there. "The president hasn't looked yet, but he will," he said to me. We then rode in silence. When we reached the station his final words summed up the man, or at least how he certainly viewed himself. "I'm a patriot, David. Never forget that."*

SEVENTEEN

VENICE

MALONE OPENED HIS EYES.

His head throbbed. He was not a drinker and had never experienced a hangover but, from listening to others complain, he imagined the agony currently raging between his ears had to be what it felt like. Where was he? Then he remembered. Still in Larks' suite.

Something was in his right hand.

He blinked the cobwebs from his eyes and saw a syringe.

He was lying on the carpet, Larks still dead in the bed. Light washed in from the outer room. His right leg hurt where something had pierced his skin, which he assumed was the needle from the syringe. His left leg remained sore from the helicopter drop. He rubbed his temples and sat up. Whatever had taken him down had worked fast and left a lingering punch.

He checked his watch. 5:20 A.M.

He'd been out a few hours.

He stood and steadied himself on the wall. His clothes were finally dry, but still reeked of the lagoon. He'd certainly managed, in a short while, to find a fair amount of trouble. The only difference this time was that by accepting Stephanie's job offer, he'd actually gone looking for it. He shook his head, tried to clear the fog, and allowed himself an empty minute.

He heard movement beyond the open doorway and cocked his head toward the noise. A shadow preceded someone's entrance. A woman. She was lean with a narrow waist and long, straight red-gold hair that swept around a middle-aged face. Three dark freckles formed a triangle on otherwise unblemished cheeks. Her blue eyes seemed dulled by a want of sleep—and given the hour, he could understand—but were otherwise focused and intent. She carried the oddly anxious look and feel of a personality he'd seen too many times to count.

Law enforcement.

"I'm Isabella Schaefer," she said. "Treasury Department."

"You have a badge?"

"Do you?"

He felt his pockets and feigned a search. "No, guess not. I assume you know who I am."

"Cotton Malone. Once with Justice, at the famed Magellan Billet. Now retired."

He caught the sarcasm. "You don't approve?"

"I want to know what a bookseller from Copenhagen is doing messing up three months' worth of my work."

More news. Neither Stephanie nor Luke had mentioned anything about others being at this party. Which made him wonder if they knew. It wouldn't be the first time the left hand of the intelligence community had no idea what the right was doing.

He motioned to the bed with the syringe. "Who killed him?"

"Looks like you did."

"Yeah, let's go with that."

"Who said someone killed him?"

"Okay, I like that one, too. That'll be the story. He just died."

"You don't get this, do you? I ask the questions, you answer them."

"You're not serious? Pulling rank? You're just a Treasury agent a long way from home, way outside your jurisdiction."

"And what the hell are you? A damn bookseller. What authority do you have?"

"I have my International Antiquarian Bookseller membership?"

"I see you truly don't get it. I found you here with a dead man, holding a syringe that, I'm sure, is the cause of death."

"And how did you just happen by?"

"I was doing my job and saw the door propped open by the latch bolt."

"You understand that was all by design. Whoever killed Larks wanted me found with him." He tossed the syringe onto the bed. "You've obviously been waiting for me to wake up. My bet is I've been snoozing from whatever killed Larks. Probably a sedative of some sort. There's a hole in my leg where the killer injected it."

She nodded. "I checked and found it."

"Gee, I feel so violated. And we hardly know each other. What does Treasury want with Larks?"

"He copied some classified documents. We want them back."

"Must be important stuff." Now he was trolling. But this woman refused to take the bait, so he asked, "Have you been on this cruise the whole time?"

He could not recall seeing her. And he would have noticed her. Truth be told, he had a weakness for redheads.

"I've been here," she said. "Waiting to take Larks into custody. Which I would have done tomorrow, as he left the ship. Unfortunately, now he's dead and the documents are nowhere to be found."

"They were inside the black Tumi case?"

She nodded. "That was my guess. The old fool hasn't gone anywhere without it."

She really had been on board.

"I need to call my boss."

"Don't bother," she said. "My boss has already contacted Stephanie Nelle. Which is why you're here with me, and not in police custody."

Finally, some interagency cooperation.

Treasury and Justice. Together again.

"I need an aspirin," he said.

She'd actually done her job. Contain and control. But he decided to try one more time. "What are these documents? Why are they so important?"

"Let's just say that they contain information the U.S. government would not want on public display."

"You mean Wikileaks missed something?"

"Apparently so."

"Then why didn't you take them from Larks when the taking was good? Why wait?"

He could see she was done answering.

"You need to go home," she said.

"No argument from me. First, though, a shower and change of clothes would be good."

A shave, too. Patches of stubble itched on his neck and chin.

"You do stink. Where have you been?"

"Rough night in town."

"I know about the money transfer, and that you were sent to the mainland to observe."

She truly was informed. More so than him, in fact. "Let's just say that meeting didn't go as planned."

"Then definitely go home, and leave this to us."

Not bad advice, actually. "What about Larks?"

She retrieved the syringe from the bed. "Not our problem. Like I said, he just died."

He recalled his confusion and concern from earlier when a woman had emerged from beneath the bed, after plunging a needle into his leg. "By the way, you never showed me a badge."

She stood before him, dressed in dark jeans and a long-sleeved silk shirt, which complemented her fair skin and red hair. She was attractive in a Kathleen-Turner-Sharon-Stone kind of way. Pretty, but not spoiled by knowing it. Confident, too. And she seemed unconcerned about projecting even a smoke screen of goodwill. He watched as she reluctantly reached into her back pocket and found a badge stamped DEPARTMENT OF THE TREASURY. SPECIAL AGENT. A photo ID read ISABELLA SCHAEFER.

"Satisfied?" she asked.

He nodded and smiled, never really thinking she was his assailant. No. That was someone else. A new player.

"Of course," she said, "there was no ID on you, besides your ship's keycard, which you would have needed to come back on board. So you were off with no wallet, no identification, nothing to point to who or what you are. But I understand why that was necessary."

"It's so refreshing to deal with a professional." He brushed past her and headed for the door.

"I don't want to see you again," she said.

He neither stopped nor turned back, saying only, "Not to worry. You won't."

EIGHTEEN

ISABELLA WATCHED MALONE AS HE LEFT LARKS' SUITE, THE DOOR snapping shut with a metallic finality. Luckily, she'd planned to be up and going by 4:00 A.M. When she'd checked Larks' room, she'd noticed the cocked-open door. Malone was right, nothing but an invitation. Inside she'd found Larks and Malone, who'd clearly been drugged. She'd told him the truth. A small puncture wound was visible on his left leg, the culprit behind it all easy to ascertain. Kim Yong Jin. Who else could it be? Both Kim and Malone had been on board the entire cruise, both keeping close to Larks. Malone personally. Kim through his stoic daughter.

What a mess.

Kim obviously knew about Malone. So she hadn't lied. The ex-agent had screwed up a lot of hard work. She'd carefully kept her distance the entire cruise, wearing wigs and other accessories to alter her appearance. She still had no idea why Malone was here. She'd reported his presence ten days ago, but Treasury had told her nothing since, just that she should keep Larks under surveillance, watch out for Kim, and monitor Malone. Most disturbing was the fact that she hadn't found the black leather satchel in Larks' room. The older man had last cradled the satchel at dinner. She assumed that today, at debarkation, something would happen. Her employer had already checked. Larks was not booked on a flight home until the day after tomorrow.

She did not like surprises and especially those that interfered with careful planning. Preparation was the key to any successful operation. And she'd fully readied herself. This was her operation and hers alone. The Treasury secretary himself had personally recruited her. Not even her immediate supervisor knew where and what she was doing. She'd been required, for the first time, to sign a top-secret nondisclosure agreement, which compelled her silence about anything learned on threat of imprisonment.

Obviously, the stakes were at their highest.

Hopefully Cotton Malone would go home. She had enough to worry about with Larks dead and Kim Yong Jin still breathing. Larks and Kim were connected. That they knew from covert wiretaps and email monitoring. Kim had actually paid for Larks' airfare and cruise, the idea being to set up a face-to-face encounter with Anan Wayne Howell. Her orders were to observe, then retrieve the copied documents. Now Kim might actually have them. And all thanks to Malone.

She shook her head.

She'd been waiting her whole life for this opportunity.

Was it gone?

STEPHANIE GLANCED UP FROM THE MANUSCRIPT AS THE DOOR TO the conference room opened and Joe Levy entered alone.

"Okay," Harriett said. "We've read what you marked."

He sat at the table. "About two months ago the NSA monitored some chatter out of North Korea that was all about Kim Yong Jin. Stephanie, you were right. This guy is supposedly an idiot. All he seems to do is drink and gamble. But then, all at once, he becomes real important and Pyongyang starts to focus on him. They're talking crazy stuff, specifically mentioning Howell's book. It seems Kim is real interested in that, too."

"I never saw a thing on this," Stephanie said. "And I get NSA tickle sheets every day."

"I put a lid on. To be provided only to Treasury."

She knew that any arm of American intelligence could claim a priority, keeping information solely within that department or agency. That could be risky business, though. If no one else knew what you knew, and everyone should have known, guess who shouldered the blame if things turned sour. Still, it was done every day, sometimes if only to shield sensitive investigations from being broadcast across the grid.

"Let me guess," Harriett said. "You pigeonholed it because in that chatter the name Paul Larks was also mentioned."

He nodded. "It had to stay here."

"What's Kim's interest in Howell and Larks?" Stephanie asked.

"It apparently started with Kim and Howell. Then Howell connected Kim to Larks. We got in late and missed out on a lot of the prior conversations, but we know that Kim is trying to prove an odd theory that concerns Andrew Mellon. Howell wrote about it there, in the book."

"About what?" Harriett asked.

"An old debt this nation owes."

They both waited for the Treasury secretary to explain.

"This is all . . . complicated. More so than I need to get into right now. Let's just say that your searching for Howell has interfered with my trying to minimize the damage Larks did by copying those documents, then communicating about them with Howell and Kim."

"What kind of damage?" Harriett asked.

"I can't go into that. And it's not important to what I need from you at the moment. Suffice it to say that we've been before this court here several times and obtained surveillance warrants on Kim, Larks, and Howell. They like to email."

"Larks and Howell are U.S. citizens," Harriett said. "This court's jurisdiction applies only to foreign nationals."

Probably another reason why the secretary had avoided the Justice Department for his warrant applications.

"They're both working with a foreign national, and together they're compromising the security of this nation. That makes them this court's business."

"Kim and Larks have been openly and knowingly communicating?" Harriett asked, with a lawyer's tone.

Levy nodded. "Many times, though Paul Larks is unaware that it's Kim he's speaking to. He thinks it's a South Korean businessman, living in Europe, whose companies are being wrongfully taxed by the United States. He has no idea of Kim's true identity, or at least that's what we believe."

Something bothered Stephanie. "You knew that there'd be a robbery in Venice, didn't you? It was Kim. He went after that $20 million. Yet you told us none of that, and put my man at grave risk."

He nodded. "We knew Kim was going to make a move on the money."

Now she was pissed. "We don't send people into something like that blind. Not ever."

The secretary said nothing.

"Whatever this is," she said, "it better be really important."

"You have no idea."

"What is it you want from us?" Harriett asked.

"To back off. Let me handle this."

Harriett shook her head. "We're done playing games, Joe." Stephanie had heard that tone before. "You're way out of your league."

"And you're not?"

"That's why I have the Magellan Billet. This *is* its league. You're taking crazy risks, talking riddles, dodging questions. I've got no choice. I have to go to the White House."

Stephanie checked her watch and knew what was happening in Venice. "That cruise ship is emptying its passengers right about now."

"Call your people," Harriet said. "Advise them of the situation."

The door to the conference room burst open.

A man entered.

Tall, broad-shouldered, with thick graying hair, dressed in a shirt, no tie, wearing a distinctive blue nylon jacket. Embroidered above the left breast was the seal for the president of the United States.

"Evening," Danny Daniels said.

NINETEEN

VENICE

MALONE FELT BETTER. A SHOWER, SHAVE, AND CHANGE OF CLOTHES
had made all the difference. His time unconscious had actually helped
with fatigue. He was rested, ready to go. He'd packed light for the cruise,
bringing only one shoulder bag, and had not deposited it outside his door
last night, as required. So he'd carry it off himself.

But first he intended to play a hunch.

He left his cabin and headed toward the ship's center, staying one
deck above the main foyer where passengers would be leaving. The atrium
was several floors high, three stylish, glass-enclosed elevators available to
shuttle people up and down. A few of the ship's many lounges could be
seen along the foyer's perimeter and all of the administrative desks were
there, convenient and accessible. On their first day aboard he'd watched
as Larks switched dollars for euros at one of them.

He wondered what Cassiopeia was doing. He missed seeing her. She
was one of the few people he'd ever actually become comfortable with.
He had friends and associates, but few close ones. Part of that was his
former job, part his personality. He just always stuck to himself. Some of
that could have been the result of being an only child. Who knew? His
ex-wife had hated his constant withdrawing. Cassiopeia had been different. She, too, cherished alone-time. They were actually far more alike

than either of them had ever admitted. It was a shame the relationship was over. He had no intention of making further contact. He'd tried, and she'd made her position clear. Any move from this point on would be hers. Stubborn? Maybe. Prideful? Sure. But he'd never begged anyone for attention and wasn't about to start now. He'd done nothing wrong. The problem was hers. But he still missed her.

He checked his watch. 7:45 A.M.

Sunshine rained down outside, softened by the ship's bronze-tinted windows. People were debarking through the main gangway into an enclosed walk that led into the cruise terminal, where luggage and Italian customs awaited. Past that were land buses, taxis, and a concrete wharf where boats would shuttle guests into town or to the airport. Most would leave by water. The cruise terminal sat at Venice's extreme west end, just before the only causeway that led across the lagoon to the mainland. In and around the terminal was the only place vehicles were allowed on the island. If this hunch played out, he'd have to be ready to move in an instant to who-knew-where.

Announcements called for passengers in predesignated categories to make their way off. He found an observation spot one deck above, near a semicircular stairway that led down to all the activity. People streamed off the ship, mostly folks in their sixties and seventies. The time of year and price of the trip cut down on families and children. Mainly professionals populated the cabins—people who cruised several times a year all over the world, enjoying their retirement. He doubted he would ever retire. What would he do? As much as he hated to admit it, he missed being a field agent. Three years ago, the idea of quitting the Magellan Billet, resigning his naval commission, and moving to Denmark had seemed like a good one. Leave the past behind and head forward. But things had not worked out that way. He'd stayed in trouble, with one crisis after another. Some he had no choice but to be a part of, others were optional. Now he was again being paid for his time.

Like the old days.

He was betting on several factors here. One, that someone had taken the black Tumi satchel from Larks' room. Two, that the someone would keep the contents inside the bag. Three, that whoever it might be was

still aboard. Four, that they had no knowledge anyone else was interested. And five, that they would be confident enough to walk off the ship
with the satchel in hand.

A long shot? No question. But it was his only shot, so he stood behind
an ornate column and kept watch below. Whatever was going to happen
would happen here. His perch provided a wide view and he caught sight
of Isabella Schaefer below, near one of the service desks, watching, too.

And there it was.

The black leather Tumi satchel, same distinctive silver buckles and
white monogram—EL—on one side. It was draped across the shoulder of
a young woman with long dark hair who hustled toward the gangway in
quick steps. He saw that Treasury Agent Schaefer noticed her, too, and
immediately followed.

Good enough for him.

He shouldered his bag and headed down the stairway.

KIM WAS SITTING IN ONE OF THE LOUNGES, NEAR THE GANGWAY
exit, watching passengers leave. Hana was off to one side, observing, too.
They'd made a point the entire cruise not to be seen together. The original idea had been for him and Larks to first talk privately, then to connect with Howell. For the first few days of the cruise, he'd called Larks'
room on a ship's phone, but none of the calls had been answered. So
Hana became his eyes and ears, watching the old man, waiting for their
chance. When Larks told him the bag had been given away, his first
thought was that maybe it might reappear here, at debarkation.

He sipped a coffee and allowed the many faces to pass across his gaze.
He appeared like everyone else, there waiting his turn to depart. Luckily
there were two Korean groups on board, one on the far side of the main
foyer, all anxious to be on their way. He was just another tourist. He
wondered what had happened with the American Malone. There hadn't
been any commotion on the ship about someone dying. As far as he
knew, Larks was still dead in his bed, undiscovered.

He saw it first, then noticed Hana saw it, too.

The Tumi bag.

Being carried by a young woman. What was her name? Jelena. He caught his daughter's gaze and nodded.

She followed.

ISABELLA WAS THRILLED.

Good things happen to good people and she believed this was living proof. Where before she was dead in the water, now her hunch had played out. The documents she sought were just ahead, inside the same black satchel Larks had toted for days, hanging from the shoulder of a woman in her mid-twenties.

Time to do what should have been done days ago. Malone was right. She could have moved on Larks at any time. But part of her mission had been to ascertain the extent of the problem, so she'd given the former Treasury official a wide leash. Too wide, actually. But that mistake was about to be remedied. All would be right once again. The only hitch was Malone, who was proof that somebody else back home had acquired an interest in all this. But to what extent and how far? Luckily, that wasn't her problem. Others would handle that.

She followed the young woman off the gangway and into a warehouse-like space where luggage was arranged in color-coded groups. Her target had apparently brought no belongings since she bypassed the confusion, stopping only a moment at customs to display a passport, then left the building.

Isabella kept pace, using the crowd for protection, and exited as well. They turned right, away from buses and land taxis, and headed for the concrete wharf where water taxis and shuttle boats waited. Maybe a dozen or more craft bobbed, ready to accept passengers. A babble of commands, mainly in Italian, quick movements, and willing hands offered many distractions. The morning was bright and sunny, the air cool and refreshing. The woman glanced out at the boats, clearly searching for someone. A variety of craft wove atop the choppy surface, each vying for space at the long wharf.

Isabella could not allow the woman to leave. So she made her move, elbowing her way through the crowd, zeroing in. Just as she reached out to corral her target, a man appeared from her left, wearing a red ball cap yanked down over his face. He was short, dressed in jeans, a purple sweater, and running shoes.

She saw him only an instant before he delivered a body check, propelling her over the edge and into the water.

TWENTY

Stephanie was not surprised Danny Daniels had appeared. Everything about the man fit into the category of unexpected. He'd always been bold and unabashed, a gregarious soul who loved being in charge. She wondered what he would do when his second term as president ended, his career in the limelight over. For a man like Danny, that would not be a good thing.

He sat at the table. "Great thing about the middle of the night is that a person can come and go as they please. Nothin' to slippin' out of the White House."

"And hello to you, too," she said.

He threw her a smile. "I'm surprised you're so cordial. I figured you'd be pissed right now."

"So you authorized the illegal entry into the Billet files?"

"That wasn't me. Joe, here, decided to go that route all on his own."

She saw that the Treasury secretary wasn't pleased to see his boss, so she decided to press the advantage. "You realize Treasury risked Cotton's life. They might even have wanted him caught in the crossfire, to slow us down."

"Oh, yeah. I get it. Friggin' stupid. Which is why I'm here. The secretary and I are going to have a chat on that." He tossed a glare across the table. "Just you and me. And then we're going to talk about what the hell you've been doing in Europe these past ten days."

Joe Levy said nothing. That was another thing about being at the top of the pyramid. Only heaven could argue with you.

"Luke and Cotton need to know what's going on," she said. "I was just about to make a call."

She'd replaced her damaged cell phone with one of two backups she always kept on hand, this one stashed at her house.

"In a minute. First, we have to talk. That's why I'm here instead of sleepin'." Daniels faced the Treasury secretary and pointed a finger. "I asked you for a simple thing. Some information on a relatively obscure subject. Next thing I know you're running an international investigation, outside the grid, risking assets who don't even work for you. I'm going to want to know why. Are you going to have answers?"

"Of course, whatever you want."

"Really? Whatever I want? The first question is going to be why you didn't tell me the truth to start with."

Levy said nothing.

"Mr. President," Harriett said. "I thought Congress was dysfunctional, but this is right up there with their antics."

"Now, that could be construed as downright insulting," Danny said. "But I understand. This is your first foray into the intelligence business . . . from the executive branch's side of the table. It's a mite different here. We don't have the luxury, as congressional committees do, of Monday-morning quarterbacking. We're on the field, in play, as it happens, and we have to make this stuff up as we go."

"A game plan is always preferred," Stephanie added.

The president said, "Joe, go get your warrants. I have to talk to these two ladies alone." He paused. "Then you and I'll have that chat."

The secretary left the room.

"He's a businessman," the president muttered, once the door closed. "Knows nothing about intelligence work."

"But you do," Stephanie said. "And you're in charge."

Only she could get away with pressing him that far. A while back, during another critical operation, they'd both discovered feelings for the other. One of those unexpected revelations that they'd wisely kept to themselves. The Daniels' marriage was over, and had been for some time, existing only as a public illusion. No anger or bitterness lingered on anyone's part, just a realization that once his second term ended, Danny Daniels would be single. Then things might change between them.

But not until.

"It is my fault," he said. "But Cotton's okay, right?"

She nodded. "Can't say the same for the $20 million and the nine other men who died."

"I've only been told in the last couple of hours that we knew Kim was going to make a move on that money. Joe decided to keep that tidbit to himself. You should have been advised as to all the risks."

"Why weren't we?" Harriett asked.

"Now, that's the rub. I think Stephanie was right. It may actually have been deliberate on Joe's part."

The admission surprised her.

"What's Kim after?" Stephanie asked.

"It's complicated."

"That's what Joe kept repeating," Harriett said.

Stephanie pointed to the printed pages on the table. "Have you read *The Patriot Threat*?"

"Every word, and the author is no idiot."

"He's a convicted tax evader," Harriett said.

"That he is. But some of what he says makes sense."

The president reached inside his jacket and produced a dollar bill, which he laid on the table. "Look on the back."

Stephanie flipped the bill over.

Lines appeared on the obverse of the Great Seal.

"I drew those," the president said.

She studied the six-pointed star. "What's the significance?"

"Check out the letters where the triangles form."

She did.

A S O N M.

"It's an anagram," the president noted. "For the word *Mason*."

"You're not seriously thinking Freemasons are involved here," Harriett said. "How many times have we heard that they're secretly controlling this country. That's utter nonsense."

"I agree. But the word *Mason* is formed from the joining of those letters. That's a fact. Which, coincidentally, also forms a six-pointed-star."

"Or a Star of David," Stephanie muttered.

"Heck of a coincidence, wouldn't you say?"

"How would you have known to do this?" Stephanie asked.

"Those classified papers Paul Larks copied. They mention another dollar bill with lines on it. Larks talked of a bill like that to Kim and Howell."

"And how do you know that?" she asked.

"Yesterday I read those classified papers Treasury is holding, the ones Larks copied. The NSA also provided me transcripts of conversations between Kim and Howell. Contrary to what Joe Levy thinks, I'm neither in the dark nor an idiot."

But she was still puzzled. "What's this about?"

"A few months ago I received a letter from a prominent Jewish organization. It dealt with a man named Haym Salomon. Do either of you know the name?"

Neither she nor Harriett did.

So he told them.

Salomon was born in Poland, but immigrated to New York in 1772. He was Jewish, highly educated in finance, fluent in several languages, and became a private banker, securities dealer, and member of a commodities exchange. By 1776 there were 3000 Jews living in the American colonies. Salomon was active in that community and fought for political equality. He became a patriot early on, supporting the Revolution, and was even arrested in 1778 as a spy by the British and sentenced to death. But he escaped New York to the rebel stronghold of Philadelphia, where he resumed his financial career.

The American Revolution was financed with no definable base. No regular taxation or public loans existed. No fiscal system had been created for collecting revenue, and the treasury, a mere pretense, stayed empty. Money was constantly needed for supplies, ammunition, food, clothing, medicine, and pay for soldiers. States were supposed to care for the troops they sent to fight, but that rarely happened. Members of the Continental Congress were short on money, too, their horses routinely turned away because livery stable keepers had gone unpaid. Continental currency was barely accepted anywhere, generally regarded as worthless. The lack of money was England's best ally, many Loyalists arguing that the Revolution would fizzle once the colonists could no longer feed their army.

In 1781 Haym Salomon came to the attention of Robert Morris, the superintendent of finance for the fledging confederation of thirteen colonies. He was enlisted by Morris to broker bills of exchange for the upstart American government. That he did, but he also personally extended interest-free loans to many of the Founding Fathers and to army officers. He became the banker and paymaster for France, an essential American ally, and converted French bills of exchange into American currency, which financed French soldiers fighting in the Revolution. He likewise performed those same services for Holland and Spain, keeping the Spanish ambassador afloat after funds from Spain were thwarted by the British blockade. From 1781 to 1784 his name appeared nearly a hundred times in Robert Morris' diary. Many entries simply read, I sent for Haym Salomon.

In total, Salomon loaned the new American government $800,000, without which the Revolution would have been lost. He never wore a uniform or brandished a sword, but he performed an enormous service. He died penniless, age 45, in 1785. His entire fortune had been spent in service to his adopted country. A wife and four children survived him. All of the documentation relative to his loans was turned over by his widow to the Pennsylvania treasurer. But those securities and certificates were subsequently lost. No repayment of those debts was ever made. His son repeatedly pressed the case from 1840 to 1860. Congress in 1813, 1849, 1851, and 1863 favored some type of repayment. In 1925 the House actually moved to have Salomon's heirs compensated.

But that recommendation never passed.

"His family tried for over a hundred years to have those debts honored," the president said. "They never were. They remain unpaid to this day. The official excuse was always that there was no adequate documentation to say they existed."

"Seems like a good one," Harriett noted.

"Except that's bullshit. Congress, in 1925, wanted to pay the heirs what was owed. A recommendation made it out of committee, but never came to a floor vote. Why? The then secretary of Treasury nixed the idea. His name was Andrew Mellon."

Stephanie began to connect the dots.

"If you multiply the percentage increase in the consumer price index from 1781 to 1925, that $800,000 loaned by Salomon becomes $1.3 billion," Danny said. "But that's too simple a measure. It leaves out a lot of value. If you use the labor method, which is what a worker would have to use in 1925 to buy that same $800,000 worth of commodities bought in 1781, you get $8.5 billion. The entire federal budget for fiscal year 1925 was only $10 billion, and that's with a $400 million deficit. So you can see why Mellon killed the idea. Full payback would have literally bankrupted the country."

"What does all this matter anymore?" she asked. "The U.S. has trillions in assets, and surely the amount is negotiable."

"That debt today is worth $17 billion with the simple CPI method, but $330 billion using the labor value method."

"Again, that's negotiable, not insurmountable, and certainly not worth all of this."

"Howell, there, in his book, thinks that Andrew Mellon either found or was given the documentation that was supposedly lost by the Pennsylvania treasurer. He hid it away and used it as leverage on three presidents of the United States. That's how he held on to his job for so long."

"It certainly sounds plausible," she said. "But we'll never know if that's true or not."

"Actually, we might be able to learn the truth. The letter I received asked that I investigate the Salomon debt. The group felt the heirs deserved something. And I agree, they do. So I had Treasury look into it. The job was given to Paul Larks. Then all hell broke loose."

"Did Larks find proof of the debt?" she asked.

"I think he did, and I also think he stumbled into something even bigger."

"Then why not just find out? All these people work for you."

"I wish it were that simple."

"I need you two on board. God knows Treasury can't handle things. I want my A-team on this."

"Coming in off the bench?" she said. "With the score not in our favor?"

"You've done your best work starting halfway through the game."

"Flattery never works," she said, adding a smile.

"But it can't hurt." He stared into her eyes. "Stephanie, this one's different. A lot has been happening the past forty-eight hours. I got a bad feeling. Me and Joe Levy are about to have a come-to-Jesus talk. He won't be a problem anymore. But we need Cotton to find us some answers."

She knew the correct reply. "We'll get it done."

He pointed her way. "That's what I came to hear. First, though, I want you both to listen to somethin'. Then, Stephanie, I need you to take me somewhere. Harriett, this is where you get off."

"That's not a problem. I have plenty else to do. And that's why we have the Billet."

"I appreciate your heads-up, though," he said. "Good job flushing Treasury out into the open."

But Stephanie still wanted to know, "Why am I taking you somewhere?"

"'Cause the Secret Service isn't going to let just anybody drive me around."

TWENTY-ONE

KIM CARRIED HIMSELF WITH EASE AND INTENTIONALLY STAYED back, following the American Malone through the enclosed gangway and into the luggage control area. Hana was ahead of him, closer to where the woman with the Tumi satchel was walking, both of them now out in a blue-gold morning on a busy concrete dock that accommodated water taxis. People seemed in motion everywhere, hopping aboard boats, luggage being handed down, orders barked then obeyed. Before leaving the cruise ship, he'd hesitated long enough to spot Malone bound down one of the two circular staircases and disembark, too. He was surprised to see him. Apparently the ploy in delaying him with Larks had not worked. Was he after the woman with the satchel too? Hard to say. But he had to know. So Kim had fallen in with the crowd and kept pace with the American.

He watched as Malone loitered, clearly following the young woman with the satchel. Hana remained off to his left, on the wharf that stretched twenty meters ahead, then right-angled and ran another thirty meters toward the lagoon. The entire dock sat at the end of a man-made inlet that also accommodated the cruise ship, which floated at anchor to his right. He knew Hana would follow on whatever boat the woman chose, gaining access one way or the other. No railing guarded the dock's outer edge, the boats nestling close and transferring passengers at any available spot along its exposed length.

A woman tumbled over the side and splashed into the water.

Amid the confusion he hadn't seen how it happened. People reacted, but there was little anyone could do as the wharf rose two meters above the waterline. The woman surfaced among the boats, one of the drivers coming to her assistance. That moment of distraction caused him to lose sight of the satchel.

He searched the crowd.

Then the woman carrying it reappeared.

She almost ran into him as she fled past, headed back toward the cruise terminal.

MALONE WAS FOCUSED ON BOTH THE YOUNG WOMAN AND ISABELLA Schaefer. A man in a ball cap and purple sweater had intentionally clipped Schaefer, sending her over the side. The move had happened in an instant, but was enough to take Treasury out of the game and alert him to the attacker's identity. Anan Wayne Howell. No question. He had the man's face frozen in his brain. And though the ball cap was there to hide features, he'd caught enough to confirm it.

Schaefer surfaced and seemed all right.

The woman with the Tumi bag never missed a beat, reversing course and heading back toward the terminal. Follow her? Or go after Howell? His orders were to find Howell. The woman had just seemed the best way to achieve that goal. His eyes searched the crowd and he spotted Howell, hustling across the dock among the passengers, the ball cap gone, a thin brush of black hair now visible.

Malone excused himself and elbowed his way past people concentrating on the water taxis. He was momentarily delayed by a stack of luggage being handed down to one of the boats. Howell was now a good two hundred feet away, on the far side, heading down the long edge toward the lagoon. A boat eased close and Howell hopped down into it. The craft jerked left and turned back for open water.

He heard a whistle.

Then another.

"Pappy."

He turned.

Luke Daniels was on the water, at the helm of the same boat from last night. Two other boats blocked Luke's access to the dock. Malone leaped onto the bow of the first one, then scooted across the low wooden roof that protected passengers from sun and spray. He jumped to the next boat and repeated the process. Luke was waiting at the stern of the second craft, and he hurdled to the deck beside him.

"Good timing," he said. "You know what to do."

"Oh, yeah."

Luke reversed throttle, maneuvered away from the congestion, then turned hard right and powered up the engines.

ISABELLA WAS BOTH ANGRY AND EMBARRASSED. SHE'D BEEN deliberately shoved. Worse, the woman with the satchel would now be long gone. One of the water taxi operators helped her up onto his boat. She sat on his deck, dripping water, then grabbed hold of herself and hopped back up to the wharf.

Damn. Damn. Damn.

A rookie mistake.

Her anxiousness had gotten the better of her. So much that she'd stopped thinking like a seasoned government agent.

And worse.

The documents could now be gone.

KIM ALLOWED THE WOMAN WITH THE SATCHEL TO PASS, NEVER giving her a look of interest. He kept walking ahead and watched as the woman who'd fallen into the water climbed aboard one of the boats. He stopped and glanced back, seeing Hana pursuing their target.

He retreated deeper into the crowd and made his way from the busy dock, back toward the bus and land taxi station, where Hana and the woman were headed. He hadn't seen what happened with the person who'd fallen into the water, but it would have been easy to do. No railing protected the outer edge and there were far too many people around than there should be. Beyond the cruise terminal, their target with the satchel ignored any form of land transportation and kept walking, leaving the premises. The sidewalk was sparse, so following her could be a problem.

He found Hana, who was standing near a group of people.

"Where is she going?" he whispered in Korean, keeping his eyes on the woman as she walked away.

There were a few options. Certainly heading into town was one. The beginnings of the pedestrian-only portion of the island, which was 99 percent of the real estate, started just past the cruise terminal. The causeway leading to the mainland also began a few hundred meters away, so a car that way was possible. Then there was the train station, maybe half a kilometer to the north.

The woman crossed the street and turned left.

Now he knew. The ocean ferries. The terminal was in sight, a hundred meters away.

"We have no choice," he quietly said. "Stay with her."

Hana's brown eyes stared back. He often wondered what that troubled mind really thought, her words so sparse and carefully chosen there was no way ever to know exactly what she was thinking. Did she hate him? Love him? Fear him? He never raised his voice or was sharp to her, assuming postures and expressions that indicated only heartfelt feelings. All she ever did was please him, never failing, always eager.

Like a good daughter.

He nodded.

And she left.

TWENTY-TWO

STEPHANIE WAS AMAZED AT THE PRESIDENT'S COMPUTER EFFICIENCY. Danny Daniels was not noted for being tech-savvy.

"Have you been taking lessons?" she asked.

He'd booted the laptop and worked the trackpad, opening the programs he wanted and enabling a flash drive that he'd found in his pocket and snapped into the machine.

"I'm not helpless," he said. "Soon I'm going to be an ex-president. And no one gives a hoot about one of those. I'll need to take care of myself."

"What about all those Secret Service agents you get for life," Harriett asked. "I'm sure they'll be able to help."

Harriett had stood to leave, but Danny had asked her to stay for a few minutes longer.

"I won't be taking those along with me," he said. "I'm following Bush 41's lead and refusin' them. I'm lookin' forward to some peace and quiet."

Stephanie doubted that. This man was not one to sit around. His entire life had been framed in the limelight. He'd started at the local level in rural Tennessee, then moved to the governor's mansion, the U.S. Senate, and finally the White House. Decades of public service, one crisis after another. He was great under pressure—she'd seen that many times. And he also could make a decision. Right or wrong. Good or bad. He made the call.

"Everybody knows about the Nixon White House tape recordings," he said. "But by the time Nixon did it, the trick was old hat. It all started with FDR."

He explained about the presidential campaign of 1940. Roosevelt wanted an unprecedented third term, but his popularity had waned and the Republican candidate, Wendell Willkie, seemed to be gaining ground. There'd been problems with misquotes in the newspapers, mainly from people present at the countless meetings held in the Oval Office. So a White House stenographer came up with an idea. Wire the place for sound. That way there'd be no debate about what was said. At the time RCA was experimenting with a new device, a Continuous-Film Recording Machine that fed noise onto ribbons of motion-picture film, which could memorialize an entire day's worth of conversations, available for immediate playback.

"The grandfather of today's recording devices," he said. "RCA donated one of the machines and they set it up in a padlocked room beneath the Oval Office. The microphone was hidden inside a lamp on FDR's desk. Over four months he used the system, from August to November 1940. He recorded press conferences, private meetings, random conversations. The public didn't know these existed until the 1970s."

She caught the qualification. *The public.* "But others knew?"

He nodded. "The recordings were stored at the FDR Library in Hyde Park. I had someone pay them a visit and they found an interesting one. So I had the information digitized onto a flash drive."

"And why would you do that?" Harriett asked.

"'Cause one and one always makes two. That dollar bill there got me started, so I went lookin'. Call me inquisitive, and thank goodness. That trait has saved my hide more times than I can count."

The three of them remained alone, the Treasury secretary still with the judge obtaining the surveillance warrants.

"On September 23, 1940, FDR had a chat in the Oval Office with one of his Secret Service agents. A guy named Mark Tipton. He was one of three agents who stayed with FDR over the course of a day, eight-hour shifts each. He and the president became especially close. So close, Roosevelt trusted him with a mission."

Danny tapped the trackpad.

"Listen to this."

FDR: *"I need your help. If I could do it myself I would, but I can't."*

TIPTON: *"Of course, Mr. President. I'd be glad to do whatever you require."*

FDR: *"It's something that godforsaken Andrew Mellon left me on New Year's Eve in '36. I'd forgotten about it, but Missy reminded me the other day about the paper he gave me. I crumpled it up and tossed it away, but she retrieved it, along with this."*

Short pause.

TIPTON: *"Who drew the lines on this dollar bill?"*

FDR: *"Mr. Mellon saw fit to do that. Right in front of me. See the lines across the pyramid? They form a six-pointed star. The letters at the corners, they're an anagram for the word* Mason. *I want you find out what that means."*

TIPTON: *"I can do that."*

FDR: *"Mellon told me that the word refers to a clue from history. He said men from the past knew that a man like me—a tyrannical aristocrat—would come along one day. Damn riddles. I hate them. I should ignore this, but I can't. And Mellon knew that. He left it to drive me crazy. I ordered an investigation at Treasury about that symbol and the letters on the Great Seal, but no one had an explanation. I asked if they were intentionally placed there when the seal was created in 1789. No one could tell me that, either. You know what I think? Mellon just noticed the letters and used them to his advantage. He made it fit whatever he was doing. He was like that. 'The mastermind among the malefactors of great wealth.' That's what they called him. And they were right."*

TIPTON: *"Is it some sort of danger to you, sir?"*

FDR: *"My initial thought, precisely. But it's been four years and nothing has come of it. So I wonder if Mellon was just running a bluff."*

TIPTON: *"Why even waste time on it?"*

FDR: *"Missy says I should not ignore it. Mellon was never one to bluff. She could be right. Most times she is, you know, but let's not let her hear us say that. She has that other piece of paper, the one I crumpled. She came in that day, after Mellon left, and retrieved it from the floor. God bless her. She's an efficient secretary. Take a look at it, Mark, and see what you think. It supposedly has something to do with two secrets from the country's past. The end of me. That's what Mellon said they were. The last thing that aging SOB said was that he'd be waiting for me. Can you imagine the arrogance? He told the president of the United States that he'd be waiting for me."*

"Waiting for what?"

"I think that's want we're supposed to find out."

A few moments of silence passed.

"He also quoted Lord Byron," Roosevelt said. *"A strange coincidence, to use a phrase, by which such things are settled nowadays. It's from Don Juan. I want you to find out what all that means, too."*

"I'll do my best."

"I know you will. And Mark, I want this kept between the two of us. Check it out, but report back everything you learn solely to me."

Danny switched off the drive. "There are other conversations, from other days, like this one. Random talks with aides, nothing of any historical significance, no reason to record any of them. The library curators tell me that just prior to all those, this one included, a press conference had occurred in the Oval Office. Those were definitely recorded. Their guess is that the staff just sometimes forgot to turn the machine off and this conversation, along with others, was inadvertently memorialized."

"So why hide it away?" Harriett asked.

"It really wasn't hidden. The recordings were found at the FDR Library by accident in 1978. They keep them in their restricted archives, not available for public inspection. This one is fairly meaningless, unless you know what we know."

Stephanie had listened in fascination. FDR's tone was rich and resonant, his enunciation perfect. Little about the private voice differed from the public one. What she heard was a casual, unbuttoned exchange with a close staff member. But there was a definite conspiratorial air.

Her mind tried to assess everything.

"This started out," Danny said, "as me tryin' to reverse a wrong. The whole Salomon thing fascinates me. Paul Larks was assigned to do some basic research. He was career civil servant, no reason not to trust him. But he went over the edge. Claimed some elaborate cover-up and how

Salomon had been cheated. Then he said the taxpayers had been cheated. He became so insubordinate, Joe finally asked him to retire. Next thing we know he's talking with Kim Yong Jin and Pyongyang is going nuts. Then you two enter the picture going after Howell, who also has a connection to Larks. It's a friggin' three-ring circus."

"Which has commanded the attention of the president of the United States." Stephanie said.

"That it has. But we're not entirely in the dark. Piecing together this tape with what Howell wrote, we know that Mellon left FDR a dollar bill and a crumpled piece of paper on New Year's Eve 1936. We also know that shortly after that Treasury investigated the whole 1935 dollar-bill redesign. Prior to that time the Great Seal of the United States was not on the dollar bill. That was added in '35 by Roosevelt himself. Apparently, though, Mellon took advantage of that presidential decision. It's a fact that the lines drawn on the bill form the word *Mason*."

There was something else. Stephanie could hear it in his voice. Her gaze caught his and, with his eyes, which she'd learned to read, he said, *Not now.*

Not here.

So she kept silent.

But he said, "I'm anxious to know how things play out in Venice. In the meantime, though, we've caught a minor break. On the recording you just heard, the man FDR was talking to, Mark Tipton, he's long dead. But his son is alive. He's seventy-four years old and yesterday we found him. His name is Edward, and that's where you and I are going. To talk to him."

Stephanie had to ask, "Where?"

"At his home."

"Why would you agree to that?"

"Because it's the only way we can find out what he has to say."

TWENTY-THREE

MALONE STOOD BESIDE LUKE AS THEY POWERED ACROSS THE lagoon, following the boat Howell had taken. He'd called Luke earlier from his room and reported Larks' death, Isabella Schaefer's presence, and what he had in mind to possibly find the satchel.

"They planned this escape good," Luke said. "Took Treasury out solid."

"Did you find out anything about Schaefer?"

"You and her have somethin' in common. You both have a bit of a reputation. Seems Isabella is a by-the-book girl. Never breaks a rule. Everything for her is right or wrong. Not much gray in her black-and-white life. One of those all-American-Mom's-apple-pie kind of agents that really get on your nerves. We had some in the Rangers. Pain in the ass. They'll end up gettin' you killed."

"And Schaefer?"

"I was told not many want to partner with her. She has a bit of a personality problem."

"It was Howell who shoved her in the water," he said.

"I caught a glimpse as he ran away, too. Bold little sucker. Apparently he knew all about Wonder Woman."

"You're quick with the nicknames, aren't you?"

"That one's not mine. That's what they call her back in DC. Behind her back, of course."

"You realize Howell knew more than we knew."

"Yeah, I get that. But the cool thing is, he seems to not know about us."

"Let's keep it that way. Don't get too close."

They were a couple of hundred yards back among a cluster of boats rounding Venice's southern flank heading toward the Grand Canal and Piazza di San Marco. A rocky channel separated Venice from Giudecca, a banana-shaped strip only a few hundred yards south of the main island. Traffic was heavy. Boats and slow-moving *vaporetti* cruised everywhere, his ears flooded by the sounds of engines and hulls slapping water. Ten days ago the cruise ship had passed this way, headed south, offering passengers breathtaking views. Then, eight days later, it had returned the same way. To his left, the bulging baroque hulk of the Santa Maria della Salute dominated the entrance to the Grand Canal. But Howell's boat did not make the sharp turn that way. Instead its course stayed due east, paralleling Venice's impressive array of towers and spires. He squinted in the bright glare and saw the Doge's Palace, along with the two iconic red-and-gray granite columns. One was topped by the winged lion of St. Mark, the city's current patron, the other by St. Theodore, its predecessor. Piazza di San Marco, just beyond, throbbed with visitors. More people milled back and forth along the waterfront in a steady parade. Another busy day at tourist central.

Howell's boat veered left and slowed.

Luke matched the maneuver, keeping his distance.

"They're headed into a canal," he said.

One that opened just past the Doge's Palace, beneath the Bridge of Sighs, forming a path north into the city bowels.

"Careful in there," he said. "We can get spotted."

The canal was only thirty feet wide, lined on both sides with tiers of old buildings, the stone mellowed by time. Once privileged palaces, they were now apartments, hotels, museums, and shops, some of the most expensive real estate on the planet. Venice was not thick with cranes, skyscrapers, overpasses, and tunnels. Time and history ruled here.

"I know you don't like to talk about things," Luke said as they slowly cruised the canal. "But I have to ask. What about Cassiopeia? Did she cool down?"

No, he didn't like to talk about that. But Luke had been there in Utah, and knew it all, so he answered him with the truth. "She's gone."

"Sorry about that. I know it hurts."

He appreciated the sentiment. About the only good thing that happened from the whole experience had been a realization that his emotions were not so dead. He'd felt attraction, intimacy, even love. And now? Regret and longing had settled over him.

"Why don't we just take this guy?" Luke asked, pointing ahead. "And be done with it."

"We will. But first I want to watch."

"Is Pappy on to somethin'?"

"Larks was killed for a reason. That robbery last night happened for a reason. Something tells me they're related."

"And how did you make that leap in logic?"

"Years of dealing with this crap."

"Our mission is only concerned with getting Howell."

"Since when? You're going to learn, Frat Boy, that in the field you can do whatever you want. Unlike Ms. Schaefer, I made a career out of breaking rules."

Luke smiled. "I like the way you think."

Howell's boat veered left and disappeared around a bend. They were creeping along and Luke negotiated the same corner, now headed straight through the city, due west toward the end of the island with the cruise terminal.

Why was he not surprised.

KIM CROSSED THE STREET AND WALKED TOWARD THE FERRY terminal. Boats leaving from there shuttled passengers to other parts of Italy, Croatia, and Greece. The ferries were oceangoing vessels, more like cruise ships, equipped with all the comforts including cabins.

The woman with the Tumi bag entered the ferry terminal and Hana hurried ahead. He kept walking, showing no anticipation. Just another passenger headed off for who-knew-where. A couple of times he checked behind him and saw no one coming in their direction. His only real concern, Malone, had balanced himself across the tops of two boats with a travel bag on one shoulder before leaping into another boat and racing away. Good riddance. Now he could focus on the task at hand.

Their own luggage remained at the cruise terminal and would need to be retrieved. But their destination had yet to be determined. Luckily, there was nothing packed that could not be replaced. Personal effects were the least of his concerns. He was working on changing both his own life and the world. *Doing the impossible,* as Disney liked to say. To that end he would spend whatever time and money was needed, his father and grandfather be damned. One day there'd be *more* than five hundred statues erected in his honor. And he would not have to embalm his body and display it under glass like a sideshow. Centuries from now people would freely speak his name with their heads bowed. He would become North Korea's greatest leader. His father, grandfather, and half brother would be forgotten. When he was done, retaking the south would be a simple matter. In fact, the south might actually ask for reunification, a request he would gladly grant. How satisfying it would be to eliminate the demilitarized zone and watch as the American army exited Korea forever. Which, if this played out as expected, it would have no choice but to do.

He entered the terminal and immediately spotted Hana at one of the counters. She finished her business and walked over, handing him two tickets.

He read the destination.

Zadar, Croatia.

The ferry departed at 9:30 A.M. His watch read 8:50.

"I will go back and retrieve our luggage," he said. "You keep an eye on our prize."

MALONE GRABBED HIS BEARINGS.

Their path had been relatively straight through the northern part of Venice, then, after a slight bend in the waterway, he spotted the wide expanse of the Grand Canal ahead. Howell's boat banked right. Luke followed. Their pace increased as they rounded another curve in the wide canal that snaked from south to north then back south again, the island's train depot now on their right. A causeway jutted from one side of the building, extending to the mainland, accommodating both rail and cars. Howell's boat motored around the terminal and exited into the lagoon. But it traveled only a hundred yards before making a sharp left, then another left. And then they were back at the cruise port, just on the far side of the main building, where a line of ferries were docked before a series of buildings.

"He made a big circle," Luke said. "I assume to make sure no one was interested."

"You got it."

"Apparently, they're not all that good at what they do. 'Cause we're here."

Luke did not follow into the lagoon. No need. They could see everything as Howell leaped from the boat onto a small dock.

"Let me out here," Malone said.

They were a hundred yards from the ferry terminal. He'd have to hurry so as not to lose him. And which boat?

"Keep my bag," he said.

"You want your gun?"

He shook his head. "If I have to get on one of those ferries, there'll be security. Better to go without it. I'll call you with what's happening. In the meantime, see about Treasury Agent Schaefer and what she's doing next."

Luke tossed him a salute. "Yes, sir."

He leaped onto shore just below a roadway and ran up. It took him five minutes to make his way to the ferry terminal. He slowed his pace, steadied his breathing, and entered. Plenty of people loitered around. His gaze scoured every face in a rapid search. Four ferries were docked outside. Each boat sizable. Then he spotted Howell, standing in line to buy a ticket, ten people ahead of him. An illuminated sign above the booth indicated the ferry for Zadar in Croatia. He stepped over and assumed a place six spots behind Howell. Close enough, but not too close. When Howell approached to buy his ticket, Malone edged forward and listened carefully, hearing only, "Zadar." No connecting ferry. He checked a lighted board and saw the boat left in twenty minutes.

He returned to his place in line.

When his turn came he bought a similar ticket.

Twelve years with the Magellan Billet and he'd never been to Croatia.

First time for everything.

KIM ROLLED HIS SUITCASE BEHIND HIM. HANA WAS DOING THE SAME. Together they headed for the gangway to board the Zadar ferry. The Croatian port lay five hundred kilometers east across the Adriatic Sea. He estimated the journey would take about five hours, placing them on the ground around 2 P.M. Hana had thought ahead and reserved a cabin for privacy. But no danger existed of Howell either recognizing or connecting him to anything, since he'd never shown his face or used his real name with either Larks or Howell.

They walked toward the gangway.

The woman with the black satchel had already boarded. They were about to do the same when two men caught his eye. One was Anan Wayne Howell, the face recognizable from Howell's website. The other was the American. Malone. Both men were heading onto the vessel.

He and Hana lingered back and sought cover behind a wide support column.

"That raises a multitude of questions," he muttered.

He saw Hana agreed.

Things had just changed.

The documents *and* Howell were now again in play.

"Come, my dear. It seems Fate has smiled upon us."

TWENTY-FOUR

STEPHANIE DROVE, WITH DANNY OCCUPYING THE REAR SEAT. HE'D actually wanted to drive himself, but she'd refused. A car with two Secret Service agents tailed just behind. An unusual trip, to say the least, but the commander in chief had left no room for doubt. He was going to see Edward Tipton, and without the normal fanfare that accompanied a presidential motorcade. She knew protocol. Standard procedure required thirteen vehicles, plus three local police cars for traffic control. Two identical presidential limousines were always included, along with armor-plated SUVs for the Secret Service, a military aide, a doctor, a small assault team, a hazardous materials response unit, the press, and communications. An ambulance assumed the rear. The whole entourage formed a long black convoy with flashing lights and plenty of attention. Not here, though. All was quiet in their two-car parade. It helped that it was the middle of the night, the streets devoid of traffic, an easy matter to flee DC into rural Virginia and a quaint neighborhood of older houses.

"The Secret Service loves to tell the story," Daniels said, "about 1996 and Clinton in Manila. Just before his motorcade was about to leave, agents in one of the cars with some heavy-duty surveillance equipment picked up radio chatter that mentioned *wedding* and *bridge*. They thought *wedding* could be a code word for a terrorist hit, so they changed the route, which had included a bridge. Clinton was angry as hell at the decision, but didn't override it. Sure enough, when agents arrived at the bridge they found explosives. Clinton dodged a big one. I was reminded of that good fortune earlier."

"And they still let you come?"

"Ain't it great. I told 'em I doubted anybody was going to kill a guy who'd be sent out to pasture soon anyway. I like this. Nice and private. I'm going to enjoy retired life."

"Like hell," she said. "You're going to drive everyone crazy."

"Including you?"

She smiled at the possibility, then asked, "How did you find this son?"

"I did some checking after listening to that recording. The Secret Service had a file on Mark Tipton. He was a good agent. Served with distinction. But he died twenty years ago. His son lives nearby, so we made contact and hit pay dirt."

She knew what that meant. His chief of staff, Edwin Davis, had done all the checking. "Where is Edwin?"

"Doing me a favor. I've worked him pretty hard the past few days."

"Was he the one who found the recording at Hyde Park?"

"Yep. Can't draw that hound dog far off the scent."

"And what favor is he doing for you in the wee hours of the morning?"

"It's a president thing. He'll be along soon enough. This with Tipton I have to do alone."

"Except you're not alone."

"I like to include you in the definition of *me*."

Only in the privacy of a car, with just the two of them, could words like that be spoken. Never had anything improper occurred between them, but she was looking forward to exploring the possibilities that might lie ahead.

They found the house, downstairs lights burning in several rooms. The man who answered their knock was short with features that clearly belonged to age—gaunt cheeks, coarsened hair, veined hands. But his smile seemed genuine and the eyes were devoid of fatigue.

They introduced themselves.

"I thank you for meeting us at this hour," the president said. "and on short notice."

"How often do you have the president of the United States come to your house? It's an honor."

"Though you don't sound overly impressed," Danny said.

"I'm an old man, Mr. President, who's seen and heard a lot. My father protected presidents nearly all his life. I don't impress much anymore. Lucky for you, though, I've always been a night person. Never did sleep much. My father was the same."

Inside, Stephanie caught a warm, homey feel from dark wooden floors, worn furniture, and frayed rugs. Lots of framed photographs adorned the tables and mantel. Not a computer or cell phone in sight, though, only a flat-screen TV. But there were lots of books on shelves and four lay stacked on a table beside Tipton's recliner. Apparently this man was a bit old-fashioned.

They sat in a dimly lit den.

Tipton crept to his chair with a broken-kneed gait. "When your chief of staff appeared at my doorstep yesterday, I really wasn't all that shocked. My father said it might happen one day."

"Your father seems like a smart guy."

"He served Hoover, Roosevelt, and Truman. He was really close, though, with Roosevelt. Being crippled, FDR always needed someone to do things for him."

She got it. Things that should not see the light of day. "We heard the recording, where your father and FDR spoke in the Oval Office."

"Mr. Davis, yesterday, allowed me to hear it, too. I assume that's why we're talking now."

They sat silent for a moment.

"You were right at the door, Mr. President," Tipton said. "I didn't vote for you, either time."

Danny shrugged. "That's your call. It doesn't bother me."

Tipton smiled. "But I do have to say, you turned out to be a pretty decent guy."

"My time's about over."

"That happens. Presidents come and go."

"But civil servants stay on, right?"

"It's what my father used to say."

"Why didn't you want to talk at the White House?" Danny asked.

The older man shrugged. "My father told me that if anyone ever wanted to discuss this, do it in private. I doubt anything that goes on at the White House is ever private."

"It is the proverbial fishbowl."

"Do you know what happened the day Roosevelt died?" Tipton asked. "April 12, 1945."

"Just what I've read in the history books."

"There are things you won't find in those books. Things only the people there that day knew. FDR was in Georgia, at Warm Springs, for a few weeks of rest. My father was with him."

Mark Tipton watched as Dr. Bruenn finished his daily examination of the president and asked his patient, "How do you feel today?"

"Other than a slightly sore neck, a bit better than usual."

Roosevelt actually looked better than he had a few days ago. Less fatigued. More color to his pallid hue, which of late stayed sickly, drained of all blood and strength. But the cheeks remained collapsed, the weight loss continuing. He probably topped off at barely 150 pounds.

"I'll make my usual report to the White House," Bruenn said.

"Tell them I'm not dead yet."

And the president added one of his trademark smiles.

But everyone knew FDR was slowly slipping away and no earthly power could stop that. Bruenn, a navy cardiologist, had quietly said yesterday, outside the president's hearing, that the heart, lungs, and kidneys were all failing. Blood pressure stayed off the charts. A stroke was a near certainty. But still the illusion was maintained. Fatigue was the diagnosis both Roosevelt and the country were told. Nothing that a little rest would not cure. But Tipton knew they were fooling no one, especially Roosevelt. He'd been with the man long enough to notice the telltale signs. Like of late, when the president ventured out, the cordial waves to well-wishers had become uncharacteristically weak. Sometimes they were nonexistent. Never in the past had FDR ignored the public. And on this trip the president had conspicuously avoided heading to the nearby rehabilitation center's warm pool for a swim, which had always brought him joy.

Bruenn left and Roosevelt reached for a cigarette, slipping it into the holder clenched between his teeth. The president found some matches and lit one, but his hand shook uncontrollably. So much that he was unable to connect the flame to the end. Tipton wanted to help, but knew better. That was not allowed. He watched as Roosevelt slid open the drawer of the desk before him and rested his elbow inside, then partially closed it, which helped secure a firm hold on the hand. The tremors had definitely grown worse.

Another bad sign.

Roosevelt enjoyed a few drags of nicotine. The president wore his Harvard tie and naval cape, ready to sit for a few hours while his portrait was painted. The artist was a friend of Lucy Rutherfurd's. The two had driven down from South Carolina and Roosevelt seemed glad Lucy was there. They'd known each other a long time, their relationship the reason why the president and Eleanor lived separate lives. Roosevelt had promised in 1919 that the affair would end, but hadn't kept that pledge. And it was clear to all, Tipton included, that Lucy brought a joy to his life he could not live without.

"Mark, what's the weather like?" FDR asked.

"Another hot, Georgia spring day."

"Just what we need, huh? Come closer, I want to show you something."

The Little White House comprised a simple cottage of white clapboard and hearty Georgia pine. The entire house under roof did not stretch as long as the Pullman railcar that had brought the president south. There were three bedrooms, two small baths, a kitchen, and an entrance foyer, all of which flowed into a central parlor that opened out to a deck. A rustic décor of hooked rugs and knotty-pine furniture dominated. Two separate cottages accommodated guests and servants. Only a single unpaved road led in and out. Roosevelt had personally selected its hilltop location and insisted on the Spartan design, sketching out the layout himself.

On the desk before the president Tipton again saw the dollar bill with red markings, the same one from five years earlier, along with the same crumpled sheet of paper he'd also first seen in 1940. On a pad Roosevelt had been jotting notes. He noticed how the handwriting down the page changed, the script at the top firm and readable, the lower part jagged and crooked, barely legible.

More effects from the tremors.

"Before the ladies arrive for my portrait sitting," Roosevelt said, "let's you and I have one of our chats."

They'd worked on this puzzle off and on since 1940, when Roosevelt first asked for help. Tipton had done what he could, intrigued by Andrew Mellon's challenge, but history was not his strong suit and the riddle remained unsolved. Mainly because the president would not allow him to enlist the aid of any outsider.

"Slide that coffin closer," Roosevelt said.

Everyone had noticed more fatalism of late. Lots of talk of death, mostly in jest, but still uncharacteristic. When they'd arrived at Warm Springs two weeks ago a large wooden crate filled with books had come along and Roosevelt had constantly referred to it as a coffin.

"I've been doing some reading of those books," the president said. "We know those letters on the dollar bill form the word Mason. I've tried every combination, but it's the only word those five letters can create. So Mason it is. Could you hand me that top book, there."

Tipton retrieved the volume from the crate.

The Life of an American Patriot—George Mason.

"It has to be him," Roosevelt said. "Mellon said this crumpled sheet is a clue from history, from someone who knew a man like me would one day come along. A tyrannical aristocrat. He certainly meant that as an insult, and God knows I took it as one. But he was insistent that this was the starting point. Open up there to the page I marked. Look at what I've underlined"

Tipton did.

Mason was one of three delegates to the Constitutional Convention who refused to sign the finished document. He said that the draft, as adopted, conveyed a "dangerous power" that would end "in monarchy or a tyrannical aristocracy." Mason declared that "he would sooner chop off my right hand than put it to the Constitution as it now stands."

"And he never signed," Roosevelt said. "Mason said the Constitution did not protect the individual and he worried about government overreaching. Of course, the Bill of Rights came along later and fixed all that. But like Mason with the founders, Mellon did not approve of my use of power, either. He actually used those exact words. Tyrannical aristocrat. He told me that history and Mason would begin the quest. That's an awful lot of riddles but, Mark, I think it's George Mason. That's who Mellon was referring to." Roosevelt held up the crumpled sheet of paper. "I'm so glad Missy kept this."

Twenty-one years Missy LeHand worked as Roosevelt's private secretary, taking care of everything. Some said she was even more than an employee, another of the president's many "private acquaintances," as the Secret Service described them. Sadly, though, Missy had died the previous July.

"I'm telling you, Mark. We focus on George Mason. He's the beginning. The coffin there is loaded with books and notes I've made. I want you to work on this and keep all this *material for me, including this dollar bill and sheet of paper. I've held on to it long enough."*

"Sir, might I ask, why is this still so important?"

"It didn't used to be. Really, not at all. But the war is coming to an end. It'll all be over soon. The Depression is gone. We're finally back on a steady footing. So I've found myself thinking of the future and what we might make of it. Mellon was so sure that this crumpled paper would be the end of me. He actually said that. The end of me. He wanted me to waste time, chase after it, but I didn't. With things starting to calm down, now I'm curious. What did the son of a bitch leave for us to find? What's so important? He said there were two secrets. I want to know what they are. So you keep on this."

"I will, sir."

They heard sounds from the living room.

"It seems the ladies have arrived for my portrait sitting. I'm told there's a picnic later, and a great kettle of Brunswick stew is being prepared."

"That was supposed to be a surprise."

Roosevelt chuckled. "I know. So we won't mention a thing."

The president finished his cigarette, then adjusted the cape around his shoulders

"Wheel me in. Can't keep the ladies waiting."

"Two hours later, a blood vessel burst in his brain and a little while after that Franklin Roosevelt was dead," Tipton said.

"What was it Mellon left him to find?" Danny said, excitement in his voice. "Those two secrets?"

Stephanie was anxious to know that herself.

"I have no idea. My father never found out. And that crate of books has been here in my house for a long time."

"No one ever inquired about it?" Danny asked.

Tipton shook his head. "Not a soul, so my dad assumed nobody knew about it but him. The crumpled sheet of paper, though, was another matter. Henry Morgenthau came to my father a few days after they buried FDR. He seemed to know all about what Mellon had done. Apparently the president told him, too."

She knew her history. Morgenthau had worked as Treasury secretary for nearly the entire twelve years Roosevelt served. He was perhaps the closest friend and adviser Roosevelt had.

"Morgenthau asked about the crumpled sheet. He wanted to know where it might be. So Dad gave it to him. He didn't ask about the books in the crate or the dollar bill."

"Can we see that dollar?" Danny asked.

"I thought you might want to, so I got it out."

Tipton opened the top book in the stack on the side table and handed Danny an old, faded bill.

She saw that it displayed ink lines, forming a six-pointed star, that connected the five letters forming the word *Mason*.

Similar to the one Danny had created.

"According to my father," Tipton said, "Mellon himself drew those lines and gave that bill to FDR. You can see that it's a true 1935 issue. We don't have bills like that anymore."

She'd already noticed the biggest difference. No IN GOD WE TRUST was printed above the ONE. That didn't come until the 1950s.

"Did your father ever find out anything about this bill?" Danny asked. "Any details?"

Tipton shook his head.

"Did he have any thoughts about that crumpled sheet?"

"He told me that what was on it made no sense. Just a few rows of random numbers."

Stephanie instantly knew. "A code."

Tipton nodded. "That's what Roosevelt thought."

"Why not have a cryptographer break it?" Danny asked.

"FDR wanted no one else involved, except him and my father. At least that's what he told him. It was only later that Dad realized Morgenthau knew some of it, too."

"Numbers could mean a substitution cipher," she said. "They were popular between the time of the two world wars. The numbers represent letters, which form words. But you'd need the key from which the code was assembled. The master document. Without it, there's little to no chance of breaking a cipher. That's why they're so effective."

"Where's the coffin?" the president asked.

Tipton pointed. "In the hall closet."

"Do you have any idea what it is we're facing?" Danny asked. "Anything?"

Tipton shook his head. "After Roosevelt died and Morgenthau took back the crumpled sheet, my father never dealt with this again. It seemed not to matter anymore. No one ever mentioned a word about it, so Dad just stored the crate away. I've held it since he died. Nobody, until yesterday, ever asked about it."

"I don't have to say that—"

Tipton held up a hand that halted the president's warning. "I've kept this to myself for a long time, I can keep doing that."

Stephanie had more questions, but a soft knock from the front door disturbed the silence. One of the agents stationed outside?

Tipton rose and answered.

The first man to enter the house was Edwin Davis, White House chief of staff. He was a tidy man, near her age, dressed in his usual dark suit, face alert and clean-shaven, nothing even hinting that it was the middle of the night. He acknowledged her with a smile and a wink. They'd been through a lot together and were close friends.

Davis faced his boss and said, "He's here."

She glanced at the president.

"When I arranged this meeting, I asked Mr. Tipton if we might borrow his den for another talk I need to keep private. He graciously agreed."

"I'm going to bed, Mr. President," Tipton said. "Please switch off the lights and lock the door on your way out."

"I'll do that. Thank you, again."

"My father would have wanted nothing less from me."

The older man headed for a staircase and climbed.

The next man to enter through the front door was in his fifties with

Asian features. His thick black hair was long and cut stylishly. He wore a tailored suit—Armani, if she wasn't mistaken—the jacket buttoned in front, his cordovan shoes polished to a mirror shine.

She knew the face.

Ambassador to the United States.

From the People's Republic of China.

TWENTY-FIVE

Isabella stood just inside the cruise terminal, near the customs stand. Passengers continued to stream out of the building, luggage trailing behind them. She was soaking wet, embarrassed, and angry. Luckily, her cell phone was waterproof, standard issue at Treasury. She'd not caught a look at the man who'd shoved her into the lagoon, only what he was wearing. She didn't want to make the overseas call but had no choice. The Treasury secretary was waiting for a report, and he'd earlier made clear that success on her end was imperative.

"The documents are gone?" he asked, when she finished talking. "That's what you're saying."

"My guess is we were made and whoever shoved me off that wharf was working with the woman."

"We don't even know who she is?"

"She only came into this during the past few hours. But if I had to guess, I'd say she's working with Anan Wayne Howell."

She'd read the transcripts from the intercepted phone calls and emails among Larks, Howell, and Kim. Though Kim had used an alias when communicating with both Americans, voice comparisons made at NSA confirmed his identity. Originally, Treasury's plan had been to use this overseas trip as the perfect way to bring it all to a head since there would be no worries here about constitutional protections. Foreign intelligence operations ran on few to no rules. Just results.

"This is not good, Isabella. You know that, right?"

She hated failure, too. "Larks was killed for a reason. Kim had to have done it. Malone stumbled into this, and Kim tried to take him out by implicating him in Larks' death. The good thing is, I don't think Kim has the documents, either. So he's probably in a quandary."

"The documents, Isabella, that's what we're after. That's all we care about. I'm sorry Larks is dead, but he chose to deal with the devil. He got what people get when they do that. We have to retrieve those documents."

She was the only agent assigned to this mission. Everything rested with her. "I found the trail before, I can find it again."

Silence filled her ear for a few moments.

"Okay, stay with it. But another agency is about to be involved."

And she knew who. "The Magellan Billet?"

"That's right. You're all Treasury has there, Isabella. This has to be contained. Do what you have to do."

The call ended.

Damn, she'd screwed up bad. But where before it was just Larks and Kim, now an assortment of new characters had entered the field. Too many for her to know for certain who was who, or what was what. She was flying blind, and that was never a good thing. Perfection. That's what her boss wanted and that's what she'd deliver.

Her father and grandfather had both worked for the FBI, her grandfather as one of Hoover's trusted assistants. Law enforcement coursed through her veins. She could think of nothing she'd rather do with her life. That was one reason why she remained unmarried. Men had never interested her, and she wondered if that might be more significant. But women carried no fascination, either. Work, that was her aphrodisiac. Her record with Treasury stood unblemished, her arrest and conviction rate superb. She'd investigated major bank fraud, embezzlements, government corruption, and countless tax evaders. Many Treasury agents were CPAs and dealt more with accounting. Her training was all law enforcement. The old-fashioned kind. Legwork and brains, working together. That's what her father taught her.

She was thirty-six, but looked older, which she actually liked. She worked long and hard and had been fortunate. People envied her, that she knew. Since day one she'd felt a pressure to succeed, and the results spoke for themselves. Some of the biggest tax evaders in U.S. history went down thanks to her. A few years ago she gathered most of the damaging evidence in the massive United Bank of Switzerland debacle, which led to sweeping changes in Swiss bank secrecy. No mistakes there. That operation ran perfectly. She hated people who cheated the government. To her tax evasion was a form of treason. Government existed to protect the people, and the people owed their allegiance. To violate that trust, to steal from it, was tantamount to declaring war. *Right is right,* her grandfather would say. That it was. When he retired, J. Edgar Hoover himself was there to shake her grandfather's hand. A photo of that moment hung in her office back in DC. One day, when her time was done, a president might congratulate her in the same way.

"I'm sorry I let you down," she whispered to her grandfather, who died before she was born.

She grabbed hold of herself and tried not to be agitated.

Across the building she caught sight of a younger man dressed in low-slung jeans, a collarless black shirt, and a pale jacket. He moved with the sinewy ease of an athlete and approached one of the Italian customs officials, flashing a badge. He was maybe late twenties, blond hair cut short, but shaggy on the edges, the face clean-shaven and warmed by a wide, toothy smile. He had a military look about him and was trying to gain entrance to the terminal, but the guard resisted. Eventually, though, he managed to make his way inside. Definitely American, and from the way he strutted in those boots, the Southern variety. Maybe even a little redneck. She knew the species, an odd offshoot of the American male.

The newcomer walked straight toward her.

"Ms. Schaefer," he called out. "I'm Luke Daniels."

"Is that supposed to mean something?"

He chuckled. "I see the reports were correct. You've got an attitude."

She'd heard the talk about her. Twenty-two partners in eleven years. None stayed long, but none of them cared like she did, either. "What kind of badge were you flashing over there?"

"The kind that can save your ass."

Interesting answer. Okay. He had her attention.

"I saw your cannonball earlier," he said. "It was Anan Wayne Howell who shoved you."

Now he commanded her full attention.

"I know where Anan Wayne Howell is right now."

She said, "He's the least of my concerns."

"Actually, he's the only lead you've got. Everybody else is gone."

Intuitive, she'd give him that. But he could also be bluffing.

"I can point you the right way," he said. "But it'll cost you."

To the Southern charm he added a grin, which annoyed her. But she kept her feelings to herself and asked, "Who has the pleasure of employing you?"

"Is that charm? I didn't expect it. I'm told you're not the most likable type."

"Maybe I'm just choosy."

"Or maybe there's another word for it, but I don't want to start off on the wrong foot. I myself don't ever buy the peaches at the top of the bin. Too many hands on them. The ones down deep are always much firmer."

What she liked was that he wasn't throwing his weight around. He clearly held the upper hand, and seemed to know her predicament. But he wasn't cocky or arrogant. Instead, he seemed genuinely interested in making a deal. Which made her wonder how much this guy knew. Or was part of his job to find out what he could from her?

"You still haven't answered my question," she said. "Who do you work for?"

"Magellan Billet."

No surprise. But they did move fast.

"Are you with Malone?" she asked.

"I'm afraid I do have to claim him."

"He didn't go home, did he?"

He shook his head. "That dog simply does not take commands."

"What's the price I have to pay for learning Howell's whereabouts?"

"I want to know what's going on. Exactly, with no bullshit. Otherwise, you can fend for yourself. But I will tell you, you're never going to find anything without me. It's all flown the coop."

She thought she could provide enough to satisfy this cowboy without jeopardizing a thing. So she said, "Do you know the name Haym Salomon?"

He shook his head.

So she told him all about a debt that now totaled in the hundreds of billions of dollars.

"Is that what's in the black satchel?" he asked when she finished. "Proof of an old IOU?"

She nodded. "An expensive IOU."

Then she waited.

It was his turn to tell her things.

TWENTY-SIX

Virginia

Stephanie tried to recall anything she knew about the Chinese ambassador. He was born to humble roots, but rose to earn a doctorate in economics. His father had been a low-ranking government official who insisted that his son become something more. Ambition, along with capitalism, had made steady inroads into Chinese culture. She'd read reports where this diplomat had been described as both sharp-tongued and quick-witted. But it had also been noted that he never challenged the communist central authority on any issue. Which, more than anything else, explained why he was here. To be given the coveted post of ambassador to the United States, a long way from the eyes and ears of Beijing, meant that he was trusted beyond measure.

Relations with China had definitely warmed since the selection of Ni Yong as its new leader. She, Malone, and Danny Daniels had played a key role in that ascension. But the country remained a perplexing tapestry of ancient customs and dark secrets. As far as she could recall, this was the first time Danny had ever sat face-to-face with this ambassador. If he had, no briefing report of any meeting had ever been circulated, which was standard procedure when a place like China was involved. For the ambassador to first agree to such a meeting, then travel from DC in the middle of the night to a stranger's home, showed clearly the level of importance.

Introductions were made, then Danny said, "I appreciate you coming tonight. From your call yesterday, it appears we have a mutual problem."

"Forgive me, Mr. President, but I asked to speak with you alone."

"Your message said that you have information about North Korea and Kim Yong Jin. This lady is knee-deep into that problem, so she needs to hear what you have to say. She'll be the one dealing with it on my end, and time is short."

The ambassador considered the situation, then seemed to concede the point and said, "I agree, time is short. For the past month we've been noticing an alarming amount of talk from North Korea about Kim Yong Jin. There are people there nearly panicked over him."

"We've picked up the same chatter," the president said. "And I imagine the reason you're here is because they also discussed your country."

The ambassador nodded. "North Korea has always been a source of contention for us. We try to help—they are, after all, our neighbor. But it is a place reason seems to avoid."

Danny chuckled. "That's a mild way of putting it. At least your two countries are allies. They hate us. So why are your people so concerned?"

"Our relationship with Pyongyang has not been the same since we acknowledged the world sanctions."

The United Nations had long imposed penalties against North Korea for its nuclear testing. The country was without a doubt developing a bomb, and no one thought that would be a good idea. A few months ago China had finally joined the economic sanctions, providing further evidence of a change in its political direction.

"I am aware," the ambassador said, "of my premier's great respect for you. I am here on his direct order. Our joining the world sanctions was something North Korea clearly did not expect. Their Dear Leader has made it known that he is not happy with us. But of course he can push only so far, as without us he truly has nothing. We are his only route of trade remaining."

She'd read the confidential CIA analysis. The Chinese had signed off on international sanctions to appease the world, but had continued quietly to supply North Korea with food, medicine, and manufactured goods.

"We have also loaned North Korea money," the ambassador said. "Dear Leader fashions himself a great builder. He has erected amusement parks, apartment blocks, even a ski resort. We recently provided him $300 million U.S. for a new bridge across the Yalu River. Money has also been advanced for highways and rail links. We believe that it is in everyone's interest to keep that country stable."

"Not to mention the mining concessions you obtained for magnesite, zinc, and iron."

She was impressed with the president's depth of knowledge. Say what you want, but he was no fool.

"Trade runs the world," the ambassador said. "We need to receive something for all our generosity."

The president smiled. "Again, why the concern? Seems like you own Dear Leader lock, stock, and barrel. What's the problem?"

"Kim Yong Jin has no such loyalty to us."

A valid point. But she said, "Mr. Ambassador, Kim is hardly in a position to do anyone much harm. From all reports he drinks too much, gambles incessantly, and is more interested in women than politics. He's been gone from North Korea since his father died, which was twelve years ago. He's a nonplayer. What could he effectively accomplish?"

"We believe he is intent on deposing his half brother, proving to his dead father, and himself, that he is not—as he was labeled—*incapable*."

"But he would have to have the means to accomplish that," she said. "Which he hardly possesses."

"We are not so sure about that. And that is why I came here tonight. I need to ask a question, one we have not been able to answer. The premier is hoping that you will be open and honest with your reply."

She and Danny waited.

"What is it from your past that so interests Kim Yong Jin? We know from our intercepts that Kim has been in communication with a former official from your Treasury Department, Paul Larks, and a fugitive from your courts, a man named Anan Wayne Howell. They talk of a great fraud and injustice from your past. What is this?"

Stephanie would love to know the answer to that question, too.

"I can only say, Mr. Ambassador," Danny said, "that there may be something that could cause us all trouble. I was not fully aware of it until the past few days. So it's impossible for me to provide any concrete details, at least at this time."

"You can offer nothing?"

"Not right now."

But she wondered just how much Danny really knew.

"It clearly appears Kim is staging a comeback," the ambassador said. "He wants his half brother gone and his birthright restored. To do that he apparently plans to harm both the United States and China. He aims high, that I will give him. If successful, he would achieve what no Kim has ever managed—a clear victory over us both."

She heard the apprehension in the ambassador's voice as he continued to fish for information.

"Here's something I can tell you," the president said. "A few hours ago Kim tried to steal twenty million dollars. It was money generated by an insurance fraud scheme, sent to Dear Leader each year on his birthday. We were there, watching, but the money was destroyed in a helicopter crash. All of that happened in Venice. Kim is there, right now, with Howell, that fugitive you mentioned."

"And the former Treasury official. Larks. Who is dead," the ambassador said, a clear signal that the other side was not entirely in the dark. Stephanie herself had only learned that information a couple of hours ago, thanks to a second call from Luke Daniels.

"We have people on site," the ambassador said. "It seems Larks' body was found in his cabin. No cause of death was immediately known."

"What people do you have there?" the president asked.

She wanted to know that, too, since they could prove a problem. Danny was performing at his best, winging things, making it up as he went along. He was part Lyndon Johnson, with his deep voice and strong-arm tactics—part Bill Clinton in Southern charm and disarming looks. Congressmen had complained for years at their inability to tell him no. He adhered to a tried-and-true formula. Reward your friends and punish your enemies.

And that he did, with a vengeance.

The question of the night, though, was which side China fell on.

"You're going to take Kim out, aren't you?" Danny asked.

"Not us. But Pyongyang has a different agenda. They are simply waiting for Kim to find whatever it is. Then they plan to claim it for themselves."

"And use it to coerce us both."

The ambassador nodded. "Now you realize the extent of our *mutual* problem. Regardless of who wins this fight between the Korean brothers, the two of us remain in jeopardy."

"The crazy half brother, disgraced and exiled, isn't as stupid as everyone thought," Danny said. "That much we now know. We have a saying back in Tennessee, where I come from. *Even the blind-eyed biscuit thrower hits the target every once in a while.*"

"And we have a similar wisdom. *With time and patience the mulberry leaf becomes a silk gown.*"

A few moments of silence passed between them. Everything about the Chinese ambassador signaled both restraint and concern.

Finally, she said, "We have our best people in Venice, right now, working on this."

"As do the North Koreans." The ambassador faced Danny. "Please know, Mr. President, that China has no grievance with the United States. We neither started nor wanted this fight. To keep the current stability between our countries is a good thing for us all. But Kim Yong Jin is another matter. He is an unknown. So let us hope we are successful in stopping him."

The ambassador stood and bid them good night. Danny did not try to stop him from leaving. Apparently, enough had been said. The front door closed and the parlor returned to its former quiet, the lights still burning low. Edwin Davis had waited outside, his job to return the ambassador to Washington.

Not until they heard the car drive off did she say, "You do realize that he's lying."

"Of course. China's after Kim, too. They surely have people over there, ready to move. But they won't make a move until they have what it is Kim's after. Beijing can't, and won't, let this opportunity pass, no matter how much supposed goodwill exists between us."

"Which begs the question, why alert us?"

"That's easy. First, he doesn't want to disrupt the goodwill that really does exist between us. And second, he had to know if it was worth the effort."

"Is it real?"

"Unfortunately this is as real as it gets, but I'm not going to make the same mistake Joe Levy made. Cotton and Luke need to know what they're up against."

"What are we up against?"

She saw that he understood her inquiry. She wasn't referring to espionage and some potential assassins. Her question was more specific.

More American.

"I'll tell you," he said. "But first, make the call to Italy."

TWENTY-SEVEN

ADRIATIC SEA

MALONE SAT AT A TABLE BESIDE ONE OF THE EXTERIOR WINDOWS, the long dining room crowded, the air reeking of scrambled eggs and bitter coffee. The ferry was more a liner with 300-plus cabins, salons, bars, lounges, even a theater. Room for more than a hundred trucks and cars occupied its lower decks. Outside, the blue Adriatic rolled by as they cruised east toward Croatia, the ride smooth and level. He'd stayed with Howell the whole way, boarding after him, keeping his distance. There were several hundred people on board across the many decks, plenty of places to disappear into, yet Howell had come straight here and filled a plate from the breakfast buffet.

Not a bad idea, actually. So he'd followed suit, having a bagel, banana, and orange juice. He hadn't eaten since yesterday afternoon. But that was nothing unusual. Back when he was a full-time agent, he'd go days without eating. The anxiety and stress of fieldwork seemed to clamp his stomach. The same had been true at JAG when he tried cases in court. Thankfully, once the pressure was relieved, his appetite always returned. At the moment, though, things were ratcheting up. He'd found Howell, so the woman with the satchel should not be far behind. In Venice she'd gone one way, Howell the other, the idea surely to throw anyone interested off track. Of course, he doubted if Howell realized that two separate factions—the Justice Department and Treasury—were now interested in him. Yet the ruse had partially worked, as they were here without anyone from Treasury in sight.

As if on cue the woman with the black Tumi bag entered on the far side, walked over, and sat with Howell.

They kissed.

Malone relaxed into the clamor of dishes, silverware, and conversation, eating his breakfast, acting disinterested in anything and everything, his actions no different from those of the hundred or so others around him. The noise, along with the din of the unabated engine became hypnotic and he resisted the urge to close his eyes.

His phone buzzed.

The display read UNKNOWN.

He decided to answer, which also made him no different from a multitude of others engrossed with their own mobile devices.

It was Stephanie.

"Your number didn't appear," he said.

"I'm at another location, on a landline."

"I have Howell and the documents in sight," he whispered to her.

"Tell me," she said.

He gave her a quick report.

"You're going to have company at some point," she said.

He listened as she explained about Kim Yong Jin, a disgraced exile who had once been the next in line to lead North Korea, and his contacts with Howell and Larks. Then she told him about a conversation with the Chinese ambassador.

"We suspect the Chinese and North Koreans may be after Howell and the documents. How about you secure them both before anything bad happens."

"This is turning into something far more than a part-time babysitting assignment."

"Don't worry," a male voice said. "I'll make sure she ups your pay."

Danny Daniels.

"Are you two always together?" he asked. "It sure seems that way every time we're on the phone."

Daniels chuckled. "We need you to get those documents back. They're actually more important than Howell. So if you have to choose—"

"Let's hope I don't have to."

"I can't think of anyone I'd rather have on site," the president said.

"Your nephew might take issue with that."

"Experience over youth. That's all."

"Were the Chinese behind that money theft?" he whispered.

"No, that was Kim," Daniels said. "He didn't want his half brother getting the money this year. But that cash is no loss to us."

His hunch had been right. All of it was related. "Do you want me to use the direct approach or a little finesse to get those documents back?"

"Your call," Stephanie said. "But get them, and bring Howell home with you, if you can. You might tell him that the Chinese have far less regard for his physical safety than we do. He's in their crosshairs. He'll be a lot safer in a federal penitentiary."

"Let's sweeten the deal," Daniels said. "Tell Howell he'll get a presidential pardon if he plays ball with us."

"That's quite a prize," he said.

"Cattle go to the slaughterhouse a lot faster when there's food in the chute."

"I'll keep that in mind."

He ended the call and went back to eating his breakfast. The ferry provided free WiFi, so he connected and used his smartphone's browser to gather more about Kim Yong Jin, keeping one eye on Howell and the woman.

The name was familiar, but he could recall few details. He read that Kim was now fifty-eight. From an old article he learned that when Kim had been caught trying to gain illegal entry into Japan he'd chosen an odd identity, passing himself off as a Dominican friar named Pang Xiong. Fat Bear. Which seemed to fit Kim physically. Every online image showed that weight had always been a problem. There were two other brothers. The current Dear Leader, who was the youngest. And a middle brother, never in serious contention for anything as their father had considered him too feminine to lead. Kim remained a North Korean citizen, though he lived in Macao. His only public comment about the current North Korean leadership came ten years ago and was not flattering. *"The power elite that have ruled the country will continue to be in control. I have my doubts about whether a person with only a few years of grooming as a leader can govern."*

Another more recent article described how North Korea had long been actively engaged in both ballistic missile and nuclear warhead production. The country remained under international sanctions, pressure to end its nuclear development coming from all sides, including now from its chief ally, China.

He then found a fascinating *New York Times* piece from last summer describing a stage show that had been broadcast live throughout North Korea. A costumed Tigger, Minnie Mouse, Mickey, and other Disney characters had paraded before Dear Leader and a slew of clapping, uniformed generals. Mickey Mouse himself had conducted women in slinky black dresses playing violins. Scenes from Disney movies were shown on screens behind the performers. Disney songs were played and sung. A spokesman for Disney was quoted as saying that none of that proprietary use had been sanctioned or licensed by the company. The band on stage was said to have been organized by Dear Leader himself, who was noted as possessing a *grandiose plan to bring a dramatic turn in the field of literature and arts*.

He smiled. What irony.

One brother was chastised and stripped of power for his interest in Western entertainment. And the other used the same thing to seemingly bolster his popularity. He could see how Kim Yong Jin might resent his half brother. But none of that explained exactly what was happening here. Lots of tendrils and bits and pieces existed, but nothing as yet had come into focus.

He finished his food and downed the rest of his juice. Howell and the woman remained at their table. He was about to head that way and get this over with when a man entered the dining room. He had a round brow on a round, fleshy head, atop a heavy, doughy body. The face was wide and seedy, his hair cut short, the neck thick and chinless. Replace the designer shirt, slacks, and jacket—which surely hung better on their hangers—with a drab green uniform buttoned to the neck and he made for the perfect North Korean stereotype.

Kin Yong Jin.

TWENTY-EIGHT

VENICE

ISABELLA HAD CHANGED CLOTHES AND DRIED HER HAIR. HER LUG-gage rested in the water taxi, beside the helmsman, along with two travel bags Luke Daniels had tossed on board. They were headed to the air-port. Just before leaving the cruise ship terminal, Daniels had taken a short telephone call. He then informed her that not only Howell but also Kim and the woman with the documents were now on a ferry to Zadar, Croatia, scheduled to arrive there in three hours.

Exactly what she wanted to hear.

That cold trail just turned hot.

She was back positive, reassured, in command. So she'd arranged for a quick flight across the Adriatic on a charter plane, which would place them on the ground just before the ferry arrived. The only thing Daniels had not mentioned was how he'd come to know all that he did.

So she asked.

"Malone's on the ferry," he told her. "We tagged Howell after he clipped you into the water and followed him."

They were alone inside an enclosed cabin that usually accommodated about ten passengers. The water taxi rode low to the water and the roar from its engines shielded their conversation.

"Maybe it's a good thing Malone doesn't follow orders," she said.

Otherwise she'd be back to square one, three months' worth of work truly wasted.

"This Haym Salomon," Daniels said. "Was he really that important?"

Telling him more on that subject wouldn't hurt a thing. "I'd say so. The Continental Congress was broke. It had no gold or silver, and in those days currency had to be backed up with real collateral. Each colony printed its own money, but hyperinflation had taken hold. Prices skyrocketed, shopkeepers quit taking Continental dollars. We desperately needed a loan from the French, but it never came. What did come was French money that flooded the American market. Scrip sent to pay soldiers who were here fighting with us."

She explained how Salomon realized the usefulness of that French scrip and started buying those bills of exchange, the goal being to establish a standard value. But there was risk. If the American Revolution failed, the bills would be worthless and Salomon would lose everything. There'd be no way to recoup his investment.

"But he believed in the cause," she said. "And what he did funded the Continental army. He invested his entire fortune in buying those French bills of exchange. Then he made loans to Congress, mainly from his own reserves. He expected those loans would be repaid once the fighting ended, but he died in 1785 before any of that could happen."

"And his widow was cheated out of repayment?"

"*Cheated* is a strong word. She provided documentation for the debts and asked for repayment, but those papers disappeared. Without them, she had no evidence of the debts. That documentation has been missing since 1785."

The boat continued to plow along, rounding Venice's northwest corner and heading for the international airport.

"During the Revolutionary War Salomon and George Washington became close. Washington was grateful for all that Salomon was doing. When the war ended, he asked Salomon what he might like in return. The man was modest and said he wanted nothing for himself, but he would like something for American Jews. So years later, as president, after Salomon had died, Washington made sure there was a tribute added to the nation's Great Seal. You have a dollar bill?"

He found one in his wallet and handed it over.

She flipped it over and pointed at the right side to the familiar eagle clasping thirteen arrows. "Look there, above the bird. Thirteen stars. Notice anything about them?"

She traced the outline of two triangles with her finger.

A six-pointed star.

"The Star of David," she said. "Washington's gift to Haym Salomon."

He was amazed. "I've never noticed that before."

"Few have. But once you see it, it's hard to miss. Kind of like that arrow in the FedEx logo."

She could see that he was fascinated. She had been, too, when first told. "I assume history was not one of your interests in school?"

"Hell, school was not an interest in school. Not my thing."

"Paul Larks was investigating some sensitive matters for the Treasury secretary that dealt with Haym Salomon and the heirs' claims for repayment. The president himself ordered that inquiry. Larks found some information but, unfortunately, the important stuff was purged by Andrew Mellon in 1925, when Congress was once again looking into authorizing repayment. A previous investigation, ordered in 1937 by FDR, confirmed that Mellon had probably taken the Salomon repayment documents."

"Which proves the U.S. government now owes his heirs $330 billion?"

"Something like that."

"I don't get it. How could this interest a guy like Kim Yong Jin?

Okay, we might owe somebody $330 billion, but that's not an international incident."

She needed this man to believe her.

Get those documents, Isabella.

She could not let her boss down again.

"Larks copied some confidential papers—"

"I get that. But you still have the originals. It's not the end of the world."

"Actually, it is. Those copies are important, particularly if you know what you're looking at. We don't want them floating around. And Anan Wayne Howell, for all his fanaticism, actually might know exactly what they mean."

She wondered how long Luke Daniels had worked with the Magellan Billet. From what she knew, that agency only hired the best. Stephanie Nelle, its longtime head, bordered on legendary. She'd even once considered applying there herself. For a long time you had to be a lawyer to be a part, but in recent years that requirement had been waived. Perhaps Stephanie Nelle might take notice of her here. A move to international espionage would be good. She'd had a few tastes of that on several other assignments.

Daniels smiled at her. "You must really think me an idiot."

She said nothing.

"I hear what you're sayin'. But I also hear what you're not sayin'. All this trouble for a bunch of copies? Bullshit. But I'm going to give you the benefit of allowing you to keep what you're holdin' back to yourself. At least for a while longer. 'Cause right now, it doesn't really matter."

She remained silent.

"Lockjaw?" he asked. "I get that myself sometimes. A word of advice. Don't try this bullshit story with Pappy. He's—"

A perplexed look came to her face, which he noticed.

"Malone. That's Pappy. Me? I'm downright congenial compared with him. He has a zero bullshit-tolerance level. Don't push him."

"I'll remember that."

She watched as he studied the dollar bill again.

"That is pretty amazing, though, about the Star of David," he said. "You almost had me with that one."

"What I said about that is true. There are many amazing things about the dollar bill." She decided to toss him one more tidbit. "In recent years the $10, $20, $50, and $100 bills have all been redesigned. Lots of bells and whistles have been added to make counterfeiting harder. Ever heard of the Omnibus Appropriations Act?"

He shook his head.

"Section 111 of that act expressly forbids Treasury or the Bureau of Engraving from using any funds appropriated by Congress for the redesign of the $1 bill." She pointed at the money he held. "That has to stay exactly like it is."

The look on his face asked why.

So she led him along.

"That *is* part of what we're here to find out."

TWENTY-NINE

KIM WAS ENJOYING HIS ANONYMITY. NEITHER HOWELL NOR THE woman had a clue to his identity. The crowded room was full of strangers, except for one face, on the far side, sitting at a window table by himself.

Malone.

The American had managed not only to escape the trap set for him, but had also found his way here. He assumed Howell had led him, as there'd been no sign of Malone from their tail of the woman with the satchel.

Hana stood at a counter twenty meters away sipping a bottled water.

For him, knowing the lay of the land, and the players in a room, came from living in an autocratic society where no one trusted anyone. Keeping everyone off guard was the most effective mechanism in retaining control. His family, occupying the apex of the political pyramid, had always enjoyed the luxury of only looking for trouble beneath them, never above. But that didn't mean you ignored your family. His father had executed his own father's brother, branding his great-uncle an enemy of the state. As a younger man, he'd never understood that. But as he'd grown older, the idea that family might pose the greatest threat had become a much clearer reality.

His half brother was living proof.

His own immediate family, though, remained benign. His children were all grown, all of them except Hana married. None to his knowledge had any interest in politics. His sons were businessmen, his daughters either mothers or teachers, living in North Korea. He hadn't spoken to any of them since he'd left. It seemed that his fall from power had also included losing his children. Hana alone remained loyal, never judging, always there. She so reminded him of her mother. They'd not been married. Instead, she'd been one of many mistresses he once maintained. On that score he and his father and grandfather were much alike. He couldn't help it. Women were a weakness. He'd met Hana's mother twenty-five years ago when he was still in favor, drawn by her beauty. His wife had never minded his dalliances, content with the wealth and privilege that being married to the heir apparent had provided. But she, too, left him after the fall, remaining in North Korea when he fled to Macao. Which he hadn't really minded. The marriage had turned depressing, draining from him much-needed talents and energy.

As he studied Howell and the woman Parks had said was named Jelena it was obvious they were connected. Their light touches and casual conversation seemed proof of a close relationship. They seemed utterly at ease with each other, content that everything had worked as planned. So what should he do next? He could proceed a number of ways.

But Jelena made the decision for him.

She stood, kissed Howell lightly on the lips, and walked away, leaving the satchel on the table. Perhaps she was visiting the restroom? Or headed somewhere else? Didn't really matter. They were now separated and he caught Hana's eyes with his own.

And he saw she knew exactly what to do.

MALONE STUDIED KIM YONG JIN, WHO WAS CLEARLY INTERESTED in Howell and the woman. He had to assume Kim knew both his and Howell's identity—as who else on board that cruise ship would have set him up for Paul Larks' death.

So what now?

The answer came as the woman with the satchel left Howell and bounded off toward the restrooms.

Kim immediately walked to Howell's table and sat in the empty chair.

"MR. HOWELL, YOU AND I HAVE NEVER MET PERSONALLY. BUT WE do know each other. I am Peter From Europe."

It took a moment, then Kim saw that Howell seemed to register the identity.

"We've emailed," Howell said. "What are you doing here?"

"I've been looking for you."

Howell looked much like his photo on the website. Mid-thirties, trim build, thinning black hair. The bio from the site had also noted a degree in political science. No work experience had been referenced and Kim doubted this man had accomplished much, besides stumbling onto what may be the cleverest weapon of mass destruction ever devised.

"How did you find me?" Howell asked, concern in his voice.

"Paul Larks facilitated that. I assume from him you know me as *the Korean*."

He caught the surprise on Howell's face as the American reached for the satchel and started to leave.

"That would not be wise."

"Go screw yourself."

Howell lifted the bag.

"I have Jelena."

Howell froze.

"She is my prisoner."

Howell's gaze raked the room in the direction the woman had gone.

"Quite right. She just left. But my associates have her hidden away. Her life is now in your hands."

He kept his voice low, directing both his words and gaze straight at his intended audience. The use of Jelena's name sent a further message that he was also informed. But he hadn't forgotten about Malone, across the room, who was certainly watching.

Howell sat.

"Much better," he said.

He allowed Howell a moment of composure.

"I have to say, I'm disappointed in both you and Larks. I paid for you and him to come here, the idea being that I wanted to meet with you both. I thought we shared the same ideals. But then I learn that you considered me *un*trustworthy. A foreigner."

"This doesn't concern you. I'm not a traitor."

"You're just a man who thinks the rules do not apply to him."

"They don't apply to anyone."

"Are you right, Mr. Howell? Is what you say true? That's what I came to find out. We do share the same ideals. I want to believe what you say."

He thought appealing to this man's ego might work. People like Howell, who'd convinced themselves of the righteousness of their cause, were easily swayed by sympathetic ears. That same tactic worked every day across North Korea.

"Are you an American citizen?" Howell asked. "Do you really pay taxes? Are you subject to our laws?"

He shook his head. "None of the above. I lied about my predicament. But only because I truly want to understand what it is you know."

"Why does this concern you?"

"It seems that anyone who is willing to aid your cause should be viewed as a friend. I doubt you have many allies. From what I know, you are a convicted criminal, a fugitive from American justice. Yet you judge my motives?"

The younger man leaned forward and whispered, "I'm not telling you a damn thing."

Howell had seemed to calm himself. His nerve had returned, along with the boldness that had surely guided him in exile.

He made his position clear. "Then she will die."

"I'll get help from the crew. Turn you in."

"And I will do the same to you. Except that you will then be available for arrest and extradition back to the United States, and Jelena will be at the bottom of the Adriatic, her body weighted, sunk to the depths."

He could see that Howell was beginning to realize this was serious.

"What do you want?"

He pointed to the satchel. "To read what's in there. After that, you and I will speak again."

The ferry continued its smooth path east across calm water.

He did not have the time for Howell's obvious agony of indecision. So he made the call for him, reaching for the case and saying, "Wait here."

THIRTY

VIRGINIA

STEPHANIE FELT BETTER NOW THAT HER AGENTS WERE APPRISED OF the danger potential. She'd meant what she'd said to Joe Levy. Never had she taken unnecessary chances with her people's lives. After ending the call to Cotton she'd called Luke, who'd just made contact with Treasury's eyes and ears, a female agent named Isabella Schaefer.

"I should have Treasury recall her," the president said.

They were still sitting alone in Ed Tipton's den. Dawn was not far away. She was tired and needed sleep, but she knew how to run on adrenaline. The president was a notorious night owl.

"Let's not," she said. "That agent has a ten-day head start on us. We could use her knowledge."

He did not argue or object. Instead he sat silent, as if weighing the emergence of a new idea. She'd made both of her calls using Tipton's landline. Danny had assured her that their host had said it was okay. But she was beginning to get the idea. "The Chinese now know I'm in the game."

"Which means they'll be watching *and* listening to you."

That meant, be careful with mobile phones. There was nothing secure about them.

"It's that damn FDR," he said. "This is all his fault. He was the luckiest bastard in the world."

"He was crippled."

"Which didn't stop him. His greatest successes came after the polio. Before that he was just another spoiled rich kid, an only child, a mama's boy. All he ever did his whole life was exactly what he wanted. He didn't know the meaning of the word *no*."

She knew a little about Roosevelt. His father died when he was eighteen and his mother had indeed become an overriding influence. As a young man he was attractive, clever, and ambitious, using family money and connections to steadily climb the political ladder. But there was nothing wrong with that, anybody in the same position would have done the same. Still, he lost two elections prior to contracting polio in 1921. After that he went 6–0. Two terms as governor of New York. Four terms as president of the United States.

"I've read a lot about dear ol' FDR," Danny said. "I never realized, but he wasn't all that bright and never amounted to much of anything at school. He talked more than he listened, and was not opposed to stretching the truth when it suited him. Teachers did not speak highly of him. He knew little to nothing about either money or economics. Why would he? His family on both sides were rich. Everything was always provided for him. His grandfather, on his mother's side, sold opium to China. Can you imagine what the press would do with that today?"

She wondered about the rant, which seemed a bit out of character.

"His first two terms as president were a failure," he said. "Unemployment in 1939, after six years of Roosevelt, was worse than in 1931, before he was ever elected. Stock values had also plummeted to new lows. And the national debt? That's his greatest gift. It grew more in the 1930s than in the previous 150 years. All he did was print money, spend it, then print more. If it hadn't been for World War Two he would have been a two-termer, gone and forgotten. War saved this country, not FDR."

"But he offered people hope," she said.

"Stephanie, he just plucked at their heartstrings and told them what they wanted to hear. He stood for flag, God, and motherhood. Today he would have been filleted by the press. His flip-flops on the major issues would have been the jokes of late-night TV. Instead he lived in a time when no one even reported he was crippled. The press was more than friendly—they were downright complacent. Look at 1940 when he campaigned on a pledge to stay out of the war. Then, in 1941, as soon as he was sworn in a third time, he implemented Lend-Lease to the Brits. Is that staying out? We supply them equipment, they take that equipment and fight. How long did he think the Germans were going to stand for that? If Japan had not attacked Pearl Harbor, the Germans surely would have made a move on us of their own. But no reporter ever took him to task. No one ever said a word. Roosevelt had a free pass."

"What's all this about?" she asked. "Why does it matter about FDR?"

"Because he was a condescending prick, patronizing and humiliating. And those aren't my words. Those came from Dean Acheson, who worked for him and saw it for himself. Now here we are, decades later, faced with the results of that arrogance."

She was still puzzled.

"The man preached moral leadership, yet he had too many mistresses to even count. We talk about Kennedy and Clinton and their indiscretions. They were amateurs compared with FDR. He lied to his wife on a daily basis. Any man who can do that will have no problem lying to the country. He chose to go after Andrew Mellon simply because he could. But he lost, big time. He underestimated Mellon. That old man was not stupid."

"You held back with the ambassador," she said. "You didn't tell him what this was all about. But you know, don't you?"

"That's another two-faced SOB. China wants what FDR was supposed to find."

"Care to tell me what that is?"

"We know that Mellon gave something to FDR when they met in 1936. It had to be that page with numbers. The code. That's what FDR was supposed to figure out. Mellon probably had possession of certain documents that could have been harmful to the United States. They probably concerned Haym Salomon. There was some sort of internal Treasury investigation in 1937. That we know, too. Larks copied its report. He also copied other classified papers."

"Cotton has the documents in sight," she said. "You heard him."

"Which gives me some comfort. I don't want those falling into the wrong hands."

The name Haym Salomon finally rang a bell. "There's a big bronze statue in downtown Chicago, near the river. George Washington, Robert Morris, and Haym Salomon. I've seen it."

He nodded. "It's been there since '41. Roosevelt called it *this great triumvirate of patriots.* It's one of the few memorials erected to Salomon. He's a forgotten figure, but appears to have been an important one. Hell, we might owe his heirs $300 billion."

"But you and I know that could hardly be what this is about?"

"I agree. But in 1936 that debt was still in the many billions and would have been a big deal. The same was true in the 1920s, when Mellon first came across the information. Repayment then could have bankrupted the nation. Not to mention the pure embarrassment of the whole thing. So Mellon, being Mellon, used what he knew to his advantage and managed to stay in power until the Depression made his blackmail irrelevant. That's when Hoover got rid of him."

"There has to be more to this than just that."

"There is."

They'd been inside Tipton's house a long time, and she sensed that their conversation should be finished in the car where they would be alone.

"Shouldn't we be leaving?" she asked.

Danny stood. "I need to get back to the White House, before things get going for the day there."

His voice had grown low and tired.

"Here's the deal, Stephanie. Mellon fashioned some sort of hunt. Something that would be, to use his words, *the end of FDR.* He provided the code and a starting point, but FDR, being the arrogant prick he was, crumpled it up and threw it away. We now know that crumpled sheet still existed in April 1945, when FDR died, and that it was given to Morgenthau at Treasury."

She heard what he hadn't said. "But it wasn't among the papers you read yesterday."

He shook his head. "No, it wasn't."

Which begged several other questions. But she held those for now and asked, "Why would Mellon hide something away that was so potentially harmful, and then give FDR a way to find it? If he hated the president, just use it and be done with it."

"It's like what Finley wrote in his diary. Mellon *was* a patriot. He hated FDR, but not America. He hid away what he had, then gave his enemy a way to find it solely for torment. He actually *wanted* FDR to find it. Surely, if it's as bad as Mellon said, Roosevelt would have destroyed it. No harm done, except that FDR would have skipped to Mellon's beat. For men with egos like those two, that was more than enough satisfaction. Today we do the same thing. We torment our enemies in the media, or on the Internet, or the social networks. We let 'em twist in the wind, just enough to drive 'em nuts."

And she had no doubt that Danny spoke from experience.

"But Mellon overestimated his importance," she said, "and FDR didn't take the bait."

"Not soon enough, anyway, as Tipton told us earlier. It seems that on the day he died, nine years after the fact, FDR had finally decided to pay attention. The problem for us is that it's still out there, waiting for *our* enemies to find." He paused, seemingly in thought, then asked, "You really think what's on that paper is a code?"

"It sure sounds like it, and makes sense."

"Then we have to find that missing crumpled sheet."

THIRTY-ONE

MALONE WATCHED AS KIM LEFT WITH THE BLACK TUMI CASE. HE debated what to do. Go after it? Or stay here? Howell's face was thick with concern. Clearly, whatever had just happened was way over that man's head. Since there was no place for Kim to go aboard the ferry, he decided to stick with Howell and see what could be learned. He rose, walked across the room, and sat at Howell's table.

"Who the hell are you?" Howell eyed him with an innate suspicion. Then recognition came to the younger man's face. "Ah, crap. You're government. What? IRS? FBI?"

"Neither. But I am a guy who can help. What just happened?"

"Does the whole damn world know what I'm doing? How did *you* find me?"

They were attracting attention.

"Keep your voice down, okay? And don't look a gift horse in the mouth. What did Kim want?"

"Who's Kim?"

"The guy who was just here. Kim Yong Jin."

"Who is that?"

"Not someone you want to mess with."

"You here to take me in?"

"That was the original plan, but things have changed. Paul Larks is dead." He saw that Howell had not known that. "Kim killed him."

Howell appeared both frustrated and scared. "This is getting way out of hand. You may not believe this, but I have no idea who that Korean is. He and I emailed some, but he used an alias. What does he want with me?"

"Actually, I can believe all of that. But I need to know what's in that satchel?"

"Look . . . what's your name?"

"Cotton Malone."

Howell threw him an odd look. "How'd you get a tag like that?"

"Long story, and we don't have the time. Answer my question."

"That guy Kim has Jelena, my girlfriend. He said he'd kill her if I didn't hand over the satchel. She's an innocent here. We met in Croatia. That's where I've been hiding. She was just doing me a favor. Larks bought my ticket for that cruise, but I changed it into her name."

He doubted Larks bought anything. More likely Kim had financed the whole venture as a way to gather the players in one place.

"What's in the satchel?" he repeated.

"Proof of a conspiracy that will bring America to its knees."

"That's a bold statement."

"Who do you work for?'

"Justice Department."

"I can't let anything happen to Jelena. She doesn't deserve this. He said he was coming back after he looked over the documents."

He zeroed tight on Howell's eyes and said for the last time, "Tell me what's in that satchel."

KIM ENTERED THE CABIN HANA HAD BOOKED FOR THEM. IT CAME with twin beds and a small bathroom with shower. They were both traveling on false passports, under aliases, which he'd obtained in Macao. He liked the ability to move about the world unobstructed and, compared with the time he'd tried to gain entry into Japan years ago, the state of the art in forgeries was far superior. Besides, no one paid him any attention.

"How is our guest?" he asked.

Hana pointed to the bed where the woman lay, laboring under the effects of the same drug used on Malone and Larks. He found it so much easier to travel with drugs as opposed to guns. No one ever questioned them. Most people today carried small pharmacies around with them.

"She was no trouble," Hana said.

They were two decks down from the dining salon, toward the bow. He saw she noticed the satchel, and he smiled at their success.

"Time for us to see if all this was worth it."

MALONE LISTENED AS HOWELL EXPLAINED THAT THE 16TH AMENDment to the Constitution came as a direct consequence of an 1895 Supreme Court decision that held taxes on incomes must be apportioned, under Article I, Section 2 of the Constitution. That would mean people living in less populated states would pay a higher tax on their income so that their portion of the overall total was equal to that of other more populated states. That fundamental unfairness had been intentional on the part of the Founding Fathers, as they were no fan of direct taxes. Apportionment became the way to discourage them.

And it worked.

Direct taxes were avoided by Congress.

But during the early part of the 20th century sentiment changed. The Gilded Age had produced clearly defined classes of "haves" and "have nots." Social unrest had firmly taken hold, and the idea of a tax to "soak the rich" became popular among liberals in both the Democratic and Republican parties. Several times Democrats introduced bills in the House of Representatives to tax higher incomes, but each time the conservative branch of the Republican party killed the measure in the Senate. That's when Democrats began to call Republicans "the party of the rich."

And the label stuck.

Causing reelection anxiety.

In April 1909 the Democrats proposed another bill for a national income tax as a ploy to embarrass Republicans and force them to publicly acknowledge their support for the wealthy. Nobody gave the bill any chance of passage—and even if it did, there was still the matter that unapportioned income taxes had, fifteen years earlier, been ruled unconstitutional. But to everyone's amazement Teddy Roosevelt and other liberal Republicans endorsed the measure. Conservative Republicans then fell into a panic. Oppose the bill and they would certainly become "the party of the rich." Support the bill and they would lose their political base—which was the rich.

So they opted for an end run.

In June 1909 President William Taft, a Republican, caught the Democrats off guard and proposed the 16th Amendment. At the precise moment when it appeared that Democrats would pass an income tax bill, the Republicans chose to submit the entire matter to the states for their approval. Even better, if the amendment was approved, it would eliminate the Supreme Court's opposition to income taxes, overruling the apportionment requirement, and allowing the tax to be imposed equally nationwide. The Republican strategy seemed brilliant on paper, as the amendment had little chance of passing in Congress and, even if it did, three-fourths of the states would surely reject it.

But they were wrong.

The Senate backed the amendment 77–0 and the House 318–14.

Then state after state ratified until, on February 12, 1913, Secretary of State Philander Knox declared the amendment "in effect."

"When the first income tax was approved in 1913," Howell told Malone, "it was only 1 percent on the first $20,000 and 7 percent above $500,000. That would be 1 percent on the first $298,000 in today's dollars and 7 percent above $7,460,000. By 1939 only 5 percent of the population was required to file a return. Today more than 80 percent have to file."

Howell sounded like a true fanatic, who loved to rely on statistics to support their position.

"The collection process changed in 1943. That's when FDR started withholding from wages and salaries. Income taxes began to be collected right at the payroll window, before they were even due to be paid by the taxpayer. That's when the whole thing went from a tax on the rich, to a tax on the masses."

He studied the salon again and saw no sign of Kim.

"I'm worried about Jelena," Howell said.

"You keep talking. I assure you, she's fine. For now."

KIM OPENED THE SATCHEL AND REMOVED A THICK SHEATH OF papers clamped together with a black metal clip. Several hundred pages, all of which appeared to be copies, except for one. He scanned through the pile, taking in bits and pieces. Clumps were stapled together.

One of the copies caught his eye.

A report.

Department of Justice

———

Office of the Solicitor

———

Memorandum
February 24, 1913
Ratification of the 16th Amendment to the
Constitution of the United States

This he knew about from Howell's book. It had been written by the then solicitor general to the secretary of state. There were references to it in other documents—that much he'd learned from Howell's book—but the report itself had never been seen publicly. Apparently it had been hidden away in secret classified files within the American Treasury Department, found by Paul Larks.

Excitement surged through him.

Part of believing Howell was believing this report existed.

And here it was.

MALONE LISTENED TO HOWELL, TRYING TO ASSESS THE YOUNGER man's credibility.

"I don't know you from Adam," Howell said. "I shouldn't even be talking to you. I've spent three years hiding from the government."

"I don't blame you for not trusting me. You're right, I was sent here to bring you back. But things have changed. Larks is dead, and your lady friend is in deep trouble. So do yourself a favor and keep talking."

"Are you always so pleasant?"

"Actually, this is a good day for me."

The younger man shook his head. "I wrote my book using bits and pieces and lots of conjecture. I admit that. But it was all I had. I heard the story about Mellon and FDR years ago. One of those urban legends American history is full of. Mellon supposedly had proof that the 16th Amendment was illegal. He also had evidence that America owed a huge debt to the heirs of a man who loaned us money during the Revolution."

"That why you don't pay taxes?"

"Damn right. It's illegal what they're doing. I started a website and tried to pass the word, but all I got was the IRS coming to visit. They showed up one day and ransacked my whole house. Oh, yeah, they had a search warrant, but they weren't after anything. They just came to deliver a message."

"Which your failure to pay taxes gave them probable cause to do."

"I know. They indicted and tried me fast. I went to the first day of the trial and saw it was all a farce, so I got the hell out of Dodge before they convicted me. Which they did, without me being there. I've been on the run ever since."

"You didn't have to surrender your passport when they indicted you?"

Howell shook his head. "The morons never even asked if I had one, and I didn't volunteer a thing. I got the passport a few years before for a Caribbean cruise. It definitely came in handy when I ran. I drove from Alabama to Mexico, then just disappeared, ending up in Croatia. I figured nobody really gave a damn about some small-time tax evader."

He figured wrong. "When did Paul Larks appear?"

"He contacted me through my website. The part about the government owing money to those heirs turns out to be true. A few months ago Larks was tasked with finding out if there was anything in the official records about a debt owed to Haym Salomon. That request came from the president himself. There wasn't much, but he did find out that Mellon, in the 1920s, may have taken proof of that debt from Treasury records. Then Larks came across stuff on the 16th Amendment in the same classified files. Stuff that shocked him. He was a quirky old guy. Kind of weird. For career government, he had little love for his employer. It pissed him off that the U.S. may have been committing tax fraud since 1913. He went to the Treasury secretary, who ordered him to forget he ever saw any of it. That just made him madder. Thank God that before he lost his job he managed to copy a bunch of stuff. That's what he was bringing to me."

"Why you?"

"He found my book online, read it, and told me he may actually have some stuff to prove I was right. It bothered him that people like me were being prosecuted and sent to jail. And it really upset him that his boss told him to forget it all. He told me what he had, which did fill in some of the gaps. Larks was right. It's wrong what the government is doing."

"Where does Kim fit in?"

"With me? Nowhere. I thought he was another guy the IRS was after. He called himself Peter From Europe. He and I talked online about the usual stuff. Taxes, jail, that sort of thing. Only with Larks did I discuss details."

Malone figured Kim was playing both ends against the middle, working Howell and Larks, learning what he could from both.

"Larks finally mentioned to me that he'd been talking to a Korean," Howell said. "But I never connected the two. Why would I? He told me that the Korean wanted to meet. There was no way I was going back to the States, but he said that was not a problem—the guy was overseas. So Larks offered to pay for my cruise and reserved me a ticket. I just changed it into Jelena's name. After talking it over some more, Larks and I agreed that we didn't want foreigners involved. We'd do this ourselves. We needed a face-to-face anyway, so we took advantage of the trip. Look, shouldn't we be doing something? Searching? Jelena is in trouble."

"It's a big ship with nowhere to go until we dock."

A picture was forming in Malone's head, but a piece was missing. "Treasury sent an agent here to get those copies back. You clipped her into the water back in Venice. How did you know she was here?"

"I didn't. I just saw her zeroing in on Jelena, so I took her out. I didn't know who she was."

"So tell me what you haven't said. And don't lie to me. I've tried to make this clear, but you don't seem to get it. I'm the only friend you've got."

He could see Howell was beginning to believe that.

"There is one document in what Larks brought that's extra special. The only original among all those copies. That's what I really wanted to see. It's why Larks came."

He waited.

"It's a crumpled sheet of paper that Andrew Mellon supposedly gave FDR."

THIRTY-TWO

Department of Justice

———

Office of the Solicitor

———

Memorandum
February 24, 1913
Ratification of the 16th Amendment to the
Constitution of the United States

Previously, the Secretary of State referred to the Solicitor's Office for determination the question whether the notices of ratifications by the several states of the proposed 16th Amendment to the Constitution are in proper form, and if they are found to be in proper form, it is requested that this office prepare the necessary announcement to be made by the Secretary of State under Section 205 of the Revised Statutes.

Eleven days ago this office forwarded to the Secretary of State a detailed memorandum concerning problems noted with the ratification process for the 16th Amendment. I will not reiterate what was stated therein, except to question why no action was taken relative to its contents. It seems that something more than silence is warranted, given the serious legal questions raised (which was why the example from Kentucky was included). Yet instead of a further investigation, the Secretary of State has now requested legal clarification as to his powers relative to declaring a constitutional amendment ratified. The Supreme Court has never directly considered this precise issue, but it has ruled in *Field* v. *Clark*, 143 U.S. 649 (1892), that

> What the president was required to do was simply in execution of the act of Congress. It was not the making of law. He was the mere agent of the law-making department to ascertain and declare the event upon which its expressed will was to take effect.

The same principle is true of the Secretary of State, relative to declaring a proposed amendment to the Constitution ratified. Congress has delegated to him the authority to declare the "expressed will" of the states relative to any proposed amendment. The Secretary of State is the sole administrative official who can make that legal determination. How that is done by the Secretary is for him alone to decide. History is instructive, though. As to all other constitutional amendments previously approved (and disapproved) since 1787, in every instance the Secretary of State declared that the requisite number of states had notified his office of their approval or disapproval. That declaration has never been questioned by any court.

Kim stopped reading.

Here was some proof that there were doubts, in 1913, about the validity of the 16th Amendment to America's Constitution, just as Anan

Wayne Howell had speculated. The amendment, he knew, was declared valid on—he checked Howell's book—February 25, 1913, the day after the memo he held was sent from the solicitor general to the secretary of state. But as Howell noted in his book, that official action merely said the amendment was "in effect," not "properly ratified." A play on words, for sure, but an important one. Perhaps done by the secretary of state in response to the solicitor's written concerns?

But what were those concerns?

The memorandum was silent on details, referring instead to another document dated eleven days earlier. He rummaged through the remaining pages and found no copy of that communication. But he did find a report, from the secretary of Treasury, Henry Morgenthau, to the president of the United States, dated January 26, 1937. This, too, had been referred to in Howell's book.

More unsubstantiated fact there.

Now here it was.

Per your presidential order, the one dollar bill was redesigned in 1935. The changes incorporated at that time were as follows: On the obverse, the blue numeral 1 was changed to gray and made smaller; the gray ONE to the right was removed; the Treasury seal was made smaller and superimposed by WASHINGTON, D.C.; and a stylized ONE DOLLAR was added over the Treasury seal. The reverse was also modified to include the Great Seal of the United States. Per your specific request (as noted on the next page) the seal was depicted with its reverse side to the left, obverse to the right.

He flipped to the next page and studied a copy of the bill's image, noting that Roosevelt had both approved and specifically asked for the seal to be depicted as noted.

He turned his attention back to the memorandum, which explained that the reverse of the Great Seal of the United States, as it appeared on the redesigned $1 bill, featured a barren landscape dominated by an unfinished pyramid of thirteen steps, topped by the Eye of Providence. At the base of the pyramid were engraved the Roman numerals MDCCLXXVI, 1776. At the top stood a Latin phrase, ANNUIT COEPTIS, which meant "God favors our undertaking." At the bottom of the seal was a semicircular banner that proclaimed NOVUS ORDO SECLORUM, taken from Virgil, meaning "a new order of the ages," a reference to the new American era. A string of thirteen pearls extended outward toward the bill's edge.

The obverse of the Great Seal featured a bald eagle, the symbol of the United States. Above the eagle was a radiant cluster of thirteen stars arranged in a six-pointed star. The eagle's breast was covered by a heraldic shield with thirteen stripes that resembled those on the American flag. The stars and stripes stood for the thirteen original states of the union. The eagle held a ribbon in its beak reading E PLURIBUS UNUM, "Out of many states, one nation." In its left talons the eagle grasped thirteen arrows. In its right talons it held an olive branch with thirteen leaves and thirteen olives. Together, those represented the opposing powers of war and peace. Another string of thirteen pearls extended outward toward the bill's edge.

Your question relative to a message hidden within the Great Seal was considered. The fact that drawing lines between letters A M S O N on the seal's reverse side not only forms a six-pointed star, but also provides letters that form the word MASON cannot be explained. The Great Seal was created over a 23 year period, starting in 1776 and ending in 1789. Many designs were considered and rejected. Symbolism abounds throughout the seal, especially with the repeated use of 13 in much of its art. But all of that was intended to reflect a patriotic flavor, a celebration of the newly formed United States of America. No evidence could be found of any intentionally inserted secret messages.

The latest redesign of the one dollar bill occurred over a period from late 1933 to the end of 1934, per your order. Many career Treasury officials participated, most of whom were hired when Mellon was Treasury Secretary, but no influence from him on the redesign has been uncovered.

The remaining copies dealt with the 1935 redesign, the reasons and justifications given for each artistic inclusion. Nothing seemed particularly relevant. Then he came across another report.

More recent.

Dated in the last ninety days.

From Paul Larks to the current secretary of Treasury.

THIRTY-THREE

ZADAR, CROATIA

ISABELLA CLIMBED DOWN FROM THE SMALL PLANE, LUKE DANIELS already on the tarmac, his sunglasses gone. The weather had steadily worsened on the flight across the Adriatic. The splendid sunshine of an Italian morning had been blotted out by the black curtain of a Balkan squall blowing in from the east, along with a noticeable temperature drop.

The flight had been quick and uneventful. They should be about an hour ahead of Malone. The ferry's docking terminal waited seven miles away, on a narrow peninsula that accommodated Zadar's town center. She'd never visited Croatia, her overseas travel confined to central Europe and England and always work-related. She never took vacations. Her accrued leave time had ballooned off the charts, so much that her supervisor had told her she had to start using it. So far she'd ignored that directive.

"I saw some taxis on the other side of the airport as we approached for landing," Luke said. "You need to know that the Chinese and North Koreans may have assets here, on Kim's trail. We could run into them."

"How would they know where Kim is?"

He shrugged. "Probably because they've been watching him, too. Just keep alert."

"I always do."

"Yeah, like you did back on the dock in Venice."

"Did saying that make you feel better?"

"Actually, it did. But let's get real, okay? How much experience do you have facing down a kill squad? This isn't a bunch of high-steppin' tax evaders. These folks will really hurt you."

She stared him down. "I know how to use a gun. I can take care of myself."

He chuckled. "Lady, you got no idea."

"Just follow my lead," she said, "and we'll be fine."

"Here's a news flash. Pappy doesn't take orders."

"Pappy isn't in charge. I am."

"Since when?"

Male abruptness seemed an occupational hazard. Of late, though, the female kind had begun to raise its ugly head. Her last two partners had been women, both loose cannons, both trying to stand out in what they believed to be a man's world. So they took risks. Made mistakes. She hated the description *a man's world*. Women could succeed. She was living proof of that, now working directly for the Treasury secretary on a top-secret mission. All you had to do was play by the rules, do as you were told, and deliver results. That always paid dividends, regardless of your sex. Everything about this mission had been explained to her in detail. She got it. The stakes were high. And she knew what had to be done, this Southern cowboy and a retired guy named Pappy be damned.

She. Was. In. Charge.

On the flight over she'd managed to learn a little about Luke Daniels. Washington had emailed that he was ex-military, special forces, decorated, with several overseas tours. He'd worked for the Magellan Billet going on two years and had the good fortune to be the nephew of the president of the United States. Which dropped him several notches on her list of respect. No one had ever helped her climb the ladder, and she resented any and all who took shortcuts.

"We need to get to the ferry dock," she said. "Before this storm arrives."

Malone waited for Howell to explain.

"Larks told me about an original sheet he found in the Treasury archives, all crumpled up. As soon as I heard what he had to say, it all made sense. We know that Mellon met with Roosevelt on New Year's Eve 1936. That comes from the diary of David Finley—one of Mellon's closest people—published in the 1970s. The meeting was to finalize the National Gallery of Art, but Mellon gave something to Roosevelt, which the president crumpled up and tossed away."

"You think it's the same piece of paper?"

"If not, it's one heck of a coincidence."

He couldn't argue with that.

"That page has random numbers on it. Larks scanned it and sent it to me."

"Then it's within Larks' email account, or on a computer at Larks' house?"

Howell shook his head. "The old guy was paranoid as hell. He told me he sent it from somewhere else. He didn't say by whom or from where, and I didn't ask. All my email accounts are under false names. A copy is stored on one of them. It's some kind of code, but I couldn't crack it. I really wanted to see the original, so he brought it over. That's part of what that Korean just took with him."

Which called into question his decision to allow Kim to walk away. Stephanie and the president's orders had been clear. Retrieve the documents.

"There's also a copy of a 1913 report from the solicitor general in that satchel. Larks sent me a scan of that, too. It's significant because it tells the secretary of state that he can pretty much do whatever he wants relative to declaring a constitutional amendment valid. It references a previous memo from the solicitor general. That previous memo, I believe, is the smoking gun. It's the one that lays out all the problems. But Larks never could find it in the archives."

He understood. "You think Mellon took it?"

"It's entirely possible."

"How in the world do you know about any of this? It seems all of the important information was sealed away. How did you piece it together?"

"I first read about this on the Internet. There's a lot of crazy stuff about the 16th Amendment. For decades people have tried to convince courts that the income tax is illegal. Was Ohio a state at the time the amendment was ratified? Some say no. I disagree. It was. Others say that the amendment did not specifically repeal previous contradictory clauses of the Constitution, therefore it's invalid. That's ridiculous. Still more say that the filing of a tax return violates the Fifth Amendment's protection against self-incrimination, or that it's a 'taking' and cannot be imposed 'without just compensation.' One guy argued that the 16th Amendment was unconstitutional since it violated the 13th Amendment's prohibition against 'involuntary servitude.' Original, but nuts. None of those are the way."

"You a lawyer?"

"Hell, no, they're useless. I'm just a guy who's read an awful lot on one subject. Read several hundred books on the same thing and you'll get a feel for how much the so-called experts don't know."

"So what's the way to win the fight?"

"Let me tell you what I found in Tennessee."

He listened as Howell told him about a trip to Knoxville that a friend of his made about a month ago, to the state archives. They picked the state at random, one of 42 that supposedly ratified the 16th Amendment. In his certification declaration of 1913, Secretary of State Philander Knox noted that Tennessee approved the 16th Amendment on April 7, 1911. Records showed that the amendment itself was transmitted for action to the governor on January 13, 1911. On January 25 a ratification resolution was introduced in the state senate.

"Right there," Howell said, "we found a problem. A provision of the Tennessee Constitution specifically said that no constitutional amendment could be introduced for ratification unless the legislature in office at the time was elected *after* the amendment had been submitted. Don't ask me why they have that rule. It's weird, I know. But it was state law at the time. In their constitution, no less. But they just ignored it and plowed ahead."

Howell then explained how the Tennessee legislature violated its own procedural rules, which provided that bills be read once, on three different days, in the House, then if passed submitted to the Senate for consideration.

And vice versa.

"That wasn't done with this ratification resolution. Even more serious, the Tennessee Constitution at the time forbade the legislature from conveying any new taxing powers on anyone that affected the people of the state. Yet they did it anyway, giving Congress the power to tax income without appropriation. That was definitely new. Then, to cap it off, there's no record that the state senate ever voted on ratification. Zero. Not a thing. So how did it get approved? And how did the U.S. secretary of state notch Tennessee in the yes column?"

The lawyer inside Malone searched for a loophole, some straw to grasp that might explain those errors, but there were none. Legislation had to be passed precisely according to law. To omit or ignore any part of the process would be absolutely fatal. And with a proposed constitutional amendment? "Almost" would never be good enough.

"And get this," Howell said. "There's not a single sheet of original documentation about any of that anywhere in the Tennessee archives. It's all gone. My friend pieced this together from secondary sources, and a real helpful clerk who knew her way around those old records."

"So none of that does you a bit of good."

Howell shook his head. "Not a drop. I need evidence. I think that other memo, the one Larks could not find, is my ticket to freedom. Before I was indicted, I made fifty-plus Freedom of Information requests to the feds. Most of the stuff they gave me was useless, but every once in a while I'd get a tidbit here and there. That friend of mine, he's since made trips to four other state capitols, searched their archives and found the same thing. Sometimes there'd be original paperwork, but most times it was gone. As if someone came along and cleaned it out. In some of the records you could see where pages had been razor-cut out of minute books."

He shifted the information into context and allowed it to float loosely through his mind.

Things were beginning to make sense.

And his problem had grown.

KIM READ THE MEMORANDUM THAT PAUL LARKS HAD PROVIDED to the American Treasury secretary.

I have made a careful examination of all documents relative to any claim of moneys owed to the heirs of Haym Salomon. It appears that documentation of the debts was in fact turned over, by Salomon's widow, to the Pennsylvania treasurer in 1785. That documentation ultimately made its way to Alexander Hamilton, who seems to have taken no action relative to it. Those papers remained in the national archives until the latter part of the 19th century, when they were returned to the Treasury Department, along with several thousand other records. But they are no longer contained within Treasury archives, whether classified or not. Without the actual commercial instruments, signed by the requisite parties, there is no way to properly evaluate whether any claim of repayment to the heirs of Haym Salomon is valid.

Contained, though, within the scant few documents that do mention the Salomon claim was some disturbing information relative to the 16th Amendment to the Constitution. Of particular note was a memorandum from the then solicitor general to the then secretary of state, Philander Knox, which specifically states that there were concerns associated with the ratification process. There was a specific reference to the state of Kentucky. So, in an effort to test the validity of what was written, I personally traveled to Frankfort and examined what records existed in the Kentucky archives. That investigation revealed that the resolution for ratification of the 16th Amendment passed in the state house (first on January 26, 1910, then again on February 10, 1910) and the one considered in the state senate (first on February 9, 1910, then again on February 11, 1910) were different in wording. Even more disturbing, the actual vote for ratification in the state senate (which occurred for the last time on February 11, 1910) was 9 for and 22 against. But the transmittal memorandum from Kentucky to the secretary of state indicated that the vote for ratification in the state senate was 27 for and 2 against. Incredibly, though rejected, the ratification measure actually made its way out of the state senate and to the governor's desk. But the measure was vetoed (on February 11, 1910). Never again was ratification considered by the Kentucky legislature. No override of that veto occurred. Yet

Kentucky is noted as having ratified the 16th Amendment on February 8, 1910. My visit to the state archives also brought to light one other disturbing fact. Many of the original records are missing. House and senate journal entries, the actual ratification resolution, and the governor's veto message are no longer there. What I learned came from unofficial secondary sources.

It is clear to me that Kentucky may have never validly ratified the 16th Amendment. This fact was brought to the attention of Secretary of State Knox, who, in 1913, apparently made no attempt to investigate the matter. Knox seems to have ignored a previous communication from the solicitor general that outlined even more concerns. That particular memorandum, which would be dated February 13, 1913, could not be located in our archives. I recommend that this entire question be given a full and complete inquiry.

He glanced up at Hana. "It seems, my dear, that we may have some of what we came for."

He found the only original page among all of the copies.

A single mangled sheet.

In his conversations with Larks, before he was apparently perceived as a threat, Larks had told him about a crumpled piece of paper with numbers. Some kind of code that Anan Wayne Howell thought had been given to the American president Franklin Roosevelt by Andrew Mellon. Was what he now held that same piece of paper? *The key?* That's how Larks had said Howell described it. What else could it be?

"Have you given thought to our exit from this boat?" he asked her.

She nodded.

He listened as she explained.

The woman named Jelena lay on the bed, still half dazed from the drugs Hana had administered.

But he'd brought some stimuli along, too.

"Wake her up enough that we can lead her," he said. "We'll take her with us. She could come in handy."

THIRTY-FOUR

MALONE TICKED OFF HIS OPTIONS, DECIDING ON THE BEST COURSE. He imagined Kim was ensconced within one of the ferry's many cabins. It wouldn't be hard to determine which one. A hundred euros to one of the stewards should garner the information. He doubted the booking was under Kim's real name, but how many fifty-plus-year-old Koreans could there be on board? Someone had seen him or maybe helped with luggage. He'd find that someone. If not, he'd just wait at the gangway.

"Larks got into a lot of trouble," Howell was saying. "That memo from 1913, where the secretary of state was told by the solicitor general of concerns, is compelling. Kentucky was specifically mentioned. Larks went to Kentucky and found problems, just like my friend discovered in Tennessee. He also found missing originals. When he reported this, Larks was ordered to forget everything he saw and knew. But the old man wouldn't let it go. Finally they made him sign a nondisclosure agreement and retired him out. He had no choice—it was either that or lose his pension."

"But Larks told you everything."

Howell nodded. "And he was bringing the proof so I could do something about it."

The drone of the engines dulled and the ship slowed. He'd already noticed Croatia out the windows, a few miles away, indicating that they were approaching their destination.

"We'll be docking soon," he said.

"What do you plan to do?"

That was a good question, but he wanted Howell to know, "If what you're saying is true, I'll make sure it doesn't get buried."

"And that should make me feel better?"

He debated whether to tell Howell about a presidential pardon, then decided to hold that piece of information a little longer.

Klaxon horns dinned out an alarm.

A low murmur of concern swept through the room.

The harsh shout of a technical voice echoed through the ship.

"Fuoco. Fuoco."

Fire.

KIM LED THE WAY, HANA BEHIND HIM HELPING ALONG THE DAZED woman, who could barely walk. They'd decided to leave their luggage to the flames. Personal belongings were the least of his concerns. Getting off this ferry before it docked—that was what mattered—and with the black satchel, which he cradled in his arms along with another carry bag for his laptop and a few essentials.

Hana had reconnoitered the decks in Venice after they'd boarded, preparing in case a hasty retreat became necessary. Before leaving the cabin, they'd set fire to the bedsheets, towels, furniture, and their extra clothing. The blaze had quickly gathered strength. He admired her ingenuity. What a perfect distraction.

They'd made their way up two decks to where the ship's lifeboats hung from davits. Compact and modular, each vessel was about five meters long, totally enclosed, painted a bright orange and white. Winches controlled their release, the controls at deck level, easily accessible.

Fire alarms sounded throughout the ship.

He stared out toward shore. A storm was brewing. Thick clouds had begun to leak rain and an easterly breeze, cold and cutting like a scythe, kicked up whitecaps. They were several kilometers west from Zadar, just past a series of archipelagoes that shielded the harbor from open sea. He approached one of the control panels where lights flashed, the switches surely activated by the alarm. They were labeled in Italian and English. People rushed past him on the deck, no one giving him any pause. He flicked one of the toggles labeled LOADING. The davit pivoted out, then its winches lowered the boat to deck level. Hana led the woman inside the enclosed cabin. He followed. He assumed there were controls inside for deployment—and there were, a set nearly identical to the outside control panel.

The ferry had slowed to a near stop.

He activated DROP and the lifeboat lowered quickly.

The moment the keel struck the turbulent water he flicked RELEASE, and they were free of the ferry.

Hana laid the woman on one of the shiny, high-backed benches. The interior was roomy, able to hold maybe twenty or more people. He watched as Hana pressed a button and the engines fired. She then threw open the throttle and spun the wheel.

And they were away.

MALONE SPRANG TO HIS FEET AND MOTIONED FOR HOWELL TO COME, too. No way that a fire alarm had just happened to go off. The entire ferry shuddered as the screws changed tempo and reversed. Raised voices came from some of the crew who ordered everyone to stay calm. He made his way outside. One of the deckhands rushed by and he asked in Italian, "What's happening?"

"Fire below."

"Jelena," Howell muttered.

He agreed. This most likely involved her. Then he noticed something aft. One of the lifeboats was dropping on its winch lines to the water. No command to abandon the ship had been given. He raced that way and arrived just as the boat freed itself and motored away. Its side hatch lay open and a face appeared, just for an instant, before an arm reached out and closed the portal.

Kim Yong Jin.

"I thought you told me there was nowhere for him to go," Howell said.

"I was wrong."

His eyes studied the remaining lifeboats. Why not? Worked once.

Howell seemed to read his mind. "Not without Jelena. I'm not leaving her."

He was not in the mood. "You can either come the easy way or come the hard way."

And he meant it. He'd beat this man unconscious and throw him on the boat if he had to. Howell seemed to sense there was no choice and nodded.

He pushed the younger man ahead of him and they rushed to a panel that controlled another of the lifeboats. Smoke had begun to bellow from the bow of the ship. People rushed back and forth, panicked at the threatening sight. A uniformed crew member appeared and yelled in Italian for him to get away from the controls. He ignored the command and lowered the boat to deck level, motioning for Howell to hop inside. The crew member pushed his way through the crowd and wrapped an arm around Malone's neck, yanking him back.

He had no time for this, and jabbed an elbow into his attacker's ribs. Once. Twice.

The neck hold released.

He spun and slammed his right fist into the crewman's jaw, sending the man to the deck. A few of the passengers bent down to help. He used that moment to hop into the lifeboat and slam the hatch shut, locking it from the inside. He found the interior controls and hit the DROP button.

They fell fast and settled in the pitching surf.

He released the winch lines and started the engines.

ISABELLA EXITED THE TAXI, WHILE LUKE DANIELS PAID THE DRIVER. They'd made the short trip along traffic-clogged streets in just under twenty minutes. Their travel bags, along with Malone's, had been left in lockers at the airport. They'd worry about them later. Right now, that ferry was their primary concern.

Zadar seemed a study in contrast. The suburbs were more modern with industrial parks and commercial zones, the old town filled with churches, monuments, and Roman ruins. Its historical center, a matrix of red-tiled low-slung buildings surrounded by thick stone walls, occupied a rectangular-shaped peninsula about three miles long and a mile wide, which jutted into the bay. A causeway connected it to the mainland. On the landing approach to the airport she'd noticed that the harbor was sheltered from the open sea by a series of islands, arranged in rows parallel to the coastline. The crenulated outlines of deep coves and inlets marred their shores. They stood outside the old town walls, at the peninsula's tip, where ships docked. That storm she'd feared had arrived, a cold, gray murk enveloping. The bare limbs of nearby trees shivered in a stiff breeze. Out in the bay, a mile or so away, she spotted the ferry and heard a siren.

"That's an alarm," Daniels said.

Smoke seeped from the ship's forward section, quickly seized by the wind. Something was wrong. They spotted a lifeboat drop to the water and motor off.

"I'll give you two-to-one odds who's in that boat," he said.

"What do you mean?"

"My bet is that's Kim's escape. He had to get the hell off that thing before it docked."

"How did he manage to steal a boat? That should not have been possible."

"Are you that naïve? Or just stupid? It's everybody for themselves out here. You do what you gotta do."

"I don't work that way. Never have. Never will."

He shook his head in seeming disgust.

Another lifeboat dropped to the water.

"And I know who stole that one," Daniels said.

He found his cell phone and dialed.

Wind swirled the misty rain across the bay like ghosts. Cold stung her face. They should find shelter, but Luke Daniels did not move, his attention locked on the two orange boats as they distanced themselves from the ferry, headed north, away from town. When the call was answered she could hear thanks to Daniels activating the speaker.

"Pappy, is that you in one of those boats?"

"It's me. Kim's ahead of us."

"We're on shore," Daniels said. "At the dock. I got Wonder Woman here with me."

She resented his condescending attitude and the insult she knew some of her co-workers at Treasury used for her.

"Kim's got the documents," Malone said. "We can't let him get away. There's an original in there we have to get back."

She caught the significance of what Malone had managed to learn, which amplified her containment problem.

"I may not be able to catch up to him," Malone said. "These tubs are not rigged for speed. Can you pace him from dry land?"

Daniels' gaze drifted from the dancing waves to the shoreline on their right, which ran in a jagged course northward where buildings and pinewoods strung close. A sheltered marina was visible, maybe two miles away.

But she saw it, too.

A highway rimmed the coast for as far she could see, sandy beaches between it and the water.

"I got it, Pappy. We'll be right with you."

THIRTY-FIVE

VIRGINIA

STEPHANIE DROVE THE CAR AWAY FROM ED TIPTON'S HOUSE. AS RE-
quested, they'd shut off the house lights and locked the front door behind them. Danny had borrowed $20 from her and tucked it beneath
Tipton's phone to compensate for the overseas calls. She'd thought it
strange, but typical. He didn't like to owe anyone.

He sat in the rear seat with the wooden crate they'd retrieved from
the hall closet. He'd switched on one of the rear ceiling lights and was
rummaging through. The glare was blocking her ability to see out the
rearview mirror, but she knew better than to ask him to cut it off. The
car with the two Secret Service agents followed closely. Dawn was less
than an hour away. Strangely, she wasn't tired, though she should be.
She'd passed the fatigue threshold several hours ago and found the point
where the body began to run on autopilot, sleep be damned.

"It's full of old books," he said. "Most of 'em are on George Mason.
And then there's this."

He stretched his arm forward and displayed between the two front
seats a copy of a thin, hardbound volume. *Taxation: The People's Business.*
Written by Andrew W. Mellon.

"I didn't know he was an author," she said.

The book disappeared back to the rear seat. "This one I know all
about. Edwin gave me a rundown on it yesterday."

"You two have been busy. Don't you have a country to run?"

He chuckled. "Actually, the thing runs itself. Especially when you're a lame duck. Nobody gives a crap what I have to say."

She knew better. "Unless you want them to give a crap."

"The copyright page says it was published by the MacMillan Company in 1924. Edwin tells me that David Finley, Mellon's close associate, actually wrote it for him, but everything in it was pure Mellon."

She heard him flipping through the pages.

Then he started reading out loud.

The problem of the Government is to fix rates which will bring in a maximum amount of revenue to the Treasury and at the same time bear not too heavily on the taxpayer or on business enterprises. A sound tax policy must take into consideration three factors. It must produce sufficient revenue for the Government; it must lessen, so far as possible, the burden of taxation on those least able to bear it; and it must also remove those influences which might retard the continued steady development of business and industry on which, in the last analysis, so much of our prosperity depends. Furthermore, a permanent tax system should be designed not merely for one or two years nor for the effect it may have on any given class of taxpayers, but should be worked out with regard to conditions over a long period and with a view to its ultimate effect on the prosperity of the country as a whole.

These are the principles on which the Treasury's tax policy is based, and any revision of taxes which ignores these fundamental principles will prove merely a make-shift and must eventually be replaced by a system based on economic, rather than political, considerations.

There is no reason why the question of taxation should not be approached from a non-partisan and business viewpoint. Tax revision should never be made the football either of partisan or class politics but should be worked out by those who have made a careful study of the subject in its larger aspects and are prepared to recommend the course which, in the end, will prove for the country's best interest.

I have never viewed taxation as a means of rewarding one class of taxpayers or punishing another. If such a point of view ever controls our public policy, the traditions of freedom, justice and equality of opportunity, which are the distinguishing characteristics of our American civilization, will have disappeared and in their place we shall have class legislation with all its attendant evils. The man who seeks to perpetuate prejudice and class hatred is doing America an ill service. In attempting to promote or to defeat legislation by arraying one class of taxpayers against another, he shows a complete misconception of those principles of equality on which the country was founded.

"Easy to see how Mellon and Roosevelt fought," Danny said. "Class warfare was Roosevelt's ticket to four terms. He played that card every chance he got. But it was a smart move. There were a whole lot more 'have nots' than 'haves,' and numbers win elections."

She could tell something was still bothering him.

It had been all night.

"Mellon was right," he said. "Raising tax rates does not raise revenues. In fact, just the opposite happens. The rich just find a way to legally shelter their money and avoid the higher taxes. And who could blame them. But every time we've lowered tax rates, revenues rose. Harding. Coolidge. Hoover. Kennedy. Reagan. Bush. They all got that."

"What's the problem?" she finally asked him.

"My Treasury secretary lied to me. Edwin found out that Larks may have stolen an original along with all of those copies. Joe Levy never said a word about that. I'd bet my ass Morgenthau classified that crumpled sheet of paper he got from Mark Tipton, the one Mellon gave to Roosevelt, and Larks swiped it from Treasury."

"And now it's out there, loose on the world, and could fall into the hands of people who might figure out how to solve the code. Ask the secretary of Treasury if he lied. Joe works for you. If he holds back, fire him."

He switched off the interior light. "That's just it. I don't think he's doing anything to hurt me. I actually think he's tryin' to protect me."

"From what?"

She approached a ramp for the interstate and entered the highway, increasing speed, the two headlights staying right behind her.

"That crumpled sheet of paper," he said.

And she agreed.

"I'm not going to fire the guy for falling on his sword. You need to read Howell's entire book."

She'd caught enough through her perusal at the courthouse to sense its overall gist. "He's an income tax fanatic. Seems to have a lot of issues with the 16th Amendment."

"Here's the deal," he said, his voice low and distant. "Our national debt is $16 trillion. The interest on that debt is right at $200 billion a year. I found a website the other day with a counter that clicks off the national debt, as it accrues by the second. I sat there and watched the damn thing. It's like a million dollars every minute. Can you imagine? It's friggin' mind-blowing."

"And you just sat there and watched?"

He chuckled. "It's kind of hypnotizing."

She smiled. Sometimes he truly was like a big kid.

"Ninety percent of the revenue used to pay that debt comes from one source," he said.

And she knew where. Income tax.

"Imagine if that tax was illegal?" He snapped his fingers. "No more 90 percent. Gone. Just like that."

She caught the implications, but had to say, "It could be replaced?"

"Really? Congress would have to pass a new amendment, then thirty-eight states would have to ratify it. That would take a lot of time, all while that debt keeps growing at the rate of a million dollars every minute. And by the way, we couldn't borrow a dime to cover any deficits since our credit wouldn't be worth spit. Even if you passed a new income tax, we'd never catch up. The trillions in accrued debt would bankrupt us. Even worse, what if we knew the 16th Amendment was illegal all along, but declared it valid and kept collecting it. That's fraud, making us liable for all those trillions of dollars we stole from folks."

"A bit far-fetched, wouldn't you say?"

"I'm not so sure. I got a bad feeling here, Stephanie, one I've learned to trust. I keep thinking about the Chinese *and* the North Koreans. And

Kim. What's he after? Then I remember that our number one creditor is China. We owe it $1.2 trillion, growing by the minute, too. What do you think would happen if we defaulted on that debt?"

She knew. It could collapse China's economy. "You think Kim is after the ammunition to take down our income tax?"

"You heard the ambassador. Unlike Dear Leader, Kim doesn't owe China a thing. He'd just as soon stick it up their ass as not. That ambassador back there was scared. I saw it in his eyes and heard it in his voice. He tried to hide it, but he was afraid."

She'd also felt the apprehension, noting a few phrases hidden in the conversation, and a hesitation where there should have been none.

They kept speeding north down the interstate, the beginnings of the day's rush hour not yet upon them. The sky overhead was fading from black to salmon. To the east, the sharp edge of a brilliant sunrise had already begun to illuminate the gray light of dawn.

"This dirty laundry of ours," he muttered, "has a real stink to it. But thanks to Paul Larks it may be about to get an airing. You've known something's bothering me. I saw it in your eyes at Treasury. This is it. Our Achilles' heel."

They rode in silence for a little while, both of them in thought.

"We can't let this happen," Danny finally said.

"I'll check in with Luke and Cotton, after I leave you at the White House."

"Do that. I need to know what they've learned on that end."

The lights of the Capitol loomed ahead. A few minutes more and they would be at the White House.

"Before we get there," Danny said from the rear seat, "there's a couple of other things you have to know. Things I couldn't say in front of Harriett."

THIRTY-SIX

CROATIA

ISABELLA RAN THROUGH THE RAIN AFTER LUKE DANIELS, THE cobbles gleaming with moisture. She wondered what he meant when he told Malone, *We'll be right with you.* The answer to her inquiry came as Daniels flagged down a taxi then, when the car stopped to retrieve him, flung open the driver's door, yanked the man out, and shoved him to the wet concrete.

He motioned for her to climb inside.

She hesitated.

"Fine, stay here. You're a pain in the ass anyway," he yelled.

Dammit. She had to go. So she rushed to the front passenger-side door, opened it, and slid in. He settled behind the wheel, slammed the gearshift into drive, and off they went, tires spinning in the swishing rain.

"You never stole a car before?" he asked her.

"Hardly."

He shook his head. "Welcome to my world."

"You realize that driver is going to call the police," she said.

"Hopefully we'll be long gone before they can find us."

He was following a road that rimmed the peninsula, outside the town walls along a quay, heading for the causeway to the mainland and, she assumed, the road that ran against the shoreline in the direction of where Kim and Malone had headed by boat. They were playing catch-up, but he was making time, passing cars, bursting through intersections, ignoring every traffic law.

And drawing lots of attention.

Horns blared and brakes squealed.

"You've apparently done this before?" she asked, trying to stay calm and holding on.

He twisted the wheel hard left and they turned north, now along the bay road. "I've had a little practice."

The taxi was a dirty and dented Audi coup. Its interior reeked of nicotine and she cracked the window enough to allow in some fresh air.

"Keep an eye out in the bay," he told her.

The rain continued to slap the car like pellets, splattering the windshield in drenching waves. She stared through the wipers and saw the ferry. The two orange lifeboats were nowhere in sight, but a spit of land jutting out into the bay, near the marina they'd spotted earlier, blocked their view. They'd need to be farther along on the road, past the outcropping, to be able to see anything.

Daniels seemed to realize that, too.

And the engine surged.

KIM STOOD BESIDE HANA.

She piloted the boat away from the ferry and toward shore. Rain was now falling in thick sheets, which was good and bad. The storm provided excellent cover, but it had also stirred the bay into a boiling frenzy. Their hostage still lay on one of the benches, not moving. The black satchel rested on his shoulder, the travel bag at his feet. They needed to find a place to disembark, preferably with few to no people around. From there, a taxi or some type of ground transportation could surely be arranged to the airport or train station.

The lifeboat churned along at a steady but slow pace. Wipers barely kept the forward windshield clear of rain. He stepped to the windows on the port side and saw the outline of one of the many islands that protected the bay. Through the starboard windows he caught the Croatian shore, lined with buildings and trees. From the rear window he spotted another lifeboat headed their way.

The American.

Who else?

MALONE KEPT THE WHEEL STEADY THROUGH THE ROUGH SEA. THE lifeboat was more like a floating cork with a motor, designed to stay up-right but not necessarily stable. Its engines were likewise engineered for durability, speed sacrificed for distance. His and Kim's escape vehicles were identical, so unless the boat ahead slowed there was no way he could close the mile-or-so gap between them. But he could keep pace, and that's what he intended on doing. He could only hope that Luke would be there when Kim made landfall.

His sea legs returned quickly, motion sickness never a problem. But it was obvious Howell was no sailor. The bobbing up and down and side-to-side had taken a toll.

"Hang your head out the hatch," he said. "Get some air, and keep a watch on Kim at the same time."

The wind's howl grew louder as the side hatch opened. Cold rain sprayed inside. He knew nothing about the local geography, only that they were headed north, in a bay protected on two sides by land. Normally this would be calm, clear water.

But not today.

He heard Howell retching up his guts.

The throttle was full ahead and they were moving as fast as they could, which wasn't anything to take note about.

But at least they were headed in the right direction.

KIM STEPPED BACK TO HANA AND MADE A DECISION.

"We need to slow down the boat pursuing us," he said. "It almost certainly contains Mr. Malone, but regardless, whoever it is needs to be occupied. Luckily, we have something that might accomplish that."

His gaze drifted to the semi-conscious woman.

"It's time we lose her," he said.

He opened the side hatch, then lifted the dazed woman from the bench and helped her to the portal. He doubted she'd be able to swim, the effects of the drug on her muscles and nerves too pronounced.

But her drowning would make for an even better distraction.

He shoved the woman out, headfirst.

MALONE SAW A BODY FALL FROM THE BOAT AHEAD. HE YELLED AT Howell, "You see that?"

"Somebody's in the water and they're not moving."

He was hoping Howell did not connect the dots.

But he did.

"It's Jelena, Malone. It's her. She's disappearing in the swells."

He realized that Kim had made him choose, which was no choice, actually, and Kim knew that. He angled the bow to port.

"More left," Howell screamed. "The current's got her."

"Come here," he screamed.

Howell rushed to his side.

"Take the wheel and work the throttle. Keep us close to her."

He rushed to the hatch.

And leaped into the water.

KIM KEPT AN EYE BEHIND THEM AND SAW A MAN JUMP INTO THE surf, the other boat veering away and slowing to a stop.

"That should occupy them long enough for us to make shore," he said.

The land to their right had steadily leveled, with fewer buildings and more pinewoods and deserted beach. Then solid earth ended and he spotted a forested point that formed another peninsula, more water and the Croatian shoreline beyond to their right.

"There. Avoid that barren stretch and head for the mainland."

Isabella could see the two boats, out in the bay, one way ahead of the other. Then she saw something emerge from the lead boat and splash into the water. A person. The second craft had now slowed, someone leaping from it into the choppy sea. The first lifeboat kept going, never hesitating. They'd rounded all the coastal obstructions and could now see the entire bay. The first lifeboat was chugging away from another peninsula toward the main coastline.

"We can get him," Daniels said. "He's coming our way."

They were still moving fast, the road here devoid of traffic in either direction. Fog kept clouding the windshield and windows, the defroster churning out more noise than heat. Brief glimpses of the chaos came when the gusts relaxed. Then a new sensation caught her eye. Red lights flashing. And a siren that wailed and howled. She whipped her head around and saw a police car behind them.

"We've got no time for them," Daniels said.

"They might not see it your way."

"They've got to catch me first."

He gave the engine more gas, which surged them forward along a straightaway. Then, up ahead, she saw more lights flashing and cars blocking the road. She counted six. That explained the lack of traffic in the other lane. They were closing fast on a barricade, less than a mile away. Uniformed men stood ready. Several had guns aimed.

"Are you going to ram them?" she asked.

Half a mile.

She waited to see what Daniels would do.

Quarter mile.

Suddenly the windshield burst to life with a spiderweb of a thousand glittering opaque lines. Someone had fired at them and now it was impossible to see ahead. Daniels seemed to sense the futility and lifted his foot from the accelerator, jamming the brakes and turning the wheel sharp right. The car's rear end swung around, perpendicular to the road, and they slid for a hundred yards on the soaked pavement before grinding to a stop.

Then, quiet.

Only the rain peppering the roof disturbed the silence.

Men encircled the car and screamed words in a language she did not understand.

But she didn't have to.

"This ain't good," Daniels muttered.

And for once she agreed with him.

THIRTY-SEVEN

STEPHANIE DROPPED DANNY AT THE WHITE HOUSE THEN HEADED for the Mandarin Oriental, where she always stayed when in town. Her travel bag had been delivered by a Justice Department staffer, who'd met the jet when it arrived hours ago from Atlanta. Luckily, the hotel had a room immediately available and her things were waiting on her when she opened the door. One of the bellmen had hauled up the wooden crate with books in it and she tipped him $5 after he laid it on the carpet.

A hot shower and some food would be great. So she cleaned herself up, then headed to the eighth floor and the Tai Pan Club where breakfast was offered. She needed to know what was happening in Venice. There'd been no reports from anybody in several hours. The last she heard Luke Daniels was headed to Croatia with the Treasury agent and Cotton was on a ferry with all the remaining players, including the satchel full of documents. Maybe they'd caught a break and things were under control. Then again, she'd learned not to rely on luck. Better to make your own.

At present, nine of her twelve agents were on assignment across the globe. She'd already delegated operational control over eight of them to her second in command. She kept Luke Daniels. Cotton was an independent, the only outside contractor presently working for her. They were utilized from time to time, but sparingly. She preferred full control over her people. Cotton was the exception, though he could, at times, prove problematic. Still, he was the best that had ever worked for her. Never, though, would she tell him that. No need, really. He knew.

Danny had encouraged her to read Howell's book, and he wanted a full report as soon as news came from overseas. So to pass the time she took him up on his suggestion and downloaded a copy of *The Patriot Threat*. Before leaving the book's home page she checked out the 43 customer reviews, with an average ranking of four stars. Most liked the unique ideas presented, but thought the premise a bit far-fetched. Several loved it, but they sounded like anarchists and nearly all of the reviewers hated income taxes.

Who didn't?

She decided to hang out in the lounge for a little while and read. The book's introduction stated that Howell was not a lawyer, but he had spent a number of years studying the federal income tax. He invited any and all readers to challenge his assertions and investigate his conclusions on their own. *Debate is healthy,* he wrote at one point.

That it was.

She glanced at the table of contents and decided to skip around, focusing first on a chapter where Howell hypothesized about the possibility that the 16th Amendment may not have been properly ratified. In the opening paragraph he freely admitted that he possessed no proof, but then stated—

Over the past two decades, many tax protesters (myself included) have claimed that the 16th Amendment is not really part of the Constitution. Therefore, the income tax is illegal. Is this argument valid? A few tax protesters have conducted extensive research, finding that versions of the amendment, as ratified in the individual states, contained minor textual errors. Some neglected to capitalize the word "States," or referenced "income" in place of "incomes." Another utilized the word "remuneration" instead of "enumeration." Still another said "levy" instead of "lay," and so on and so on. So the question becomes, if the requisite number of states did not all vote on the same identical text for the 16th Amendment, can the amendment really be considered ratified?

You have to admit, it is a good question. When Congress, or a state legislature, enacts a law, the two governing chambers must always approve the same text. If not, then there is no law. Instead, there are two separate votes on two separate versions of that law. Similarly, if the states did not all vote on the same language, one could argue that they did not all ratify the same 16th Amendment.

There is a certain logic to this conclusion, but the courts have consistently held that minor textual variations in the versions the states voted upon are unimportant. Those same courts assert that every state legislature that acted on the amendment intended to either ratify or reject it, *exactly as proposed by Congress.* When they voted, they understood themselves to be voting to approve or reject the 16th Amendment, *as proposed by Congress.* Judges who have considered the issue have all held that "the text of that amendment, as set forth in the various state instruments of ratification, was there for recitation purposes only. Any errors in that text were not proposals to change the amendment being ratified, they were just inadvertent errors that do not detract from the overall intent of the state legislature to ratify the amendment, as proposed."

Another ruling courts have used to defeat tax protesters is that the official declaration (by the appropriate government official) of the effective date on a constitutional amendment is definitive. In 1913 the Secretary of State was the government official charged with determining whether an amendment to the Constitution had been properly ratified (today, that task is performed by the Archivist of the United States). Courts, although regarding themselves as empowered to determine the meaning of the Constitution and the laws, regard themselves as *not* competent to say when the definitive text of the Constitution and its amendments starts to be applied. In 1922, the Supreme Court held in *Leser* v. *Garnett,* 258 U.S. 130 (1922), that when the Secretary of State certifies that an amendment to the Constitution has been ratified, no court is empowered to look behind that claim to determine whether or not it really was. Of course, that ruling came nine years after Philander Knox certified the 16th Amendment. But the same principle was applied in 1913. So what would happen today if an amendment was proposed and three-fourths of the states do not ratify it, but the Archivist of the United States ignores that reality and declares it ratified? The Supreme Court says courts cannot question that patently wrong action. Common sense would say that of course the courts would question that. Which in and of itself begs a question.

A final bit of reasoning courts offer to defeat tax protesters is that the 16th Amendment has been around for over 100 years, it has been considered and applied by courts, including the Supreme Court in innumerable cases, therefore it's valid. As one judge wrote, "While this alone is not sufficient to bar judicial inquiry, it is persuasive on the question of validity." Let's stretch this to its logical conclusion. If a law was illegal from the start, yet was still adopted, would the simple fact that it's been around a long time be enough to now make it legal?

Clearly not.

Here's reality: Courts simply don't want to hear that the 16th Amendment may be invalid. The implications from that conclusion are too horrific for them to even consider. So judges have fashioned their own form of twisted logic to shoot down any and all challenges. The problem is that their reasoning does not hold up to scrutiny. And when the day comes that someone can actually present concrete proof not only of the amendment's non-ratification, but that the declaration of its effectiveness by the Secretary of State in 1913 was flawed from the start, the courts will have no choice but to consider it.

Here's one final point. Some say that even if the 16th Amendment was not properly ratified, that does not mean Congress could not impose an income tax. That's true. Congress could still impose an income tax, but it would have to be apportioned, as required by Article I, Section 2. Of course, that would never happen. The fears of the Founding Fathers relative to "direct taxes" have not abated. If anything, they are even stronger today. No Congress would approve an income tax that has radically differing rates depending upon where one lived.

And don't forget about that "horrific part" the courts really fear. Imagine for a moment if the 16th Amendment is invalid, has been invalid from the start, and the Secretary of State in 1913 knew enough to at least be suspicious—yet still declared it "in effect." By any definition that's fraud. Not only would the current application of the 16th Amendment cease immediately, but the United States would be liable for trillions and trillions of dollars it illegally stole from its citizens. Considering that possibility, it's easy to see why the courts work so hard to uphold its validity.

She stopped reading.

Everything Howell wrote made perfect sense. His arguments were sound, the implications clear, some of it echoing the fears Danny had expressed in the car. She could understand now why he was concerned. He'd obviously read the book. She also tried to recall something else the federal appellate court had written in Howell's case, right after it stated that "for Howell to prevail, we would require, at this late hour, an exceptionally strong showing of unconstitutional ratification." She tapped the keyboard on her laptop and found the trial court's opinion online, locating the passage at the end.

Howell (through his appointed counsel) has made no such showing, only boldly concluding that the amendment was improperly ratified. No evidence has been presented to prove this assertion, nor has Howell cited any factual or legal authority binding on this court (or for that matter on Secretary of State Knox in 1913) for his contention that the 16th Amendment was improperly ratified. In short, Howell has not carried the burden of showing that this 100-year-old amendment was unconstitutionally ratified.

Was the proof Howell sought contained within a black satchel presently crossing the Adriatic Sea on its way to Croatia? China, North Korea, and Kim Yong Jin seemed to think something substantive was there.

She agreed with Danny.

This crisis was decidedly different.

And she, too, had a bad feeling.

THIRTY-EIGHT

CROATIA

KIM KEPT A WATCH OUT THE REAR WINDOWS, PLEASED THAT THE other lifeboat was far in the distance, occupied with a rescue. Even better, a fog had slithered in, swallowing everything in its path, offering excellent cover. That and the rain should mask their escape. They remained half a kilometer offshore, churning across the frothy bay. Neither he nor Hana seemed affected by motion sickness, though they should have been. The deck beneath his feet rose and fell with unsteady regularity.

"We need to know where we are," he said to her.

They were definitely north of Zadar. He'd spotted the port city as they'd made their escape. Right now they were paralleling the mainland, protected to the west by barrier islands and rocky archipelagoes. The storm, though, had come from the east and was not abating. Thankfully, the shoreline remained visible. Hotels, resorts, and various other buildings lined the beaches, where surf roared up in a welter of foam.

The black satchel remained draped over his shoulder, sealed tight. He could not allow rain to harm anything inside. He needed time to examine everything, without any pressure. Heading straight for the airport or train station now appeared unwise. Malone was still out there, and he may have help. So a room at one of the seaside resorts he'd spotted seemed like an excellent respite.

Ahead, he spied more buildings clustered together.

And docks.

He pointed. "We'll end our journey there."

MALONE FELT THE SEA CLOSE OVER HIM, THE COLD WATER LIKE A physical blow, taking his breath away, sucking strength from his muscles. He surfaced, the swells easily four to five feet high, and searched for Jelena.

But she was nowhere to be seen.

He sucked a breath and dove under, swimming hard. His clothes quickly became dangerous weight, but he kept going. Up and down he went, his eyes trying to find some sight of her in the rolling waves. He wondered if she might have been drugged. That seemed Kim's preferred weapon. If so, there was no way she could swim.

Calm down, he told himself.

"Jelena. Jelena," he yelled over the wind.

He kicked hard, kept himself afloat, and fought to control his panic. He'd learned in the navy about a sense of hopelessness associated with floating alone in a bobbing sea. A raging storm only added to that anxiety, and the cold numbed his legs, so he worked them harder. Fog had appeared out of nowhere. Visibility was down to maybe fifty feet. He hoped Howell had kept the wheel true, following his path into the water. If not, he could be swept away, just like Jelena.

Then the lifeboat appeared out of the mist, to his right.

"Here," he yelled as loudly as he could.

Its rounded bow turned toward him, the windshield wipers still working hard. Cold water forced his eyeballs back in their sockets with a stabbing pain. Between strokes to keep himself afloat he thrust his arm in the air to draw more attention. Howell apparently saw him and eased close. This was not going to be easy. Howell appeared in the open hatch.

Their eyes met.

He shook his head.

"No. No," Howell mouthed.

Shock filled the younger man's face, then sadness.

He climbed inside. His muscles ached and he was breathing hard. Howell staggered to the other side of the enclosed cabin, a hand to his face, tears in his eyes.

Malone's lungs kept grabbing deep breaths, the oxygen in his blood stabilizing. Cold chewed into his muscles and he still tasted the raw tang of salt water. Beneath the wood benches were surely blankets, and he found one and wrapped himself inside.

He glanced out the windows.

Nothing but fog.

Kim was gone.

ISABELLA HAD ARRESTED PLENTY OF PEOPLE, BUT NEVER HAD SHE been led away with her own hands bound behind her back. The local police had not been in a good mood, wrestling them both from the taxi, then quickly removing them from the scene. Luke Daniels had wisely kept his smart mouth shut, as had she. Whatever would be sorted out would not be done in the rain. She would need to speak with someone much higher on the authority pole—on both sides of the Atlantic.

They were transported back toward Zadar's center and a four-story building that sat on the mainland, facing the old town peninsula. On the drive she saw that the ferry had arrived and docked, no more smoke emitting from it. They sat alone in the rear of the police car, two officers in the front seat.

"When we sort this out," she whispered to Daniels, "you and I are parting ways."

He threw her a glare. "And I thought we had somethin' special."

"That cocksure attitude is what let Kim get away."

"Bad luck let Kim get away. I was givin' it my best shot."

She could only hope that Malone had been able to stop Kim. Those documents could not be lost.

The car was parked, but before the officers could exit a cell phone rang with a soft chime, like church bells. Both of their units had been confiscated after their arrest, but the one ringing was not hers.

"That would be me," Daniels whispered.

The officer on the passenger side in the front answered the phone.

"Luke. Are you there?"

They could hear Malone thanks to the speaker being activated.

"Who is this?" the policeman asked.

"Who the hell are you?"

"Policija."

MALONE REALIZED THAT THE VOICE ON THE PHONE WAS NOT LUKE Daniels, and though Croatian was not one of the languages he was particularly proficient at he caught the meaning.

Police.

He decided to throw a little weight around. "This is Cotton Malone. United States Justice Department. Do you have Agent Daniels and Agent Schaefer with you?"

ISABELLA HEARD WHAT MALONE SAID AND SAW THAT THE OFFICER had understood every word. The two policemen stared at each other, seemingly trying to decide how to reply. Finally, the officer holding the phone said, "We have them both. They are under arrest."

"What charge?"

"Car theft. Reckless driving. Endangering the public."

"Those are agents of the United States government, on a mission. I suggest you contact the American embassy immediately."

"We take no orders from you, and have no way to know who you are and if you speak the truth."

"You will know who I am, once I get there."

She liked Malone's moxie. Straight up. Direct. No bullshit. Daniels had said he had a low tolerance level.

But the two policemen did not seem concerned.

They ended the call.

MALONE SLIPPED THE PHONE BACK INTO HIS POCKET AND RETOOK the lifeboat's helm, powering up the engines. What the policeman said worked two ways. He had no way of knowing who he'd been talking to, either.

But he couldn't deal with that right now.

Fog still engulfed them, the wind and rain continuing, its spray as solid as buckshot. If Luke and Isabella had found trouble, that meant Kim was long gone with the documents. They needed to get gone, too. The lifeboat was stolen property and, by now, the ferry was in port and the police involved. He had no time for any of that. Stephanie could handle the locals later, that was her job. His was to find Kim and those documents. He'd made a miscalculation on the ferry in allowing the North Korean to walk away. Of course, at the time he'd had no idea of their importance or how brazen Kim could be. His only chance now was Howell, who sat motionless on one of the benches.

He kept his eyes out the front windshield, trying to pick a way through the murk, the blunt nose of the lifeboat bucking the sea. "I'm going to need your help."

"He killed her. Just tossed her out and let her drown."

No time existed for remorse. "Pay him back." He added a compelling urgency to his voice that he hoped Howell caught.

"Damn right. I'll do it. But I got a stake here, too. My freedom was in that satchel."

"You may not need it."

"What do you mean?"

THIRTY-NINE

HANA STOOD IN THE CLASSROOM, SILENT, AS REQUIRED. FROM DAY one all of them had been taught to stand straight, bow to Teacher, and never speak unless asked a direct question. The school building was similar to where she and her mother lived, a plain concrete square with filthy vinyl covering its windows. Teacher stood at a podium with a blackboard behind him. He wore a uniform and carried a pistol holstered on his hip. She did not know his name, but that was unimportant. Obedience was all that mattered. The forty students stood separately, boys on one side, girls the other. She knew only a few of their names. Camp rules discouraged close friendship and alliances were forbidden, as both bred collision.

"You have to wash away the sins of your mothers and fathers," Teacher said to them. "So work hard."

Most of every day was spent reminding them of their uselessness.

School had begun at 8:00 A.M. Absences were never allowed. Just last week, she'd helped a sick Sun Hi across the camp. The girl was perhaps Hana's only friend, though she was unsure of that word's exact definition. If it meant that she enjoyed being with her, then a friend she was. When Teacher provided them time to remove lice from their hair, she and Sun Hi would clean each other. Between classes, when Teacher allowed them to play "rock, paper, scissors," they always gathered together. They'd both been born in the camp. Names were allowed for Insiders simply as a means of identification. But identities, personalities, character—those were forbidden. Still, she was drawn to Sun Hi, if for no other reason than just to be with someone her age. Someone not her mother.

Simple interaction between two prisoners was not discouraged, as it helped root out rule breaking.

School always began with chonghwa. Harmony. Time when Teacher criticized them for all that they had done wrong the day before. More reminders of their lack of worth. Only this time the sins were not those of their parents, but their own.

She was nine and had slowly learned to read and write. Each year they were issued a single notebook. Pencils were fashioned from a sharpened piece of charred wood. Writing exercises were confined to explaining how she'd failed to work hard. Reading involved a mastery of camp rules. Today Teacher seemed especially angry. His criticisms had been harsh, but no one uttered a sound. If asked anything, the proper response was the same for them all. *I shall do better today.*

"Be alert," Teacher yelled at the class.

She knew what was coming. A surprise search.

One by one they approached and Teacher patted them down, then he rifled through their pockets. No one possessed anything that violated the rules except Sun Hi, who carried five rotten kernels of corn.

"You bitch. You stole food?" Teacher said. "We cut the hands off thieves."

Sun Hi stood trembling, saying nothing, as no question had been asked.

Teacher displayed the blackened kernels in his open palm. "Where did these come from?"

A question. Which must be answered.

"The . . . field."

"You dare steal? You worthless excuse of a person. You're nothing. Yet you think you can steal?"

His words came fast, his voice loud. His right hand had twice reached for the gun at his hip, but he had not, as yet, drawn the weapon. Shooting prisoners was a daily occurrence, though it had never happened inside her school.

"Look at this worthless nothing," Teacher said to the class. "Spit on her."

They all did as he ordered, including herself.

"Kneel," Teacher demanded of Sun Hi.

Her friend dropped to the floor.

Each of them wore the same black pants, shirt, and shoes issued a year ago. Now mere tattered rags covering little skin.

"Repeat for me subsection three of camp rule three," Teacher said to Sun Hi.

"Anyone who steals . . . or conceals . . . any foodstuffs will be . . . shot immediately."

"And what have you done?" Teacher asked.

"I have . . . broken that . . . rule."

She heard the fear in Sun Hi's voice.

None of the students moved, each stood straight and still.

Concealing food was one of the camp's worst crimes. They were taught that from the time they could speak along with the fact that anyone who violated that rule deserved harsh punishment. The will to steal was just another fault they'd inherited from the treasonous blood of their parents. Worthlessness only bred more worthlessness.

Teacher reached for his wooden pointer, the one he used during lessons. His right arm whipped through the air, the thin line of wood crashing into the side of Sun Hi's head.

The girl collapsed to the floor.

"Get up," Teacher yelled.

Sun Hi slowly righted herself, dazed from the blow. Another came. Then another. Not a sound slipped from her mouth, the face twisted with fear and failure. She started to collapse again, but Teacher held her upright by the hair and continued the attack, every blow aimed to the head.

Lumps emerged on the scalp.

Blood began to leak from her nose.

Sun Hi's shoulder tilted, an elbow dug into her side, the frail body listed sideways, then her eyes went glassy and she pitched forward. But Teacher kept pummeling, gritting his teeth in a weird grin, his eyes an even mixture of hate and contempt. Finally, he released his grip and allowed the girl's body to topple to the floor.

He stared down at his student, breathing hard. Then he stepped to the open door and tossed the five kernels of rotten corn out into the wind. He cleared his throat of disgust and said to the class, "No one is to touch those."

Sun Hi lay bleeding, not moving, the face swelled in sorrow.

There she stayed for the rest of the day, while they learned their lessons.

Disappointment always made Hana think of Sun Hi. Her friend had been dead fourteen years. And that was what she had been. A friend. Of that she was now certain.

No one in the class ever spoke of Sun Hi again. It was as if she'd never existed. No one questioned the punishment, either. All realized that it had been necessary. Sadness and regret were two emotions she'd learned only *after* leaving the camp. Behind the fences survival was all that mattered. No prisoner ever judged another for anything. Nor did they ever judge the guards or Teacher.

But that day changed her.

Though she was only nine, she resolved that no one would strike her with a wooden pointer until her head burst open. And never would she spit on a friend again. If those refusals meant she died, then that was what would happen. Suicide, of course, always remained an option. Many followed that path, especially Outsiders. But any surviving relatives were severely punished for that defiance, which made that route all the more tempting. The thought of her mother being disciplined pleased her. But killing yourself inside the camp was a problem. Some tossed themselves down the mine shafts. Others chose poison. The quickest way was to rush the fences and wait for the guards to shoot. But the worse that could happen was for an attempt to fail. Then only more hard labor, hunger, beatings, and torture came.

On the day Sun Hi died Hana had known nothing of what lay beyond the camp. But she decided then to find out. How? She did not know. But she would find a way. Her mother's crimes were not hers. Sun Hi stole five kernels of corn because she was starving. Teacher was wrong. The guards were wrong. That day, while only nine, she stopped being a child.

"You are so smart," Sun Hi would tell her.

"And you so obedient."

"That's what my name means. Obedience and joy. My mother gave it to me."

"Do you like your mother?" she asked.

"Of course. It is the sins of my father that placed us here."

She'd never forgotten Sun Hi, with her perpetual runny nose and wet-mouthed grin. Hana's mother had named her at birth Hyun Ok. Which meant "clever." But she hated anything and everything associated with her mother so she never spoke that name. The guards and Teacher called her bitch, as they did every other female. She liked the label Sun Hi had given her when they were allowed time to play in the forest or swim in the river, before five kernels of corn changed both of their lives.

Hana Sung.

It meant "first victory" and she'd never quite understood why Sun Hi thought of her that way. But she liked the name, so she kept it, never speaking it around her mother.

Twice in her life she'd made a choice. The day her friend died and the day her father found her. Both had generated irrevocable decisions. And both were special because *she* made them.

The time was approaching for a third.

Which she, too, would decide.

FORTY

STEPHANIE KEPT READING *THE PATRIOT THREAT,* THE TEXT actually quite interesting, the reasoning thorough, its conjecture clearly delineated from facts. Howell dealt with the rebuttals against the 16th Amendment as skillfully as any lawyer. His arguments seemed a careful merger of legend, history, speculation, and hypothesis. Enough that she wanted to know more. Especially about Andrew Mellon, who seemed at the heart of it all. She recalled the sections read earlier at the court-house about Mellon and Philander Knox. They were close friends, so much that Knox in 1920 convinced Warren Harding to appoint Mellon as his secretary of Treasury. She found one of the portions that had been flagged by the Treasury secretary and the words that had intrigued both her and Harriett Engle.

Some say that, before his death, Knox passed a great secret on to Mellon.

The next few pages expanded on this bold assertion, sections that had not been flagged by Joe Levy for them to read.

Philander Knox was more a pawn than a rook or a bishop. His ability to move across the political chessboard seemed limited to only one space at a time. His success came from doing what others wanted. He personally wanted to be president, but was never able to make that a reality. Several questions remain unanswered about him.

First, assuming there may have been problems with the ratification process in 1913, why would Knox ignore those concerns
and declare the 16th Amendment "in effect"? Knox was a Republican. His boss, Taft, was a Republican president, and the amendment itself had been proposed by Taft and approved by a Republican
Congress. Remember, the entire idea in 1909 had been for the
amendment to fail, either in Congress or during the ratification
process. But Congress overwhelmingly approved the language and
the states, one by one, started to ratify.

By 1913 the country had swung decisively toward the left.
Progressivism became popular, and supporting the rich elite
would be political suicide. All three candidates for president in
1912, Taft, Teddy Roosevelt, and Woodrow Wilson, supported
ratification. The Democrat Wilson won that election, handing
the Republicans a decisive defeat. By February 1913, when Knox
acted on the ratification (as one of his final chores as Secretary
of State), the last thing the nation wanted to hear was that there
might be problems. That type of "eleventh hour" revelation might
even have been construed as a Republican dirty trick. Even if
Knox had declared the amendment invalid, the Democrats who
were, by 1913, in power would have just re-proposed and re-
submitted it for ratification, taking all of the credit. So nothing
politically productive would have come to the Republicans by
challenging ratification.

Biographers note that Knox was proud of being the center of
all that attention. Legally, he was the sole decider of the 16th
Amendment's future and he chose to let it stand. But some semblance of conscience may have shown through. Instead of declaring the amendment "ratified," as had been done with all previous
and subsequent constitutional amendments, he chose the curious
language of certifying it merely "in effect." Was that a message?
A hint at the truth? We'll never know. All we do know is that during his short campaign to secure the 1920 Republican presidential
nomination, Knox several times commented that he "saved the
Party back in '13." Nowhere, though, is that assertion ever explained.

The second remaining inquiry is a corollary of the first. If any of this is true, why would Knox ultimately reveal what he'd done? The answer to that comes from Harding's snub of Knox. By March 1921 when Harding was inaugurated, Knox, though still a sitting United States Senator from Pennsylvania, had become a bitter man. It seems reasonable that, at some point, he may have told his close friend Andrew Mellon about what happened in 1913. As the incoming Secretary of Treasury, perhaps Knox thought Mellon should know that there may be problems with the income tax? Or perhaps he just thought Mellon a sympathetic ear? Or maybe he was simply expounding on his seeming importance? Regardless, Philander Knox died on October 21, 1921, and with him went any chance of further explanations.

Of course, she knew things that Howell did not. Information that filled in the gaps and turned some of his speculation into fact.

She definitely agreed with Danny.

The Treasury secretary was hiding something.

But what? How bad could it be?

She paged to the end of Howell's book and read the final paragraph.

My legal case is not atypical. There are thousands of people who have been tried and convicted of either failing to file a tax return, tax evasion, or tax fraud. Many of those people were sentenced to jail, myself included. But what if the speculation is true and the 16th Amendment is somehow tainted? What if that fact was known from the moment Philander Knox declared the amendment "in effect"? It's no secret that our government keeps secrets. Sometimes it's in our best interests that things remain hidden. But other times the cloak of secrecy is used for nothing more than political advantage or to hide mistakes. Lyndon Johnson tried that with Vietnam. Nixon with Watergate. Reagan during Iran-Contra. Of course, all of those attempts failed and the truth was ultimately revealed. What will history say of the 16th Amendment? Is all that has been said all that will be said? Or is the final chapter yet to be written? Only time will tell.

Her phone buzzed.

She'd set it on vibrate so as to not draw attention, though the lounge surrounding her had become sparse on people. The LCD display indicated it was Cotton. Finally. She stood, walked to a far corner, and faced the papered wall. "I've been waiting."

"It's a mess."

Not what she wanted to hear.

"We have a multitude of problems," he said, "all of them bad."

FORTY-ONE

CROATIA

ISABELLA SAT IN THE CELL WITH LUKE DANIELS. TWO HOURS HAD passed since they'd been brought inside from the rain. During that time she'd said little. Neither had Daniels, who appeared unconcerned, lying on another steel bench, eyes closed. Rest was the farthest thing from her mind. Getting out of here and back on the trail, that was what mattered.

She'd asked when they first arrived to use her cell phone, but the locals refused. From the abbreviated call in the car, Malone had most likely realized they were in trouble. So hopefully he'd send help. Never had she been in this kind of situation before, so its resolution was not all that clear. Apparently, Daniels harbored no worries.

She stood, walked over, and shook him awake.

"What the—" he said, rousing from his snooze.

"You're snoring."

He sat up and wiped the sleep from his eyes. "I don't do that."

"If you say so."

He checked his watch.

"You have to be somewhere?" she asked.

"No, Your Highness. It's just that things should be happening about now."

"Care to explain?"

He smiled and shook his head. "Not really."

"You being Speed Racer got us into this mess."

"And how do you know about *Speed Racer?* That show was on back in the '60s. How old are you?"

She did not answer him. Instead she said, "Why not just hire the cab to take us where we wanted to go? Why steal a car? Then drive like an idiot. You could have hurt someone."

He sat back against the wall. "You need to go home, get your calculator, and chase tax evaders. This line of work is not for you."

"I get the job done," she said. "And without causing so much trouble. It's not necessary."

He stared at her with eager eyes. "I wish it weren't. But sometimes you gotta do what you gotta do. We can only hope Kim didn't get away."

On that he was right. The documents had to be found. Those were her orders. But to do that she had to find Cotton Malone. Which did not seem like an easy task. And thanks to the wiseass sitting across the cell from her, Malone may be the only lead left.

Metal doors opened beyond the bars and she saw a man in a damp suit enter the holding area. He was middle-aged with a balding head, an untidy mustache, and a bow tie. He walked alone, the doors closing behind him. He approached the cell and introduced himself as a deputy attaché with the American embassy.

"I drove down from Zagreb," the man said.

Daniels stood. "About time, we've got things to do."

"The charges against you are quite serious. The Croats want to prosecute."

"And I want to win the lottery, but neither one of those is goin' to happen."

"There's no need to be obstinate," the man said.

She couldn't resist. "You should see him when he really gets mad."

Daniels chuckled. "Real cute. Look, we're on a mission, dispatched through the Justice Department for me, Treasury for her. Were you advised?"

Their savior nodded. "Oh, yes, I received a briefing from the secretary of state himself. He told me to get you out of here immediately."

"Then why are we talking through these bars?"

She wanted to know, "What about Cotton Malone? Do you know anything about him?"

The man nodded. "I just spent the last half hour with Mr. Malone."

Now she was interested. At least she knew Malone was nearby. "Where is he?"

"At the American Corner. It's within the city library, not far."

He explained that the corner comprised a collection of books and DVDs about American life, history, and society. There were eight such repositories scattered around Croatia, the first ever opened here in Zadar. The host library provided shelf space, utilities, an Internet connection, and an on-site coordinator. The embassy contributed a television, DVD player, and several computers.

"It's a way local people can learn about us firsthand, on their own. I helped set the program up."

"I can see you're proud," Daniels said. "But can you get us out of here."

The man nodded. "Of course. Mr. Malone said I was to bring you straight to him at the library."

Something was bothering her. "You said the secretary of state called you personally?"

He nodded and produced his cell phone. "Right on this. Quite exciting, actually. The embassy is two hours away in Zagreb, but I was already on the way here to Zadar for the day on other business. The secretary told me to first contact Mr. Malone and take him to the library, then come straight here."

His tone was curt and precise, straight to the point, which she liked.

But his directness clearly irritated Daniels.

Which she also liked.

"The charges are all being dropped," the envoy said. "We'll make restitution to the cabdriver for his vehicle, along with a little extra to compensate for his trouble. Luckily, no one was hurt, which will make this much easier to handle."

"And my phone?" Daniels asked.

"Oh, I'm glad you reminded me."

He fished two units from his jacket pocket and handed them through the bars. "For both of you."

"I need to make a call," Daniels said.

"They don't work in here," the envoy noted. "It's a police station, you know."

"Then get us out."

She agreed. The quicker she rid herself of Luke Daniels the better. Now that she knew where Malone was located, she'd get there herself and talk to him directly. Hopefully, he had the documents, or at least knew where they were located.

"The officers will be right along to open the cell."

"Thank you," she said, offering a smile. "Mr. Daniels and I are not meant to be kept so close together. I'm anxious to be on my way."

"But that's not possible," the envoy said.

She saw the comment grabbed Daniels' attention, too. "What do you mean? Let her be on her way, by all means."

"I was told to bring Ms. Schaefer along. She was not to go off on her own. Those were my orders."

She wanted to know, "From who?"

"The secretary of state said those came directly from the president of the United States."

FORTY-TWO

Stephanie examined the cache inside a closed room with the secretary of Treasury, who'd brought out everything Paul Larks had supposedly copied.

"Joe, you have to explain. Why was this stuff classified? It's a bunch of nothing."

He shrugged. "That's a good question. But the decision to classify was made by other people a long time ago. I assume they had their reasons."

"Is this everything Larks took?"

He nodded. "It's all there. That's it."

She knew he was lying. Cotton had briefed her on what he'd learned at his end, including the presence of a 1913 solicitor general memo and an original crumpled sheet with numbers that Paul Larks had stolen.

Neither was here.

"Joe, I'm going to assume that you're trying to help. That whatever is going on is so bad you want to protect the president, protect the country." She paused. "But you have to stop lying to me."

He seemed to sense something from her tone. "What do you know?"

"My man on the scene has learned a lot."

"Far more than my eyes and ears."

She waited.

"It's bad," he muttered. "Real bad. There could be a problem with the 16th Amendment. What Howell wrote in that book? It's amazingly close to the truth."

"Tell me about the original sheet Larks stole. With the numbers on it."

"It's the problem."

"I need more."

He stood. "Follow me."

They left the room and walked down a long hall to a set of double doors marked PRIVATE. People milled back and forth, as the Tuesday work morning had begun in earnest. After speaking with Cotton she'd left the hotel and come straight here. Any briefing of the president would wait until she knew more. Cotton had been right, a lot of things had gone wrong on his end. And things were rapidly deteriorating on her side, too.

But there might be a way to turn it all around.

Past the double doors were fewer people. She'd never been in this part of the building before. But she could only remember coming to Treasury once. Before this encounter, the department had not figured prominently into Billet business. The Secret Service handled most of its covert needs. The secretary led her to another closed door that he unlocked with a metal key he carried. Inside was a small workroom with a table and chairs. Files were stacked in neat rows, some of the paper lying scattered. A shredder sat next to the table.

"This is where I've been working on all this," he said. "Ever since Larks let the cat out of the bag. This is every piece of paper from our archives that even remotely mentions anything associated with what we're dealing with. I had my agent Isabella Schaefer, the one who is now in Italy, assemble it."

She approached the table and waited for him to explain.

He closed and locked the door. "The problem is, we don't have a copy of that original Larks stole. Once he left for Europe, we seized Larks' home computer and searched his email accounts. There was nothing in either. We've only been listening in on Larks' calls for the past three weeks. We know there were a lot of communications to Howell prior to that. We only know that crumpled sheet is important thanks to a memo Henry Morgenthau wrote to FDR. That we do have. It was located in a set of classified files Larks did not examine. And thank goodness he didn't. If he'd taken that, we might not know anything."

"Has your agent reported in?" she asked.

He shook his head.

She told him about what had happened with the police in Croatia and how she'd had the White House intervene. Edwin Davis had handled things with the Croatian government, and the secretary of state sent a representative to Zadar to secure the release of both agents.

"Ms. Schaefer has been indisposed," she told him. "I had the White House order her to go with my man. I hope you don't mind, but it seemed better to keep them all together."

He nodded. "Of course, I understand. This is your game now."

"Not entirely. I still don't know what you know."

"Are you sure you want to?"

She had no choice. "Tell me."

He reached down to the table, lifted one of the papers, and handed it to her. She saw that it was a memorandum from Secretary of Treasury Henry Morgenthau to Franklin Roosevelt, dated December 5, 1944. Across the top, in large type were the words FOR THE PRESIDENT'S EYES ONLY.

I have the answer to the questions you posed last week. I had agents interview several current and former employees of Treasury, people who were there in the 1920s. We learned that in 1925 former secretary Mellon was interested in a possible financial claim that the heirs of Haym Salomon may have against the United States. Congress, at the time, was considering some form of repayment and made a formal inquiry to Treasury as to any documentation that may exist in our archives. There were, in fact, documents. These were removed and given directly to Secretary Mellon. Those documents were never returned and remain unaccounted for. If you would like a personal briefing, I can provide one on the Salomon claim. Because of its sensitive nature, I would prefer not to commit those thoughts to writing.

I remain troubled by what you told me concerning Secretary Mellon's actions on December 31, 1936. This quest he left for you to decipher is not only insulting, it borders on treason. This country is now at war and we cannot afford to have anything jeopardize the efficient operation of government. It's vital we maintain a strong and decisive posture. Mellon's comments that whatever he left could be "the end of you" is disturbing. The dollar bill you showed me and the anagram of letters is particularly troubling. Is that a coincidence? If so, it's one only Mellon seems to have been cognizant of. But the reference to "tyrannical aristocrat" is not hard to decipher. I am a student of history and those words were once uttered by George Mason, from Virginia, one of several delegates who refused to sign the Constitution in Philadelphia. Which would also explain the significance of the word Mason formed by the six-pointed star. The crumpled page of numbers you showed me is definitely a code. I would suggest having our cryptographers examine it.

It is possible that the missing Salomon documents could be what Secretary Mellon left for you to find. I am told that those could be not only financially damaging, but overtly embarrassing. As you related, Mellon noted that the page with numbers deals with "two" national secrets. What the other might be, I do not know. My suggestion would be to follow the trail and see where it leads.

She silently filled in the blanks with what she already knew. Obviously, FDR had discussed the Mellon situation with someone other than his Secret Service agent Mark Tipton. But that was no surprise. She knew Roosevelt had made a habit of delegating the same task to multiple people, telling each not to speak of it with anyone else. It served as a way for him to obtain varying viewpoints. Ed Tipton had told her and Danny that FDR had focused on George Mason. Indeed, the wooden crate was full of books on Mason. Now she knew how that focus had been obtained.

"Henry Morgenthau hated Mellon," Levy said. "He wholeheartedly supported Roosevelt's tax vendetta against Mellon. Of course, that backfired in both of their faces."

"Which is a lesson for not doing it."

"I get it, Stephanie. I'm playing games, too. But this isn't 1944. The world is a different place. This country is different. Roosevelt had a war to worry about, but he was dead six months after that memo from Morgenthau. And all of this was forgotten."

She could see that there was more. "What is it, Joe?"

He handed her a tattered sheet of brownish paper. An original memorandum from the solicitor general to the secretary of state, dated February 24, 1913.

"Larks found this and copied it. I withheld it from what the president viewed yesterday and from what I showed you earlier. The stuff about Salomon is one thing, but this is altogether different. This is the second secret Mellon was referring to."

She read it, then said, "This talks about concerns with the 16th amendment. It specifically mentions Kentucky."

"Which Larks visited. He discovered that the state may have never ratified the amendment, yet Knox certified that it did."

She motioned with the copy. "And the other memo? The one sent eleven days earlier that seems to have even more concerns?"

He shook his head. "It's not here. And that's the truth."

She gestured again with the page. "Is there any evidence that Morgenthau saw this memo from the solicitor general?"

"If he did, he never mentioned it in any surviving documents. But in those days, finding anything in our archives would have taken weeks of hand searching. It was easy for things to get lost."

"Maybe he didn't want to know."

"That's possible. But there's no evidence anywhere that he even looked. He was definitely focused on the Salomon angle, and realized that there may be something else, but there's nothing to suggest he ever went looking. Again, they were all preoccupied with the war, then FDR died. I also did some other checking. The solicitor general who wrote that memo you're holding, from 1913, left office and died three months after sending it."

"So tell me what's so awful that you're willing to risk your job and career?"

"Larks read that 1913 memo and got some kind of wild hair up his butt. He went to Kentucky and found problems, which didn't help. I told him to forget about it and leave it alone, but he wouldn't stop. Finally, I sent Isabella Schaefer, the agent now in Croatia, not only to Kentucky, but three other states, and she found similar problems. Questionable procedures, lax rule following, missing originals. More than enough to call into question whether those states properly ratified the 16th Amendment. By then Larks had gone nuts, demanding a formal investigation. There's no way we could do that. So I eased him out and sealed his lips behind a classified stamp and threat of jail."

"And without any proof, he'd just be another wild conspiratorialist."

"That was my thinking. But the old man got a step ahead of us and made copies. Then we found out he stole that original, keeping the best evidence for himself. A single page with random numbers—"

"Crumpled up."

He looked surprised. "That's right. How did you know?"

"Kim Yong Jin has it now."

Shock filled Levy's face. "Stephanie, I don't think that amendment was properly ratified. It could be void, and may have been even from the start. I think Mellon knew that, and used it to his political advantage."

And she knew the rest. "But this was never meant to get out. It was something between Mellon and FDR."

The lawyer inside her calculated the fallout. Danny had been right in the car on the drive back from Virginia. If the person certifying the 16th Amendment had been placed on notice that the ratification process may have been flawed, yet he certified the amendment passed anyway, that was fraud. Which meant that every single cent collected through a wrongfully adopted 16th Amendment was subject to suit and restitution. Those millions of lawsuits would destroy the American economy. Not only that, current revenue collections would cease until a substitute revenue source could be legally enacted. Maybe a direct tax, subject to apportionment? Or some sort of national sales tax or flat tax? Or a new amendment to allow a legal income tax without apportionment? All options. But those would take time to enact, all while the U.S. government would be without over 90 percent of its revenues.

"Kim wants to use this offensively against us," Levy said. "And he can. He'll be able to destroy us, without ever firing a shot. He'll actually turn our own legal system against us. He could do what North Korea has been threatening for decades. We laugh at them. What are they? Just a tiny, insignificant country on the other side of the world. But look at the damage he could do."

Which also explained why the Chinese were so interested. Over a trillion dollars in defaulted debt would seriously injure them as well. She had to admit, the scheme was clever. Smart, too. And they would have never seen it coming but for a few fortuitous flukes that had pointed them in the right direction.

"You see why I tried to contain this," he said. "If the president was to know any of this, then he'd be part of the conspiracy. As it is now, he's got deniability."

"I get it, Joe." She pointed at the shredder. "You planning on a purge?"

He nodded. "Every piece of this is becoming confetti. That's what should have happened to it long ago."

She did not necessarily disagree. "Not yet. Okay? Let's finish this, first. In the meantime we're going to keep this between you and me."

"What about Kim? If he's got that original crumpled sheet, he might be able to find whatever it is Mellon left for Roosevelt."

"He might, but Kim has a problem. He's four thousand miles away, in Croatia, and what he wants isn't there. The trick will be to contain him long enough so we can locate it here first."

"But he has the only clue to know where to look."

She smiled. "Maybe not."

Then there was that *other* problem.

And with Justice and Treasury now being allies—

"Joe, I'm going to need your help to end this."

FORTY-THREE

CROATIA

MALONE WAITED INSIDE THE ZADAR CITY LIBRARY, A GRAYISH-blue, single-story building that—back in the 1920s, he was told—had served as an officers' club for the Italian military. During a recent re-modeling its three wings had been connected with all-glass corridors that, at their center, accommodated a pavilion-like cafeteria forming a transparent inner courtyard. The library sat on the mainland, facing the old town peninsula. Beyond the glass, the fog was gone but rain contin-ued to fall, though not with the intensity of earlier. In the distance, the ferry still sat docked at the north end of the peninsula.

He'd managed to ease the lifeboat back to shore, ditching it on a stretch of beach near one of the hotels north of the town center. Fog and the squall had limited his choices, the important thing being to get back to dry land and on Kim's trail. He'd spoken to Stephanie and reported everything that happened, including that Luke and Isabella Schaefer might need some help. He had no doubt she'd take care of things. His problem was Howell and Kim. During a return call from Stephanie he'd reported where he and Howell had landed. They'd stayed put until a car arrived, driven by an odd-looking fellow in a bow tie, who produced State Department credentials and drove them straight to the library, explaining why along the way.

Tucked in one of the wings inside was a section that contained books, biographies, novels—anything and everything American for the uninitiated. Also, there were three desktop computers, connected to the Internet, that the envoy said were at their disposal. That had been nearly an hour ago. Howell was sitting off to himself, still shaken up over Jelena. He, too, was bothered by what happened and sat quietly watching as a dozen or so birds arrived in the bay. They wheeled low, then hurled themselves into the water with closed wings and out-thrust heads forming a spear-beaked missile in search of food. To the west, where the sky met the sea, the pale watery gray shaded to a sepia haze.

He heard movement and turned. The envoy had returned with Luke Daniels and Isabella Schaefer.

"I can't leave you two alone for more than five minutes without you getting arrested?" he asked.

"It was all his fault," Isabella said, pointing to Luke.

Which he believed. He explained all that had happened on the ferry, then said, "We couldn't find Jelena. Kim tossed her out, just to slow me down."

"She didn't have to die," Howell said. "She wasn't part of this."

"Until you involved her," Isabella said. "You sent her on that cruise."

Howell's eyes widened. "To get some documents from a crazy old man. I had no idea North Koreans were involved in this."

"That's what happens when people stick their noses where they don't belong."

"Lay off him," Malone said. "His girlfriend just died."

"I don't take orders from you." Schaefer pointed a finger at Howell. "You're going to jail."

"Actually, he's not. He's got a presidential pardon coming."

"For what?"

He shrugged. "Why don't you call Danny Daniels and ask him. All I know is he told me this guy has a free pass. Done. So back off."

Howell stared at him. "What does he want? My help? Or silence?"

Malone nodded. "This is more serious than you just not filing tax returns. You, more than anyone else, should realize that. And I think you owe Kim Yong Jin."

Howell stood. "You're damn right. What do you want me to do?"

He liked the younger man's spunk. "You told me that you have a scan of that solicitor general's memo and the page with numbers."

Howell nodded. "They're in a secured email account under a false name."

"Can you access that account from here?"

Howell nodded.

He pointed to one of the computers. "Do it."

As Howell sat and began to type he faced Luke. "Kim has enough of the puzzle to connect the dots. But not enough, I don't think, to hit pay dirt. I'm betting he doesn't understand the whole picture. That's why he needed Howell. We know things he doesn't and, most important—"

"He's on the wrong side of the ocean to actually find anything," Luke said.

He nodded. "And if we can contain him here then we can keep this under control."

"But you're assuming he's working alone," Isabella said. "What if he has people in the U.S., waiting to hear from him."

"There it is again," Luke said. "That ray of sunshine I've come to love. Unfortunately, she's right. We don't know that."

"I'm betting he doesn't. Nothing about this guy signals team player. So I'm assuming Kim is here with only that woman who jammed a needle in my leg." Malone faced Isabella. "I don't suppose you have any idea who she might be?"

"Hana Sung. His daughter. She was on the cruise, trailing Larks while you did."

He heard the unspoken insult of his failure to notice her. "Only on TV does the good guy always know that someone else is watching. There were three thousand people on that boat. That's a lot of faces to keep track of. And let's not forget, you're the one who gave Larks way too much rope."

"Don't you think I know that? I get it. You guys are the pros. I'm the rank amateur, who messed it all up."

He actually needed this woman's assistance, so he decided to cut her some slack. "That's one way to look at it. Another is you made a call at the line of scrimmage, as the play was happening. We all do that. Sometimes it works, sometimes it doesn't. So let's not sweat it and finish this thing."

"I got it," Howell called out.

They stepped to the computer and he gazed at the screen, which displayed an image of a crumpled page with four lines of numbers.

869, 495, 21, 745, 4, 631, 116, 589, 150, 382, 688, 900, 238, 78, 560, 139, 694, 3, 22, 249, 415, 53, 740, 16, 217, 5, 638, 208, 39, 766, 303, 626, 318, 480, 93, 717, 799, 444, 7, 601, 542, 833

As Malone suspected, the sheet was a cipher. Stephanie had told him every detail she'd learned, and now it was up to him to solve it. He searched his eidetic memory. *Tyrannical aristocrat. George Mason. History and Mason begins the quest. A quote from Lord Byron. A strange coincidence, to use a phrase, by which such things are settled nowadays. And Mellon said he would be waiting for Roosevelt.* That's what Stephanie had told him. Random elements, all somehow connected.

"I know what this is," Isabella said.

He was curious to hear what she had to say.

"It reminds me of the Beale cipher? Ever heard of it?"

He shook his head.

"There's a story that around 1820, a man named Thomas Beale and twenty-nine other men found a treasure in the Blue Ridge Mountains of Virginia. For whatever reason, they reburied it and hid its location behind three pages of numbers, just like this. One of the ciphers has been solved. The other two remain a mystery."

"And you know this, how?" Luke asked.

"I do have interests outside of work. Codes fascinate me." She motioned to one of the other computers. "May I?"

Malone nodded. "By all means."

She sat and typed, working the keyboard and finding an online image of the Beale cipher sheets. And she was right. The pages were similar. Random numbers, one line after the other.

115, 73, 24, 807, 37, 52, 49, 17, 31, 62, 647, 22, 7, 15, 140, 47, 29, 107, 79, 84,
56, 239, 10, 26, 811, 5, 196, 308, 85, 52, 160, 136, 59, 211, 36, 9, 46, 316, 554,
122, 106, 95, 53, 58, 2, 42, 7, 35, 122, 53, 31, 82, 77, 250, 196, 56, 96, 118, 71,
140, 287, 28, 353, 37, 1005, 65, 147, 807, 24, 3, 8, 12, 47, 43, 59, 807, 45, 316,
101, 41, 78, 154, 1005, 122, 138, 191, 16, 77, 49, 102, 57, 72, 34, 73, 85, 35, 371,
59, 196, 81, 92, 191, 106, 273, 60, 394, 620, 270, 220, 106, 388, 287, 63, 3, 6, 191,
122, 43, 234, 400, 106, 290, 314, 47, 48, 81, 96, 26, 115, 92, 158, 191, 110, 77,
85, 197, 46, 10, 113, 140, 353, 48, 120, 106, 2, 607, 61, 420, 811, 29, 125, 14, 20,
37, 105, 28, 248, 16, 159, 7, 35, 19, 301, 125, 110, 486, 287, 98, 117, 511, 62, 51,
220, 37, 113, 140, 807, 138, 540, 8, 44, 287, 388, 117, 18, 79, 344, 34, 20, 59, 511,
548, 107, 603, 220, 7, 66, 154, 41, 20, 50, 6, 575, 122, 154, 248, 110, 61, 52, 33,
30, 5, 38, 8, 14, 84, 57, 540, 217, 115, 71, 29, 84, 63, 43, 131, 29, 138, 47, 73,
239, 540, 52, 53, 79, 118, 51, 44, 63, 196, 12, 239, 112, 3, 49, 79, 353, 105, 56,
371, 557, 211, 505, 125, 360, 133, 143, 101, 15, 284, 540, 252, 14, 205, 140, 344,
26, 811, 138, 115, 48, 73, 34, 205, 316, 607, 63, 220, 7, 52, 150, 44, 52, 16, 40,
37, 158, 807, 37, 121, 12, 95, 10, 15, 35, 12, 131, 62, 115, 102, 807, 49, 53, 135,
138, 30, 31, 62, 67, 41, 85, 63, 10, 106, 807, 138, 8, 113, 20, 32, 33, 37, 353, 287,
140, 47, 85, 50, 37, 49, 47, 64, 6, 7, 71, 33, 4, 43, 47, 63, 1, 27, 600, 208, 230,
15, 191, 246, 85, 94, 511, 2, 270, 20, 39, 7, 33, 44, 22, 40, 7, 10, 3, 811, 106, 44,
486, 230, 353, 211, 200, 31, 10, 38, 140, 297, 61, 603, 320, 302, 666, 287, 2, 44,
33, 32, 511, 548, 10, 6, 250, 557, 246, 53, 37, 52, 83, 47, 320, 38, 33, 807, 7, 44,
30, 31, 250, 10, 15, 35, 106, 160, 113, 31, 102, 406, 230, 540, 320, 29, 66, 33, 101,
807, 138, 301, 316, 353, 320, 220, 37, 52, 28, 540, 320, 33, 8, 48, 107, 50, 811, 7,
2, 113, 73, 16, 125, 11, 110, 67, 102, 807, 33, 59, 81, 158, 38, 43, 581, 138, 19,
85, 400, 38, 43, 77, 14, 27, 8, 47, 138, 63, 140, 44, 35, 22, 177, 106, 250, 314,
217, 2, 10, 7, 1005, 4, 20, 25, 44, 48, 7, 26, 46, 110, 230, 807, 191, 34, 112, 147,
44, 110, 121, 125, 96, 41, 51, 50, 140, 56, 47, 152, 540, 63, 807, 28, 42, 250, 138,
582, 98, 643, 32, 107, 140, 112, 26, 85, 138, 540, 53, 20, 125, 371, 38, 36, 10, 52,
118, 136, 102, 420, 150, 112, 71, 14, 20, 7, 24, 18, 12, 807, 37, 67, 110, 62, 33,
21, 95, 220, 511, 102, 811, 30, 83, 84, 305, 620, 15, 2, 10, 8, 220, 106, 353, 105,
106, 60, 275, 72, 8, 50, 205, 185, 112, 125, 540, 65, 106, 807, 138, 96, 110, 16, 73,
33, 807, 150, 409, 400, 50, 154, 285, 96, 106, 316, 270, 205, 101, 811, 400, 8, 44,
37, 52, 40, 241, 34, 205, 38, 16, 46, 47, 85, 24, 44, 15, 64, 73, 138, 807, 85, 78,
110, 33, 420, 505, 53, 37, 38, 22, 31, 10, 110, 106, 101, 140, 15, 38, 3, 5, 44, 7,
98, 287, 135, 150, 96, 33, 84, 125, 807, 191, 96, 511, 118, 40, 370, 643, 466, 106,
41, 107, 603, 220, 275, 30, 150, 105, 49, 53, 287, 250, 208, 134, 7, 53, 12, 47, 85,
63, 138, 110, 21, 112, , 51, 63, 241, 540, 122, 8, 10, 63, 140, 47, 48, 140, 288

"The second of the three ciphers was solved using the Declaration of Independence," she said. "It explains all that here. You assign a number to every word in the Declaration, then match that to the code. The first number in the Beale cipher is 115. The 115th word in the Declaration of Independence is *instituted*. That starts with *i*. So the first letter of the code is *i*."

A classic substitution cipher. Simple and easy, provided you knew which document had been used as the key. Without that knowledge the cipher became next to impossible to solve.

"Looks like you just earned your keep," Luke said to her. "Pappy, I think she might be on to somethin'."

He agreed. It seemed possible.

"All we have to do is find out what document Mellon used," Howell said.

Malone's mind was already working on that, but first, "You told me that Kim contacted you using an alias. Peter From Europe. Do you still have that email?"

Howell nodded. "I keep everything."

Kim had to be pleased with himself, managing to obtain the stolen documents then escaping the ferry. Malone had made a mistake allowing that opportunity, but he now saw a way to regain the upper hand.

"Kim still has the original cipher," Isabella pointed out.

"Which I'm assuming Treasury has no copy of," he said.

She shook her head.

"Which explains," Luke said, "why they're all fired-up anxious to get it back."

"We can't allow Kim to keep it," she said.

"Believe me, it'll do him no good," he said. "There's too much he doesn't know."

Luke smiled. "And that will usually hurt you."

Exactly.

FORTY-FOUR

HANA STOOD UNDER THE SHOWER, HER SKIN ALIVE FROM THE steamy flow. Bathing still remained, for her, a luxury. Every time she turned on a faucet and allowed clean, fresh water to engulf her she thought of the camp. No one bathed there, unless allowed, and only then when it rained or in the cold river. She never knew just how awful her life had been until she was free. Insiders simply knew no better. The camp *was* their world. There she'd been a short thin child, her hair just a brush of fuzz, her scalp always covered with a filthy white cloth tied at the neck. By the age of six beatings from her mother became a regular occurrence. And always over food. Until the age of seven, each day her mother had gone to work in the fields, leaving her alone. The morsels left for her to eat never made it to midday. As soon as her mother was gone she'd devour not only her portion but her mother's, too, never considering the fact that her mother may starve. Why would she care? Your own belly was all that mattered. The guards encouraged such conflicts and never objected if prisoners hurt one another. That violence simply saved them the trouble, as they'd all die soon enough anyway.

She wondered if there would come a time when she did not think of the camp. Probably not. Fourteen years had passed, yet the memories had not faded. She thought back to the day after Sun Hi was murdered, when she approached her mother for the last time. By then they barely spoke, her world evolved to nearly total silence.

"Why am I here?" she asked again.

Her mother did not answer. As always.

They were not all that dissimilar in size and weight. She'd grown and her mother had shrunk. No affection at all existed inside her for this person who'd given her life. In fact, she hated that such a thing had ever happened. And not because of what she might be missing outside the fence, but solely because of what was happening within. Sun Hi was gone. And she'd only now realized what that loss meant to her. A strange feeling of fear had swelled inside her since yesterday, watching Sun Hi die on the floor, and for the first time in her life she felt entirely alone.

A shovel stood propped against the block wall. Her mother carried it to and from the fields each day. She gripped its wooden handle and swung the blade in a wide arc, catching her mother square in the stomach. Intentionally, she'd made sure the rounded flat side made first contact. Her mother slumped forward, grabbing her midsection. A second crashing blow with the rounded end sent her mother to the floor.

She tossed the shovel aside and pounced, yanking back her mother's head. "You will never beat me again." And she meant it. "I asked why am I here? Answer me."

Violence seemed the only thing that worked inside the camp. The guards routinely meted it out. Teacher seemed to have enjoyed killing Sun Hi. The older children abused the younger. And once, not all that long ago, she'd been forced to watch as her mother pleasured one of the guards, not an ounce of emotion seeping from either of them. After he finished, the guard had slapped and kicked until his conquest managed to crawl away.

Her mother's gasping breathes eased. The eyes were alight, not with fear, but with something else. Something new.

"You . . . are a . . . Kim."

"What is that?"

"It is what . . . you are."

"Explain or I'll beat you again."

Her mother smiled.

"That . . . is a Kim."

She hadn't understood any of that at the time.

Then everything changed.

Unlike her mother she'd only spent a short time in the fields and had never been sent to the mines. Instead she'd worked in one of the factories, making glassware. Other sites produced cement, pottery, and uniforms. Her life should have been as meaningless as her mother's. But a week after Sun Hi died, as she walked home from the factory, the guards cuffed her hands behind her back and blindfolded her. She was tossed into a jeep and driven a long way on a bumpy road. Then she was led inside a building, where the blindfold was removed. The room was windowless and empty, except for a chair where she sat. She'd heard stories of places like this and wondered if today the guards would finally have their way with her. The door opened and a short, stout man with a pudgy face wearing plain, dark, uniform-like clothing entered. His hair was cut short, like the guards, with no sideburns. But instead of the emotionless features she'd seen on those around her all her life, this man smiled.

"I am your father," he said.

She stared at him, unsure how to reply. Was this a trick?

"Your mother and I once knew each other. We were in love. But my father sent her here. I never knew that, until recently. I never knew you existed, either."

She was confused.

"I asked that you be brought to me," he said. "What is your name?"

"Hana Sung."

He smiled. "Did your mother name you?"

"Someone else chose it. But I like it."

"Than you shall be Hana Sung."

"You knew my mother?"

He nodded. "She and I were close. But that was many years ago."

"I was born here."

"I know that. But you will live here no longer."

"Who are you?"

"Kim Yong Jin."

And she knew then what her mother had meant.

She truly *was* a Kim.

That day her father saved her from the camp, but any concept of gratefulness remained foreign to her, both then and now. At that first encounter all that had raced through her mind was that maybe, just maybe, she would eat no more spoiled cabbage or rotten corn. No more grasshoppers, locusts, or dragonflies. Even worse, no more regurgitating what had been eaten, then eating it again, as a way to fool her hunger. The grapes, gooseberries, and raspberries found sometimes in the forest she would miss, but not the rats, frogs, and snakes that she'd also hunted down.

"What of my mother?" she asked him.

"I cannot help her."

Which had actually pleased her. After the shovel attack they hadn't spoken a word, though they continued to live together. Each went her own way and, surely, if the opportunity presented itself, one would turn on the other to the guards, so they both stayed wary.

"I am an important man," her father said.

"Can you give orders?" she asked. "Like the guards?"

He nodded. "No one here will question a thing I say."

"Then I want you to do something for me."

He seemed pleased that she'd made a request.

"I want someone punished for hurting my friend."

"What did he do?"

She told him about Sun Hi, then said, "I want him punished for that. If you are important, then you can do that."

Two hours later she was led into another windowless room. Teacher hung upside down, his ankles in shackles, the body just high enough from the floor that his outstretched arms could not touch. His head was flushed with blood, his clothes stank of urine.

"What would you have me to do with him?" her father asked her.

"Kill him, as he did Sun Hi."

"I thought that might be what you'd say, so I had this brought with him."

A guard appeared with a pointer in hand.

The shower water rained down on her and she allowed the lubricated sensation of the soap to soothe her rattled nerves. Religion had been forbidden in the camp, and her father believed in nothing. Neither did she, really. Insiders only believed in themselves. She'd stood that day and watched as Teacher's skull was pounded with the pointer, each smack sharp and clear. Unlike Sun Hi, who took her beating in silence, he screamed in pain like a puppy. Welts appeared that burst open, blood dripping from them to the floor.

He struggled at first, then eventually gave up and died.

"You are an important man," she told her father.

"I will be the next leader of this country."

During the past fourteen years she'd watched her father's rise, then fall. He'd taken her from the camp, then eventually with him when he fled the country to Macao. She'd been educated first in North Korea, then in Chinese private schools, where she became familiar with world history beyond the camp fences.

Some of which had astounded her.

Long ago, nearly 2.5 out of 10 million people died in what the world called the Korean War. The north had actually invaded the south, with no clear victor from the fight. Millions of North Koreans were starving, the country so isolated and corrupt that no nation wanted anything to do with it. Her father had been born a communist prince, raised in luxury and educated abroad, all while people by the tens of thousands died every year from malnutrition. She'd come to learn that breeding and bloodlines defined everything in North Korea.

As did power.

Her father was once a four-star general in the Korean People's Army, though he possessed no experience for the job. While inside the camp she'd been taught no notion of the country, the world, or its leaders. Only after being removed, during the short time she attended state schools, had she been told that America was evil, South Korea even worse, and North Korea was supposedly the envy of the world. Unlike every other schoolchild outside the fences, in the camp she'd never carried and praised a photo of Dear Leader, nor one of his father or the father before. Prisoners were not even important enough to brainwash. Her life had been nothing but a constant reminder of genetic sins. Then to be told that she was actually part of the national leadership, part of the fabric that condemned so many people to exist behind the fences—that had been too much.

She'd would never forget the prisoners.

Not ever.

She'd watched her father kill a defenseless old man, then toss a drugged woman out to drown. He placed no significance on other people's lives. Kims were just like the guards and Teacher. Her great-grandfather created the camps, her grandfather expanded them, and her half uncle kept them going. Hundreds of thousands remained prisoners, more added by the day. The Kims killed Sun Hi, as surely as if they'd personally beat her with that pointer. And she had no doubt that her father, once installed as supreme leader, would continue that legacy. He said otherwise, but she knew better.

He *was* a Kim.

She finished her shower and shut off the water, her body scrubbed clean and immaculate. Steam engulfed her, the wet marble walls warm to the touch. She stood naked, water dripping from her skin. One thing was certain.

She was no Kim.

Names fascinated her, perhaps because for the first nine years of her life they'd meant little to nothing. She'd taken the time to study her father's and learned that Yong referred to bravery and Jin a jewel.

He was neither.

Her own name was different.

Hana Sung.

First victory.

Which pointed the way.

FORTY-FIVE

KIM FINISHED HIS LUNCH, DELIVERED BY ROOM SERVICE HALF AN hour ago. He'd made a good choice with the hotel, an upscale establishment that faced the bay and offered a level of personal service he'd come to expect.

After abandoning the lifeboat he and Hana had made their way into a small suburb north of Zadar where they found a taxi. The driver had suggested the hotel and delivered them to the front door. He'd kept a close hold on the black satchel and Hana had brought along the travel bag from the ferry. All in all, their escape had worked perfectly. He was now free of the American, with the documents, ready to move forward.

Hana was showering and he needed to do the same. He wore a soft robe from the bedroom closet, as their clothes were being laundered. They'd need to buy some more, which he could do later or tomorrow. Their suite was the hotel's largest, with two bedrooms, two baths, and a spacious living room. French doors opened out to a terrace that overlooked open water. The day had turned chilly, the wind finally eased, the fog lifted to a thin gray film. Waves continued to march in the bay, the pulse of the sea strong, constant, and relentless.

The documents from the satchel were spread out on the table, a cache straight from the private records of the U.S. Treasury Department. He knew the sole original was the most important. It had been unfortunate that he hadn't been able to speak with Howell further. He'd intended on forcing more information on threat of harm to his lover. Unfortunately, that lever was now gone, as was Howell. So he'd have to figure out the rest on his own.

He'd brought along his laptop in the travel bag, which was now connected to the hotel's wireless network. A quick check of the day's news revealed a disturbing story from North Korea. Six high-level government administrators had been arrested, tried, and convicted of "attempting to overthrow the state by all sorts of intrigues and despicable methods with a wild ambition to grab the supreme power of our party and state." The conspirators had been labeled "traitors to the nation for all ages."

All six had been immediately executed.

He studied the list of names and noted four were sources he'd regularly used within the government. One had been his informant about the money transfer in Venice.

That was no coincidence.

His half brother was on to him.

He'd expected repercussions from the $20 million, but not quite so fast. How had Pyongyang traced the debacle in Venice? He'd heard nothing more from the men hired to steal the $20 million, but their fate was immaterial. Unless they'd been taken prisoner and interrogated, little existed connecting him to them. No one had followed him onto the ferry. How could they? Everything happened so spontaneously. Telling the world about those six executions was a way for his half brother to send a message. Decades of inertia had long anchored North Korea in cement. What had his father said? *We must envelop our environment in a dense fog to prevent our enemies from learning anything about us.* So when that fog was intentionally lifted, that meant something.

The laptop dinged, signaling an incoming email.

He glanced at the listing and noticed the sender. PATRIOT. That was the tag Anan Wayne Howell had always utilized. He had many emails stored away that bore the label.

He slid the machine closer and opened the message.

> You left me on the ferry. I'm assuming that was you in one of those lifeboats and some American agent named

Malone in the other. He confronted me after you left, then took off when the fire alarm sounded. Which was fine by me. He came to bring me back to the United States. I'm assuming you started the fire. Jelena was nowhere on the ferry, so I'm also assuming she's with you. I can tell you now, there's no way you're going to make any progress with those documents without me. There are things you don't know. I want Jelena back, unharmed. I also want my freedom. You have what I need to prove my innocence. Let's deal. Interested?

Yes, he was.

Thankfully, Howell seemed in the dark about what had happened on the water. But that was understandable given the storm and the fog. Visibility had been next to nothing. Malone was who-knew-where, and Howell had apparently fled, now contacting the only person who might be able to help. Unfortunately, Howell was right. There were things Kim did not know, and he did not have the time to discover them on his own. Those six executions alone were reason enough to speed up the process. Discovering the legal and historical particulars of this puzzle were one thing. What he did with that information, once known, was an entirely different matter. That would involve careful maneuvering among lawyers and publicists, the press and the courts. Bringing the United States to its knees would not be easy, but it also no longer seemed impossible.

His fingers worked the keyboard, formulating his reply.

MALONE WAS BETTING THAT KIM YONG JIN WOULD REACT AS A gambler. From the little he'd read, and from what he'd observed, Kim surely fancied himself as someone smarter than everyone else. And that kind of arrogance usually led to mistakes. So he'd drafted an email for Howell to send, taking advantage of what he perceived to be Kim's main weakness.

Ambition.

He now understood the stakes.

Kim wanted to destroy the United States, and if some of that misery spilled over to China then so much the better. To his credit Kim had stumbled onto something that might just work. He'd meant what he'd said earlier. They had to contain Kim here, and hope no one on the other side of the Atlantic was waiting for instructions. Stephanie had told him earlier that the NSA, thanks to a court order, was listening specifically to Kim's cell phone. As usual, though, all international calls in and out of the United States were also being monitored. Millions of them, the NSA recognition software on the lookout for words like *income taxes, 16th Amendment, Andrew Mellon, Roosevelt,* among others.

"Do you think he saw the email?" Isabella asked.

"And if he did," Luke said, "will he take the bait?"

He was certain. "It's his only play. There are things he just doesn't know."

They were still inside the American Corner, that entire section of the library temporarily closed off. His clothes were damp and crusty from the seawater.

The desktop rang.

All of their gazes locked on Kim's reply.

I am prepared to deal.

KIM WAS TAKING A BIG CHANCE, BUT HE THOUGHT IT A CALCU-lated one. Howell, as an American fugitive, after three years of running, would have no love for any agent like Malone. He wouldn't necessarily care much for Kim, either, but in Howell's mind Kim had Jelena, and that he did care about. All he had to do was play out the bluff.

A new message appeared from Howell.

We need to meet and I want Jelena there, to make sure she's okay. Once that happens, I'll tell you things that will open your eyes. I don't know what you have in mind, nor do I care. But if you expose all of this as the fraud that it is, that only helps me. I don't want to go to jail. I've spent years studying this, and I didn't write everything I know in the book. In fact, you have the most important piece to the puzzle. That original sheet of numbers. But for that to do you any good, we have to chat.

ISABELLA HAD TO ADMIT, WHAT MALONE WAS DOING SEEMED clever. He was working a con, using the con man's own fears and expectations against him. Not unlike when she worked a tax cheat, making him or her think she was there to help, easing her way closer and closer to the truth. She'd investigated so many, her conviction rate an impressive 93%. It helped that she was selective, walking away from the questionable ones, zeroing in on the real criminals. Unfortunately, no such luxury existed here. You played the hand dealt. Luke Daniels had been right. Malone was tough, and smart.

But so was she.

Another reply came from Kim.

How do you suggest we accomplish all this?

"The fish is on the hook," Luke said, with a smile.

Malone nodded at Howell.

"Reel him in."

FORTY-SIX

STEPHANIE MADE TWO MORE OVERSEAS CALLS ON A LANDLINE TO Cotton, then left the Treasury building through its main entrance. She and Joe Levy had agreed to keep what they knew to themselves, at least for a little while longer. Levy was right. Official deniability could become important, so for now the less the White House knew, the better. Everything screamed caution. *Tread lightly, walk slowly.* A lot was happening. She knew some, but had to know more.

From her reading of *The Patriot Threat* she recalled numerous references to the National Gallery of Art. Howell had noted that Mellon died in 1937, just as construction on the gallery began. The museum did not officially open until 1941. According to Howell, even from the grave Mellon had directed a great many things about the project. The museum's first director, David Finley, remained loyal to his old boss and did exactly as Mellon requested. Cotton had suggested some further exploration. Mellon had created the code with a purpose, so the more they knew about the man the better.

A call to the National Gallery's central office had directed her to one of the assistant curators, a young woman who was a supposed expert on Mellon. A few years ago the first definitive biography of the man had finally been published, and this curator had worked for the author as a research assistant. So while Cotton and Luke maneuvered things in Croatia, she decided to troll a little bait of her own.

She'd driven past the National Gallery a thousand times, but had only ventured inside once or twice. Art was not something that had ever really interested her. The massive gallery occupied a northeast corner on the Mall, facing Constitution Avenue, in the shadow of the Capitol. Its exterior was a monument to classicism with lofty portals at each end, Ionic porticoes in the center, and a dome jutting skyward. Harmony and proportion dominated, all formed out of warm, rosy-tinted marble.

Inside she was directed to the second floor where she found Carol Williams, a pleasant-looking woman with short black hair.

"This is my first experience with an intelligence agency," Carol said. "Curators rarely deal with things like that, but I'm told you want to know about Mr. Mellon?"

She nodded. "A little insight could prove helpful."

"Could I ask why?"

"You could, but I can't answer. I hope you understand."

"Spy business?"

She grinned. "Something like that."

Carol motioned at their surroundings. "You've definitely come to the right place to learn about Mr. Mellon. Here, in the rotunda, is a perfect example of his influence. He wanted a dome on the building as a focal point for the outside, to offset the mass of the long wings. He caught a lot of grief for that decision. People thought only the Capitol should be domed. Here, inside, you can see he was right. This space offers the perfect meeting point for the great halls. A true centerpiece."

Overhead rose a coffered dome with scalloped niches and a glass oculus at its center, strikingly similar to the Pantheon in Rome. A circular procession of thick, green marble columns held the roof aloft, matted from behind by cream-colored limestone walls. A tingling fountain sat in the center.

"The bronze figure in the fountain is Mercury, cast sometime in the late 18th or early 19th century. Mr. Mellon acquired it as part of his collection."

"Why do you call him *Mr.,* as if he's still here?"

"He is still here."

A strange reply.

"This building is totally reflective of him. This was his monument to the country, and since he was paying the bills his wishes were generally honored."

She listened as Carol explained how Mellon chose the architect and approved every aspect of the design. He selected Tennessee marble for the outside and most of the interior décor. He wanted the exhibit rooms harmonious, but not elaborate, intended to convey both period and place. So plaster was used for early Italian, Flemish, and German works. Damask for later Italian. Oak paneling displayed Rubens, van Dyck, Rembrandt, and other Dutch masters. Painted paneling accommodated the French, English, and American canvases. No other adornments were allowed in the galleries, save for a few sofas. Never, Mellon insisted, should the building dominate its contents.

"He had a good eye," Carol said, "and a good sense of things. It would have been easy for him, with all his money, to build a palace. But he intentionally refused to do that. Instead he built a place where works of art could be appreciated."

"You admire him?"

"For his art? Definitely. His taste? Oh, yes. But there were other aspects of him that were less than admirable. He was, after all, a clear product of his time. First, from the Gilded Age where fortunes were built upon greed and ruthless ambition. Then from the prosperous 1920s where those fortunes either expanded or collapsed. Mr. Mellon's multiplied a hundredfold."

Her hostess motioned and they left the rotunda, entering one of the long sculpture halls that spread east and west. Overhead, a barrel-vaulted ceiling with skylights allowed in the late-morning sun. Statuary lined the center between pediment doorways that led to more exhibition rooms. Visitors paraded back and forth, admiring the sculptures. She noticed that the hall was another simple, elegant space that did not overpower.

"Did history interest him?" she asked.

Carol nodded. "His father, Thomas, once said that *in the short voyage of a lifetime, we can see the eddies and ripples on the surface, but not the under-currents changing the main channel of the stream.* Only history can determine the causes that bring that about. The son believed that, too. History was important to him. His book on taxation is still regarded as authoritative. Many of the things he wrote about then continue to apply today."

She recalled Danny reading portions to her in the car.

"He was not a proponent of big government," Carol said. "To him, less was more. He never felt government should be taking care of people. He believed people should take care of themselves. And that wasn't a cruel attitude. He just cherished personal independence. The New Deal, to him, infringed on that freedom, with government mandating everything for you. Social Security, unemployment insurance, a minimum wage. Those he opposed. He was definitely a product of his circumstances. Prior to 1932, ideas of wealth redistribution and social welfare were not popular."

They stopped near the gallery's end, before another of the rectangular doorways.

"Did Mr. Mellon appreciate any historical figures? Like George Mason?"

Carol's face lit up. "How did you know? He admired Mason a great deal. It took courage to not sign the Constitution, but Mason stood his ground. That was the type of independence Mr. Mellon respected. He was a contributor to the renovation of Gunston Hall, Mason's ancestral home in Virginia. It was restored in the 1930s and is now a lovely museum."

Which might explain why Mellon chose to utilize that name in the start of his quest. The fact that, upon the Great Seal, a six-pointed star and five letters combined to form the word *Mason* was surely just a coincidence. Albeit a fortuitous one for Mellon, which he used to aggravate the 32nd president of the United States. And no matter how much FDR protested, he'd clearly been intrigued. Enough to assign a Secret Service agent and the secretary of Treasury to investigate. Unfortunately, Roosevelt did not live long enough to see any of that through.

They left the hall and entered a spacious garden court.

"This is more of Mr. Mellon's influence," Carol said. "He wanted people to feel refreshed and uplifted, not worn out or tired. So he had these green spots added where visitors could rest among plants and flowing water."

THE PATRIOT THREAT | 253

More sunlight poured in from skylights in another barrel-vaulted ceiling and added to the obvious feeling of being outdoors. Stalks of varied greenery stretched up twenty feet. Roses, begonias, and chrysanthemums added a blaze of color. Everything was meticulously tended. They sat on one of the stone benches abutting the walls and she listened as the curator told her more about Andrew Mellon.

"His father, Thomas, required that all of his sons memorize every word of 'Epistle to a Young Friend.' It's by Robert Burns. Have you ever read the poem?"

She shook her head.

"Burns wrote it in 1786 to someone who was about to head out into the world. It's a poem of advice that deals with practical wisdom and self-sufficiency. One verse was Mr. Mellon's favorite. *To catch dame fortune's golden smile, assiduous wait upon her. And gather gear by every wile that's justified by honor. Not for to hide it in a hedge, nor for a train attendant. But for the glorious privilege of being independent.*"

She smiled at the verse's cleverness.

"As a boy of ten, Mr. Mellon would recite the poem then, together, he and his father would repeat out loud that seventh verse. Burns wrote the poem to a young man named Andrew. Of course, that was Mr. Mellon's first name, too, a coincidence he loved."

What she'd heard on the tape with FDR flashed through her mind. Roosevelt told Mark Tipton that Mellon had quoted from Lord Byron. *A strange coincidence, to use a phrase, by which such things are settled nowadays.*

Strange, indeed.

"That verse from Burns defined Mr. Mellon," Carol said. "He literally lived his life by it."

"What Roosevelt did," she said, "going after him, at the end of his life for tax evasion. That had to be devastating."

Carol nodded. "For someone of his stature, being portrayed as a cheat and a crook was awful. He attended court proceedings every day, which dragged on for months. He personally fought every charge and won. Unfortunately, he died before the decision was announced."

"Any idea why Roosevelt targeted him?"

"Politics. There's no other way to view it. Who was going to stand up and defend one of the richest men in the country against the president of the United States? Particularly when half the population was out of work. Roosevelt saw in Mr. Mellon an easy target, a way to bolster his own political image. A free shot, with little to no repercussion."

Except that Roosevelt lost and Mellon went on the offensive. But this woman would know none of that. She thought about quizzing her on some of the particulars Mellon had discussed with Roosevelt, but knew better. The connection with George Mason had been worth the trip over. But she did recall something else from the tape recording in the Oval Office, when Roosevelt and Mark Tipton were speaking. *He said he'd be waiting for me. Can you imagine the arrogance? He told the president of the United States that he'd be waiting.*

That was New Year's Eve 1936.

"What did Mellon do in the final months of his life?" she asked.

A group of schoolchildren entered the court, for the most part quiet, but still excited. Two adults kept them in check as they made their way toward the fountain and the sunken garden at the center.

"By 1937 he was, essentially, retired. He'd turned over control of his businesses to others, withdrawn from public life, and the tax trial was finally over. He did a lot of art collecting during that time, most of which is on display here. But he also knew he was dying. So his main focus was on the plans for the National Gallery."

"I'm curious, why didn't he name this after himself?"

"On that he was smart. He wanted the gallery to grow, to acquire many works of art from varied sources. He thought collectors would be more willing to donate to something recognized as the nation's as a whole, rather than a single individual's. And he was right. We've acquired an enormous number of objects thanks to the fact that this is the *national* gallery."

She asked, "What happened when he died?"

"He was at his daughter's home on Long Island. The cancer had taken a toll, but he remained focused on getting this building started. Construction had begun in June, but he died August 26, 1937. A few days later, there was a massive funeral in Pittsburgh."

She could see that Carol Williams was a true fan, and she had to admit, "He left quite a legacy. This is an amazing place. Those children, there, seem to find it fascinating."

"Tens of thousands come every year."

"When did Mellon learn he was dying?"

Carol thought about the question for a moment, then said, "November 1936. He was immediately given radium and X-ray treatments, which drained him."

Which meant that when Mellon met with FDR on New Year's Eve, he knew he was terminal.

He said he'd be waiting for me.

"Have you ever visited his grave site in Pittsburgh?" she asked.

"That's not where's he's buried."

That caught her attention. "I just assumed that since the funeral was there—"

"The entire family lies together. Mr. Mellon, his son, daughter, and their mother, Nora, his ex-wife. All four of them in one place. A bit ironic since none of them were particularly close in life. Mr. Mellon and his ex-wife divorced thirty years before he died, and not in an amicable way. Paul and his father barely got along. Brother and sister weren't much better. But in death, there they are, side by side, forever."

She smiled at the irony. "And where is this family reunion?"

"Upperville, Virginia. At the Trinity Episcopal Church. It's a small grassy graveyard surrounded by a stone wall."

The schoolchildren continued to enjoy the fountain. She had several more questions, but they became unimportant as a man entered the garden court. He was dressed in a dark suit and tie.

The same outfit from Atlanta, if she was not mistaken.

He walked straight toward her.

Chick-fil-A Man.

FORTY-SEVEN

CROATIA
6:10 P.M.

ISABELLA WAS AMBIVALENT TOWARD COTTON MALONE. HE SEEMED the same arrogant, self-absorbed alpha male that she dealt with day in and day out. To him she was surely unimportant—first, because she was a woman, and second, because she worked for Treasury, as opposed to the CIA, NSA, or some other agency with jurisdiction outside the United States. But she'd been on this trail long before anyone from the Magellan Billet had ever heard of the problem, and she knew more about it than anyone else.

She'd left the American Corner and retreated to the library's café, now nursing a cup of green tea. Coffee had never interested her, nor had drugs or cigarettes. A glass of wine? Now, that was something she could enjoy, and she did, alone, in her apartment, most nights after coming home from work. She never drank with her superiors or colleagues, preferring to always maintain her wits in their presence. Some of her fellow female agents thought differently, not realizing that no matter how much they tried they'd never be "one of the boys."

Few people occupied the tables, the library quiet on this rainy afternoon. She sat with her fingers clasped behind her head, lost in her hair, one leg drawn up, knee in the air. Her gaze was locked out beyond the glass walls.

From down one of the corridors Malone appeared.

He entered the café, walked straight to her, and asked, "May I sit down?"

She nodded and appreciated him asking.

"I get it," he said. "This is your baby. You've been on this from the start. And then we come in and take over."

"The secretary of Treasury himself assigned me. I've searched the classified archives. I've been to state capitols researching records. You have no idea."

"Actually, I do. I think I've figured this out. That crumpled sheet of paper is going to lead us to proof that the 16th Amendment may have been void from the start. Even worse, it's fraud since the government knew the amendment may have been improperly ratified, but went ahead with it anyway. Kim is going to use that to bring us and the Chinese down in one shot."

He actually did understand. And since he knew it all, she felt free to say, "I'll tell you now, there are problems associated with ratification. It's serious. I've seen those problems firsthand in state records. But I get the program. You guys are the big boys, and I'm just from Treasury—"

"Bullshit. You're a trained agent. A damn good one I'm told."

"Who was body-blocked into the water by a federal fugitive."

He chuckled. "If you only knew some of the crap that's happened to me. And besides, I'm the one who really screwed up here. I let Kim get his hands on those documents."

That he had, but she appreciated his admission.

"Did the president really order me here?" she asked.

He nodded. "Absolutely. I told him I wanted you to stay with this. We need your help."

"Luke thinks I'm a pain in the ass."

"You should hear what he says about me."

"I have. He actually respects the hell out of you. He won't say it, but it's clear."

"I was told charm was not your specialty."

"But it apparently is yours."

And she meant it.

"I didn't come here to play you," he said. "I came to ask for your help. That was good thinking in there about the Beale cipher. You may be on target."

She wondered about all this mea culpa. "How did you figure this out?"

"I've talked to Stephanie Nelle. Things are happening in DC. Your boss and mine are now working together. This is a joint operation that's about to get complicated. The Chinese and North Koreans are both involved. They want what Kim is after, then they want Kim dead. Like I said, I need your help."

She gestured with her tea. "Want me to keep your coffee cup full? Make sure there are snacks for everyone?"

"Is it that bad?" he asked. "Do you get that much lack of respect? 'Cause I have to tell you, I worked twelve years for the Magellan Billet and the women there were just as good, just as tough, just as smart as any man. Most times, they were better. Never once have I ever treated a female agent different from a male. I'd never even consider doing that."

She was beginning to think that she may have misjudged this man.

"What I need," he said, "is for you to play with the team. This isn't a job for the Lone Ranger anymore. It's going to take a combined effort and you have a luxury that I don't enjoy. Kim doesn't know you exist. Luke, either. That means you both are going to have to take point. Can you handle that?"

Now she knew exactly why he'd come. To judge for himself if she was up to the job. She wanted in, of that she was sure, so much that she was willing to give this man the benefit of the doubt. "I can do it."

"That's what I want to hear. And besides, I owe you one."

She was curious.

"You kept watch over me in Larks' room while I was out cold. You wanted me to think you hung around just to chew me out, but you were also making sure no one came back for a second look."

That she had. Agents did that for one another.

"Thanks," he said. "Now tell me about Kim's daughter, the one you failed to mention in Larks' room after I woke up."

"You understand why I kept that to myself."

He nodded. "I would have done the same thing. I was a stranger, an unknown. You just wanted me out of the picture."

"Her name is Hana Sung. She's North Korean, early twenties, black hair, short, pretty. We know little to nothing about her, other than she's illegitimate, but most of Kim's children fall into that category. She boarded the cruise ship with him and shadowed Larks most of the time."

"I never made her."

"It would have been impossible. She kept her distance and faded into the other Koreans on board. I wouldn't have made her, either, except that we had some intel that alerted us to be on the lookout for her, including a picture."

"You knew she killed Larks?"

She shrugged. "Either her or Kim. Who else could it be?"

"The North Koreans are some of the most ruthless agents in the world. You're going to have to keep your eyes and ears open, 'cause they can come from anywhere. Don't get yourself killed, okay?"

She could see that his warning was genuine, and she appreciated it. "I'll watch out. What do you have in mind?"

He stood. "Drink your tea and relax a bit. There's not going to be much time for rest in the hours ahead."

She watched as he left the café, her opinion of Harold Earl "Cotton" Malone quite different than a few minutes ago. Silence returned and she allowed the calm to soothe her nerves. Here she was, right in the middle of an international intelligence operation. Chinese? North Koreans? Luke Daniels was right. This was far different from what she was accustomed to handling.

But she liked it.

FORTY-EIGHT

Washington, DC

STEPHANIE STOOD FROM THE BENCH AND FACED THE MAN FROM Treasury. She kept her cool and asked, "Are you following me?"

He did not answer, and she understood why.

She looked down at Carol Williams and said, "Could you excuse us? I appreciate your time. I'll give you a call if I need more information."

The young curator left.

"New friend?" he asked.

"None of your business."

"I wish that were true. I don't want to be here any more than you want me here. I told you back in Atlanta that you should leave things to us."

"And I told your boss not an hour ago that this was now an American intelligence operation, of which you are not a part."

They were speaking low, beneath the ambient noise from the fountain and the schoolchildren, who continued to enjoy the garden court.

"What are you doing here?" she asked.

"I came to tell you a few things."

He sat on the bench. She had no choice but to sit, too.

"No chicken sandwiches today?" she asked.

"You still sore about your phone?"

"I'm still sore about a lot of things. I thought Joe Levy and I had an understanding that he was going to leave this to me."

"Look, don't shoot the messenger. My boss told me to find you—"

"And since you were having me shadowed anyway, that wasn't so hard."

He chuckled. "Something like that."

"So what's so important?"

"There's been some reorganization within North Korea. It's late breaking, and the secretary thought you might want to know."

She listened as he explained that six government officials had been convicted of treason, then summarily executed.

"Happens all the time there," she said.

"There's more."

"What makes you so cocksure of yourself?"

He shrugged. "Those friends in high places I told you about at our first little chat."

She still wasn't intimidated. "Tell me more."

"The Dear Leader's other brother, the middle one, has been executed, along with his wife and their three grown children. Two of those children were married, so the spouses and their four children were also killed. Seems like a thorough housecleaning."

Definitely a message was being sent from brother to brother. And a fast one. Only about eighteen hours had passed since the loss of the $20 million. In that time North Korea had assessed the situation, determined the culprits, and fashioned an appropriate response. Not bad. By eliminating his middle brother and all of that brother's heirs, Dear Leader was saying to his older sibling that his remaining nieces and nephews were next. From what she could recall, all of Kim's children and grandchildren still lived in North Korea, making them easy targets.

He said, "The official reason given was 'acts of treachery regarding a business dispute.' I guess that's what they call the loss of $20 million. Wasn't it your agent who screwed that up?"

"My man did his job. At least that money won't be used to buy any nuclear components. I'd rather see it as ash."

"Can't argue there, but I bet the family of that middle brother wishes things had gone different."

She stared at the man. "Is there anything else?"

His hand slipped into a pocket and he pulled out a $20 bill. "I hear you're into hidden symbols and secret messages on money. Here's one you might not know about."

She watched as he creased the bill in half, lengthwise, then folded the left and right sides upward, the bill now shaped like a house with a gabled roof.

He pointed at his creation. "See anything?" He pointed.

"Right there," he said, "above the fold. It's the Pentagon, burning, on 9/11." He flipped the bill over. "And here are the twin towers."

He was right. Both images were strikingly poignant.

"What are the odds?" he asked her.

"Is this some Treasury Department trivia?" she asked.

"You work with money all the time, you come across things. Frankly, I think it's spooky as hell."

"You came here to show me that?'

He shook his head. "Nope. I came to see your reaction."

"To what?"

"We know where Kim is in Croatia."

She did not mask her surprise. "How could you possibly know that?"

"Are we just too stupid at Treasury to know anything? The NSA is still monitoring Kim's phone and email. We got a hit and a trace. Seems he's getting sloppy, or desperate. I guess that depends on your point of view."

"And why are you telling me?"

"It's *your* guys on the ground, so my boss wanted you to know. And we decided not to broadcast it to the world on a cell phone line."

"Tell Joe Levy I appreciate the news flash, but I don't need a babysitter."

"My boss doesn't trust you. There's a lot at stake here."

"I could have all of you arrested."

He chuckled. "But you won't. That draws a lot of attention, especially from the White House, which you don't want."

She said nothing.

"There's one other tidbit. You know the Chinese are involved, but they've also brought in the North Koreans. NSA picked that up, too. Beijing decided to curry some favor with their neighbor to the south and told them everything they know. The North Koreans are going to do the dirty work, while the Chinese sit back and watch. Gives them deniability. Thankfully, they're all dumber than dirt, but unfortunately they're also crazy as hell, so there's no telling what might happen. You got nobody here on this with you. Zero. You're flying solo. So my boss just thought you could use a little help from an old friend like me."

"And when I find whatever there is to find, you'll be there to make sure it's properly destroyed."

He shrugged. "That's entirely possible."

"Where is Kim?"

"He retreated to a Croatian luxury resort on the Virsko Sea. The

Hotel Korcula. He's in a two-bedroom suite. You want the room number?"

"What is it?"

An irritating smirk formed on his lips. "3506. Bet you thought I didn't know."

She stood. "Tell your boss I'd rather be shot by the Chinese, or the North Koreans, than have you help me. Stay off my tail."

"I'm good with that. I don't like you, anyway."

She glanced around the courtyard. The schoolchildren were moving on. She counted six more people on the other benches. Two women, four men. Nobody paid her or Chick-fil-A Man the slightest heed. Actually, she did feel a bit alone. The only two agents she trusted with anything associated with this mess were engaged in Croatia. This end was hers. And she was stymied until Cotton solved the cipher. His last scrambled text message indicated that he was close.

She walked off.

Leaving Chick-fil-A Man alone.

FORTY-NINE

CROATIA

MALONE WAS BACK IN THE AMERICAN CORNER WITH LUKE AND Howell.

"Wonder Woman going to play ball?" Luke asked.

"You know, she might actually surprise you."

"She's green as an unripe banana, Pappy."

"She's your partner on this one, so make it work. Hell, I got you last time and it was okay."

Luke seemed puzzled. "Actually, I thought that was the other way around."

Malone faced Howell. "Have you given any thought to what you and I talked about?"

"You don't have to worry about me, I can do it."

"I do worry. Kim has killed two people in the past twenty-four hours. A third would not be a problem for him."

"Let him try."

He pointed a finger. "That's what I mean. Right there. Cockiness *will* get you killed, and that's going to do none of us any good, especially you."

Howell seemed to get the message. "If it matters, I'm scared to death. But I'll get it done."

"That's what I want to hear. Fear's a good thing, in small doses. Now tell me about where you've been hiding."

Before he'd left to visit with Isabella he'd explained his plan to both Luke and Howell. What he needed was a place where his show could be staged. Howell had suggested a locale deep in Croatia.

"Solaris is a small village about two hours by rail from here, up in the mountains. Jelena was from there. I was just wandering, trying to vanish, and one day I stepped off the train. I met her and she asked me to stay."

He listened as Howell told them that there were only a few hundred residents, the town located near the eastern border between Dalmatia and Bosnia. Serbs once dominated the area, but when Croatia retook the land in the 1990s they were all expelled in ethnic cleansing.

"Lots of ruined buildings and empty places are still there," Howell said. "It's largely rebuilt, but still economically depressed. Though the Croats didn't realize it at the time, they needed those Serbs."

"Did any of them come back?" Malone said.

Howell shook his head. "Precious few."

"Bet it made a good place to hide," Luke noted.

"I thought so. Then I met Jelena and decided it was a great place to hide."

Howell sounded upbeat for a moment.

"You're going to have to string Kim along and keep him dangling," Malone said. "Use the truth. Less thinking on your part that way. Lies can be tough to keep straight under stress. He'll want to hear the story, so tell him bits and pieces, but never the whole thing."

"Isn't that risky?" Luke asked. "He knows too much already."

He shook his head. "He's not going anywhere. We just need him rocked to sleep until that train stops in Solaris. I'll be there, waiting." To Howell, he said, "Luke and Isabella are your backup. We have the upper hand since Kim doesn't know they exist. But watch out for the daughter. She's the wild card. We know nothing about her, except that she likes to stick people with needles."

If this played out right, he should be able to corner Kim in a remote Croatian village, a hundred-plus miles inland, with nowhere to go. International communications would exist, but be spotty at best. And how many Koreans could be there? His places to hide would be few, his escape options limited. All in all, an excellent trap.

"One thing," he said to Howell. "You cannot ever let him think that you know Jelena is gone. At that point your value to him becomes zero. He will kill you."

"I get it. I know how to play this game. You forget I've been on the run for three years."

"What about the Chinese?" Luke asked.

"Still an unknown, but Stephanie is working on finding out, as we speak, if they're really here."

Luke nodded. "In this part of the world, they use a lot of freelancers. So you never know from where they'll strike."

"That doesn't sound good," Howell said.

"It's not good," Malone said. "The Chinese and North Koreans want what Kim has, and they'll kill any of us to get it."

"We won't let that happen," a new voice said.

He turned and saw Isabella.

"That's the main thing you and Luke have to be worried about," Malone made clear. "Let Howell handle Kim. You two make sure that any strangers stay out of this. If trouble is coming, it will be with you."

The envoy from the embassy rounded the corridor and reentered the American Corner. Malone had sent him on an errand, which apparently had been accomplished. The man in the bow tie now carried a leather briefcase.

"You got 'em," Malone asked.

The envoy laid the case on one of the tables and opened it, removing two semiautomatic pistols. Malone took one, then handed the other to Luke. The envoy reached back inside and produced a third.

"That one's yours," he said to Isabella.

She palmed the weapon.

The envoy gave them each a spare magazine.

"What are you going to do with Kim, once you have him?" Howell asked.

That was a good question, one he and Stephanie had yet to answer. He could guess what she'd like to happen. There was no way they could allow a prosecution. That would be way too much of a public forum. Hiding him away was both impractical and ineffective. No. Dying was what she'd want. Just like a month ago in Utah, with another fanatic.

That had turned out okay for Stephanie, not so much for himself. In the process, he'd lost someone he cared a great deal about.

But that was then, and this was now.

He motioned to Howell. "Send the email to Kim."

KIM HAD RE-DONNED HIS CLOTHES, WHICH THE HOTEL HAD cleaned and pressed. Hana's had likewise been rejuvenated. She'd already dressed and was downstairs checking out their options for leaving. His watch read 6:40 P.M. This day had turned out to be quite eventful. He was still disturbed by the news report of the six executions, made even worse by a second report on the slaughter of his other half brother's entire family, which also gained worldwide press attention. Not that he harbored any special feelings toward any of them. They were essentially strangers. But the message being sent his way came loud and clear.

Dear Leader was angry.

The fate of his own children and grandchildren weighed heavy. If any doubt existed about whether they could become targets, it had been erased by what he'd read today in news accounts. Some observers had postulated that the entire execution story was false, fabricated by journalists with a bias against North Korea. That happened quite often, actually. Just another repercussion of a society having totally closed itself off from the world. But he knew with certainty that his half brother's family was gone. That was the way of the Kims. Nothing would interfere with their grasp of power. His younger half brother surely knew about the lost $20 million. And though he hadn't been responsible for that fortuitous occurrence, he would definitely shoulder the blame. No way existed for him to protect his children or grandchildren but, to be honest, he had no desire to do that. They'd all abandoned him when he was replaced, their loyalty quickly transferred to their half uncle. Time for them to see the error of their ways. Kill them all, for what he cared.

The laptop dinged.

He'd been waiting nearly half an hour for an answer to his question. *How do you suggest we accomplish all this?*

Take the 7:40 p.m. train east from Zadar to Knin. I'll be on it. Have Jelena with you. What you want is located in Solaris. We'll talk on the ride.

He hit REPLY and said he would be there.

The door opened and Hana reentered the suite.

"Two men are lurking downstairs," she said. "They're here for us."

Another chill frosted his spine.

The battle had just drawn closer.

Thankfully, Hana was here. He'd learned to trust her. Fourteen years in a labor camp had honed both her suspicions and her survival instincts. The storm was gone, though the day remained dreary. Nightfall was not far away, and they had less than an hour to make the train.

He stared at her and said, "We must leave."

FIFTY

HANA LIKED THE FACT THAT HER FATHER DEPENDED ON HER. In that he was different from her mother. The camp forced both isolation and independence. No one could really care for anyone else. Sun Hi's death proved that reality. Her mother had repeatedly given herself to the guards, thinking they would take care of her. But she'd been wrong. No mercy had ever been thrown her way. Guards cared nothing for prisoners. They were mere pieces of property to do with as they pleased.

By the time her father found her she was working in the factory every day. Her body had developed enough to attract the guards' attention, and it would have been only a matter of time before one of them had taken her. But she'd already decided that whoever that might be would pay a heavy price. Unlike her mother, she would kill or maim him and take whatever punishment came, which would have surely been death.

But she'd been spared that ordeal.

Once identified as a Kim she'd been treated for the first time as a person. The fear on the guards' faces that day when her father claimed her had been pleasing. Watching Teacher die had satisfied her even more. It had taken nearly an hour, but he finally succumbed. Afterward, she asked that he be cut down and left to lie on the filthy floor until the day ended.

Just like Sun Hi.

"You have a cold heart," her father said to her.

"I have no heart."

He gently laid a hand on her shoulder. She hated being touched, but knew better than to repel the gesture.

"Your time here is over," he said. "Life will be different."

But she knew that was not true. Though she may be leaving the camp, the camp would never leave her.

She was a product of its evil.

As impossible to change as the camp rules.

She left the hotel suite for a second time and headed back down to the lobby. Her father had listened carefully as she explained what she wanted him to do. He'd assured her that he would follow her directions. She was reasonably certain that the two men she'd spotted had no idea of her identity. They hadn't seen her earlier, of that she was sure, and she told herself to make sure that they did not see her now.

The Hotel Korcula was a renovated mammoth with walls of swirling marble, gilded details, and wood-paneled elevators. She'd explored its upscale restaurant and surveyed what was described as the Emerald Ballroom. The lobby was spacious, dominated by three large aquariums full of colorful fish and swaying plants. She stepped off the elevator and avoided the main reception area, turning right and walking down a short corridor to where the restrooms were located. She entered the ladies' room and saw that the space was empty. The bathroom facilities were as upscale and elegant as the rest of the hotel. Three marble sinks lined the stone counter before a long mirror. She stood before one of the sinks, washed away her anxiety with some cold water, and waited.

KIM HAD CHECKED. THE TRAIN EAST FROM ZADAR TO KNIN WAS an evening express with only four stops. Two just outside Zadar, and the next to last in Solaris, about twenty miles from the end of the line in Knin. The trip should take less than two hours. He had no choice but to go. He needed to understand everything and Howell was the fastest way to accomplish that goal. He was carrying the black satchel and their travel bag. He was trusting Hana to make their escape possible, though he was still concerned about who had been able to locate him so fast. It had to be his half brother. Who else? And the fact that he'd been found only added to the sense of urgency. Before he could formulate the final stages of his miraculous comeback, he had to secure whatever there was to find and learn whatever there was to know. To accomplish that, he had to outsmart his opponent.

He rode the elevator down, stepped off on the ground floor, and turned left. He entered the lobby and marched past the aquariums, his eyes noticing the two men Hana had described. Both were clean-shaven Europeans, dark-haired, dressed in long coats. Neither concealed their interest in him, immediately stepping his way.

He stopped, made a parade-ground turn, and walked back down the short corridor to the elevators, turning right as Hana had instructed. No need to glance back. He knew they were coming. Double doors for what was labeled THE EMERALD BALLROOM were visible ahead and he kept his course straight for them.

"Stop," a male voice said behind him in English.

He kept walking.

"I told you to stop," the voice said again.

He entered the ballroom, a cavernous, carpeted hall with a towering ceiling decorated by whirls of plaster. No one was inside, the chairs surrounding the bare tables empty, the only light coming from a few incandescent fixtures that kept the place from becoming a cave. Hana had described the interior perfectly. He heard the double doors open, then close behind him.

"Halt," the voice said.

He stopped and turned.

The two Coats blocked his way out.

They stepped closer.

One of them produced a gun and said, "We'll take that black satchel."

"I do wonder, did Pyongyang send you?"

Before either man could reply, both shrieked in agony and lurched forward, arms reaching back over their shoulders. One of the men turned, but never made it all the way. Both collapsed to the carpet, revealing Hana standing behind them, each hand gripping a syringe, thumb on the plunger. She'd waited in the restroom down the hall until he'd lured the men here, carefully making her way inside and taking them down with the same sedative used on Larks and Malone.

Unlike his other children, who'd become traitors, this one was a joy to behold.

HANA TOSSED THE SYRINGES AWAY AND IMMEDIATELY SEARCHED both men, finding their guns and wallets. Both weapons were equipped with sound suppressors. Apparently they'd come prepared. They were identified as Austrians, nothing on them pointing to whom they may be working for. She pocketed the wallets. The less the authorities knew about these men the better. She handed one of the guns to her father and kept the other. She accepted the travel bag from her father, slipping the strap over her shoulder. He kept the satchel.

"We'll need a taxi out front," he said. "Keep the gun hidden."

She concealed the weapon behind the travel bag. Her father did the same utilizing the satchel. They left the ballroom and headed back toward the lobby. Just as they made their way across its center, two more men appeared from her left. An additional problem materialized near the exit doors. The first two shifted positions and rounded one of the aquariums, intent on cutting them off from any retreat toward the elevators.

She whirled and revealed the gun, firing.

Not at them.

But into the aquarium's glass front.

A wall of water erupted outward, washing over both men, splashing to the marble. Both men lost their balance and slipped to the floor among the fish and plants. Chaos erupted from the twenty or so other people scattered about. They took advantage of the commotion and darted for the exit. The other man near the doors drew a weapon. She was about to take him down with a shot to his thigh when her father fired two suppressed rounds into the chest.

The man collapsed to the floor.

"Hurry, my dear," he said.

She kept moving through the exit doors, past the body, and out to an exterior walk among a wall of plants that led to a ground-transportation arrival area. Never losing a step they came to the drive and waved for one of the waiting taxis.

The vehicle motored up and they hopped into the rear seat.

"The train station," her father said.

FIFTY-ONE

MALONE SETTLED DOWN IN THE PASSENGER SEAT OF THE MERCEDES coupe, the embassy envoy driving. The trip from Zadar to Solaris would take a little over an hour. Along the way the train had stops to make and would not leave for another twenty minutes, so the head start and the straight shot by highway should vault him ahead of Luke and Isabella.

He planned to use the time in the car wisely, trying to see if he could decipher the rows of numbers. Stephanie had told him about George Mason during their two calls, secure-texting him a few minutes ago and advising him about Mellon's philanthropy toward Mason's family home, which showed even more of a connection.

He knew his American history and was familiar with George Mason, one of the unsung Founding Fathers. The Virginian had believed in a weak federal government and strong states' rights. And though he helped mold its language, he refused to sign the Constitution, arguing that it did not adequately protect the individual. His arguments eventually led to the Bill of Rights. And when James Madison drafted those proposed amendments, he drew heavily on an earlier document—the Virginia Declaration of Rights—adopted in 1776, written by George Mason.

The similarities between the two were remarkable. Both, in nearly identical language, confirmed the freedom of press and religion, the right to confront an accuser, the ability to call witnesses and have a speedy trial before a jury. Cruel and unusual punishments were forbidden, as were baseless searches and seizures and the deprivation of due process. Even the Second Amendment's right to keep and bear arms found its roots in the Virginia Declaration. Madison had actually helped Mason draft those earlier articles so, in 1789, he incorporated Mason's final thoughts into his proposed Bill of Rights. Jefferson, too, had drawn on them when crafting the Declaration of Independence. Stephanie had told him that Andrew Mellon used the term *tyrannical aristocrat* when speaking to Roosevelt. If Isabella's suspicions were correct, the four rows of numbers he now held could be something similar to the Beale cipher. The five letters from the dollar bill formed the word *Mason*. The Beale cipher had apparently utilized the Declaration of Independence as its key. So maybe Mellon had used another document, one that provided protection from *tyrannical aristocrats*. One connected to someone named Mason. Malone had printed out a copy of the Virginia Declaration of Rights to test his hypothesis. It was a long shot, but a calculated one. If this path proved unproductive, once the business in Solaris was over, he'd try something else. But this seemed as good a place as any to start.

"It must be exciting to travel about and deal with all this intrigue and danger," the envoy said.

They were headed out of Zadar on what appeared to be a freshly paved two-laned highway, its smooth surface unblemished, the thick road lines visible in the headlights freshly painted. The time was approaching 8:00 P.M., the sun gone to the west.

"It's not what you think," he said.

And it wasn't.

Having your life in jeopardy every second may be a rush for some, but not for him. He liked the task, the mission, the results. Years ago, when he shifted from the navy to the Justice Department he'd wondered if that move was the right one. He quickly discovered that it was. He had a talent for thinking on his feet and getting things done. Not always according to plan or without some collateral damage, but he could deliver results. Now he was back in the saddle. An agent, in charge of an operation, one that could have dire consequences if he screwed up.

"I've been stationed all over," the envoy said. "Germany, Bulgaria, Spain. Now here in Croatia. I love the challenges."

He needed this man to shut up, but the gentleman inside him refused to say so point-blank. Luckily, when he didn't comment on the career observation, the man returned his attention to the road.

After Luke, Isabella, and Howell had left for the train station, he'd read more about the Beale cipher. The tale spoke of how a treasure was buried in 1820 by a man named Thomas Jefferson Beale. The secret location was somewhere in Bedford County, Virginia. Supposedly Beale entrusted a box containing three encrypted messages to a local innkeeper, then disappeared, never to be seen again. Before dying, the innkeeper gave the three encrypted ciphers to a friend. The friend spent the next twenty years trying to decode the messages, able only to solve one. That friend published all three ciphers and his solution to the one in an 1885 pamphlet. Interestingly, the original messages from the box were ultimately destroyed in a fire, so only the pamphlet remained.

He'd downloaded that pamphlet to his phone and read about the Declaration of Independence as the key for one of the ciphers. How that discovery had been made was never adequately explained. Which led him to believe that, at least with the Beale cipher, perhaps the solution may have come before the cipher. Which was not the case here.

As Isabella had noted, the first number of the Beale cipher, as shown in the pamphlet, was 115. The 115th word of the Declaration of Independence was *instituted*. So the first letter of that word, *i*, became the first letter of the decoding. The idea would be to repeat that process with each number, garnering a new letter each time. He agreed with Stephanie's assessment that Mellon had wanted FDR to solve the code, so he would not have made it overly difficult. And from everything he'd read, the Beale cipher would have been a known commodity in Mellon's time. Also, something else Stephanie had said made the connection more plausible. She'd learned that Mellon was buried in Upperville, Virginia, at the Trinity Episcopal Church. An interesting fact considering Mellon's connections were all to Pennsylvania.

What had Mellon told FDR?

"I'll be waiting for you."

He'd brought a pen, along with the hard copies of Mellon's cipher and the Virginia Declaration of Rights. It would take a few minutes, but he had to number every word.

So he started at the top.

1   2   3 4   5 6 7   8   9 10

A Declaration of Rights made by the representatives of the

11   12   13 14   15   16 17 18 19

good people of Virginia, assembled in full and free

20   21   22 23 24 25 26 27 28

convention which rights do pertain to them and their

29   30 31 32 33   34   35   36

posterity, as the basis and foundation of government.

37   38 39 40 41 42 43 44   45   46 47

Section 1. That all men are by nature equally free and

48   49 ,50   51   52   53 54 55

independent and have certain inherent rights, of which,

56   57   58 59 60 61 62 63   64   65   66

when they enter into a state of society, they cannot, by

67   68

any compact,

It took another twenty minutes before he came to the final word and wrote the number 901 above *other*. His driver had stayed quiet, seemingly realizing he needed to concentrate.

He studied Mellon's cipher again.

869, 495, 21, 745, 4, 631, 116, 589, 150, 382, 688,
900, 238, 78, 560, 139, 694, 3, 22, 249, 415, 53, 740,
16, 217, 5, 638, 208, 39, 766, 303, 626, 318, 480, 93,
717, 799, 444, 7, 601, 542, 833

The first number was 869. He searched for the word that corresponded to that number and found it. *Equally.* He noticed that other words also began with *e*. A quick scan showed more than twenty.

He wrote an *e* on the page.

He was assuming that, like the Beale cipher, the numbers corresponded to the first letters on the key, but it could be the opposite and refer to the last. He knew that some substitution ciphers even utilized a certain position within a word—like the third letter of each—which could really complicate matters.

The next number was 495. *Demand.* There were multiple words that also began with *d,* the first appearing in the prologue with *declaration.*

He added a *d* beside the *e*.

The third number, 21, led to *which* from the prologue. He kept going until, at the sixth match he had a word.

Edward.

The odds of that being wholly coincidental were next to zero. He apparently was on to something.

"Mr. Malone," the envoy said. "I dare not disturb you, but I must pass on a message that came before we left Zadar."

They were still cruising on the highway, shrouded in darkness.

"You're just now mentioning this?" he asked.

"I wanted to earlier, but I could see you were absorbed in your work so I left you alone. After all, we have another half hour before arriving and you weren't going anywhere."

This man was more of a diplomat than he'd given him credit for.

"Ms. Stephanie Nelle, your superior, I believe, passed a message through the embassy's secured channel."

He waited as the envoy reached inside his suit jacket and removed a folded sheet of paper, which he handed over.

He read the paragraph.

The last sentence caused him the greatest concern.

They took the bait and made a move on Kim in Zadar. It failed. Kim escaped, but killed a man in the process. The Chinese and/or the North Koreans are definitely there.

That gave him pause.

And he hoped Luke and Isabella could handle things.

FIFTY-TWO

HANA STARED OUT INTO THE NIGHT THROUGH THE WINDOW. THE cold darkness beyond seemed threatening. Night and day in the camp had always been the same, neither offering any respite from suffering. The train churned along on a bumpy ride through the Croatian countryside, nothing but black beyond the glass. She and her father were inside a first-class compartment that accommodated four seats, two on each side facing the other, the door shut but unlocked.

"Why kill the man at the hotel?" she asked him.

They hadn't said a word since fleeing Zadar.

"It was necessary. We can't have any interference. Not now."

She'd been told all of her life that killing was *necessary*. Either to enforce camp rules, to prevent escapes, or to free a prisoner from generational bondage. *Death is liberating*. That's what Teacher had told them every day. If that was true, she hoped Teacher was enjoying his freedom.

Her father seemed wholly comfortable with killing whomever he pleased. Three had died over the last twenty-four hours.

"I learned earlier," he said, "that our Dear Leader killed my other half brother and all of his family. Your uncle and cousins. He did that to show me that he could."

She wanted to say, *Just like you,* but knew better.

"We have to stay vigilant," he said. "And never can we be weak."

"What of your other children?"

She wanted to know what he thought.

He shrugged. "There is nothing I can do for them, and I doubt they would want me to. None of them stayed loyal, except you."

Because she'd had no choice. She was barely ten when her father was disgraced, still unaccustomed to the world beyond the fences. So when he chose to leave the country, she'd had no choice but to follow. True, as she grew older she could have left, but she had no desire to return to North Korea. She hated anything and everything associated with that place. Only once had she gone back, on a personal errand her father arranged, there for only a day. It happened ten years after she'd fled the camp. She was nineteen, fully recovered from years of malnutrition, and had wanted to see her mother. Her father secured permission and she'd reentered the camp that day inside a limousine, the superintendent there to personally greet her. Neither of them spoke of the past. She was taken directly to her mother, who was now working in the pottery factory, her days in the fields obviously over.

Her mother appeared weaker than she recalled, still wearing the same filthy sack-like clothes that stank of sweat, slime, and blood. And while her own hair had grown long and thick and her body had blossomed—the gaunt hollowness and pale skin no longer there—her mother had shrunk further. Most of the teeth were gone, the eyes sunk deep from lack of food, a prelude she knew to more serious problems.

"I thought you were dead," her mother said. *"I was told nothing. So I assumed you were gone."* The words were delivered with the flat lack of emotion she so vividly recalled.

"My father came for me."

A look of surprise appeared on the tired face, which was exactly what she'd come to see.

"And he did not save me?"

"Why would he?"

And she meant it.

She still wanted an answer to the question she'd asked so many times. *Why was I a prisoner?* Her father had told her about the love affair and how his father had disapproved, her mother sent to the camp, no one at the time knowing she was pregnant.

"Because he loved me," her mother said with a sadness in her voice. *"I was a great beauty, full of life and excitement."* Then a coldness returned to her eyes. *"I never told you why we were here, because I never wanted you to know of him."*

A curious answer, which compelled her to ask, "Why would you do that?"

"He sent me here."

"That's a lie." The swiftness of her rebuttal surprised her.

"What did he tell you? That his father sent me here?" Her mother laughed. "You're so foolish. You were always foolish. He sent me here. He wanted me gone. He enjoyed what he wanted from me then, when he tired of me, I was sent here to disappear."

She'd never believed much of what this woman said. The camp forced prisoners to remain enemies, constantly distrusting one another. But the angry look in the sad eyes that stared back—which for the first time she could recall seemed to convey true pain— said her mother was telling the truth.

"He is a ruthless man. Never forget that. Don't be fooled. He is as what came before him. You stand here in your fine clothes, your belly full, smug in your freedom. But you are not free. He is Kim. They have no loyalty beyond themselves."

Her mother spit in her face.

"And you are Kim."

Those were the last words they ever spoke. Since no semblance of anything resembling love had ever passed between them, she hadn't given the woman another thought. She learned a year later that her mother was dead, caught trying to escape. How many times had she witnessed such *teachable moments,* as the guards described executions.

She could easily imagine her mother's fate.

A wooden pole would be pounded into the hard earth. Prisoners would assemble, the only time more than two were allowed to gather. One of the guards would shout at how the ungrateful bitch had been offered redemption through hard work, yet rejected the generosity shown. To prevent any rebuttal, her mother's mouth would have been stuffed full of pebbles, her head sheathed with a hood. Then she would be tied to the pole, shot, her body heaved into a cart for disposal in one of the mass graves, the occupants' identities as meaningless in death as in life.

But she'd never forgotten what her mother told her that final day.

He sent me here.

She watched her father as he read more of the documents from the black satchel. Who were those men at the hotel? Why had they come? They had to be from Pyongyang. Who else would care? The Americans? Possibly. She was sure no one had followed them from the hotel and they'd made it onto the train with no incidents. But something told her they were not alone. There was danger here.

"I'm going to check the train," she said.

Her father glanced up from his reading. "I think that is an excellent idea."

Before she could rise the door to the compartment slid open and she saw a man. Mid-thirties, sparse hair, slight build. She knew the face.

Anan Wayne Howell.

"Where is Jelena?" Howell asked.

"Nearby," her father said. "Once we have our chat, you may have her."

But she knew that was a lie. Howell would most likely end up dead, too. How many more would die? Fifty? A hundred? Ten thousand? Millions? The fact that she could not say with any certainty was proof enough that her father was indeed Kim.

"Sit down," he said to Howell. "My daughter was just leaving."

She rose and stepped out into the narrow corridor. Howell allowed her to pass, then entered the compartment.

She slid the door closed.

It seemed that with every word she became more distant. Her father lied with such ease. Nothing about his tone or countenance changed, whether his words be truth or fiction.

So nothing he said could be believed.

Even more proof that he was Kim.

Isabella had followed Howell through the train. He was searching. She watched through the window in the far exit door, which offered a view into the next car, as Howell apparently found what he sought, disappearing into one of the first-class compartments.

A young woman appeared in the hallway.

Hana Sung.

That meant Kim was there.

She quickly claimed a seat across from a woman with two small children, who tossed her a faint smile. She returned the gesture and heard the door at the far end of the car open, then close. She was sitting facing away in a four-seat configuration. She waited until Hana Sung passed, heading for the exit that led toward the cars at the rear of the train. Sung should have no idea of her identity. On the cruise they'd both kept their distance from Larks and a variety of wigs had changed Isabella's appearance by the day.

So far, so good.

Howell was in place and Kim's eyes and ears were on the move, temporarily blind and deaf.

Advantage to the good guys.

FIFTY-THREE

KIM FACED THE AMERICAN.

"I'm not telling you a thing until I see Jelena," Howell said, the voice sharp and raw.

"I'm not sure how you believe yourself to be in a position to demand anything. We will talk. Then, once I have what I need, you will have your lady."

He could see that Howell wasn't happy, but that the younger man realized he had no choice. "What do you want to know?"

He motioned with the original crumpled page. "What are these numbers?"

"They're a substitution code Andrew Mellon created."

"Have you solved it?"

Howell shook his head. "I didn't, but Cotton Malone did. He told me so on the ferry."

"And why would he do that?"

"Because he wanted to know if he was right?"

"Was he?"

"Dead on. His solution makes perfect sense." Howell paused. "I want to know what you're going to do with all of this."

"I plan to end the income tax."

"Which will end America."

He shrugged. "The seeds for that destruction were laid in 1913 when the amendment was falsely certified as legal. You were convicted because of that wrongful act. I only want to right that wrong."

"It will still destroy the country."

He was perplexed by the comment. "Which you didn't seem to mind when you published your book and told the world about your theory. Now it's somehow my fault that you proved to be right? You are the one who started all this."

"I was fighting for survival."

"As am I."

"What will you do? Funnel whatever there is to some anti-tax organization and to the cable news networks? That should generate enough buzz that it can't be swept under the rug."

He grinned. "Fortunately, America is full of people who want to adopt a cause. I shall simply hand them one. I'm sure there will be plenty of members of your Congress who will want to champion the issue. The lawsuits will be numerous and endless."

"Income tax is over ninety percent of federal revenues. If it's voided, then the United States goes bankrupt. You do realize the effect that will have across the globe."

"Catastrophic, I assume. But living in a closed society, such as North Korea, will then become an advantage. We are not dependent on the world for much of anything. And we're certainly not dependent on the United States. So its fall will have little consequence for us. Isolation will become our greatest asset."

"What about China?"

He shrugged. "It will hurt, but they'll adapt. One thing is certain. They will have a newfound respect for North Korea, and its new leader. They will not ignore or ridicule me. If you like, I can extend citizenship and you can live there, too."

"Like you're going to allow me to hang around and claim some of the credit."

"That's where you are wrong. I would not mind that at all. You conceived the idea, but I perfected it. And should you not resent your government? It lied to you and to millions of its citizens, demanding tax money that was legally not its to take. You were even sentenced to prison.

America loves to proclaim itself a land of laws. It denounces governments across the world who ignore the rule of law. We shall see how accepting America is when those laws are turned against itself."

He was enjoying this moment of triumph. The last decade had been one failure after another. Only in the past few months had things begun to turn around. Now he seemed on the threshold of greatness. But he forced his mind from the grand scheme and onto a more immediate problem.

He motioned with the crumpled sheet.

"What does this mean?"

HANA MADE HER WAY THROUGH EACH OF THE PASSENGER CARS, moving from first class back to standard, surveying the passengers. There weren't all that many, the train perhaps a quarter full. The gun she'd removed from the man at the hotel rested against her spine, beneath her jacket. No security checks had been required to board the train, for which she'd been grateful. Two years ago her father had insisted she take shooting lessons. The world was a tough place, he'd said, and she should be able to protect herself. She hadn't argued since feelings of security were always welcomed. The entire purpose of the camps had been to strip prisoners of all self-respect and keep them in a constant state of panic. It was a form of control she'd come to both recognize and deplore. She was a person. An individual. Her name was not *bitch*. She was as unique as each grain of sand on the beach.

And her mother's sins were not hers.

So far her recon had raised no alerts.

The train slowed.

They were coming to the first station.

She made her way to one of the exits between the cars. A few of the other passengers rose and headed that way, too. Apparently, this was the end of the ride for them.

The train stopped inside a lit building.

People moved on and off.

She stepped down to the platform and studied both directions, checking to see who was coming on. Two cars away she spotted a man about to board. Young, dark hair, Korean face. He carried nothing, his hands jutted inside coat pockets. He tossed her a stare that contained a look of triumph, seemingly unconcerned about being inconspicuous. He wanted her to know he was there, daring her to do something about it.

A bell rang signaling the stop was over.

She stepped back onto the train.

ISABELLA HAD BEEN ABLE TO EASE BACK A FEW CARS, KEEPING PACE with Sung. When her target stepped down to the station's platform, she'd watched out the window and spotted an Asian man hopping onto the train. A glance ahead and the same man now headed straight into her car and assumed a seat, his hands remaining inside his coat pockets.

This was trouble.

Hana Sung had thought so, too.

She'd caught the instant of apprehension on the young girl's face.

The bell rang, signaling they were leaving. She rose and headed back toward the rear cars where Luke Daniels was waiting. She found him engrossed in a conversation with an older man. When he saw her, he excused himself and came a few seats up to where she'd sat.

"A new friend?" she asked in whisper.

"I thought it would help blend me in. Getting down with the locals."

"Howell is with Kim. Sung is on the move. And we've got company."

She described the potential threat waiting three cars ahead.

"He's the bird dog," Luke said. "Here to get the scent and flush the fox forward. The hunters are waitin' ahead."

"There's one more stop before Solaris," she said.

"And our job is to get there in one piece. But there's no tellin' what the other side has in mind."

She had to admit, this was way more exciting than a tax cheat. But she also realized she was a little scared. Contrary to what she'd boasted, this was her first street fight without gloves.

"All kiddin' aside," he said, his voice low, "keep sharp. Don't get yourself hurt. Okay?"

"I will, if you will."

He smiled and pointed a finger at her. "There's that charm again. I could grow to like that."

Back in Zadar she'd chastised his recklessness but, truth be told, she was now comforted knowing that Luke Daniels knew how to handle himself. What was about to happen was anybody's guess. The not knowing was the worst part. But she was confident that they could handle things.

The train started to move, leaving the station, gathering speed.

"What now?" she asked.

"We give Howell the time he needs."

FIFTY-FOUR

MALONE KEPT WORKING ON THE CIPHER.

He'd switched on one of the car's interior lights and used its amber glow to illuminate the pages before him. The envoy from the embassy had informed him a few minutes ago that they were approaching Solaris. That meant the train was not far behind. He wished he could have been aboard himself, but realized that was impossible. Luke could handle it. So could Isabella. It was Howell that worried him. He'd warned the younger man about keeping his emotions in check, but understood the pain of losing someone you cared about. Though Cassiopeia had not died in a literal sense, she was still gone. And the anxiety that came from such a loss definitely clouded judgment. He was a pro, yet it still affected him. He could only imagine what it was doing to Howell. But he'd had no choice in the matter. Kim only wanted Howell. Hopefully Luke and Isabella would catch a break and have things under control *before* any outsiders managed to get involved.

He'd been slowly matching the 42 numbers from Mellon's cipher with the corresponding words in the Virginia Declaration of Rights. Thankfully, he'd guessed right and found the key. After matching the last number in the cipher he read the finished message.

Edward Savage Eleanor Custis
Martha Washington 16

He didn't have time to ascertain its meaning, which should be easy to determine given the Internet and search engines. He wanted to know what was happening on that train. But he had to stick to the plan, so he asked the envoy, "Exactly how far away are we?"

"Less than ten minutes. The train should arrive at 9:50."

Which gave him a solid fifteen minutes of lead time. "Head straight for the station. It shouldn't be hard to find."

"I checked before we left and know precisely where it is located."

He folded the page with Andrew Mellon's decoded message and handed it to the envoy. "After you drop me off, find a landline and have the embassy transmit what I decoded to the Magellan Billet, through a secure channel. No cell phones on this one."

The envoy nodded his understanding.

"I don't want to spook anybody who might be waiting, so drop me a mile or so from the station and I'll walk in."

He checked his iPhone and saw that there was service.

Perfect.

Stick to the plan.

He dialed the number.

STEPHANIE WAS OUTSIDE, ON THE MALL, IN THE SUNSHINE, HAVING fled the confines of the National Gallery. She'd taken half an hour and eaten something in the museum's café, located belowground in a connector that bisected the street above. Chick-fil-A Man had disappeared and no one had followed her to the café or out. She was stalling for time, waiting for a reply to the message she'd sent Cotton through the State Department. Last she heard he was on his way to the Croatian interior, a town called Solaris. Everything depended on things playing out exactly as they'd anticipated. Thank God it was Cotton on the other end. He was the one person she could always depend on. He'd never let her down.

The White House had called twice and she'd dodged both attempts. She realized that could only be done for so long, as the president of the United States was tough to ignore.

Her phone rang.

She was walking among the grass and bare trees just before the Smithsonian's Museum of Natural History. The Capitol anchored the far end of the Mall behind her, the Washington Monument rising ahead. People milled back and forth in the afternoon sun, the air typically crisp for November in DC.

"I solved it," Cotton said.

"Where are you?"

"Just about to enter Solaris and meet the train."

"Tell me the message Mellon left for Roosevelt."

"It's a strange one. I'll text it to you now."

She waited a moment until her phone signaled receipt, then she read. "That is strange."

"You can figure it out on your end. It shouldn't be hard."

"The secretary of Treasury is having me followed. Stupid me actually thought we were on the same side."

"What do you intend to do?"

Bells in the distance chimed for 3:30 P.M.

She said, "I'm going to find what Mellon left and destroy it."

HANA STAYED ONE CAR AHEAD OF THE KOREAN WHO'D ENTERED at the first stop, keeping a careful watch from afar. The train was slowing for its second stop, then it would be less than half an hour to Solaris. She assumed her father and Howell were still inside the first-class compartment. The man she was watching had yet to survey any of the other cars.

What should she do?

They were trapped, and he knew it.

For years she'd been thinking about her life, and over the past few days its future course had become clear. The Americans. The men

at the hotel. The one here on the train. She resented all of their interference. What would happen here would be *her* choice and *hers* alone.
So she decided to take the offensive. One man would be easy to contain.

The train stopped in another lit station.

People came and went, just like last time. Through the glass, into the
next car, she saw three more Koreans enter and join the first man.

Four?

That could be a problem.

But the gun nestled at her spine reassured her.

ISABELLA SAT AS LUKE DANIELS HEADED FORWARD THROUGH THE
cars, surveying who was coming and going on the final stop. She took a
moment and checked her phone, discovering there was no service. Unlike trains at home this one did not come with any WiFi.

They were, literally, on their own.

Treasury agents were not schooled for this type of operation. But
that didn't mean she couldn't handle herself. Daniels' concern for her
safety seemed genuine. For the first time his cocky façade had dropped
and the man beneath had peeked through. She told herself to cut both
him and Malone more slack. They were trusting her with their lives,
each of them now dependent on the other. Three against whatever was
thrown their way, and she was determined to do her part.

The bell rang, signaling another station gone.

She glanced around the seat and saw Luke returning.

The train began to move.

He sat beside her.

"We've got four problems three cars ahead. Hana Sung is a car behind them. She has to know they're there. This is about to get ugly."

"You got any ideas?"

"Pappy taught me the direct approach is most times the best. So I
think we need to take these guys out."

She was ready to play with the team.

"I'm listening."

MALONE WATCHED THROUGH THE WINDSHIELD AS THE CAR approached Solaris, the road passing through a rough defile between sharp, precipitous rocks. Dalmatia itself formed the southern part of Croatia, the coastal region a narrow strip about three hundred miles long. Shakespeare called it Illyria. Its fjords and islands had once been the haunts of pirates. Greece, Rome, Byzantium, the Turks, Venice, Russia, Napoleon, and the Hapsburgs had all left their mark. So had the 1990s civil war when thousands died. Many thousands more were slaughtered in ethnic cleansing, when Yugoslavia disintegrated into a snake pit of rivalries. Here, at the country's extreme eastern boundary, had been ground zero.

Solaris sat on a hilltop amid a dense forest, its narrow paved streets crawling upward toward a brightly lit, twin-towered cathedral. A milky fog had formed and shrouded everything in a spooky mist. They'd driven in through one of the old city gates, a remnant from when thick walls had offered safety, a Venetian lion standing guard. Inside, he noticed lots of gray stone buildings, most in various stages of decay or renovation, signaling that Solaris just another workaday provincial town. Few people were in sight. Every shop was closed. They seemed to have chosen the right stage.

"The train station is about half a kilometer ahead," the envoy said.

"Then let me out here."

The car came to a stop.

He opened the door and cold, wet air invaded the cabin's warmth. "Once you're away from here, send that message I gave you."

"It shall be done. Not to worry."

"And hold on to these papers. Back at the embassy, scan and then send them electronically to the Magellan Billet. Keep the originals locked away."

The envoy nodded his understanding.

He stepped out to the street and nestled the gun between his belt and spine, beneath a leather jacket.

"You take care, Mr. Malone," the envoy said.

He shut the door and watched as the car eased away. He was left among the closed shops and empty streets, the cool misty air disturbed only by a solitary church bell signaling half past nine. The cobblestones beneath his shoes were slippery with moisture. Solaris was clearly not a night place. Howell had told him there were a few cafés, but they were located farther up the hill, near the cathedral. It was doubtful any were open this late. The train station sat close to the city walls, where the tracks pierced a break and skirted the highlands on their way east to the border and Bosnia, about fifty miles away.

Here he was again.

In the line of fire.

FIFTY-FIVE

KIM CHECKED HIS WATCH AND REALIZED THEY WERE GETTING close to the train's third stop at Solaris. So he asked, "Why are we going to this town?"

"All of my work is there. You'll need to see it. This is more complicated than you realize."

Howell still had not told him what he wanted to know, so he pointed again to the crumpled sheet. "What does this code say?"

"When I see Jelena, then you'll know. Not until. I assure you, there's no way you'll ever figure it out alone."

Unfortunately, that statement seemed accurate. And he assumed without the solution his quest would end so he decided to humor this American until they made it to Solaris.

"Where is Jelena?" Howell asked.

"I had her transported by car. She'll be there. My employees are wait-ing for a call—after you produce what I want."

"Do you have any idea the chaos you're about to cause?" Howell asked. "Isolated or not, North Korea will feel the impact of an American collapse."

But he truly did not care. While that was happening he would be se-curing his birthright. Those generals who called him *unreliable* and *reckless* would flock his way, all eager to pledge their loyalty. His half brother would finally look the fool, unable to say or do anything to undo his ineffectiveness. His own return to Pyongyang would be triumphant. Finally, a leader who had made good and destroyed the great American evil.

He'd already considered his new title.

His grandfather was labeled Eternal, his father Great, his half brother Dear Leader.

He would be Revered.

A line from an Italian cantata was his favorite. *Di lui men grande e men chiaro il sole.* Less great and brilliant than he is the sun. It was a reference to Napoleon, but he'd adapt it to Korean and its intent would set him apart.

All he had to do was play Howell a little while longer.

HANA DECIDED THIS WAS THE MOMENT. SHE WAS TIRED OF TRYING to rid her mind of the camp, and she'd long ago given up any semblance of happiness. For her, crying or laughing or tears never came. Life presented no joy. Only the nightmares were constant. She hated to be touched, resented criticism, and lived in virtual silence. It was no matter that fourteen years had passed—she still thought of herself as an Insider, the camp her entire world. Accountability, anger, and revenge had all been learned on the outside, and those three now pointed her toward a singular path.

Time to empty the heart, shed its secrets, and expose her fears.

And though she did not regard herself as a Kim, that did not mean she could not act like one.

KIM FACED HOWELL AND SAID, "THE DESTRUCTION OF THE UNITED States is the only way to prove my point. I actually think most of the world will enjoy watching America fall. You preach to us all about your openness and democracy, yet none of that seems to matter when it comes to your own people. You keep secrets, just like we all do. There's deceit and corruption, just like everyone else experiences. This fraud is the perfect example of American hypocrisy. If your system is so precious, so special, so right, it will survive what I am about to unfold."

"You're insane."

He laughed. "I think of myself as an innovator. That's what you are, too. You just lacked the means. Luckily, I don't have that problem."

"You're a murderer."

The tone had changed. Howell's eyes flashed white-hot and he suddenly realized that this man had been lying to him.

"You killed Larks. Then you threw Jelena out to drown. You murdered her for no reason."

"So you were on the boat with Malone."

Howell nodded. "And you won't be getting off this train."

He was curious about the bravado. Did that mean the Americans were here? The black satchel lay in his lap, his right hand inside the whole time he and Howell had been talking holding the pistol obtained back at the hotel. He withdrew the weapon and aimed it straight at Howell.

"Just know that when you shoot me, your little scheme is over because you're not going to learn a thing without me. Fire away. You still won't get off this train, and your grand plans will be over."

A quandary, for sure, but not insurmountable.

The compartment door opened.

Hana had returned.

She entered, closed the panel, and said, "Four Koreans are here."

Howell sat smug. "It's easy to kill a defenseless woman and an old man. Let's see what you do with them."

He kept the gun aimed. "Mr. Howell knows that we're running a ruse here, and he seems to think his life has value to me. Fortunately for him, it actually does." His mind was racing. "Where are these four men?"

"Two cars back."

"Stay here," he said. "I'll see what can be done."

He slipped the gun back into the black satchel, but left the thick sheaf of clipped pages on his seat.

Hana found her own gun, which Howell now saw.

"Don't tempt her," he said. "She is less patient than I am."

Then he left the compartment.

MALONE WALKED THE STREETS OF SOLARIS, PASSING A JEWELRY store, rug dealer, and several closed food shops, the dark buildings all huddled close together. At an antiques store he hesitated before a picture window that displayed goblets, vases, tables, and drapes. He'd never been into antiques. He liked things to look old, but not necessarily be old.

He rounded a corner and spotted the train station at the end of a block. The building was one of the largest in town, a profusion of sculpted niches, doorways, arches, and iron grilles, its stone painted a pale pink and lit to the night. A few people came and went through its main doors. If Stephanie's intel was correct there should be a foreign field team somewhere nearby. The note he'd read in the car from her had informed him that the Chinese or North Koreans had made a move on Kim, which meant they were here.

This was clearly a two-front war.

One was happening in DC with Stephanie, the other here. What they were doing seemed akin to trying to hold five balloons underwater at the same time. Difficult. But it could be done. Actually, it had to be done.

He clung to the shadows and used the mist for cover. Lights burned on the street before the station, their glow muted by the fog. Three cars were parked at the curb, and he watched as another vehicle appeared from a side street and cruised toward the station.

His watch read 9:40.

The train would arrive in ten minutes.

The car stopped and a man emerged from the passenger side.

An Asian.

No freelancers. But after all, this was a rush job, and they surely thought that the middle of nowhere would offer them a relatively safe haven. That might be true, except that they'd been lured. His main hope was that they'd yet to figure that part out.

Luke and Isabella were covering the train.

The station was his problem.

So as the one man entered the building through the double doors, he made his way toward the car.

FIFTY-SIX

Washington, DC

Stephanie waited for the car to find the curb and Joe Levy to emerge. She'd called him from the Mall just after Cotton's overseas report and informed him that the code on the crumpled sheet of paper had been broken and she now knew the location of what Andrew Mellon had left for Roosevelt to find. The secretary of Treasury seemed excited and wanted to be there when she made the discovery, so she'd told him to meet her in front of the Smithsonian Castle.

The turreted red sandstone building was reminiscent of something from the Tudor age, which she knew had been intentional as a way to align the building more with England than Greece or Rome. Its spires and towers were iconic, more like a church than a museum, and it had stood on the southwest corner of the Mall since the mid-19th century. Unlike the National Gallery, which she rarely frequented, the castle was a familiar haunt. She was good friends with its curator, which had made it easy for her to make contact and explain what she needed to examine.

"Okay," Levy said, "I'm here. What have you found?"

"Mellon hid his prize in a clever place. Cotton deciphered the code and I now know where that is."

"Thank God. I was afraid this would become uncontrollable."

Traffic whizzed by in both directions on Independence Avenue, busy for a Tuesday afternoon.

"Shall we go and see?" she asked.

She led the way through the gardens and into the castle, her badge allowing them to bypass the metal detector and visitor security checks. Inside rose a majesty of arches and vaulted ceilings, the gray-green color scheme warm and inviting. Once the ground floor had all been exhibits, but now it housed offices, a café, and a gift shop, along with a handful of special displays. Waiting for them was a thin man with a happy face, patches of sparse gray hair dusting the sides of a smooth scalp. He stood inside the vestibule, beyond the checkpoint where visitors were having their bags examined.

She'd known him for years.

"Joe," she said, "meet Richard Stamm, the longtime curator of the Castle's collection."

The two men shook hands.

"Your phone call was quite intriguing," Stamm said. "The desk you mentioned has been here, at the castle, for a long time. It's one of our special pieces."

"Can we see it," she said.

They were led through the ground floor, away from the café, past the gift shop, and into the building's west wing. A short corridor opened to a single-story hall, it too painted in the gray-green theme. Arches lined each side. Display cases filled the gaps in between, holding what a placard announced were America souvenirs—relics, keepsakes, and curios. Beyond one of the arches, against an outer wall, stood an ornate cabinet. Visitors milled back and forth, admiring the other displays. Stamm pointed to the cabinet and told them that it had been built in the latter part of the 18th century by the great German master David Roentgen.

"It's a classic rococo writing cabinet."

It stood over ten feet tall and spread six feet wide, its façade a riot of dazzling architectural order crowned with a clock. Stamm explained that it was made of oak, pine, walnut, cherry, cedar, curly maple, burl maple, mahogany, apple, walnut, mulberry, tulipwood, and rosewood. Ivory, mother-of-pearl, gilt bronze, brass, steel, iron, and silk added both contrast and accent. Finely detailed colored marquetry panels decorated its front and sides. The cupola above the clock was topped with a gilt bronze of Apollo.

"It may well be the most expensive piece of furniture ever made," he said. "Three were created. One for Duke Charles Alexander of Lorraine,

another for King Louis XVI of France, and a third for King Frederick
William II of Prussia. This was Frederick's. That's him there in the
portrait medallion, on the central door. It's like a royal entertainment
system, full of ingenious mechanisms and hidden compartments. Most
of them open to the music of flutes, cymbals, and a glockenspiel. The
clock also has some lovely chimes. It's an amazing piece of workman-
ship."

"For the truly rich," she noted.

Stamm smiled. "Frederick paid 80,000 livers for this, which was an
enormous amount at the time."

"How long has it been here?" she asked.

"I checked to be sure, and my memory was right. Andrew Mellon
acquired it in the 1920s. He donated it to the Smithsonian in 1936, with
the proviso that it had to be displayed somewhere in the Castle at all
times."

"This desk has been here since then?" Levy asked.

Stamm nodded. "Somewhere, inside the castle. Conditions are not un-
common with gifts. If we accept the restricted donation, then we honor
the request. Sometimes we do reject a gift because of the conditions. Not
with this, though. I imagine it was simply too tempting. The curator at
the time had to have it, which I can understand."

She admired the exquisite cabinet.

"I took the information you provided on the phone and checked out
the desk," Stamm said. "You were right, there is a paper hidden inside."

"Did you read it?" Levy asked.

He shook his head. "Stephanie told me not to touch it, so I left it
alone. It's still inside."

"Joe doesn't know what I told you," she said to Stamm.

He led them closer. "I know most of the secret places in the desk. But
what you were able to decipher told me about a new one and how to open
it. That was exciting."

He removed a skeleton key from his pocket and inserted it into a slot
in the central door. Once turned, it set in motion a multitude of springs
and latches. A wooden panel slowly unfolded to create a writing surface.
Above it a lectern formed, angled to accommodate a book or a sheet of
paper. At the same time two compartments emerged on either side that

held inks, sand, and writing utensils. The whole metamorphosis was swift and smooth, done to the tune of tinkling music.

"It's like a Transformer today," Stamm said. "It appears as one thing, then becomes another. And it's all old-school technology. Levers, springs, weights, and pulleys."

He pointed out a few of the secret compartments. Small ones in nests, long slender ones with mother-of-pearl, swivel drawers concealed behind other drawers, all of them gliding open without a sound and easily slid back into place.

"There are maybe fifty or so secret spaces," Stamm said. "That was the whole idea. To have spots to hide things. I genuinely thought I knew them all."

He pointed to a section above the lectern where she saw more gilt bronzes and festoons of leaves and grapes. A Corinthian capital sat between two portraits in marquetry, a man on the left, woman on the right, each peeking out at the other from a side curtain, adding a whimsical touch. Stamm lightly gripped the small column between the images and twisted. "I would have never done this before for fear of damage. But a quick turn of the column releases a latch."

The image of the man on the left suddenly moved and the wooden panel upon which it appeared sprang open, revealing a secret compartment. Stamm gently hinged the panel out ninety degrees. She saw an envelope inside, brown with age.

"I'll be damned," Levy said.

She reached in and slid out the packet. Written on its face, in faded black ink, was

For a tyrannical aristocrat

She realized that they were standing in a public hall, though out of the main line of traffic, people moving back and forth, so she quickly slid the envelope into a coat pocket and thanked her friend.

"I need you to keep this to yourself," she said.

The curator nodded. "I get it. National security."

"Something like that."

"I don't suppose you could at least tell me who left that."

THE PATRIOT THREAT | 305

"Andrew Mellon hid it for FDR to find. But that never happened. Thank goodness we're the ones to actually discover it."

"I'll be interested to hear, one day, just what this is all about."

"And I'll let you know as soon as I can. Without going to prison."

She and Levy left the hall as Stamm went about returning the desk to its more benign self. They avoided the entrance they'd used coming in, which led back to the street, and exited the Castle toward the National Mall. She wanted a quiet place where they could read what was inside the envelope.

They followed a wide graveled path toward the museums on the far side. People moved in all directions. An empty bench ahead, beneath trees devoid of summer foliage, beckoned and they sat.

She removed the envelope from her pocket, "It's definitely from Mellon. FDR said he used these words, *tyrannical aristocrat,* when referring to him. It seemed to really piss him off."

"You realize," Levy said, "that what's inside there could change the course of this country."

"I get it. That's why we have to make sure no one else sees this but us."

She was about to open the envelope when she heard footsteps behind them. Before she could turn a voice said, "Just sit still and don't move."

She felt the distinctive press of a gun barrel at the base of her neck. The man who'd spoken stood close, another man pressed equally close to Levy, obviously trying to shield their weapons.

"We will shoot you both," the voice said. "Two bullets through your head and be gone before anyone knows the difference."

She assumed the weapons were sound-suppressed and that these men knew what they were doing. Levy seemed nervous. Who could blame him. Having a gun to your head was never good.

"You do realize that I am the secretary of Treasury," Levy tried, his voice cracking from nerves.

"You bleed like anybody else," the voice said.

To her right she caught sight of another man, walking down the graveled path, wearing a dark overcoat, dark trousers, and the same shiny Cordovan shoes that she remembered from last night.

He stopped before them.

The ambassador to the United States from China.

FIFTY-SEVEN

CROATIA

KIM LEFT THE FIRST-CLASS CAR AND PROCEEDED BACK TO WHERE Hana said the four men were waiting. He decided that the time to lead had come and fear was the last thing he would show. So far he'd acted decisively, never hesitating in ending Larks', Jelena's, and the man at the hotel's lives. No one would be allowed to stand in his way, and that included the four Koreans he saw sitting together ahead. He cradled the black case to his chest, the gun with sound suppressor still inside, and entered the car. He approached the four and sat across the aisle in an empty row of seats, their faces all set in a frosty immobility. Only eight other people were in the car, all at the far end.

"Are you looking for me?" he asked quietly in Korean.

ISABELLA COULD SEE INTO THE CAR AHEAD AND SPOTTED KIM, apparently confronting the four problems. Luke was facing her, his back to the action.

"You're not going to believe this," she whispered.

And she told him.

"Crazy fool is tryin' to unnerve them," he said.

"He's carrying the black satchel."

"Let's get closer," he said. "You go ahead and move to a seat at the end of this car, near the exit door. I'll be along."

She stood, walked down the center aisle, counting six others scattered among the empty seats. She claimed a spot near the exit door, facing toward Kim, whom she could see through the half glass in the doors between the cars. Luke appeared and sat in the row across the aisle, he, too, watching ahead.

"Where's Howell?" she heard him mutter over the clank of the wheels on the tracks.

She was wondering the same thing.

Howell had been sent to occupy Kim.

But that wasn't happening.

"It has to be the daughter," she whispered. "She's got him."

HANA STUDIED THE MAN CALLED ANAN WAYNE HOWELL. HE watched her with a stern gaze that did not betray even a hint of fear. She'd observed Howell and the dead woman in the dining room on the ferry. They were obviously close, their touch and looks those of lovers. She envied him. Never had she experienced affection. Not with her mother, her father, her siblings, or anyone else. She'd even escaped the guards' lust and kept her virginity. Perhaps only with Sun Hi had she ever experienced any form of close connection with another human being.

"Did you throw Jelena into the ocean, or did he?" Howell asked.

"I have never killed anyone."

Her English was perfect, learned in Macao at a private school where she'd lived for the past twelve years. It had taken time for her to catch up with the other students, but she'd been determined to free her mind of ignorance. And she had. Reading was one of her few delights. Howell's eyes signaled that he did not believe her declaration, but she did not care what he thought.

She knew the truth.

"What's wrong with you?" Howell asked. "There's not a speck of feeling on your face or in your eyes. It's all blank, like you're a machine."

He was the first person to ever say that to her. Not once in fourteen years had her father ever inquired about how *she* felt. Everything had always been centered on him. His thoughts. His desires. Especially during the past few months, as his excitement rose in proportion to his potential success.

She said nothing and continued to stare at him.

"I'm leaving," Howell said.

She produced the gun from beneath her jacket.

Howell froze.

KIM FACED THE FOUR MEN, THE BLACK SATCHEL IN HIS LAP, ITS ZIPPER open, the gun inside easily accessible. "I asked a question."

The man closest to him, on his right, said, "We're here for that satchel and for you."

"And did my bastard of a brother send you?"

"The people of the Korean Republic sent us. You have been named an enemy of the state, as was your other brother."

"Who was slaughtered, along with his entire family."

"You cannot escape this train," the man said in Korean. "We have people waiting in Solaris."

"Might I inquire how you know so much about my whereabouts."

"We have friends helping, supplying excellent information. And they have the means to know."

That meant the Chinese. Then it occurred to him how. They were monitoring his mobile phone and computer use. He'd honestly thought nobody cared what he was doing. Definitely a miscalculation, but not insurmountable given his present location. Isolation worked both ways, and he intended to take advantage of the situation.

"The Chinese are not our friends," he said to the man, who was apparently in charge of the other three. "Far from that, in fact."

He gestured with his head to the satchel in his lap. "I assume you want the documents this contains?"

The man nodded. "All of them, especially an original crumpled page with numbers on it."

Amazing. How much did these people know? And just who exactly were the Chinese monitoring?

"Do you think me a fool?" he asked.

"I think you are a reasonable man. There are four of us here and more waiting when this train stops. There is literally nowhere for you to go. Can we not do this without violence?"

He seemed to consider the inquiry.

"Let us start," the man said, "with you handing over those documents."

He lost all of his curiosity at these men's intentions as another more vital desire rose within him. Survival. So a nod of his head seemed to accept the inevitable, and the hint of a tolerant smile masked his right hand as it slipped into the case and found the gun. He did not bother to withdraw the weapon. That would provide too much of an opportunity for his targets to react.

Instead he angled the satchel to the left and pulled the trigger.

ISABELLA COULD SEE THAT SOMETHING WAS HAPPENING IN THE next car. Kim jerked the black satchel, first left, then right. The four men sitting across the aisle from him were only partially visible, but over the train noise she heard faint pops and saw part of the satchel burst open. One of the passengers in the car ahead leaped to his feet and the exit door was flung open. A bearded man in an overcoat rushed her way. Through the glass she saw others bolting for the exit at the other end of the next car.

Luke saw it too. "What the hell?"

KIM FIRED THREE SHOTS, LEAVING NEAT HOLES IN THE TWO MEN TO his left and one to his right. The man in charge, sitting closest to him, had clearly been caught off guard but recovered and managed to pivot in his seat and thrust with his legs. The man's feet slammed into the satchel and threw Kim back, but he managed to keep a grip on the gun, which he now withdrew from the case.

His target was quick.

Slipping to the floor, and finding a gun of his own.

FIFTY-EIGHT

STEPHANIE SAT STRAIGHT ON THE BENCH AND NEVER MOVED, HER gaze locked on the Chinese ambassador.

"We've been watching and listening to you," he said. "But your agents inside China do the same to us." He shrugged. "It's the way of the world."

No real surprise, so she said, "Once you left Virginia last night, you knew I'd be running the show from this end. Of course, China would never risk an international incident. We are, after all, supposedly friends. But North Korea is a friend, too, whom you were talking to long before you came and spoke to me and the president."

"They rely on us for help. Which we provide—"

"In exchange for those mining concessions the president mentioned. North Korea, for all its problems, does have a lot of minerals in those mountains."

"That it does. But let's not be so sanctimonious. Your country has allies that it helps, too. Some, I'm sure, occasionally to the detriment of others. You will admit this current situation is, to say the least, extraordinary."

The ambassador held out his hand for the envelope.

She hesitated, then handed it over.

"You're just going to give it to him?" Levy asked.

She faced the secretary. "Please tell me my choices."

His silence confirmed that there weren't any.

But she wanted to know more so she said to the ambassador, "You obviously had me followed today. There were eyes and ears in the National Gallery?"

The ambassador nodded. "One of the people in the garden court, when you spoke to Ms. Williams, then to the Treasury agent, monitored it all. Quite amazing what technology can do."

That it was. Remote listening equipment was standard issue. No need to place a device near anybody. Just get within fifty yards, point the laser receiver, and listen away.

"And from that conversation you learned exactly where Kim was in Croatia."

"Precisely. The North Koreans are there. They even tried to kill him, but failed. I'm told, though, that they now have Kim cornered on a train."

She pointed at the envelope and asked, "Will the North Koreans actually get to see what's inside?"

"That was the bargain."

"You're taking an extraordinary risk accosting two federal officials on the National Mall."

"I don't think it's such a problem. Nobody seems to care. But after all, it had to be done."

Which she understood. "There's no way you were going to allow Pyongyang to take the lead here. They could just as easy double-cross you. So you had to get this for yourself, while they did the heavy lifting overseas."

"Which they are much more suited to accomplish. And I do this as much for you as for us. At least now we can contain things, which you would have never been able to accomplish. I came to the president last night to find out if this was real. I left there knowing that it was."

"And there's no telling what Dear Leader might have done, is there?"

"He can be a bit . . . unpredictable."

"Were you inside the Smithsonian?" Levy asked. "Watching us?"

He nodded. "I was able to see thanks to a covert video feed from an agent we had there in the exhibit hall. That desk is quite amazing. We have pieces like it in China, from long ago. Andrew Mellon apparently went to a lot of trouble to torment your President Roosevelt."

"Does your premier really know of this operation?" she asked.

"He does. And he remains your friend, grateful for all the help you provided him. But this is a matter of national concern. The potential destruction of the American economy could cripple us, too."

"So you plan to hold on to what's in that envelope, and hope that it's enough of a stick to keep us in line."

"What did your President Reagan say. Trust but verify. We believe the same thing. You can be assured that if the potential here is catastrophic, we would be the last to utilize that. As I've said, your interests and ours are similar. As are North Korea's, by the way. Dear Leader has no interest in seeing his half brother succeed."

"Though he wouldn't mind being the one who actually takes us down," she said.

"I assure you, that is not going to happen."

"And we have your word to make us feel better," Levy added with sarcasm.

The ambassador smiled. "I understand your pessimism. But all Dear Leader wants at the moment is his half brother dead. Since he just annihilated his other half brother's entire family, that should consolidate his power. No threats would remain to him. He can go back to his isolation and continue his bravado, which no one pays much heed to. So you see, our taking control of this envelope will not be a problem for the United States."

"Except that our dirty little secret won't be a secret anymore."

The ambassador slipped the envelope inside his coat. "That is the price to be paid, but it could have been much worse. The North Koreans themselves could have taken command of the situation and acquired this information. Lucky for you, we decided to make sure that did not happen."

Officially, the United States maintained no diplomatic relations with Pyongyang. In the past all necessary communications were funneled through the Swedes. But that had not been an option here.

She decided to allow the conversation to end.

She doubted the ambassador planned to linger much longer anyway. The Mall was quiet, and there were security cameras everywhere.

"I'm going to leave," he said. "The men behind you will linger a few moments, then leave, too. After that, let us consider this matter closed."

The ambassador bowed slightly, then turned and walked away, heading toward the American history museum and a car that waited on the street before it. She watched as he climbed inside and the vehicle drove away. After another minute, the men behind them left.

She and Levy sat on the bench.

The day was fading away, the air turning cooler.

She faced Levy and smiled.

He smiled back.

It worked.

FIFTY-NINE

CROATIA

MALONE DECIDED THAT THE MAN IN THE CAR WOULD BE FIRST, and he hoped that these two were all that he'd have to worry about on this end. The street was quiet, nearly no one around, all of the shops and stores closed. The train was due in shortly, so he needed to be in position and ready. He also wondered what was happening in DC, since everything depended on Stephanie's show.

He assessed the situation and made a decision.

The direct approach was usually best.

He fled the shadows and headed into the street, negotiating the fifty feet of damp cobblestones between him and the car. He approached the driver's side and banged on the rear windshield.

"Taxi. Are you for hire?" he called out.

He caught the startled reaction from the man inside.

He pounded on the rear window again. "I need to go. Are you available?"

The car door opened and the driver emerged. Another Asian, his face agitated. He wore a long overcoat and gloves. Big mistake. Not giving his adversary a moment to think Malone slammed his bare right fist square into the man's jaw. The blow stunned the driver and he used the second of shock to grab a handful of hair and smash the man's face into the car's roof. He felt muscles go limp as consciousness faded. He kept a grip and stuffed the body back inside, laying him across the two front seats. He spotted a plastic grocery bag lying on the floorboard and retrieved it. A few rips and he fashioned a strip strong enough to bind the hands behind the back. For added measure, he pocketed the car keys and retrieved a pistol off the unconscious Korean. No need to leave a weapon around for someone to use.

One down.

He checked his watch.

Less than five minutes until the train arrived.

He locked and closed the car door, then headed inside.

ISABELLA SPRANG FROM HER SEAT AND FOUND HER GUN, MOVING toward the half-glass door. She stepped aside into a row of empty seats and allowed three people from the car ahead to complete their hurried escape from the gunfire. Kim had disappeared to the right, one of the Asians toward the front.

Two more pops.

Louder this time.

She instinctively ducked, then advanced to the door. A hand grabbed her from behind.

"What are you doing?" Luke asked.

"My job."

"I get it. How about we do this together."

She nodded.

Luke held his gun.

Another shot from the car ahead grabbed both of their attentions.

HANA HEARD GUNFIRE AND KNEW THAT HER FATHER WAS KILLING more people. He'd left with the gun in the satchel for a reason. She'd counted six rounds and wondered how many of the four men were left. Howell also realized something was happening.

"You're not getting off this train," he said to her.

What did this man know that she didn't? There was no way he was aware of the Koreans, as he'd been here, inside the compartment with her father, when all four had boarded.

The Americans.

They were here, too.

KIM FIRED A SHOT IN THE DIRECTION OF THE REMAINING PROBLEM, but the man was no longer on the floor. It took a second for him to realize that his target had sought refuge in the first row of seats. Partitions protected the rows, extending from the top of the seats to the floor, which meant he could not ascertain anything from below.

And looking up would expose him.

The exit door ahead slid open.

He risked a peek.

The man was fleeing.

He pursued.

ISABELLA FELT THE TRAIN SLOWING.

"We're coming into Solaris," Luke said.

"We have to get to Howell."

She saw that he agreed. Surely by now some of the panicked passengers had alerted the crew. But the train was long with many cars, and it might take another minute or so for someone official to come investigate. Through the glass in the doors she saw Kim exit the car ahead.

Luke motioned.

They followed.

Three-quarters of the way through the next car she saw the bodies of three dead Asians.

"That makes two left, including Kim," Luke said.

"You're forgetting the daughter."

He nodded at his error.

"Who probably has Howell."

HANA HAD THOUGHT ABOUT THIS MOMENT FOR A LONG TIME, EVER since she realized that her father was evil. If her mother was right, then he was responsible for the misery she'd experienced during the first nine years of her life. No guard, no teacher, no one would have been able to hurt her if not for him sentencing her mother to exile. And though she despised her mother, for this one time she believed her. Kims created the camps and Kims kept them going. Sun Hi had been born there because of Kims. And she died there for the same reason. One afternoon a few months back her father had sat her down and told her about a book he'd read, *The Patriot Threat,* written by the man sitting across from her. It foretold a possible way to destroy the United States of America, and maybe even China. He'd seemed excited by the possibilities, enthused at the prospect of revenge on his half brother. He'd spent nearly every waking moment since trying to make that a reality. They'd traveled all over, him plotting and planning, she watching and waiting. He never asked and she rarely volunteered anything about herself. For men like her father—self-absorbed, egotistical, and maniacal—what others thought rarely mattered. As long as she remained willing, appeared vested, and questioned nothing he simply assumed she was his ally.

She'd learned that trick in the camp.

But unlike her father, the guards were rarely fooled. Of course, being able to beat, torture, and kill at will made their task much easier. Her father, at least, had a few rules to which he must adhere. Not many. But enough to tie his hands and cloud his judgment. True, he had taken her from the camp. She meant *something* to him. She was just not sure what.

And that seemed the only question left to answer.

Everything else was clear.

Especially what to do now.

How many people had she seen killed in the camp? She tried once to count, but had not been able. How sad that it was so many she could not even determine their number.

So many lives lost.

And all because of Kims.

For a long time she was simply too young to do anything. Only in the past few years had she matured enough to watch for opportunities. Sadly, she knew she would never be happy, nor content, nor rid of the horrible memories. Any semblance of a life had been denied her. Thankfully, the instinct for survival all Insiders developed never left her. She was, in many ways, that same prisoner who'd meant nothing to no one.

But she was also Hana Sung.

First victory.

Howell was fidgeting in his seat, clearly anxious.

There may not be another opportunity.

She raised her gun.

SIXTY

STEPHANIE ENTERED THE NATIONAL GALLERY WITH JOE LEVY AT her heels. They'd walked over from their bench at the far end of the Mall and gained access through the building's impressive south entrance. Wide marble steps led up to the second floor. Chick-fil-A Man was waiting for them at the top, in the portico, among a forest of massive columns.

"Did you record everything?" she asked him.

He nodded. "Got it all, nice and clear."

"Good job."

And she meant it. He'd played his part to perfection. The technology the ambassador had boasted that China utilized was also available to the United States, and had been used to return the favor. Everything said a few minutes ago at that bench was now memorialized. She led the two men inside the building, just past the doors and before the security checks, into what was labeled FOUNDERS ROOM. Wood-paneled walls showcased framed oil portraits of men and women, the most prominent of which was Mellon's, hanging high above the fireplace. She marveled at the irony that everything had ended up right back here.

The moment the Chinese ambassador departed Ed Tipton's house she'd gone under a microscope. Which was why, as Danny had explained during the drive back to DC she'd been included in the meeting. Plenty of NSA intercepts had already determined that the Chinese were deeply involved and that they'd been communicating with the North Koreans. Danny had told her all about those just before she'd dropped him at the White House. He'd also correctly concluded that there was no way to be rid of the Chinese, and that they were most likely double-dealing with the North Koreans, none of which would be good for the United States.

So he told her a story.

"Any turkey decoy can get a tom into shotgun range," he said. *"That's about forty yards. But a lot can go wrong in forty yards. Blink an eye or move your leg a little when you fire, and your turkey gets away. Now, if you want that bird archery close, you need a decoy, and it takes a helluva good one to draw the bird in. If you don't think your turkey decoy looks real, the bird won't, either. I used to love huntin' turkeys. If you're lucky enough to be able to chase unpressured birds, then it's easy. Just stay on the trail till you take 'em down. But pressure changes everything. Pressured turkeys don't run toward bad calling, fidgety hunters, or decoys that don't look real. To score those everything has to be right, especially the decoy. That's what we have here, Stephanie. A pressured turkey, headed straight for us. What we need is a good decoy."*

So she and Cotton had fashioned one.

Assuming the Chinese would be listening to her mobile calls, they'd intentionally utilized open cell phones to create the perfect turkey decoy. The call she'd made to Cotton from the eighth floor of the Mandarin Oriental had most likely been a safe one. No one was nearby to intercept. She'd used a landline in Joe Levy's office to make the more critical calls to Cotton, where they'd worked out the details. She then arranged for a visit to the National Gallery, the idea being to use the locale as a means to funnel information to the other side. Chick-fil-A Man had been sent to confront her, their entire conversation staged, similar to what had happened in Atlanta only this time they were all on the same side. If it worked once before, she felt, why not again? They'd prolonged the confrontation as long as possible, and she had to admit that the thing with the $20 bill was fascinating. But the main idea had been to provide anyone who might be listening with Kim's Croatian location. The NSA had zeroed in on the Hotel Korcula thanks to Kim's use of his laptop, which they'd been monitoring for some time. If the Chinese had succeeded and killed Kim, then it would have been all over. Sure, the crumpled sheet of paper would be in Chinese hands, but since she was way ahead of them, there'd be nothing for them to find. No harm, no foul. If the attempt failed, then Kim would have simply been flushed farther into Cotton's trap. Either way, the good guys win.

Before grabbing a bite to eat earlier, she'd retreated to Carol Williams' office and, on a landline, learned from an asset the embassy had dispatched to the Zadar hotel of the attack, with one man dead, shot by Kim, who was accompanied by a young woman. The unknown was how many resources the Chinese had on the ground in Croatia and whether they could rebound and mount an attack on the train. But that was a risk Cotton had known he was taking.

Once the code had been solved, Cotton had called on her cell phone and announced that fact to the world, sending her an encrypted text with the correct solution. That she passed on to Joe Levy via another secured text while leading her nosy listeners to a desk in the Smithsonian Castle, one she'd long known existed.

If you don't think your turkey decoy looks real, the bird won't, either.

Thankfully the Smithsonian had the resources to accommodate her urgent requests. Its conservation lab was a master at restoring old books, but it also possessed the ability to reproduce antique documents. So while still at the Treasury Department she'd called Richard Stamm, and he'd readied the perfect decoy in less than two hours. An envelope stained and bleached to look eighty years old, along with a single sheet of paper with faded print from an old manual, ribbon typewriter, which the conservation lab had on hand. Cotton had suggested the wording, and she'd refined it.

Mr. President, I hope this quest has proven as enjoyable for you as it was for me to create. I wanted to see if you would actually do as I instructed and it's good to know that you did. Unfortunately, there is nothing to find. No danger exists to this country, except the ones you will inflict upon it. Surely, by now, I am dead. But if for some reason you have found this message before I pass, please be sure to let me know your thoughts. I will give them the same courtesy and consideration that you have always shown to mine.

She'd seen the writing cabinet at the Smithsonian before and knew of its many secret compartments. So the envelope with the fake message was delivered to Stamm, who hid it inside. When she called Joe Levy from the Mall on her cell phone the Chinese again were listening. And like that pressured turkey, they ran straight for an irresistible decoy. All she and Levy had to do was play their parts to perfection.

Now the Chinese had their prize, only it was no prize at all. They would conclude that the entire affair was just a way for a rich man to torment a president, part of a vendetta from long ago that had no relevance today. Cotton's actual deciphering of the code had been delivered to Carol Williams by Chick-fil-A Man, face-to-face, just after the earlier encounter in the garden court.

Edward Savage   Eleanor Custis
Martha Washington 16

Hopefully, while she and Joe Levy finished their performance on the Mall, Carol had solved the riddle. Like Danny had said a few hours ago outside the White House, as he exited her car, *Remember, the second mouse to the trap is the one who always gets the cheese.*

Carol Williams entered the Founders Room. Visitors wandered in and out too, the building's coat check located just beyond. They drifted near the fireplace, among a cluster of comfortable upholstered chairs, beneath Mellon's portrait. Chick-fil-A Man stood at the doorway to keep watch, but little danger existed anymore. The turkeys were long gone.

"It was easy," Carol said. "I didn't even need the Internet. This one I know."

Stephanie's phone vibrated, the caller unknown.

She decided to answer.

"Ms. Nelle, this call is a courtesy, ordered by my superiors," said the male voice, which she recognized.

The Chinese ambassador.

"Our friends to the south were not happy with what I secured from you. It was not as . . . substantial as they'd hoped. Whether it be true or false matters not to us. Regardless of what you think, we are simply trying to keep two allies happy. But being in the middle of this fight has proven most unpleasant. We are done. It is over, as far as we are concerned. But I cannot say the same for our friends to the south. They are the ones currently handling the operation overseas and they have decided to eliminate all remnants of the problem. I pass the message on as a show of good faith that we are not your enemy."

She sucked a deep breath.

"They have trained personnel on the ground in Croatia," the ambassador said. "They made a move on Kim, which failed. They now have sent their assets to finish the task. They have orders to kill Kim, his daughter, Howell, and anyone else who may be on that train, which includes any American assets. As I said, they are angry."

This man was clearly informed.

"Thanks for the warning."

"Not at all. It is, after all, what friends do for one another."

She ended the call.

It's a two-front war, Cotton had told her.

And he was right.

She quickly sent one more text.

SIXTY-ONE

CROATIA

MALONE HEARD THE TRAIN APPROACHING, MAYBE A MILE DOWN the tracks. He'd checked the schedule board and saw that this was the last one due here for the night. Only a handful of people were around, the station nearly empty. Inside the station was a cavernous hall with a lofty ceiling supported by iron beams. The remaining Korean stood on the loading platform, off to the side, near one of the iron supports that held up an overhang. Both of the man's hands rested inside his coat pockets, one of them probably holding a weapon. Malone's gun was just beneath his leather jacket. What was their plan? Were there assets on the train to secure Kim and then these two would be waiting to take him away? Or were these two the only ones involved, here to claim Kim as he disembarked? He'd done his part to make things difficult here. But what were Luke and Isabella facing?

His phone vibrated.

He'd been waiting for the text.

Under control here. All done. Worked perfectly. No Chinese on your end. It's NK. They are greenlighted to move on all of you.

He knew what that meant. There was no way Kim Yong Jin would be allowed to just walk away. For good measure, they'd also take out anyone else who happened to be nearby.

And he'd provided them the perfect venue.

This Croatian isolation worked both ways.

Which meant things were about to get messy.

ISABELLA KEPT MOVING FORWARD, ADVANCING TO THE CONNECTing space between the cars. There were still passengers in some of the seats ahead of her, the bodies and commotion now behind them. Farther on, in the next car, began the first-class compartments.

The train was slowing.

Luke stood to her left, she to the right of the door into the next car, both of them with guns drawn. She ventured a quick look and saw Kim moving down the center aisle, still holding the black satchel, which surely contained a gun.

"We need to stop him," Luke said.

She nodded her understanding.

"Let's do it," he said.

KIM WAS LOOKING FOR HIS ADVERSARY, INTENT ON KILLING THE final obstacle to his success. The man had fled toward where Hana and Howell waited among the first-class compartments. One more car and he'd be there. His left arm held the satchel while his right hand was inside, wrapped around the gun. None of the passengers here seemed concerned, as they surely had no idea what had happened behind them. The clank of wheels to rails seemed more than enough noise to mask the suppressed shots. He glanced out the exterior windows and saw lights. That and the ever-slowing speed indicated they'd arrived in Solaris.

"Kim Yong Jin."

He stopped and turned.

A man and woman stood at the far end of the car, guns pointed toward him.

HANA SENSED THAT SOMETHING HAD GONE WRONG. SHE LOWERED her gun, grabbed the clipped stacked of papers, and stood from her seat.

"Where are you going?" Howell asked.

She ignored him and slid open the compartment door, stealing a quick look into the car behind her. Through the glass in the doors she saw her father, facing away, a man and woman at the car's rear with guns aimed at him.

Then another man.

The first Korean who'd boarded the train.

He was standing in the space between her exit door and the entrance for the next car. He held a gun and was carefully peering around the window's edge toward her father, his back to her.

She aimed at the door two meters away and fired.

KIM HEARD GLASS BREAK BEHIND HIM.

He whirled and dropped down at the same time, expecting to see the last Korean bearing down on him. Instead he caught sight of Hana through the now obliterated half of the door to the next car.

Then the Korean appeared, coming to his feet.

The squeal of brakes to wheels, then wheels to rails signaled the train was stopping. He saw the man dart left and disappear. The two problems behind him had also sought cover. He decided to give them more reason to stay down. He tossed the satchel aside and fired three shots in their direction, then rushed the door and slipped out.

The Korean was gone.

Hana emerged from the car ahead.

"Get Howell."

The train was fully stopped.

They had to leave.

Now.

MALONE TIMED HIS MOVE TO COINCIDE WITH THE TORRENT OF noise that accompanied the train's arrival, assuming that would be the moment of maximum distraction. Hopefully, his target would not expect an attack from the platform, the focus on the train and what may have happened there. So far he'd stayed back, out of sight, using another of the iron supports for cover. The platform itself was dimly lit, which helped. Several workers busied themselves in preparing for the arrival, the train easing to a full stop.

A man leaped from one of the lead cars while the wheels were still moving. Asian. Holding a gun. The man on the platform yelled something not in English, the first whirling around and realizing that he now had an ally. He pointed up to the train and signaled for them to retreat.

Three more people emerged to the station.

Kim and his daughter, both toting guns, and Howell.

What the hell happened?

ISABELLA KNEW INSTANTLY WHAT THEY HAD TO DO, AS APPARENTLY did Luke. Kim had fled ahead so they needed to exit the train from the doors just behind them. The few passengers in the car slowly rose from the floor, where they'd all plunged when Kim starting shooting.

Everyone appeared okay.

They slid open the door and hopped down to the station.

She immediately spotted Kim, Hana Sung, and Howell.

And the shooting started.

SIXTY-TWO

Stephanie and Joe Levy followed Carol Williams out of the Founders Room then into the rotunda with the fountain that she'd visited earlier. They turned right and walked down the same long sculpture hall that led to the garden court—except this time they veered into a series of exhibition rooms. The first displayed French canvases, the next British artists. A few visitors loitered here and there, admiring the works. It was approaching 4:00 P.M., closing time a little more than an hour away. In a gallery labeled 62 she noticed that the two open doorways were blocked. NO ADMITTANCE signs were posted at each.

"The American rooms are being renovated," Carol said. "They've been closed for a month, but follow me."

They bypassed the barricades and entered a set of galleries where the canvases were gone, the bare walls and hardwood floors being repaired. on. Workers milled about with paint and stain and the air smelled of varnish.

"We took down most of the canvases," Carol said.

They entered a rectangular room with pale-blue walls and cream-colored trim. Its ceiling was backlit glass panels dotted with floodlights angled down at canvases that remained hung, but covered in white cloth. The floor was the same hardwood planks, which had yet to be refurbished.

"They're working their way here," Carol said. "But what I think you're after is right there. I had the sheet removed."

The exposed image was substantial, around ten feet long and eight feet high, framed in heavy gilded wood the color of burnished gold.

Carol stepped toward the painting and pointed to its left side.

"The little boy is George Washington Parke Custis. He was Martha's grandson by her first husband, but after his parents died he came to live with Martha and George. Of course, that's George Washington sitting beside his namesake. Martha is across from her husband. Her granddaughter, Eleanor Parke Custis, stands beside her. She and George adopted both children as their own, so this is the actual First Family. The man in the background, behind the two women, is probably one of Washington's slaves, but no one knows for sure."

Stephanie listened as Carol explained more about the work. Edward Savage, its creator, had been an 18th-century American painter. Portraits were his specialty, but his most famous creation was this group started in 1789 and finished in 1796.

The Washington Family.

"It's the only portrait of the First Family painted from life," Carol said. "They actually posed for Savage, then he painted this from sketches he made. Washington, as you see, was depicted in uniform, his hat and sword on the table, his left hand resting above a set of papers, the idea to symbolize both the military and civilian aspects of his service to the country. Martha sits before a map of the federal city, her closed fan pointing to what is today Pennsylvania Avenue. The grandchildren are there to symbolize the nation's future. The servant in the background is particularly noteworthy, as it was rare for slaves to be depicted in early American art. He stands overdressed in livery, in the shadows—there, but not. A reminder that Washington remained a gentleman farmer and planter.

"What's really interesting are the people themselves. They sit stiff and awkward. Little life to them, and the faces, notice how none of them looks at the others. Their gazes are all off, focused separate, which was surely more symbolism. None of them was particularly close to the others. True, they were a family, but we would call it dysfunctional today."

Stephanie studied the image, impressed with both its color and its detail. Behind the figures a vista down the Potomac seemed to complete the patriotic illusion.

"What you sent over," Carol said, "Edward Savage, Eleanor Custis, Martha Washington. They all add up to this painting. Mr. Mellon bought it in January 1936. It's hung here, in the gallery, since we opened in 1941 per his specific instruction. I checked on that to be sure. It's one of the permanent pieces in the museum."

All of the dots connected. That was nearly a full year before Mellon met with Roosevelt on December 31, 1936. But she needed to know more. "Where was it before the gallery opened, from 1936 to 1941?"

"In Mr. Mellon's Washington apartment. It stayed there, even after he died in 1937, until we opened."

Making it easily accessible if Roosevelt had bothered to go looking.

I'll be waiting for you, Mr. President.

That's what Mellon told Roosevelt.

Literally, at least for a time.

Stephanie held a smartphone in her right hand, its camera pointed at the portrait. On the walk from the Founders Room she'd dialed the number and established an encrypted connection. The unit had been provided by Treasury, so no one would be intercepting this transmission. As Carol Williams gave her explanation, the phone had heard, too.

Two other people appeared behind them, a man and a woman, the museum's director and chief curator, who introduced themselves.

"I involved them," Carol said. "I hope it was all right."

She wasn't listening. Instead, she was pondering the riddle. Andrew Mellon had left clues that directed FDR straight to this portrait.

But what now?

"Ask all of the workers here to leave, please," she said. "We need privacy."

The museum director looked unsure, so she decided to make the point clearer.

"That's not a request," she said. "Either work with me or I'll shut this place down and do it my way."

Joe Levy looked surprised at her abruptness, but there was no time for niceties. Things were playing out in Croatia and she had a timetable. The director gave the order and the chief curator cleared the galleries around them. She stepped closer to the painting and tried to make sense of what Mellon had done. He'd gone to a lot of trouble, everything executed with a precise purpose, so there was no reason to think that the final parts were any different.

Edward Savage   Eleanor Custis
Martha Washington 16

She focused on the granddaughter, Eleanor, and asked Carol about her.

"They called her Nelly. She lived a long time and spent her life protecting George's image. Look closely at how Savage depicted her, though. The right hand is lifting the map, as if signaling that there was something beneath it."

And she saw that the observation was correct.

She aimed the phone toward Eleanor's image, which also encompassed her grandmother Martha.

Then it hit her.

Mellon's clues.

Edward Savage was for the painting itself. *Eleanor Custis* for a message beneath. So did *Martha Washington* complete the riddle? First she studied the painted floor beneath Martha's hemline, where the toes of one shoe could be seen resting atop the checkerboards. Nothing there. She stepped closer and examined the outer frame in the lower right corner. Clearly it was old and had been hand carved, its edges abundant with chips and gauges. The wood was a good eight inches thick.

So why not?

She dropped to her knees and studied the frame's underside that faced down to the floor. About four inches in from the bottom right corner she saw a round plug embedded into the wood. She immediately examined the opposite left corner and found a similar plug. One difference, though. The one on the right contained tiny engravings, rough, but still legible.

XVI.

16.

She aimed the phone at what she'd discovered.

"Bingo," she whispered to it.

A small toolbox lay atop a padded drop cloth on the other side of the gallery. She laid the phone on the floor, rushed over, and found a hammer and screwdriver. The others watched her in silence. She came back and positioned herself beneath the frame. Three feet or so of clearance existed from there to the floor. She adjusted the phone's angle, then jammed the screwdriver into the slight depression that encircled the plug. She was just about to pound the hammer when the museum's director and curator both yelled for her to stop.

"You can't do that," the director told her. "That's a national treasure. I cannot allow it."

"Stay out of this," she said.

"Go get security. Now," the director told the head curator.

The woman ran away and the director lunged toward her, reaching for the hammer. He yanked the tools away and said, "You're insane."

She allowed him his moment and simply reached for the phone. "What do you want to do?"

"You know damn well what I want," Danny Daniels said through the speaker.

The director seemed shocked. He clearly recognized the voice.

"Sir," Danny said. "Please hand those tools back to Ms. Nelle, and get the hell out of the way."

Though a command, for Danny, it had been delivered in an uncharacteristically cordial tone.

"Take it from me," Joe Levy said. "You don't want to argue with him."

The director definitely appeared to be in a quandary and she could sympathize. His entire job was to protect everything within the museum and here she was about to deface one its original treasures. But Andrew Mellon had specifically wanted that plug removed. If she was right, he'd been the one to actually place it there. So she doubted her violation would inflict any historical damage.

"I'm waiting," Danny said through the phone. "You don't want me to come over there."

The director handed back the tools.

"I also need you and the other lady, Ms. Williams, to leave," Danny said. "Please make sure Ms. Nelle and Mr. Levy are not disturbed, and that no one comes anywhere near the gallery. Have those security guards you summoned seal the area where you are right now. And shut off any cameras that are recording."

"I assume it matters not that I don't actually work for you," the director said.

"You're kiddin', right? You think some civil service rules are going to stop me from kickin' your ass."

The director could see he was outgunned, so he nodded his assent, then he and Carol Williams left the gallery.

"Make sure we're alone," she called out to Chick-fil-A Man, who nodded, then followed the others out.

"They gone?" Danny asked.

She still lay on the floor. "Yep."

"Open that sucker up."

SIXTY-THREE

CROATIA

MALONE WATCHED AS THE FIRST MAN FROM THE TRAIN JOINED HIS compatriot in the station and they realized that Kim was armed and on the move.

"Everyone down," he screamed in English as he found his own weapon.

The few people on the platform who understood him looked his way, saw the gun, then fled toward the station doors. Kim also reacted to the warning, jamming the barrel of his gun into Howell's ribs. Malone gave that act some respect, but the two Koreans seemed not to care. They'd taken cover behind a metal bench and aimed their weapons. Their mission did not include returning either Kim or Howell alive.

And here was a golden opportunity.

ISABELLA SPOTTED KIM AND HOWELL FIFTY FEET AWAY, THE STA-tion platform dim, people fleeing. Both she and Luke were exposed with no cover. But Kim's attention had been drawn in the opposite direction.

To Malone.

Whom she saw had drawn his gun.

Hana Sung, though, was staring straight at her and Luke.

A row of luggage carts stood lined to their left, which offered some protection.

She leaped that way as Sung aimed her gun and fired.

MALONE HAD SEEN ISABELLA AND LUKE EXITING THE TRAIN, AND while the father worried about him, the daughter was shooting at them, rounds popping out in rapid succession.

A woman screamed.

Another man yelled.

In Korean.

Kim turned his attention away from Malone and toward the other two. More Korean words passed between them. Isabella and Luke had lunged for cover behind a row of luggage carts. Kim forced Howell ahead, toward the doors that led from the platform to the station, using his captive as a shield. It would only be an instant before Luke and Isabella started firing. He hoped they realized that Howell was in a bad predicament.

"Luke," he yelled. "Two more to your left. Both armed."

Bullets came his way from the Koreans as they now realized his presence. Luckily he'd found cover behind one of the iron pedestals that held the ceiling aloft. Rounds pinged off the metal, tossing sparks, ricocheting in every direction.

He steadied himself and prepared to return fire.

KIM'S HEART FLUTTERED WITH PANIC. ALARM BURNED AT THE back of his ears. This town was a trap, one set by both the Americans and North Koreans. He had to flee. Hana had occupied the man and woman from the train, and the two Koreans were shooting at someone else off to his right. Unfortunately he had to cross that line of fire to escape. His left arm wrapped Howell's neck, the gun still tight to the man's ribs.

One of the Koreans stopped firing and turned back his way.

Anan Wayne Howell was of no use to him any longer. He'd been played on the train. Surely Howell had been told not to mention that he knew Jelena was dead, but the younger man's emotions had gotten the best of him. Still, though Howell was of no value in one respect that did not mean he was completely useless.

He pivoted left and placed Howell between him and the rising danger.

A shot came his way and thudded into Howell's chest.

The man's breath left him in a gasp and the body jerked from the impact. Another round and a second bullet slammed into Howell.

Neither penetrated through to Kim.

He released his grip on the American.

MALONE WINCED AS HOWELL WAS SHOT TWICE.

He fled his cover, aimed at the Korean shooting, and took him down with one shot. The second man then went on the offensive, firing Malone's way, which caused him to dive to the concrete floor.

Rounds whizzed past him and dinged off the train.

He rolled and used another iron pillar for cover.

The last he saw, Kim and Hana Sung were fleeing the platform into the station.

And the remaining Korean followed.

ISABELLA CROUCHED BESIDE LUKE, THEIR POSITION NOT THE BEST in the world. They had some cover, but not much. Rising up and shooting would involve exposure, but she saw that Luke was willing to risk it. So was she. A lot of rounds were being expended. Their eyes met and signaled that they would do it together. Luke nodded and up they went.

The platform had gone quiet.

A body lay on the concrete near the train, a second off to the left in the shadows.

"Malone," Luke called out.

"Here."

And she saw a dark figure emerge from behind one of the support pillars. He held a gun at his side and rushed toward the man down near the train.

They did the same.

It was Howell.

Luke rolled him over. Howell was breathing, but spewing blood with each exhale, more fluid pouring from two chest wounds.

"Hang in there," Luke said. "We'll get you some help. Stay with us."

Her heart sank.

"Kim used him as a shield," Malone said.

"We had some issues on the train," she noted. "All hell broke loose just before we got to the station. Three more are dead on board."

"The daughter was holding a stack of papers," Malone said.

She'd seen them, too.

"I'm going after them," he said. "You two get some help. Don't let him die."

And Malone ran off.

HANA FOLLOWED HER FATHER AS THEY RUSHED FROM THE TRAIN station and onto the street. She'd seen many a town just like this in China and North Korea. Compact and quiet, the paths through it narrow and angular with abrupt endings. Even worse, they knew nothing of the local geography. Above them stood the chief glory, a cathedral with twin bell towers and ornamental windows, its brightly lit belfries framed by the night, then blurred by the fog.

"We go that way," her father said.

And he ran up the inclined cobblestones toward the church, turning a corner and disappearing into the darkness.

She glanced behind them and noticed no one.

All of the commotion remained inside.

In the distance she heard sirens.

And knew what that meant.

MALONE RAN THROUGH THE STATION TOWARD ITS STREET EXIT. THE few attendants on duty were all in a panic, providing enough confusion for him to make his way through the building. He slipped the gun, still in hand, beneath his jacket. Outside, in the mist, he spotted Kim and his daughter rounding a bend, headed up an inclined way between the closed shops toward the cathedral. He saw nothing of the second Korean who'd also left the platform. He doubted he'd fled, so he told himself to proceed with caution.

Sirens in the distance were drawing closer, maybe only a few blocks away.

He hustled off in Kim's direction.

ISABELLA COULD SEE THAT HOWELL WAS IN A BAD WAY. TWO SLUGS TO the chest could do a great deal of damage. Luke cradled Howell in his lap, the man's eyes open, his breathing labored, blood still spewing with each exhale. That meant a lung had been pierced. One of the station workers had called the police and an ambulance. Several of the passengers from the train stood off to the side, watching. She wondered if there was a doctor anywhere among them, but her callouts in English for one had gone unanswered.

"Hang in there," Luke told Howell again. "Stay with me. Help is coming."

Luke's gaze up to her asked if that were true, but she could only shake her head and hope.

"Malone shouldn't have gone alone," she said. "One of the guys shooting at us is out there, too."

"I agree," Luke said. "Go."

She hadn't expected that.

"I'll stay here with Howell. Go. Help Malone."

She did not need to be told twice, leaving the platform and entering the station. Her gun was inside her coat pocket where she'd concealed it when she and Luke had rushed to Howell. Out the front doors and she caught a glimpse of Malone through the fog, fifty yards away, rushing up an inclined street. The sirens were nearly here, the night air overhead strobed by red glows drawing closer.

She headed after Malone.

Another figure appeared.

To her right. Thirty yards away. Holding a gun and advancing. It had to be the second Korean she'd seen escape the platform during the gunfight. She stopped, gripped her weapon with both hands, and yelled, "Stop. Now."

Her target hesitated an instant, turned her way, then decided to risk escape, rushing off down the street. The night and the mist complicated things, but the uphill path slowed him just enough. She led him like a bird in flight, then fired. The round slammed into him, jarring his balance. He whirled and tried to swing his gun around.

She shot him again.

He dropped to the cobbles.

MALONE HEARD A BANG AND TURNED.

Twenty yards back a man holding a gun staggered in the street.

A second bang and the form collapsed.

He rushed back, his own weapon ready, and saw Isabella, just outside the train station, poised to fire.

She lowered her pistol.

A police car appeared behind her, wheeling to the station. Another followed. Uniformed officers emerged. One saw her with the gun and drew his own. Malone was far enough away that he could slip back into the darkness, but Isabella stood exposed in the penumbra of light from the station's exterior. She wisely remained frozen, her gun still aimed his way, her back to the police. All of the officers had now drawn pistols and were screaming orders her way.

Isabella saw him.

"Go," she said loud enough for him to hear. "Get out of here."

Her gun clattered to the street and her arms were raised in surrender. Slowly, she turned and faced the police, who advanced her way with their own weapons still trained.

No one had seen him.

She'd covered his back and taken one for the team.

Which allowed him a chance to get Kim.

SIXTY-FOUR

Stephanie wedged the screwdriver into the circular indentations. With the hammer she tapped the metal tip until it was embedded a good inch, then she worked the handle back and forth. The old wood gave way. She yanked the screwdriver out and repeated the process around the circle, then rested the metal tip at the center. Three taps and she pierced the plug. Chunks of it gave way and fell to the floor. Joe Levy had bent down and was watching her.

"Just bust it out," he said.

"I agree with him," Danny said through the phone.

She knew he could better see what she was doing from the camera's vantage point on the floor, where chips of a two-hundred-plus-year-old frame lay scattered. She took their advice and worked the screwdriver left and right. The plug was obliterated and its remaining pieces rained down. She folded her finger up into the cavity and freed more remnants until an opening about three inches wide was revealed.

"I wish we had a light," she said.

"We do," Joe said, pointing to the phone.

He was right. She reached for the unit and activated the camera flash, pointing the bright rays up into the darkness.

"There's something there," she said. "At the edge of the frame. The cavity beyond is wider than the opening."

She laid the phone back down, reached up with two fingers, and felt paper. She found an edge and maneuvered whatever it was to the center where she could see an envelope. She folded it along its length and brought it down. The exterior was brown with age, not unlike the facsimile the Smithsonian had fashioned for her earlier. On the outside was typed

A strange coincidence, to use a phrase,
by which such things are settled nowadays

She showed the words to the phone camera.

"Lord Byron," Danny said. "From *Don Juan*. Like Roosevelt said on the tape."

She remembered.

"*'Tis strange, but true. For truth is always strange. Stranger than fiction,*" Danny said through the phone. "More from Byron. Which definitely applies here."

"I never knew you were a poetry buff."

"I'm not. But Edwin is."

Something hard was inside the envelope, and she opened the flap to see a skeleton key. She displayed it for the camera. There was also a single page, tri-folded. She slipped it out. "I doubt Mellon thought it would be eight decades before this was read."

The paper seemed in good shape, helped by the fact that it had rested sealed inside the frame, the painting itself always in a climate-controlled environment, especially since 1941. What better place to preserve something than within the National Gallery of Art?

"What are you waiting for?" Danny asked her.

She stood from the floor.

Levy grabbed the phone and aimed its camera over her shoulder. She carefully opened the page, the fibers still resilient, its typed ink readable.

I recently acquired this painting just for this quest. Its symbolism was too tempting to resist, so I thought it would make an excellent repository. It hung in my Washington apartment until the day I died. I waited for you to send an emissary, but none arrived. So I still await you, Mr.

President. How did it feel to step to my tune? That's what you made me do the last three years of my life, and each day I sat in court I pondered how I would repay you. I won that fight and knew that the day we spoke at the White House. But I assumed you knew the same thing. A part of me realized that you would never go looking so long as I remained alive. Never would you give me the satisfaction of knowing that you might believe what I say, or that you feared me. But you reading these words is proof of both. Please recall that I told you that the page of numbers I left would reveal two American secrets, either of which could be the end of you. The first concerns Haym Solomon. This country does owe his heirs a huge debt. I removed all documentary evidence of that from the government archives in 1925, thereby preventing Congress from making any repayment. I freely admit that I used that knowledge to maintain a hold on my cabinet appointment. It was a difficult choice those three presidents faced. Spit in the face of a patriot, or authorize a billion-dollar repayment. I did no different though than anyone else before, or after me. Power must be taken and kept or it will be lost. I now leave the Salomon documents to you. It will be interesting to see what you do with them. That choice will be yours alone. I doubt you are the champion of the common man that you want so many to believe you to be. The other secret is far more potent. The Sixteenth Amendment to the Constitution is invalid. This was known in 1913, but purposefully ignored. Proof of that also helped maintain my hold on power. I still have that evidence. What you do with that will be equally interesting. Everything is waiting for you, Mr. President, as am I.

She finished reading the note out loud, her mouth close to the phone, her voice low.

"Joe, I see why you were willing to keep this to yourself," Danny said. "Looks like the possible just became reality."

"Unfortunately," Levy said.

Her mind was racing. "Could you go get Carol Williams?"

Levy handed her the phone and hurried off.

"What do you want to do?" she asked Danny.

"We're thinkin'."

That meant Edwin Davis was also watching. Good. His level head could come in handy.

"Anything from Cotton?" he asked.

"Not a word. But he could have his hands full."

She heard footsteps and quickly pocketed the note and key. Levy re-entered the gallery with Carol Williams. She caught the quick glances the younger woman gave to the bits of frame on the hardwood floor.

"Believe me," she said, "it's not damaged. Your Mr. Mellon wanted that done. It's easily repaired."

She recalled something they'd discussed earlier. "You told me that Mellon is buried in Virginia. So they had the funeral in Pittsburgh, then brought him south for burial?"

Carol shook her head. "That's not what happened. He died in New York and they returned the body to Pittsburgh. Flags were flown at half-mast and the service itself took place in the East Liberty Presbyterian Church, where he'd worshiped as a boy. It was all a bit unusual for the Mellons. Normally they paid their last respects at the home of the deceased. The casket stayed closed. At his request."

Which immediately raised questions in her mind, as she knew it would in Danny's.

"Three thousand people came. There were so many flowers that the local florist had to send to Chicago for more roses and chrysanthemums. I read some of the newspaper articles. Even President Roosevelt sent flowers."

She realized how hollow that gesture had been.

"His casket was taken to Homewood Cemetery. The family had a mausoleum there. He was laid to rest with his brother."

"So how did he end up in Virginia," she asked.

"His son died in 1999. He had the Virginia connection. The son lived a long time, surviving them all. So before he died he had his mother, sister, wife, and father all brought to the church in Upperville. Like I told you before, a reunion in death for a family that had never been united in life."

"That means," Danny said through the phone, "in 1937 Mellon was in Pittsburgh."

She got it.

The sound of the president of the United States' voice clearly un-nerved Carol.

"You know where I need to go," she said.

"It's less than two hundred miles," Danny said. "I can have you there in under two hours."

"I want to come, too," Levy said.

Danny chuckled. "I thought you might. You've been along this far, so why not."

SIXTY-FIVE

CROATIA

KIM KEPT TO A STEADY PACE UP THE BARREN STREET, CAREFUL ON the slick stones. Unfortunately, he wore leather as opposed to rubber soles, which ordinarily he preferred. He was grateful for the fog, though, which was moderately close to the ground, thicker up the lengths of the weathered houses that encased the narrow way. If this path accommodated any traffic it was surely only one-way.

The lights of the cathedral bled through the fog and he used them as a beacon. He had no idea where they were headed, only that it was away from the station and the gunfire. It had been a miracle they escaped. During the chaos he'd recognized one of the shooters. He'd been off to himself, using one of the pillars for cover, but he was reasonably sure it had been the American, Malone.

Hana had handled herself with skill, forcing some of their attackers to seek cover. The two Koreans, whom he'd seen clearly, had definitely been sent by his half brother to kill him. The other two from inside the train he wasn't sure about, but they'd appeared American. He needed to accelerate his plans, but Anan Wayne Howell was gone. How to proceed from this point was a mystery, but he'd find a way. Hana carried the documents, which he'd need. And Howell said that Malone had solved the code.

That meant he could, too.

He just needed time.

MALONE STAYED BACK, MORE HEARING KIM AND HIS DAUGHTER than seeing them. Kim must be wearing leather heels, the click off the cobbles easy to follow. Thankfully, his own shoes were rubber-soled, each step silent and sure.

Behind him the foggy night sky continued to be red-and-blue-strobed from the police cars. Hopefully Isabella had distracted the authorities enough so that he could finish this. He wasn't sure where Kim thought he might be going, but he appreciated the fact that they were no longer near the train station. He hoped Howell would make it, but doubted it. Taking two bullets to the chest was usually fatal. He hated that he'd placed the man in jeopardy, but doubted he could have kept Howell away. Death always seemed a consequence of what he did. He still thought about his friend Henrik Thorvaldsen, and what had happened in Paris. And then there was Utah, just a month ago, and the events that had cost him Cassiopeia Vitt. An anger began to boil inside him, and he told himself to keep cool. This was no time for sentiment or emotion.

He had a job to do.

And the future of the United States might depend on it.

ISABELLA'S HANDS WERE CUFFED BEHIND HER BACK, ANOTHER ONE of those plastic bands that the police here seemed to tighten too much. Arrested twice in one day. That had to be a record for a Treasury agent. But she'd done her job and covered Malone's back.

Now it was up to him.

An ambulance finally arrived at the station and two uniformed men rushed inside with cases.

"Do you speak English?" she asked the officer gripping her arm.

He nodded.

"I'm an agent, working the United States Treasury Department. My identification is in my pocket. The man inside is an agent, too. I need to see about them."

The officer ignored her. Instead, she was led to one of the police cars, shoved into the backseat, and the door closed. Through the front windshield she spotted the body of the man she killed, police standing nearby. She'd noticed no one had headed up the street.

Her diversion worked.

"Now it's up to you," she whispered to Malone.

HANA STOPPED AND TURNED. THOUGH SHE SAW NOTHING BUT darkness and mist, she knew someone was behind them. The camp had taught her about danger. From the guards, other prisoners, even family. Attacks were common, and prisoner-on-prisoner violence was never punished. On the contrary, it seemed to be encouraged. Even she'd finally succumbed to its lure, attacking her mother with a shovel.

"What is it?" her father asked.

She continued to stare back down the street. Lights only existed at a few of the intersections, barely visible in the murk. All the buildings were rudely constructed of stone, topped by tiled roofs, most with unpainted balconies jutting outward, everything stained by time and weather. No movements anywhere betrayed a problem, the storefronts and doorways quiet.

She decided to raise no alarm, shaking her head that all was fine.

The dim and shadowy church loomed just ahead where the street leveled into a triangular piazza. She spotted a post office, theater, and some cafés, all closed. A clock tower rose opposite the church, its tower lit to the night, the mist making the dial hard to see.

No one was around.

The casement door for the church stood ajar, throwing out a slice of warm light into the palpable darkness.

Her father headed for it.

MALONE EMERGED FROM THE DOORWAY.

He'd taken refuge just as the click of heels stopped ahead of him. The recessed portal had provided a perfect hiding place, the wet bracing air and darkness his friends. Kim was not far away, as he'd heard the older man ask something in Korean. There'd been no reply, but he could hear footsteps once again.

Moving away.

KIM ENTERED THE CHURCH AND IMMEDIATELY NOTICED THE WAFT of incense and beeswax. *The smell of Christians,* he liked to call it. Its lofty interior was partially lit from hanging brass fixtures. Thick pillars supported a roof, the stone a mixture of pink and white. Frescoes decorated the apses and vaults. Rows of wooden pews that spanned out from the high altar waited empty. Satisfied they were alone, he stepped back to the entrance and carefully eased the thick wooden door open, peering out at the piazza. The street from which they'd come remained quiet.

"It seems we may have made it away," he said.

He closed the door.

MALONE HAD WATCHED AS KIM AND HIS DAUGHTER ENTERED the cathedral. The church was large, but not overly so, fitting for such a compact place as Solaris. On the way up from the train station he'd spotted several streets leading off this main route, none of them marked by names. He assumed the entire town was a labyrinth of lanes leading to more hidden piazzas, like the one before the church. He could not follow Kim inside through the main doors, so he'd detoured down one of the side paths into an alley between two shops that led to the town walls. Darkness here was nearly absolute, and though his eyes were adjusted to the night, he had to walk carefully.

He decided to risk some illumination and found his iPhone. Its LCD display provided enough light for him to safely locate the end of the alley where the town walls rose only a few feet away. He turned left and followed the stone down another alley behind the buildings that fronted the street. As he hoped, the path led to the rear of the church and a small wooden annex.

Two doors opened inside.

Both were locked.

A window was protected by an iron grille.

Thankfully, the locks on both doors were modern brass and keyed, common to a zillion other doors. In his wallet he always carried two picks. He found them and worked the tumblers. Only a few seconds were needed to hear their release. The picks made him think of Cassiopeia, who never went anywhere without hers, either.

He opened the door a few inches, its bottom scraping on something hard, and slipped inside a small room, beamed with oak, that led to what were certainly vestment and other storage rooms. A short hallway ended at a curtain that he assumed opened to the nave.

A ladder to his left, attached to the exterior wall, caught his attention.

He decided that might be the best vantage point.

So he pocketed his gun and climbed.

Isabella was startled as the car door was opened. She'd grown accustomed to the quiet. She was led from the vehicle, back out into the chilly night. One of the policemen cut the bands binding her wrists and she rubbed away the soreness and stretched her arms. The envoy from the embassy emerged from the train station along with Luke Daniels.

They both approached.

"Howell's dead," Luke said.

She hated to hear that. She told them what happened with the Korean and where Malone had headed.

"Why the police change in attitude?" she asked the envoy.

"Mr. Malone asked me to take care of a matter. Once done, I returned and discovered what occurred. I telephoned the embassy and the next thing I knew presidents were involved. These local police are not happy, but they do follow orders."

She was listening, but also staring up toward the mist-shrouded church. "We need to head up there."

"I agree," Luke said.

And they hustled off.

SIXTY-SIX

HANA ABSORBED THE SCENE OF LOFTY SPLENDOR AND WONDERED if fate had again intervened. How ironic that they would find a church. The interior was dim and musty, the towering stone walls natural and powerful. Ornate carvings, statues, and gilded elements brought contrast to an otherwise muted scene.

She stood hollow, cold, and ready. To her right, in one of the apses, small candles were arranged in a bronze rack, their flames flickering in the darkness. She stepped their way, still holding both the clipped documents and her gun. Her father lingered near the center aisle, catching his breath from their sprint up the steep street. He was overweight and out of shape, and with all his grandiose plans she'd often wondered why he cared so little about his health.

"Leaving this town could prove a problem," he said to her in Korean.

"Especially since you killed Howell."

He glared her way. "I didn't kill him. My half brother did."

"Is that how you justify it in your mind?"

He seemed perplexed by her rebuttal.

"What is this about?" he asked.

"Speak English."

A command. The first she'd ever issued his way.

"You do not care for your own language?"

"I do not care for *your* country."

He seemed intrigued by the statement. "All right," he said in English. "What is this about?"

"How did my mother end up in the camp?"

She'd never asked that question of him before. Talking about her past was the last thing she wanted to do, and never had he expressed any interest on his own. It was as if she'd just appeared to him as a nine-year-old and what had happened before was insignificant.

"Why do you ask this?"

She knew his tricks. Answering a question with another question was his way of diverting a conversation.

"How did my mother end up in the camp?"

"Why is that important now?"

"How did my mother end up in the camp?"

He needed to know that she wasn't going to budge.

"I sent her there."

His words shocked her. She hadn't expected the truth. So she asked the obvious, "Why?"

"We do not have the time to discuss this now."

She leveled her gun at him. "I think we do."

"And if I refuse? Would you shoot me?"

"I would."

He stared hard into her eyes, and for the first time she allowed him to see through them. The camp had taught her about desperation. Little was lost to those who had nothing to lose. Like here. And she wanted him to know that.

"Your mother and I carried on a love affair. She wanted it to be more permanent. I could not allow that. She insisted, so I sent her away."

"To that place."

"I considered it more humane than killing her."

"And did you know she was pregnant?"

He shook his head. "I learned of you years later, just before I came to the camp to find you."

"You told me then that *your* father sent her there."

"I lied. I thought it best. You were so young."

She lowered the gun. "I hated her for me being there. I blamed her for everything bad that happened to me. She told me once that her sin was falling in love. I've come to realize that I was wrong in hating her. Instead it is you I should despise."

He seemed wholly indifferent, unaffected by her rebuke. "Then I should have left you there where you would by now surely be either dead or used up by the guards."

"You are beyond evil."

"Really? And what were you when you asked that I have that teacher tortured, then killed?"

"That was justice for *his* wrongs."

"Is that how *you* rationalize it? You kill and it's justice. I kill and it is barbaric. Have you ever considered that I might be entitled to justice, too?"

Actually, she had, but she'd decided that his justice probably came when his father disowned him. Never had he shared with her the truth of what happened. That fanciful tale she'd read back on the cruise ship was surely lies. Once, on the Internet, she'd found news articles that described what happened. Sure, they were from a Western perspective, but she trusted that information far more than anything from him. All of the commentators agreed that her father was inept, reckless, and irresponsible. To a degree they were right. But she also knew that he liked people to underestimate him.

And she would not make that mistake.

MALONE LISTENED FROM HIS PERCH, TEN FEET ABOVE WHERE KIM and Hana Sung stood. A waist-high wooden wall formed a railing that encircled the building, the balcony there for more worshipers, its wooden pews all empty. Below, the nave seemed immersed in timelessness, full of motionless shadows. The warm air carried the stale pall of all the anonymous people who thronged here each day and breathed it over and over. He hadn't expected a confrontation, but there was obvious tension between Kim and his daughter. He'd risked a look down and watched as Sung lowered her weapon.

He gripped his own gun, ready to react.

KIM WAS PERPLEXED. HE'D NEVER SEEN HANA IN SUCH A MOOD. IN her eyes and on her face was nothing but anger. Emotion had always been foreign to her, and he'd grown accustomed to that solemnity. Which was why he hadn't lied about the camp and her mother. He truly did not realize that it mattered. But apparently it did.

"Give me the documents," he said to her.

She stood three meters away, near the prayer candles that continued to flicker in the apse, their light dancing across the wall frescoes. She tossed the clipped bundle to the floor, where it thudded at his feet. The disrespect was both obvious and offensive. He bent down and lifted the stack. For an instant he understood his father's anger at his own lack of respect. Never before had any of his children shown him such rudeness. All they did was avoid him. Hana, to her credit, was here. But why?

"You hate me that much?" he asked.

"I hate what you are."

"I am your father?"

"You are a Kim."

"Then you must also hate yourself."

"I do."

She was clearly troubled, but he'd meant what he said a few minutes ago. There was no time for this. He needed her to think clearly and help him escape from this town.

"Hana, we can discuss this once we are away from here. I came into this church simply as a way to flee the street and think. I need your assistance in getting us out of here."

"You care nothing about the camps," she said. "They will continue under you."

No sense denying the obvious. "Enemies have to be punished. I could kill them—"

"No, you can't. Murder has consequences."

She was more astute than he'd imagined. "That is true, but it is also necessary, at times. The camps offer a simpler, more controlled way to deal with problems."

"You are no different than your father and grandfather."

No, he probably wasn't. Kims were meant to rule and rule they would. But he would be different, just not in ways she seemed to want.

"You allowed Howell to die without a thought," she said. "The same was true for Larks, the woman on the boat, and the man in the hotel. Their lives meant nothing to you."

"All of which was necessary to achieve our goal."

She shook her head. "Not my goal. Yours."

Then a thought occurred to him. Her obstinacy. The anger. He stared at the stack of papers in his hand. He still held his gun, but was able to shuffle through the pages. "Where is the original?"

Nowhere had he seen the crumpled sheet, darker in color, thinner, more fragile than the others.

Hana stayed silent.

"Where is it?" he demanded, his voice rising.

MALONE KEPT LISTENING, A SAYING FROM SUN TZU'S *ART OF WAR* spinning through his mind. *When your enemy is in the process of destroying himself, stay out of the way.* Sound advice, particularly here where containment meant everything. When he and Stephanie had talked, laying out the plan, setting the stage, one thing had been stressed. Nothing about this could leave Solaris. It had to end here. So they'd purposefully pointed the Chinese, luring them down a concocted path, hoping anyone and everyone would follow.

And they had.

Time to intervene, but first he, too, wanted to know the answer to Kim's question.

Where was the crumpled sheet of paper?

ISABELLA, WITH LUKE, FOLLOWED THE STREET UP THROUGH A HONEY-comb of dark houses. All of the clamor remained behind them as the embassy envoy had assured them that no police would come their way.

The fog had thickened, limiting visibility to maybe fifty feet. Beyond that everything blurred away into a wall of vapor. They'd proceeded with caution, keeping watch on the buildings and the many side streets, seeing and hearing nothing. Now they'd found the lit cathedral and an irregular-shaped piazza that fronted it. All remained shrouded by an unnatural quiet.

"Where the hell is he?" Luke whispered.

KIM HAD WAITED LONG ENOUGH FOR AN ANSWER TO HIS QUESTION, so he aimed the gun at his daughter. "Where is the crumpled sheet? I will not ask again. You were right when you said I am a Kim. You obviously know what that means—after all you are one, too. If I have to shoot you, I will."

"Why did you come for me? Why not just leave me in the camp?"

"You were my daughter. I thought you deserved not to live there."

"But my mother did?"

"Your mother was just one of many women I encountered. They were objects of pleasure, nothing more. My wife, with whom I have my legitimate children, will always be my wife. And what do you care? You hated your mother. You told me that the first day we met. Why is she so important now?"

He kept the gun aimed.

HANA REALIZED THAT SHE'D MADE A HORRIBLE ERROR. THE WOMAN she'd despised her entire life was blameless. Truly, her only sin had been *falling in love.* Her punishment? A lifetime of banishment to a place of unimaginable horror, where problems were sent to be forgotten—without consequences.

Her mother had no choice.

But her father had possessed many.

This nothing of a man was the cause of all her agony. For an instant she was sad that her mother was gone. A feeling of longing, similar to what she'd felt for Sun Hi, filled her heart. Fourteen years she'd pondered this. But only in the past few minutes had she truly understood the depth of her pain.

And she knew what had to be done.

One hand held her gun. The other she slipped into her pocket and found the original sheet. She'd removed it from the stack while still on the train with Howell, crumpling it into a ball. Howell had liked that, saying nothing, only smiling at her desecration.

He killed your lady, she'd said to Howell. *Not me.*

And the American had nodded his understanding.

She displayed the ball of paper to her father.

"Are you insane," he said. "Those fibers are eighty years old. We may never be able to open it back up."

The wad rested on her open palm.

She turned and, with a flick of the wrist, propelled the ball through the air and onto the burning candles. Her father gasped and rushed to try and stop the inevitable, but the fragile paper quickly disintegrated.

"You bitch," he screamed.

She heard the word that every female prisoner had been called since birth. She'd come to associate that slur with defeat, but for the first time in her life she actually felt empowered. She'd conceived, planned, and executed her every move, down to the final part, the one that would deny her father all that he sought. She stared with defiance into his angry eyes, knowing exactly what he would do.

And he did not disappoint her.

He aimed his gun and pulled the trigger.

MALONE HAD NOT EXPECTED KIM TO SHOOT HIS DAUGHTER, BUT the man had done so with no hesitation. Hana Sung destroying the code was perfect. Kim was now dead in the water, unlikely to have any copies or facsimiles. Everything had happened on the train, and Kim had not even known its significance until Howell told him. Kim was surely counting on leaving here with everything in his possession, figuring it out later.

But now that plan would never happen.

HANA FELT THE BULLET SLAM INTO HER STOMACH, THEN PASS right through her. The pain was at first unnoticeable, then excruciating, radiating upward and exploding in her brain.

"I gave you life," her father said. "Gave you freedom. I could have left you there to rot, but I didn't. And you repay me with this?"

She needed him to finish. It was time for her to die. She should have died long ago with Sun Hi. Instead she survived and spat upon her friend. The shame from that had never left her. For a long time she'd debated what to do. Kill her father? No. Then she would be no better. Instead he must be offered the opportunity to kill her, and his choice would be telling.

Blood gushed from the wound, and she fought to stand.

She would die on her feet with no expressions of pain—strong, determined, and silent—like Sun Hi. Maybe they'd see each other once her spirit traveled to wherever spirits went. She hoped there was a place. What a shame if there be nothing but blackness.

One final insult swelled inside her.

More of her redemption.

She spat at her father.

But he stood too far away for anything to touch him.

He shot her again.

MALONE ROSE UP AND AIMED HIS GUN DOWNWARD JUST AS KIM fired for the second time. Sung dropped to the stone, blood oozing from her in ever-widening rivulets. He assumed she was dead.

"Drop the gun," he said.

Kim did not move, keeping his back to him, but the North Korean said, "American. You must be Malone. I saw you in the train station."

"I told you to drop the gun."

"Or you'll shoot me?"

"Something like that."

"She was a lovely girl," Kim said. "So much like her mother. A shame she was also a fool."

"You kill your children easily."

"The choice was hers, not mine."

He kept the gun aimed, amused at how Kim thought a little small talk would buy him time to assesses his options.

Unfortunately, there weren't any.

"I tried to love her," Kim said. "But I assume you saw what she did. Burning that sheet, which you surely know about."

"It's done," he made clear. "This is over. The only question is, will you walk away in one piece."

"Of course I will," Kim said. "Why would I not? You stand above me, in the balcony. I can tell from your voice. And I am down here. I doubt you will shoot me for no reason."

"Turn around. Nice and slow."

He'd purposefully not repeated his command to drop the gun. Kim slowly turned, the pistol still firmly gripped at waist level. He saw the sound suppressor at the end of the barrel and now knew why the shots had been so muffled.

"I'm going to leave," Kim said. "Here are the remaining papers." He tossed them to the floor. "As you say, this matter is over."

"Except for the five murders you've committed."

"And what would you do? Try me in a court? I doubt it. The last thing America wants is to provide me with an open forum. I may not have the answers, but I can ask enough questions to cause the United States a lot of embarrassment."

That he could.

Which actually begged the question that the arrogant fool apparently wanted answered.

Would Malone shoot him?

He lowered the gun and decided to give the bastard a fighting chance.

"I see," Kim said. "This is to be my trial."

The challenge had been issued. Leaving here meant going through him. Kim's daughter had pegged him right. This man's family had ruled millions of people for a long time. And they'd accomplished that feat through lies, force, violence, torture, and death. Never had a single person voluntarily voted for them. Their power was hereditary, dependent on corruption and brutality. Placed under a microscope, or exposed to the light of day, or even debated in the simplest terms, their evil quickly came into focus. They would never amount to anything where people possessed a free and informed choice.

"Just you and me," he said.

Kim stood rigid, the gun at his waist.

He knew Stephanie Nelle wanted this problem eliminated. She hadn't said as much, and never would she. Officially, the United States did not resort to assassination. But it happened. All the time.

"Is this a duel? A shootout? Like in the westerns?" Kim chuckled. "Americans are so dramatic. If you want me dead, just shoot me."

He said nothing.

"No, I don't imagine you would do such a thing," Kim said. "You don't seem like a man who kills for no reason. So I'm going to toss my gun down and leave. That's much better than me being given a public trial. We both know that. Then this matter can truly end."

Kim's thin lips twisted into an acrid smile.

Ordinarily, he'd agree, but there was the matter of Larks, Jelena, and Hana Sung. The waist-high wall before him shielded his gun from Kim's view. His right thumb slowly cocked the hammer back and clicked it into place. Kim's arm with the gun straightened and he began to aim the weapon toward the floor, as if about to discard it. Malone kept his gun at his side, wondering if Kim might actually call his bluff and walk away. But men like Kim Yong Jin always thought themselves smarter than others, and this version did not disappoint him.

Kim swung his arm around and up.

Malone raised the gun and fired, all without the benefit of a solid aim, but he did not miss. The bullet tore through Kim's chest and hurled him backward. One hand shot up for support but found none. The weapon pinwheeled out of Kim's hand.

He knew what had to be done.

He fired two more shots.

ISABELLA HEARD RETORTS.

Definitely gunfire. Both she and Luke turned toward the source.

The cathedral.

They rushed to its main doors and found the latch open. They each assumed a position on either side of the stone jamb. Luke pushed the wooden slab inward. Its hinges whined some resistance. She stole a glance inside, the gun gripped with both hands. Past a small vestibule and into the nave, she saw a body lying in the center aisle. Luke spotted it, too.

"Malone," she called out.

"I'm here. It's all clear."

They both relaxed their weapons and entered the church.

Kim Yong Jin lay still on the floor. To her right she saw the daughter, the body in a posture only achievable in death. Malone stood above them in a balcony that encircled the church.

She caught the warm sickly stench of blood.

"He killed her. I killed him. What about Howell?"

Luke shook his head.

"That's too bad."

She saw the stack of documents lying beside Kim and retrieved them.

"The original of the code is gone, burned over there at the candles. Nobody will ever see that again."

"Then that ends this," Luke declared.

"Not quite yet," Malone said.

SIXTY-SEVEN

STEPHANIE SAT IN THE HELICOPTER AS SHE AND JOE LEVY FLEW across Pittsburgh. Below, rush hour clogged the highways. Since they had no time to sit in traffic, a chopper had been waiting at the airport. The trip north on a Department of Justice jet had taken less than two hours and they should be on the ground shortly.

She knew Mellon had first been buried in Homewood Cemetery. Part memorial, part park, founded in the late 19th century, it sat at Pittsburgh's affluent east end and served as the final resting place for the city's elite. She'd never known there was a difference between a cemetery and a graveyard, but Joe Levy had enlightened her.

"Graveyards are just that," he said. "Land set aside for burials. Usually churches or a government maintain them. Cemeteries are much more. Rules and regulations control the plots. There are dos and don'ts. They're more elaborate and provide for perpetual care. Like institutions, in and of themselves."

"Is this an interest of yours?"

He smiled. "I like history. So I read a lot."

She'd heard Cotton say the same thing many times, and flying over Homewood she began to understand what Levy was saying. In the fading light she saw acres of rolling landscapes, open meadows, winding roads, a pond, and lots of tall trees. Monuments were everywhere, some just markers, others more like temples, a few larger than houses. One in particular caught her eye, shaped as a pyramid.

"It's really impressive," Levy said as they gazed out the cabin windows.

Evening was rapidly fading, the sun setting to the west. The pilot swung the chopper around and landed in a paved parking lot devoid of cars, except for one. A man waited for them beyond the rotor wash and they quickly exited the helicopter. He introduced himself as the superintendent and explained that a call from the White House had alerted him to their visit.

"I understand you want to see the Mellon tomb."

And they climbed into the lone vehicle.

Darkness enveloped during the drive through the quiet grounds. No lights illuminated anything. But why would they be needed?

"The Mellon plot is located in Section 14, among an array of our more elaborate mausoleums," the superintendent told them. "It was built for James Mellon, when he died in 1934. Andrew, James' brother, was laid to rest there, too, in 1937, but he was moved decades later to Virginia."

This man had no idea why they were there and she offered nothing.

"James Mellon was president of our board of directors until his death. He exerted a profound influence on the cemetery's development."

A touch of pride laced the statement.

They wound through the shedding trees. A carpet of leaves shone in the headlights, lining the road on both sides. Finally they stopped, and the superintendent indicated that they should all exit.

"I have flashlights in the trunk. I thought you might need them."

He retrieved three and handed two over. Stephanie switched hers on and played the beam off toward the mausoleum where she saw white marble walls, a pedimented front, and columns that cast the look of a Greek temple. Iron doors blocked the way inside beneath the word MEL-LON carved in stone. A bronze statue sat between the road and three short steps that led to the entrance. A haggard-looking man, cradling a little girl on his lap. She stepped closer and saw the word MOTHERLESS carved into its base.

"That was in James Mellon's garden," their host said. "There are a lot of tales about it. Some say it represented the premature death of a Mellon woman, and the father took up the charge of raising the child. But the simple truth is James had it made in Scotland as a lawn ornament. The artist named it *Motherless*. After James died it was moved here as adornment. No mystery at all."

But it was striking.

"I was told," the superintendent said, "that you wanted to be brought here. Unfortunately, I can't open the doors. That would violate our rules. Only the family can allow that."

She needed this man to leave. "Could you excuse us. Come back in half an hour or so."

She saw the perplexed look on his face, but he left with no argument. She assumed the White House had also requested privacy.

They stood silent until the car's taillights faded down the road.

"That key," Levy said. "You think it opens the lock?"

"Let's find out."

They walked across the soft grass and stepped up to the iron doors. A notched hole was visible in the right bronze panel. She removed the key from her pocket, the one Mellon had left inside the painting, and slipped it in.

Which fit perfectly.

She worked the stem right, then left, and freed the lock, releasing the latch with a distinctive click.

"Looks like we don't need the family's permission," she said.

They opened the doors and shined their lights inside. More white marble could be seen, the walls lined with markers where Mellon relations lay. She studied the dates and saw that there hadn't been a burial here since 1970. One section was blank, its marble front gone, the stone niche beyond it empty.

"That must have been for Andrew," Levy said. "Before he was moved."

She agreed.

"What now?" Levy asked.

She surveyed the interior, trying to make sense of what Mellon had left. And then she saw it. Marble outlined with a thin border of gold. She stepped across. The panel measured about eighteen inches square. Atop its face was carved a Roman numeral.

XVI.

"Not exactly X marks the spot," she said. "But close enough."

The Roman numerals had been etched into a separate piece of thin marble, maybe four inches square. So far Mellon had kept things simple and direct. No reason to doubt he'd stopped now.

She tested the Maglite in her right hand. Sturdy. More than capable. So she reversed the flashlight in her grip, then slammed its weighted butt into the numerals.

The stone easily shattered.

Just as she suspected.

She cleared away the remaining bits and pieces and saw a gold lock.

"You know it fits," Levy said.

She inserted the key and turned, revealing that the panel was actually a door.

Their combined lights exposed a compartment about two feet deep. A stack of brown and brittle parchments lay inside, a few rolled and bound by leather straps. Other sheets were lighter in color. Vellum, she assumed, stacked loosely about six inches high thanks to bulky waves and curves. She aimed the light while Levy carefully removed them.

"They're promissory notes," he said.

She watched as he studied a couple.

"Incredible. These are from the Second Continental Congress. This one acknowledges a loan made to the colonies by Haym Salomon. It specifies the amount, an interest rate, and due date. 1790." He stared up at her. "It's like Mellon said in the note from the painting. Here's proof of the debt."

"Are they all similar?"

He carefully examined the fragile documents. "Some are from the Continental Congress, others from the Congress of the Confederation, which was what the Continental Congress became in 1781, when the Articles of Confederation were approved. But, yes, these are the promissory notes for debts owed to Haym Salomon."

"Which today would be in the hundreds of billions of dollars."

"That's certainly one way to calculate it."

She noticed the signature on some of them. Distinctive and iconic. John Hancock. Then she recalled. He'd served as president of the Continental Congress.

Another envelope and some paper remained inside the compartment. She carefully removed both. The envelope was identical in size and condition to the one from the museum, its flap open, only a single folded sheet inside. Beneath the envelope were two sheets of browned paper, the type upon them still readable.

And significant.

Department of State

Office of the Solicitor

Memorandum
February 13, 1913
Ratification of the 16th Amendment to the
Constitution of the United States

The Secretary of State has referred to the Solicitor's Office for determination the question whether the notices of ratifications by the several states of the proposed 16th Amendment to the Constitution are in proper form, and if they are found to be in proper form, it is requested that this office prepare the necessary announcement to be made by the Secretary of State under Section 205 of the Revised Statutes. The 61st Congress of the United States, at the first session thereof, passed the resolution which was deposited in the Department of State July 31, 1909. It called for an amendment to the Constitution of the United States, which, when ratified by the legislatures of three-fourths of the several States, shall be valid to all intents and purposes:

The Congress shall have power to lay and collect taxes on incomes, from whatever source derived, without apportionment among the several States, and without regard to any census or enumeration.

The Secretary of State has received information from 46 states with reference to the action taken by the legislatures on the resolution of Congress proposing the 16th amendment to the Constitution. The two remaining states (Florida and Pennsylvania) never considered the issue. It appears from this information that of the 46 states that did consider the amendment 4 states (Connecticut, Virginia, Rhode Island, and Utah) have rejected it. The remaining 42 states have taken action purporting to approve. The question is whether a sufficient number of those approvals support ratification.

A breakdown of the 42 states shows: The resolutions passed by 22 contain errors of capitalization or punctuation, or both; those of 11 states contain errors in the wording, some of them substantial; 3 states (Kentucky, Tennessee, and Wyoming), though indicating that they have ratified, have fundamental legal problems associated with their actions, enough to warrant a conclusion that they did not ratify; and 7 states (Delaware, Minnesota, Nevada, New Hampshire, South Dakota, Texas, and Vermont) have enough missing or incomplete information relative to their ratification to warrant a careful study as to whether ratification even occurred.

Thirty-six states are required for ratification. If there be significant legal and constitutional issues with more than 6 of the 42 states that supposedly approved, then ratification is in doubt. It is my opinion that there are significant issues regarding ratification in at least 10 states. One in particular, Kentucky, is illustrative. My investigation reveals that the State Senate there rejected the amendment by a vote of 22-9. I have learned that Secretary of State Knox personally examined the official journals from the Kentucky Senate which, from my subsequent examination, reveal that the state senate clearly rejected the amendment. Yet, inexplicably, the Secretary of State has certified Kentucky as a ratified state.

Let me say that, under the Constitution, a state legislature is not authorized to alter in any way an amendment proposed by Congress, the function of the state consisting merely in the right to approve or disapprove the proposed amendment. Thirty-three of the 42 states that considered the amendment altered it (some in minor ways, others more substantial). Ten states have serious legal issues associated with their ratification votes. If called today to pronounce judgment, it would be my opinion that the amendment has not been properly ratified. It is recommended that the Secretary of State's declaration announcing the adoption of the 16th Amendment to the Constitution be delayed until such time as a full and thorough investigation can be made. Given the importance of the amendment in question this seems the only prudent and reasonable course. This office stands ready to assist in any way deemed necessary.

She looked at Joe Levy.

They'd both read the memorandum.

"It's true," he said. "It's all true. They rammed it through. For whatever stupid reason, Philander Knox let it go into effect."

"This is the first memorandum referred to in the one Larks copied from your archives. That one was dated February 24, 1913. I remember that the solicitor noted he'd sent a previous opinion, eleven days earlier, that had been ignored. This is it."

The proverbial smoking gun.

She also recalled what Howell had written about why Knox would have done that. "He probably saw the amendment as essential. After all, the Republicans had proposed it. And the last thing the Republicans would have wanted was to void it on technicalities. They were going out of power. Woodrow Wilson and the Democrats were coming in. I doubt any of them really considered the income tax much of a problem. It only applied to a tiny portion of the country—who'd find ways to avoid it anyway. Nobody then dreamed what that tax would become."

The look on the secretary of Treasury's face mimicked what she was thinking. What were they going to do now? Before making any decision, she decided they should examine Mellon's final message.

She opened the envelope and removed the single sheet.

Levy held the light and they read together.

Your quest is over and you now know both secrets. In 1921 Philander Knox told me of the issues associated with the 1913 ratification of the 16th Amendment. My old friend chose to ignore those illegalities. He thought he was doing his party and his country a great service. Maybe so, but he overestimated his importance. I managed to convince him not to reveal what he knew. Then I ensured that the secret would remain safe forever. I dispatched agents around the country to remove all relevant documents from various state records, thereby rendering it impossible to prove anything about ratification. Those ten states that worried the Solicitor General are no worry at all. So you see, Mr. President, I made your decision on this point easy. And if I had not, what would you have done? Void the amendment? Refund every tax dollar illegally collected since 1913? We both know you would have concealed the information, protecting America, just as I did. So you see, we are more alike than you ever thought. My only regret was that I could not protect the country from you.

"What would Roosevelt have done?" she asked.

"Exactly what Mellon said. Nothing. Remember, Roosevelt was the one who expanded the tax to a broader base and started withholding from people's paychecks. He needed that revenue."

"Why not just re-pass the amendment?"

"How could he? That would have been an admission that all of the collections from 1913 forward were improper. Think of the lawsuits."

And she recalled what Howell had referenced in his book. What Mellon said to his friend David Finley. *In the end he'll find what I left for him. He'll not be able to help himself from looking, and all will be right. The secrets will be safe and my point will have been made. For no matter how much he hates and disagrees with me, he still will have done precisely what I asked.*

And his final declaration.

I'm a patriot, David. Never forget that.

"Mellon made sure that the 16th Amendment would not become a problem," she said. "He tormented Roosevelt, knowing there was no danger."

But she realized that he probably also used what he knew to maintain a hold on the Treasury Department through three presidents.

"Unfortunately, that danger still exists," Levy said. "There's enough here to raise a lot of legal questions. The 1930s were a different time, with different rules. You could actually keep a secret then. There's no way we can survive this debate today. This would be a political nightmare."

And she remembered what the Eleventh Circuit had wanted in Howell's appeal. *An exceptionally strong showing of unconstitutional ratification.* This may not be enough, but Levy was right. It could certainly start the ball rolling.

"We're standing here in the dark," he said, "and that's the way it should remain. This can't see the light of day."

He was right.

But their next course of action raised many ethical questions, ones she'd always prided herself on being able to answer.

Now she wasn't so sure.

He seemed to sense her hesitancy.

"It's just you and me on this one," he said to her.

That it was.

She led the way outside, carrying the solicitor's memo. Levy toted the Salomon documents. Everything around them was dark and quiet. From her pocket she found a lighter, which she'd brought along just in case. She flicked the flame to life and set fire to the memo. Levy offered up the old vellum, which instantly disintegrated.

They stood silent and watched it all burn.

The ashes scattered into the night.

SIXTY-EIGHT

Isabella was impressed with Cotton Malone's bookshop. Everything was organized, the shelves clean and orderly, a definite Old World feel. Books had never been much of an interest for her, but they clearly fascinated Malone.

"You own this place?" she asked.

"All mine."

Darkness had arrived outside, the lit square beyond the plate-glass windows—called, she was told, Højbro Plads—crowded with a rush of people. Malone had obviously chosen a great location for his business. Luke had provided her the quick bio on Malone's early retirement and his move to Denmark. There was an ex-wife, a son, and a girlfriend. Cassiopeia Vitt. But that relationship had ended a month ago.

They'd all flown from Croatia earlier. She and Luke were headed on to the United States tomorrow. Malone had suggested dinner and a layover in Copenhagen. Luke laid his travel bag on the hardwood floor while Malone tossed his on the stairs. They'd retrieved both of them from the Zadar airport before leaving. Luke had told her that Malone lived upstairs on the fourth floor. What an interesting life this ex-agent had forged.

Malone had said little since last night. The bodies of Kim, Hana

Sung, and the two foreign agents had been taken by the Croatian police. She doubted anyone from North Korea would claim them. Howell's corpse was assumed by the U.S. embassy and would be shipped back home. Malone was right. The president had issued a full pardon, so Howell had died a free man. Secretary Levy had called and told her to hand over the sheaf of copied documents to the embassy for destruction. She was to personally witness the shredding and she had, just before they flew west.

The bookshop was closing, the store manager heading home. Malone locked the front door behind her as she left. All of this had started late Monday night in Venice and ended twenty-four hours later in Croatia. People had died, more than she'd ever witnessed, one of whom she herself had taken down.

Her first kill.

It happened so fast that she hadn't had time to digest the implications. On the plane ride Luke had sensed her reservations and explained that it never got any easier, no matter what the circumstances, and Malone had agreed.

"*There's no internal investigation in the spy business,*" Malone told her. "*No suspension with pay. No press attention. No psych evaluations. You shoot, they die, and you live with it.*"

And he spoke from experience.

He'd killed Kim.

"It's all tidied up," Malone told them. "Everybody who knows anything is dead. The documents are gone, the code destroyed."

Including, she knew, everything from Howell's anonymous email account, which the Magellan Billet had already accessed and erased.

"How about you two," Malone asked, pointing to she and Luke. "All good between you?"

"He grows on you," she said.

Luke shook his head. "Don't sell yourself short. You take some adjustin' to deal with, too. But I'd do it again." Luke held out his hand, which she shook.

"Me too," she added.

"You both did good," Malone said. "And I second what Frat Boy said. Anytime, Isabella."

Secretary Levy had been sketchy on the details from his end so she asked Malone, "What happened in DC?"

"Let's have some dinner and I'll tell you what I know."

STEPHANIE SAT IN EDWIN DAVIS' WHITE HOUSE OFFICE, WHICH was located down the hall from Danny Daniels. She and Joe Levy had returned from Pittsburgh last night. To alleviate any concerns she'd sent a text to Edwin confirming that everything was under control and that she would make a full report in the morning. So she and Danny now sat alone, in the office of the chief of staff.

"You going to tell me what happened?" he asked.

She reported the events in Solaris, culminating in the death of Kim and his daughter. The documents had been retrieved and destroyed, including the crumpled sheet of paper. Then she described her ruse in Washington and how she diverted the Chinese, allowing her and Joe Levy an open-field run to what Mellon had left behind.

He chuckled. "Now, that was the perfect turkey decoy. Good job."

She also told him about the ambassador's call and his warning on the North Koreans.

"Which might also explain something that happened overnight," he said.

He told her that China had declared a "red line" on North Korea, proclaiming that it would not allow any war, chaos, or instability on the Korean peninsula. Peace, their foreign minister had declared, can only come through denuclearization and they would work to make that happen. The days of pointless confrontation were over.

"That's downright revolutionary," Danny said. "They flat-out told the North Koreans that they better straighten up and fly right or else. And Pyongyang can't ignore Beijing. We may actually be able to get rid of the North Korean nuclear program. That announcement was another way for China to show they're on our side."

"Generous of them, considering their antics here."

"I hate that Howell had to die, though. That man wasn't stupid. He made a lot of sense."

Nothing remained that could cause them any problems. When she and Levy burned what Mellon left, they effectively ended everything. Was it the ethical thing to do? Probably not. But it certainly was the smart play. Little would be gained by raising questions about the 16th Amendment. The United States of America was a world power and nothing could be allowed to interfere with that status. People had paid their taxes for decades and they would continue. Only one thing bothered her.

"You realize that there are people in prison for failing to pay taxes," she said. "Who have no business there."

"I know. I've thought about that. Before I leave office, I'll pardon the ones I can. We'll couch it in some neutral manner, like nonviolent federal offenders with a sentence of so-many years or less. That way it doesn't solely zero in on tax evaders. That should work. I'll make that right."

She knew he would.

In the end she, Edwin, Joe Levy, and Danny would know it all. Cotton, Luke, and Isabella Schaefer would know some, but they were seasoned agents, sworn to secrecy. So things were safe.

"How about the people at the National Gallery?" she asked. "They okay?"

"There were some ruffled feathers. The director didn't appreciate me ordering him around. And he wasn't happy that one of his paintings was desecrated. But when Edwin told him that his budget next year would be increased by twelve percent he said I could abuse him anytime."

She smiled.

Always a dealer.

"You'll be glad to know that Luke may have met his match," she said. "Cotton tells me that Ms. Schaefer from Treasury handled him, and herself, with style."

"You thinkin' about hiring her?"

She shrugged. "I'm always on the lookout for good people."

"Joe Levy might fight you on that one."

Always a possibility.

"I looked into that other matter," he said to her.

And she knew what he meant. Luke reported that Isabella Schaefer had told him about the Omnibus Appropriations Act, which forbid Treasury from using public money to redesign the $1 bill.

"She's right," he said. "It's buried deep in the bill, but it's there. We've redesigned every denomination, save the $1 bill. Edwin poked around and found out that the prohibition has been there for decades. Nobody knows why. Makes you wonder, doesn't it?"

That it did.

"You're not going to tell me, are you?" he asked. "About what you found in Pittsburgh."

"There was nothing there."

He gave her a sly smile. "Is that Joe's story, too, and you're both stickin' to it?"

Last night, after returning to DC, she and Levy had made a stop at Treasury. In the locked room where all the documents were assembled, together they'd shredded every page. Levy's observation at the cemetery had made sense. The world was a different place from 1937. And what Andrew Mellon left could alter the balance of power across the globe. Too much was at stake. But she did offer, "Just know that, in the end, Mellon really was a patriot."

"How about this," he said. "Once I'm no longer your boss and retired to pasture, we'll have a little chat on this subject. When it doesn't matter if I know."

She tossed him a smile. "I'll look forward to that."

MALONE SAT ACROSS THE TABLE FROM LUKE AND ISABELLA. HE'D led them across Højbro Plads to the Café Norden and his usual table on the second floor, against the window, with a view down to his bookshop.

"Last time I was here," Luke said, "we were being chased by men with guns." The younger man pointed a finger at him. "And you almost blew my head off."

He grinned. "I thought it was a pretty good shot, myself. Right past your ear and into the bad guy."

"I'd like to hear that story," Isabella said.

"I'll tell you on the way home. That way it'll be my version instead of this old-timer's."

They'd all enjoyed a bowl of tomato bisque and he'd told them what happened across the Atlantic. Stephanie had called on a secure line before they left Croatia and explained the outcome.

"You goin' to be okay?" Luke asked.

He had no regrets about killing Kim. Not that he reveled in pulling the trigger, but there were some people who just needed to die.

Kim Yong Jin was one of those.

"The world is a better place without that piece of crap," he said.

"That's not what I mean," Luke said.

Interesting how the younger man had sensed his reluctance. Being here brought back thoughts of Cassiopeia. He could not deny that. They'd enjoyed many meals at this same table. But he could not think about that. Not now. Instead he allowed the last bits of energy to evaporate from his body. He'd lived off adrenaline the past forty-eight hours, sleeping little.

So he stood and said, "I'm going to let you two enjoy the rest of the evening. I think I'll head back to the shop and go to bed."

Luke did not press for an answer to his question, which he appreciated.

He'd booked two rooms at the Hotel d'Angleterre.

"The hotel is a few blocks that way." He pointed toward the back of the restaurant. "Just follow this side street and you'll see it. I'll see you both in the morning, at breakfast there. Then I'll drive you to the airport."

"You take care, Pappy," Luke said.

He noticed the softer tone, that of a friend, which he now considered Luke to be. He'd also noticed that Wonder Woman had become Isabella, which might mean something, too.

She stood and kissed him lightly on the cheek. "I second that. Take care."

Warmth laced her words and a smile illuminated her features. She wasn't nearly the badass she wanted everyone to believe her to be.

He threw them both a smile, then descended the stairs back to ground level and left through the café's main door. A welter of thoughts from the past month swirled through his mind. Interesting how he was so precise as an agent, executing his assignments with surgical precision, everything always handled and resolved.

Like here.

Nice and neat.

But not in his personal life.

That seemed to stay in chaos—a frustrating and relentless pattern of expectation, disappointment, then hope.

A familiar feeling of loneliness swept through him, one he'd grown accustomed to before meeting Cassiopeia, but one he'd been glad to see gone once he came to love her.

And he had loved her.

In fact, he still did.

All of that was over, though.

Now life went on.

WRITER'S NOTE

As usual, there was fieldwork associated with this novel. The cruise that Larks, Kim, Hana, Malone, and Isabella take across the Mediterranean and Adriatic Seas is one Elizabeth and I enjoyed. We visited all of the places the characters saw, including Venice and Croatia. We also made a trip to Hyde Park and the Franklin Roosevelt Library, along with three excursions to Washington, DC. A few years ago I explored the Little White House at Warm Springs.

Time now to separate fact from fiction.

The meeting between Andrew Mellon and Franklin Roosevelt (prologue) happened on December 31, 1936. The two men were fundamentally different (chapter 46) and personally detested each other. As depicted, Roosevelt had no choice but to accept Mellon's donation for the National Gallery of Art, and the meeting's purpose was to finalize that gift. Of course, I added the part about Mellon's revenge. Roosevelt did in fact have Mellon prosecuted for tax evasion. When a grand jury refused to indict, Roosevelt pursued the case civilly. That litigation ended in Mellon's favor with a full exoneration. And as Mellon notes, Roosevelt was not the first to use the Bureau of Internal Revenue (as it was then known) against enemies. The story of Senator James Couzens is historical fact. Also, the derogatory campaign ad Roosevelt makes reference to is taken from history, and the comment from Harry Truman about Roosevelt's lying is real.

Venice is accurately portrayed (chapters 1, 4, 6, 23), as are Isola di San Michele (chapters 1 and 4), the cruise ship terminal complex (chapters 19, 21), and ferry terminal (chapter 23).

Kim Yong Jin is fictional, but he is based on Kim Jong-nam, the eldest son of the late North Korean ruler Kim Jong-il. Jong-nam was the heir apparent when, in May 2001, he tried to sneak himself and one of his children into Japan to visit Disneyland. The details of that fiasco provided in chapters 2 and 27, along with Kim's exile to Macao, are factual. Kim Jong-il did in fact disown Jong-nam and his younger son, Kim Jong-un, became heir and eventually head of North Korea in 2011. In the novel I refer to this person only as Dear Leader. Most of the Kims' history, as related throughout the story, is taken from reality. Political purges, which include sham trials and swift executions, are commonplace in North Korea (chapters 9, 44, 45).

The insurance fraud scheme described in chapters 4 and 10 is factual. Millions of dollars were realized each year, all presented to the North Korean leader on his birthday. Those illegally obtained funds were used to finance everything from luxury goods to nuclear components. Of late, though, international attention to the scam has made its continuation more difficult.

Sadly, the North Korean labor camps, which are an integral part of Hana Sung's life (chapters 13, 39, 44), exist. At present it is estimated 200,000 people are confined in unimaginable horror. The best primary source on the subject is *Escape from Camp 14*, by Blaine Harden, which tells the story of Shin In Geun, the only known person to escape and tell the tale. Most of Hana's experiences herein are based on Shin's experience. And though recently Shin has publicly acknowledged that some of the accounts related in the book may not be true, he continues to insist that he, and thousands of others, have suffered behind the fences. Typically, the North Koreans acknowledge nothing, saying only *There is no human rights issue in this country, as everyone leads the most dignified and happy life.*

The Foreign Intelligence Surveillance Court functions in the same manner and at the same locale as in chapter 14. All of the statistics cited about that court are accurate.

Several interesting personalities are portrayed in the story.

First and foremost is Andrew Mellon. His bio, and that of his father, Thomas, noted in chapter 15, are accurate. Mellon did in fact retain control of the Treasury Department through three successive presidential administrations. My speculation as to how that might have happened, though, is just that. Mellon also greatly admired Robert Burns' "Epistle to a Young Friend" (chapter 46). In 1924 he published *Taxation: The People's Business,* and the excerpt from that book quoted in chapter 35 is verbatim. Mellon's 1937 funeral, burial in Pittsburgh, and eventual reburial in Virginia happened (chapters 46 and 64). The Homewood Cemetery and Mellon mausoleum in Pittsburgh, along with the family plot in Upperville, Virginia, are there (chapter 67). The only fictional addition was the marble door with XIV carved into it. The definitive biography of this fascinating man is a 2006 volume, *Mellon: An American Life,* by David Cannadine.

Philander Knox is another curious character. His background and faults (as described in chapter 16) are accurate. He was secretary of state in 1913 when the 16th Amendment was supposedly ratified. He was also a close friend of Andrew Mellon. As first detailed in chapter 16, it was Knox who convinced President Harding to first appoint Mellon secretary of Treasury. Likewise, Harding refused to appoint Knox to any cabinet post, a decision Knox openly resented. Whether there was any subterfuge regarding the 16th Amendment, or if Knox passed some secret on to Mellon, we will never know. All the reasons offered in chapter 40 as to why Knox might have ignored any irregularities in the ratification process (though my speculation) are grounded in history.

David Finley was indeed close with Andrew Mellon, considering him a friend and mentor. After Mellon died in 1937, Finley oversaw the construction of the National Gallery and became its first director. Finley went on to achieve legendary status in American art circles, instrumental in the creation of the National Trust for Historic Preservation.

Haym Salomon is one of the unsung heroes of the American Revolution. His exploits (as detailed throughout the story) are factual (chapter 20). The Continental Congress stayed broke, and it was Salomon who found the money to fund the fight (chapter 28). Those nearly one hundred references in Robert Morris' diary that simply said, *I sent for Haym*

Salomon, are real (chapter 20). The monument in Chicago (chapter 30) is one of the few to Salomon that exist. His $800,000 in loans would indeed be worth many billions today, and those debts remain unpaid. Congress did consider restitution several times (chapter 20) but never approved anything. In the hope of repayment, the documentation relative to those debts was provided to the Pennsylvania treasurer in 1785, but subsequently disappeared (chapter 28). That Andrew Mellon found this evidence, then hid it away, is entirely my invention.

Outside the state of Virginia George Mason is a relatively unknown Founding Father (chapter 51). But he was important. He did refuse to sign the Constitution, and his references to a *tyrannical aristocracy* (chapter 24) are documented. Gunston Hall is Mason's Virginia home, but any contributions made to its restoration by Andrew Mellon are fictional. Mason was the principal author of the 1776 Virginia Declaration of Rights, which Jefferson drew upon for the Declaration of Independence and Madison utilized to frame the Bill of Rights (chapters 51 and 54). It remains one of the most important documents in American history.

The $1 bill is somewhat of a character, too. It was redesigned in 1935, at Franklin Roosevelt's insistence (prologue). The Great Seal was then added, and Roosevelt ordered that the pyramid be placed on the left and the eagle on the right. The image in chapter 32 is from the actual memo where Roosevelt noted this preference in writing. The 1935 issue did not have IN GOD WE TRUST, which was added in 1957 (chapter 24). As to the six-pointed star formed by connecting five letters across the seal of the United States (atop the pyramid), resulting in the anagram for the word *Mason,* there is no explanation why it's there. But it is. Regarding the thirteen stars in the Great Seal, above the eagle, that also form a Star of David (chapter 28), legend says George Washington did in fact ask for this inclusion as thanks to Haym Salomon. But no one knows for sure. Again, there is no denying that the image is there. Section III of the Omnibus Appropriations Act (chapters 28 and 68) actually does forbid the altering or changing of the $1 bill. And eerily, the $20 bill shown in chapter 48, when properly folded, does reveal images strikingly similar to what happened on 9/11.

Disney turns up in several places. First, relative to Kim Yong Jin's fall from grace, then with a Disney-themed program on North Korean television (chapter 27). That broadcast actually happened in July 2012. Finally, the print of Walt himself (chapter 7), with the slogan *It's kind of fun to do the impossible,* hangs on both Kim's office wall and mine.

Audiotaping by Roosevelt in the Oval Office happened. He was the first president to utilize this tool. The conversations noted in chapter 22, though, are fiction. The actual tapes are stored in the Roosevelt Library at Hyde Park. The scene described from the day Roosevelt died (chapter 24) is reasonably accurate. The examination by his doctor happened, and the conversation between them is factual. Of course, the addition of Mark Tipton was mine, though there would have been a Secret Service agent present at all times. The Little White House at Warm Springs still stands and is now a national park. All of the derogatory comments Danny Daniels makes relative to Roosevelt (chapter 30) are taken from historical accounts, some of which paint an image of the man quite different from his public persona.

Zadar lies on the Croatian coast with its sheltered harbor and islands (chapters 33, 34, 36, and 38). The city library is accurately described, as is the American Corner (chapters 41, 43, and 49). Solaris is my invention, a composite of several east Croatian border towns.

The Beale cipher exists, and the Declaration of Independence proved relevant in deciphering one of its three codes (chapter 43). The image reproduced in chapter 43 is from the actual Beale cipher. The puzzle Andrew Mellon leaves behind is my invention. To create it, I applied the Beale cipher to the Virginia Declaration of Rights, just as Malone does in chapters 51 and 54.

There is a desk inside the Smithsonian Castle, located on the ground floor in the west wing. Curator Richard Stamm showed it to me, and it does contain a multitude of hidden compartments. Though intriguing, I decided instead to use the 18th-century Roentgen secretary's cabinet on display at New York's Metropolitan Museum of Art. As noted in chapter 56, it may be the single most expensive piece of furniture ever made, loaded with secret compartments. I moved that desk to Washington, DC, and made it a Mellon gift to the Smithsonian. The Smithsonian conservation lab (noted in chapter 60) is an amazing place, where rare books and old documents are saved every day.

The National Gallery of Art is an American wonder, created by

Andrew Mellon. Its elegant exterior, the Founders Room, rotunda, dome, fountains, galleries, and garden court all can be visited (chapters 60, 62, and 64). In Gallery 62 hangs Edward Savage's *Washington Family*. Mellon bought the painting on January 29, 1936. It hung in his DC apartment (even after his death in 1937) until 1941, when it was moved to the National Gallery, where it has remained ever since. All of the symbolism noted in chapter 62 was intentional on Savage's part. Amazingly, there's even a plug in the lower right corner of the massive frame (one I discovered *after* I had fabricated my own), there to accommodate an iron support.

China is North Korea's most important ally, providing vital commerce and cash (chapter 26). China is also America's number one foreign creditor. Income tax does account for over 90 percent of federal revenues (chapters 7 and 35). Sadly, all of the statistics concerning the national debt (chapter 35) are true. That debt accrues at a staggering rate of over $1 million every minute, and there are indeed websites with counters where you can watch it grow. Also, what Danny Daniels says about the correlation between higher tax rates and lower revenues (chapter 35) is correct.

This novel deals with income taxes. Whether the 16th Amendment was properly ratified is a fascinating legal question. My exposure to this issue first came when I discovered *The Law That Never Was*. It's a treatise by a man named William Benson, who took the time to visit all 42 states that supposedly ratified the amendment, documenting exactly the processes followed and analyzing whether they conformed with that state's law. Some of what he found is disturbing and compelling. Whether it be true or not, I'll leave to others to ascertain. This is a novel—which by definition is not real. But I did include two of the more glaring examples Benson uncovered—Kentucky and Tennessee (chapters 33 and 34). Interestingly, Benson also encountered (as did the characters in the story) the problem of missing originals. His arguments are not wholly irrational. The federal courts, though, have consistently avoided the issue, their logic and reasoning weak (as detailed in chapter 37). The appellate opinion reproduced in chapter 12 is fictitious, but the language is quoted verbatim from several actual decisions.

In 1922 the Supreme Court held that a secretary of state's declaration that a constitutional amendment has been ratified is conclusive, not subject to judicial review (chapter 37). Whether that be sound reasoning or not, the issue has never again been considered by the Supreme Court. The 16th Amendment was born out of early-20th-century politics, and was actually designed to fail, but didn't (chapter 31). Initially, it applied only to a small segment of the country (less than 5%), who could avoid the tax through loopholes intentionally built into the first revenue act passed in 1913. It was Roosevelt, in 1943, who took the tax mainstream with withholdings now coming straight from people's paychecks (chapter 67).

Several memoranda are reproduced throughout the novel, all of which are my creations save for the one dated February 13, 1913 (chapter 67). It is loosely based on an actual memorandum from the solicitor general dated February 15, 1913. Images of this document populate the Internet. That memorandum raises several legal questions about the ratification of the 16th Amendment. One sentence of my memo is quoted verbatim from the actual document:

> Under the Constitution, a state legislature is not authorized to alter in any way an amendment proposed by Congress, the function of the state consisting merely in the right to approve or disapprove the proposed amendment.

But that is precisely what happened during the ratification process. The proposed amendment was altered by state after state in a variety of ways. And the secretary of state at the time, Philander Knox, ignored not only that reality but also the solicitor general and declared the 16th Amendment "in effect."

Why not "ratified"?

A meaningless distinction?

Or a reaction to the legal advice he'd received?

We'll never know.

What exactly would happen if the 16th Amendment was somehow tainted from the start? Thirty-six states were needed at the time for ratification. Forty-two considered it. What if more than six of those states have serious legal issues regarding their adoption votes? Many say that's the case. The problems discussed within the memo cited in chapter 67 came from their research.

But the courts refuse to listen.

And with good reason.

The issue exposes a huge vulnerability.

At one point in the novel (chapter 29) Kim Yong Jin calls the 16th Amendment's possible illegality "the cleverest weapon of mass destruction ever devised."

And he may be right.